Getting It All
Sapphire Falls, book four

Erin Nicholas

ISBN: 978-0986324550

Editor: Heidi Moore
Cover artist: Valerie Tibbs
Copy edits: Kelli Collins
Digital formatting: Author E.M.S.
Print formatting: Kim Brooks

DEDICATION

To the girls who remind me daily that I'm not in this alone—
Mari Carr, Rhian Cahill, Cari Quinn, Shelli Stevens and PG Forte.
To the girls who keep my secret and send me gushy texts just when I need them—
Shannon, Jodi and Maureen.
And finally to the girls who do everything they can to make me look good in spite of myself—Heidi Moore and Kelli Collins.

None of this would be what it is without you all!

CHAPTER ONE

Delaney Callan wanted Tucker Bennett more than any man she'd ever met.

No, it went beyond want. She *needed* him. Bad.

And it had nothing to do with the faded blue jeans that molded to his butt and thighs or the royal-blue T-shirt that stretched over wide shoulders, thick biceps and flat abs.

Or the deep rumbly voice that said, "Hey, Delaney." Or the grin that he gave her that felt familiar even though she'd only ever seen it in photos.

It had everything to do with how pleased he seemed to see the boys.

And her. That grin was really something. But it was more the boys.

She'd never wanted a guy as much as when Tucker grabbed the back of six-year-old Jack's pants as he started to climb up one of the wrought iron shelving units to try to reach a coffee cup.

She had been out of her seat and reaching for Jack when Tucker strode through the door, jingling the little bell overhead, and immediately swung the little boy up and over his shoulder like a sack of potatoes. A giggling sack of potatoes. Like he had a sixth sense, Tucker then grasped the back of eight-year-old David's shirt, keeping him in place as David started for the sample tray on the counter—for the fifth time.

He spun David into his chair at the little round table near the window and then dropped into the chair Jack had occupied with the boy in his lap.

Having someone else handle the boys without even blinking, with a big panty-melting grin in place even, was hot. Pure and simple.

She almost cried it was so hot.

Of course, she was completely exhausted, her body was

more caffeine than water, and she hadn't had sex in so long she wasn't sure she could find all the right parts anymore. But she was pretty sure it was really hot anyway.

In retrospect, Delaney realized that bringing four tired, bored, restless, hungry boys to a quaint bakery and candy shop might have been an error in judgment.

She'd have to add it to the list of those she'd made lately.

She and Tucker had chosen Scott's Sweets as their meeting spot since it was right along the highway and Delaney had never been to Sapphire Falls before. Not that it was a huge town, but taking the boys to a place with cookies had *seemed* like a good idea.

It wasn't like Tucker had kept them waiting either. They'd been there for about ten minutes. It had only taken her nephews three minutes to start trouble.

"Hi, Tucker."

Her grin must have been a little too enthusiastic, because he blinked at its brightness before nodding. "Good to see you."

"You too." He had no idea.

The eight hours on the road today had been tough. Worse than yesterday's eight hours.

Of course, the past four months had pretty much sucked twenty-four-seven, and Delaney really thought it was possible she would never feel rested and content ever again.

But being here in Sapphire Falls, Nebraska, with Tucker Bennett was a really good start toward that. She thanked God, literally, that her brother-in-law had spent every summer in Sapphire Falls with his boys since the oldest, Henry, had been born twelve years ago.

Summer break had started for the boys three days ago. She'd packed them up and pointed the car toward Sapphire Falls the minute she'd been able.

Tucker knew the boys. They stayed at his house every summer, all summer. Tucker had helped their dad teach

them to fish and ride dirt bikes and do chores around the
farm. They always talked excitedly about the dirt-bike
races and the summer festival and swimming in the pond
and driving the tractor. This summer in Sapphire Falls was
exactly what the boys needed.

And frankly, what Delaney needed.

The help. From someone who knew the boys so well,
someone they were familiar with and liked. Someone their
father had trusted implicitly. Someone their father had
asked her to bring them to see.

Jack sat on Tucker's lap, happily picking colored
sprinkles off the top of his brownie and putting them in his
mouth one by one. As if he was a pro at sitting still and
behaving. He barely even wiggled. A miracle in and of
itself. Up until that moment, he'd been jumping up every
two minutes to reposition the chair, getting on the floor to
play with his matchbox cars, getting up to run to the
bathroom, going to the bakery display case six times and
asking for refills on his water twice.

Of course, if she was on Tucker's lap, she wouldn't be
inclined to leave it anytime soon either.

Delaney caught herself and shook her head, sitting up
straighter.

"Hey, Henry," Tucker said to Delaney's oldest nephew.

"Hey, Tucker." Henry didn't quite smile, but he looked
interested at least.

That was the most positive expression the kid had worn
in a month.

"Your dad told me you'd grown a lot this year, so I
have a new bike out at my place for you to try."

Delaney held her breath, watching Henry.

Most people tiptoed around the subject of the boys'
mom and dad. Most adults weren't sure how to talk to kids
after their parents had died.

Delaney didn't do that. She brought both Rafe and
Chelsea up on a regular basis. She said things like, "your

mom would have loved this", or, "that's how your dad always did it".

But most people avoided the topic entirely, not wanting to make the boys sad.

She appreciated that Tucker didn't do that.

She was also grateful that Tucker had assured Rafe that the boys would have their Sapphire Falls summer like always. She knew that included dirt bikes. She didn't get it. She knew nothing about the bikes or motocross. But the boys loved it and that was enough for her.

"That's awesome," Henry said, actually letting a small smile escape.

Delaney's heart clenched at the sight. There just hadn't been enough smiles and giggles and excitement from any of the boys over the past three months.

"And hey," Tucker said, turning to Charlie. "Remember that ramp we built last summer?"

Charlie leaned in, the iPad he'd been playing with forgotten in his hand. Wow, Tucker Bennett continued to impress.

"Yeah?"

"We put it into the track at my place," Tucker said. His smile was as wide as any she'd seen around the table, and Delaney thought she felt a little clench in her heart at that as well.

She frowned. That could be a problem.

There were all kinds of reasons to be attracted to Tucker. He was incredibly good-looking for one thing, and while she was in mourning, she wasn't dead. He was also a hero to the four little boys she loved with all of her heart. He'd been a big part of their lives, their entire childhoods to this point, and that meant she automatically had a soft spot for him. He was also the best friend to the man who had been *her* best friend for thirteen years—her brother-in-law, Rafael.

Rafe and Tucker had been best friends from fifth grade

through twelfth grade right here in Sapphire Falls. Tucker automatically got points just because Rafe had counted Tucker among the people he was closest to.

And Tucker was willing and able to help her out with the boys for the summer while the world stopped spinning quite so fast around them. Chelsea's sudden death three months ago, then the cancer taking Rafe only two months later, had put Delaney and the boys into a situation none of them could have been prepared for. Every day since had been a challenge. And a blur.

But when she'd driven past the sign that said *Welcome to Sapphire Falls*, she'd been able to take a deep breath and feel something positive for the first time since...Christmas maybe. She hardly remembered.

She felt terrible about that. The boys needed her, and they needed her to be positive, uplifting, supportive. She'd been all of those things, but frankly, she'd been faking it. Now maybe it could be true.

This was Sapphire Falls. The best place on earth. To the four little boys at the table with her right now, this town even beat Disney World. After all, there were dirt bikes here.

Here, of all places, she could be happy and positive and upbeat. Perky even. She could get things figured out, get a plan together. From what she'd been hearing about Sapphire Falls for the past thirteen years, this was where everything worked out and everyone felt good.

She knew it was crazy to think that just being here would magically fix everything.

But she didn't have any better ideas.

And the boys really wanted to ride dirt bikes this summer.

"You got the track done?" Charlie asked, handing Delaney his iPad.

Wow, completely giving up possession of it? That was huge.

"Yep, finished about a month ago. My brothers and I have been out on it and it's great," Tucker said with a huge grin.

About a month ago. Right around the time Rafe had passed away. Delaney felt a lump in her throat and looked around the table, wondering if that phrase was triggering anything for them and ready to jump in with…something. She never knew what. In spite of the online sites and books, she was never sure what exactly to say.

But the boys looked fine. They were all staring at Tucker, excitement in their eyes.

Delaney sat back in her chair and looked the farmer over again.

Staring at him was no hardship. She might just spend some time doing that now that the boys seemed settled.

Yeah, she was very, very glad to be here.

Tucker tried to ignore Delaney's eyes on him. Having her watching him was making him itchy. Not in a bad way, but in an inappropriate way.

Damn, he'd known she was gorgeous. He'd seen enough pictures over the years. And he knew she was awesome, amazing, wonderful, unbelievable—he'd heard those adjectives from Rafael for thirteen years now.

But wow. In person, with yellow frosting smudged on her white T-shirt, four matchbox cars in one hand and the lopsided bun on top her head nearly falling free, she looked…real.

She was really here. Surrounded by little boys he loved.

He'd prepared himself to see her. To finally meet this woman that his best friend wouldn't shut up about. He knew that Rafe had been madly in love with his wife, Chelsea. He knew that Rafe talked Delaney up because he loved her like a sister. He also knew that Rafe wanted

Tucker to love her.

It was actually kind of crazy that they'd never met, but Rafe and Chelsea had eloped and had been married by a justice of the peace. Neither Tucker nor Delaney had been there. And there had been no funeral for either Chelsea or Rafe, per their instructions.

Tucker ran a hand over his face and carefully kept his smile in place. He knew he was being watched—and not only by the gorgeous woman to his right. The boys were giving him their full attention and he had to keep his emotions in check. Even if he was faking it.

This was important to Rafe.

Tucker had a feeling that Rafe was keeping an eye on them, and he was sure Rafe wouldn't hesitate to haunt him at night if Tucker didn't do what he wanted him to.

Tucker wanted to chuckle at that. He wouldn't mind a haunting from Rafe. He missed his friend and felt like they had more to talk about. But he couldn't chuckle without explaining what was so funny, and he didn't want the boys or Delaney thinking he was crazy.

He also couldn't choke up. He intended to talk to the boys about Rafe, because he wanted them to feel comfortable talking about their dad when they needed to. But he couldn't choke up every time. He knew that he was supposed to be the hero here. The guy who helped put the pieces back together. He'd always enjoyed being a role model for the boys, and he was very much looking forward to being Delaney's knight in shining armor.

And that was saying something. He specialized in knight in shining armor and it seemed that Sapphire Falls had a lot of damsels.

He glanced at Delaney and found her still watching him. Almost as if she was puzzled by something.

He quickly focused on David instead.

Yep, there were a number of emotions he needed to learn to control—the urge to pull *her* into his lap in front of the boys in the middle of Scott's Sweets was definitely one of them.

It was crazy that thirteen years had passed with Delaney and Tucker being Rafe's best friends and they'd never even been in the same room. Rafe had wanted Tucker and Delaney to get together for as long as Rafe had known Delaney.

And if she hadn't lived twelve hours away, it might have happened.

But she'd lived twelve hours away.

Until now. Now she was here. With the boys—his best friend's four sons who Tucker loved as if they were his own.

They weren't here to stay. Only for the summer. At least, that was the plan according to Delaney's emails. They were staying in Sapphire Falls so that the boys would have a summer like all the others—a good time, a memory, a way of remembering the fun times with their dad.

Tucker felt his throat tighten as he thought about the summer without Rafe. The first summer Tucker had spent without his friend since they were ten.

Twenty years. Twenty summers.

He cleared his throat and contributed just enough to the conversation amongst the kids to keep them chattering about the dirt-bike track and the season and the machines.

But his mind wouldn't stay on anything the boys were saying.

Delaney was here.

She was beautiful, for sure, but she also looked worn out. There were dark smudges under her eyes, her glossy brunette hair was mostly escaping the messy bun and she looked thinner than he remembered from pictures. Then again, it had been a while since he'd seen one. Rafe had been sick since last September, and his picture taking had slowed way down. Still, she looked not-eating-well thin rather than trim from healthy workouts.

He bet she'd stopped eating well about three months ago. Probably the night her sister was shot and killed in a random convenience store hold-up. Then the rest of her appetite had probably disappeared a month ago when she'd become the guardian of her four nephews when their dad finally succumbed to the brain tumor that had been slowly stealing his life for eight months.

Tucker ached with it all. He'd lost his best friend, a man he'd grown up with and seen five times a year over the past twenty years. The guy he emailed inappropriate cartoons and jokes to, the guy he texted while watching Nebraska football, the guy who was always only a phone call away whether Tucker had good news or bad.

But Delaney had lost her sister *and* her brother-in-law. A brother-in-law who had been more like a brother. Rafe and Chelsea had gotten married when Delaney was only sixteen and she'd lived with them until she was about twenty. The three of them had been on their own down there in Nashville for the past thirteen years.

He couldn't even imagine what she was going through. An overnight mom with no one to help her out.

Well, that was where he came in. The four boys were all boy. He knew that they were energetic and curious and bright and rough-and-tumble. Exactly as boys should be.

Henry was twelve and definitely the leader of the bunch. He was a rule follower, the good kid, the good student, the good role model. He was more of a traditional ball-sport athlete, preferring basketball, baseball and football to dirt biking, but he was a good rider too. For the past three summers, he'd played baseball with the kids in Sapphire Falls and had developed some nice friendships. Tucker hoped that would be good for him since he was facing the first summer here without Rafe.

Charlie was ten and the bookworm of the group. He loved to read and to build things. He could take anything apart and put it back together. He had helped Tucker build

some ramps and lay out a miniature of the dirt course
Tucker now had on his property. But Charlie especially
loved engines, and he and Tucker's older brother, TJ, had
bonded over a lawn mower last summer.

David, the hellion, was eight. He pushed everyone's
boundaries and buttons just for the hell of it. He was loud
and dirty and spent more time being disciplined than the
rest, but he had a quick sense of humor and he loved
everything about farming. Tucker's other brother, Travis,
had let David help drive the tractor and watch a pig give
birth last summer, and David had been in heaven. It seemed
that farming calmed the kid. While he instigated most of
the tussles and fights with his brothers, he was gentle and
patient with the animals.

And finally, the six-year-old. Jack loved dirt bikes,
loved riding, was a daredevil and loved to go fast. All the
boys liked riding and had taken to it naturally and with
enthusiasm, but Jack lived for it. He'd be on a bike from
sunup to sundown if allowed. Tucker couldn't wait to see
what the kid could do now, being a year older and a little
bigger.

"Do I get a bike?" Jack asked him, wiggling on his lap
to look up at Tucker.

He had smudges of brownie in both corners of his
mouth and his big brown eyes were his dad's.

Tucker cleared his throat and forced a smile. "Yep, got
another one for you too, little man."

Last year, Jack had shared with David, but Tucker and
Rafe had talked about it, and the boys were riding for
different reasons and so needed different bikes. David
wasn't all that competitive. He liked riding for the ramps
and dips and tricks rather than actual racing. He was hard
on his bike—and himself. Ending up on his butt in the dirt
didn't bother David a bit, and Rafe had always said it was
the perfect outlet for all of his antagonistic energy. David
needed a bike he could beat up. Jack, on the other hand,

was all about racing and winning. He wanted to go fast and he wanted to cross that finish line ahead of everyone else. Tucker had found a sleek, almost-new bike that Jack could race.

"Well, this is a nice thing to walk in on."

Tucker looked up to find a beautiful blonde smiling at him and the boys. She put a hand on the back of his chair and leaned in.

"Hey, Jenna." Jenna Simpson was one of the damsels in distress in Sapphire Falls.

"I was looking for you," she said.

She smelled good. Tucker couldn't help his smile. The smelling-good thing was only one perk of being close to a girl. "Were you?"

"My truck's acting up again. I'm thinking it's the fuel line again. Could you take a look?"

Tucker loved a woman who drove a truck and who knew what the parts underneath the hood were called. He also loved that most of the single women his age came to him with these kinds of things—car repairs, basic home repairs, various other made-up issues. He liked being the guy the girls could turn to.

"Um, yeah, I could do that."

Jack squirmed on his lap, looking up at Jenna. "You smell like lemonade."

Right. Jack. And the other boys. And Delaney.

He cleared his throat. He had other responsibilities now.

But Jack was right. Jenna did smell like lemonade.

Jenna gave Jack a big smile. "Well, thanks, I think. Do you like lemonade?"

Jack nodded. "Lots."

Tucker chuckled. So Jack was going to be the ladies' man too.

Jenna lifted her gaze from Jack to Tucker. "There is really something about a hot guy holding a cute kid," she said.

Jack tipped his head to look up at Tucker, his face upside down. "Are you hot?" he asked.

"He is," Jenna assured Jack before Tucker could reply.

"You should have lemonade," Jack said. "That's cold."

Jenna laughed and Tucker bit his tongue.

It was the damndest thing really. Jenna was perfect for him. She was from here, beautiful, smart, sweet, drove a truck, wore cowboy boots, didn't get upset if her hands got a little dirty and she could bake. Man could she bake.

She met every item on his mental checklist.

And he was attracted to her. He could certainly have some fun with her between the sheets.

Yet he still wasn't dating her.

His brothers said there was something wrong with him.

His brothers might be right. If he dated her, he could have sex and cherry cobbler all the time. But he was holding out. He'd always known the right woman would come along eventually. And he had just enough sex and cherry cobbler to get by until she did.

He glanced at Delaney again, hesitantly now with Jenna flirting with him…and Jack. But Delaney had her elbow on the table, her chin propped on her hand, watching it all with mild interest. She really did look tired.

He definitely hadn't forgotten she was here. In fact, with Jenna standing so close, it seemed that his awareness of Delaney had been cranked up several notches. She not only had yellow frosting smudged on the front of her T-shirt, but she had a smear of chocolate on her arm and a few sugar crystals on her cheek near her ear. He'd guess she'd smell like sugar. Or sugar cookies.

He probably hadn't noticed all of that initially because he'd been trying *not* to stare at her, and because, well, the yellow frosting was on her left breast.

And there was a niggling voice in the back of his mind saying *maybe you've just been waiting to meet her.*

Damn if that voice didn't sound a lot like Rafe's.

Raphael Williams Castillo, known as Rafe Williams to everyone in Sapphire Falls, had been like another brother to Tucker growing up. The brown-eyed, brown-skinned mischief maker had come into Tucker's life in the summer before fifth grade and they'd been nearly inseparable after that. Tucker's brothers, Travis, TJ and Ty, had felt the same way about Rafe, and he'd been a part of most of their brotherly shenanigans. But Rafe had loved dirt biking and hunting more than Tucker's brothers, so the two boys had spent plenty of time on their own.

Of course, TJ, Travis and Ty had never passed up a dinner invitation to the Williams' place. Rafe's father, Marshall Williams, a Nebraska farmer through and through, had met Rafe's mother, Sofia Castillo, on a vacation to Mexico. It had been love at first sight and they'd gotten married two weeks later. They hadn't returned to Sapphire Falls for a few years though. It had been too hard for Sofia to leave her family. But eventually, Marshall had sweet-talked her out onto the farm. And she had ruined all of the Bennett boys for Mexican food forever. There would never be a tamale that could measure up. Ever.

"You want to come over tonight?" Jenna asked, pulling Tucker's attention back to the current moment. "I can cook."

And usually, that would be enough to get him there.

He shook his head. "I've got company."

"Oh, they're staying?" she asked, looking around the table again. Her gaze landed on Delaney—seemingly for the first time. "All of them?"

Tucker nodded. "Yep. All summer."

"These are Rafe's boys, right?" Jenna asked.

She knew they were. Everyone in town knew the boys. They were here every summer and loved Sapphire Falls. They loved the cheeseburgers at the diner and the soft-serve ice cream at the Stop, the gas station/convenience

store/pizza place/ice cream shop, and the nachos at the
Come Again, the only bar in town.

"Yep," Tucker said again.

"So where's Rafe?"

Everyone at the table suddenly froze. No one moved,
no one made a sound. Tucker felt his chest tighten. His
gaze immediately went to Delaney. She looked like Jenna
had just slapped her.

Fuck.

He thought everyone knew. They'd run an obituary for
Rafe. He'd gotten lots of, "I'm sorry," and, "Sorry to hear
about Rafe," when he'd been out and around town and he'd
gotten a few cards, along with requests for Rafe's mother's
address in Mexico. She'd moved back to be closer to her
family after Rafe's dad had died about ten years ago.
Tucker still sent her birthday and Mother's Day cards.

Apparently, Jenna hadn't been paying attention.

"You really look like your dad," she commented to
Charlie before anyone could say anything.

Charlie simply nodded, his face devoid of any other
emotion. He'd been told that since he'd been born.

"Jenna—" Tucker started, not really sure where he was
going with it. He didn't intend to ignore her question and
he wanted to address it in front of the boys so they knew it
was not a taboo subject.

"Rafe passed away a month ago."

The soft but firm voice pulled everyone's attention to
Delaney.

She was sitting up straight and meeting Jenna's eyes
directly. "I'm sorry you didn't know."

Delaney looked around the table and met each of the
boys' gazes with clear affection and support. "The boys and
I are spending the summer here in Sapphire Falls,
remembering him and celebrating all of the wonderful
things that he loved about this town and all of the good
times the boys had with him. It's really important to him

that the boys have an amazing summer here with Tucker."
Finally, she looked at Tucker. "We love to talk about him,
but sometimes it still hits us hard."

Several things hit Tucker hard.

The hardest to ignore was that Delaney's love and
protectiveness of the boys made him want her.

He also noticed that she'd said this summer was
important to Rafe. As in present tense. Not that it *had been*
important to him, but that it was *now*.

He liked that.

"I'm so sorry."

Tucker looked up at Jenna. She looked legitimately
stricken.

He gave her a smile. "It's okay." He looked around the
table. "We're all going to be okay."

Henry met Tucker's gaze but he didn't say or do
anything. Charlie was looking at his lap. David was glaring
at his cookies. And he couldn't see Jack's face, but he
could feel the little boy holding himself tight.

He finally met Delaney's eyes again. "Everything is
going to be okay."

She gave him a little nod. "Definitely."

"I hadn't heard," Jenna said. "I just feel awful. I'll bring
over…a casserole or something." She sounded completely
flustered.

"I could really use some help." A voice broke into
Jenna's stumbling.

Everyone turned to look at Adrianne Riley, the owner
and baker of Scott's Sweets. She wore a big smile and a
purple apron over a simple T-shirt and jeans. "I have a huge
batch of fudge I'm trying to finish and I could use some
more hands."

"I'll help!" Jack immediately began squirming and
Tucker let him slide to the floor.

Jack took Adrianne's hand.

"I could use someone taller to stir," she said, looking at

Henry.

Henry didn't say anything, but he pushed his chair back and stood.

"How about you guys? I could use a taste tester," she added.

That got David's attention. "I'll do it!" He was up and out of his chair in a blink.

"Um, don't let him near the burners," Delaney said. She looked at David. "Or the mixers. Or the knives. Or…most of your kitchen," she finished weakly.

Adrianne chuckled. "Got it. I'm thinking Charlie can help me keep an eye on him?" She directed the question to the final brother still sitting at the table.

Charlie got to his feet. "Okay."

Charlie could indeed help keep an eye on David. If he didn't get distracted by all the new machinery and tools in the kitchen.

"Um, you might want to keep *him* away from anything that…can be taken apart," Tucker said.

Adrianne gave him a wink. "We're good."

Tucker really liked Adrianne.

"I'm going to go," Jenna said as the boys headed for the kitchen with Adrianne.

The two youngest were holding Adrianne's hands and already asking a million questions, the two older ones following behind.

Adrianne was fine with the boys. She had two of her own, and even at their young ages, they were a handful and a half.

She seemed to love it.

"I'm really sorry, again," Jenna said sincerely, her voice soft and sad.

He looked up at her. "It really is okay. Not your fault."

"I know you were really good friends," Jenna said. "If you need anything, let me know."

He knew that she wanted more than a couple of tumbles

in bed and a few car repairs from him. And he also knew that her sympathy was real. That was how it went around here. He'd known Jenna most of his life. Yes, there was dancing at the bar and beer parties at the river and flirtations that sometimes went too far and didn't end until morning. But at the bottom of it all were real friendships and caring that stemmed from knowing people and their families and sharing a love of their hometown.

"Thanks. I will." He meant that too. If he needed a cup of sugar, to borrow a cooler, a ride somewhere, a shoulder to lean on...or a soft body to get lost in for a few hours, he could call Jenna and she'd be there.

"Nice to meet you," Jenna said to Delaney. "I'm sorry for your loss."

Looking at Delaney again, Tucker knew he wouldn't be calling Jenna, for anything, for a long while.

It also occurred to him that he hadn't even introduced the women. His mother would have smacked him.

"Thank you," Delaney said, even giving Jenna a small smile. "I'm sure we'll see each other around this summer."

"Okay. Bye."

Jenna left the shop without making a purchase and Tucker had to wonder if she'd come in because she'd seen his truck rather than because of a need for candy.

As the bell jingled over the door and then bumped shut behind Jenna, Tucker and Delaney were left relatively alone.

For the first time ever.

He knew things about her that he didn't know about some of the women he'd grown up with.

He knew she was a peanut-butter fanatic. He knew she had watched every episode of *NCIS: LA* three times, all seasons. He knew she loved country music and her favorite artist was Brett Eldredge.

Of course, he knew all of that from Rafe. Rafe made fun of her peanut-butter obsession, had watched all the

NCIS: LA episodes with her and had given her tickets for a Brett Eldredge show for her birthday.

Now Tucker wanted to know a lot more, and he wanted to find it all out for himself.

Tucker let himself focus on Delaney. He'd been avoiding letting his gaze rest on her for more than a glance at a time because…well, frankly, the urge to pull her into his arms and let her rest her head on his shoulder was nearly overpowering. But now, looking at her, he saw more. Besides tired and messy, she looked like she was being held together by chewing gum and rubber bands—loosely and not well.

He barely knew her and he could tell she was on the verge of tears.

Tucker had grown up one of four boys himself. So he knew about three percent of the things about women that he should. But he did know that women cried for a whole host of reasons.

He wasn't about to try to guess the reason for Delaney's seemingly imminent tears, but he did know that she wouldn't want the boys to see them and he also knew that she needed to let them out.

Without thinking, he reached for her hand and sandwiched her tiny one between his. "I'm glad you're here."

She didn't look startled at his touch, and she didn't pull away. In fact, her fingers curled around his. Which was interesting. And stupidly, inappropriately arousing.

Yes, he liked to take care of women. Yes, he felt close to this one because of their shared love and loss of their best friend. Yes, she looked like she desperately needed someone on her side, holding her up and holding her together.

But he also really wanted to kiss her.

"I'm really glad to be here," she said. "The boys need you."

So do you. He didn't say it. She might not appreciate that a bit. But she did need him. Even without Rafe telling him that she did, Tucker would have thought so.

"I love those boys. This will be a great summer, I promise."

Tucker knew that she was intending to take the boys to Colorado to be closer to her parents. Tucker also knew Rafe and Delaney had argued about that. Rafe didn't want her to go, but he acknowledged that she didn't have many options. Delaney hadn't wanted to stay in Nashville with all of the memories there. She wanted a new start for her and the boys. Her only family now was in Colorado and that seemed the best choice.

But only because she didn't know Sapphire Falls. Yet.

Sapphire Falls was a better place for her and the boys than Colorado, without question. Delaney and her sister had been estranged from their parents for thirteen years. Their parents had thrown Chelsea out when she got together with Rafe, and Delaney had followed her sister only a few weeks later. Tucker didn't know every detail about that, but he did know that Rafe and Chelsea had taken Delaney in and they had been the three musketeers ever since. To say that Rafe had been concerned about Delaney leaning on her parents now would be an understatement. Rafe had hoped this summer with Tucker would ensure she would come back to Sapphire Falls often to visit.

And now, within the first five minutes Tucker had ever actually spent with her, over a table covered with cookie and brownie crumbs, with her looking like a wilting flower in the hot summer sun, Tucker definitely wanted to convince her to do more than visit.

Tucker pulled his hands away and sat back. *Whoa.* That was fast. And…a lot. Even for a guy drawn to women in need, that was a lot.

"We should get you all out to the farm. You can relax. You look like you need a shower."

A heartbeat later, he realized how that sounded. And it hadn't sounded like a come-on. *That* he could have dealt with.

Her eyes widened. She looked down at herself, lifted her hand to hair and then looked back at him.

And started laughing.

Tucker felt relief wash through him as his mouth curled. Okay, so he hadn't offended her. Or she was too tired to do anything but laugh hysterically. Either way, he wasn't getting slapped.

"You have no idea how much I'd love a shower," she said.

That wasn't a come-on either, he knew, but his imagination didn't care.

He cleared his throat as his mind ran with the image of her taking her hair down from the bun and it cascading over her naked back.

Dammit. He'd been quickly attracted to women before. He had an active imagination. But there was no way in hell he was going to make a move on a woman in mourning, overwhelmed with her new life responsibilities and completely out of her element.

Their situation was complicated.

She was staying at his farm with the boys as Rafe always did. They couldn't have a fling. Unless of course it lasted all summer...

"I'm going to apologize ahead of time for the sugar high and the coming crash for the four boys in the other room," Delaney said.

He grinned. "I've got a *farm*."

She raised an eyebrow, indicating she had no idea what he was talking about.

"Plenty of fresh air and room for them to run and work off some of the energy and plenty of chores to be done if they're grumpy or fighting."

She actually took a deep breath at that. "They need that.

So much. Eight hours in the car two days in a row… I know I should have broken the trip up more, but I was so anxious to get here."

She meant because of the boys. She meant because she wanted to get out of Nashville and away from the sad memories. She meant because she needed his help. But damn if Tucker didn't want her to mean more than that. He wanted her to be anxious to see him for *him*.

And how was that even a tiny possibility? She didn't *know* him.

Surely Rafe had talked about him as much as he'd talked about her. Surely when they got back from their summer trips the boys told her about him. Okay, the chances were better that they told her all about the farm and the dirt bikes and the swimming hole and the festival. Tucker knew he was important to the boys, but he and all of that were wrapped up together in their minds.

He was just going to have to show Delaney who he was and that there were lots of reasons to be glad to see him.

He grinned at that.

This had all the makings of a fantastic summer.

"Let's get the hoodlums out of here," he said, stretching to his feet and holding his hand out to her.

She took it without hesitation and let him pull her to her feet.

They stood close—probably too close—and looked into each other's eyes for a moment.

But in the brief bit of time, Tucker felt the connection. The *I know you* that didn't make a lot of sense but felt pretty damned real.

Then the moment was gone. Delaney stepped back and turned toward the swinging doors to the kitchen to retrieve the boys. He'd been so caught up in her, he hadn't noticed the talk and laughter coming from the kitchen.

Man, he owed Adrianne.

"I need about three dozen to go," he told her as he

strode into the back room.

Adrianne looked up from the work counter where she had Jack putting candied flowers onto squares of white fudge. Henry was stirring at the stove and Charlie and David were popping chocolates out of candy molds and arranging them on trays.

"Take whatever you want. The boxes are under the front counter," she told him. "Okay, boys, soap and water is right over there."

Tucker watched Delaney as she watched the boys all abandon their jobs and head for the big sink along the far wall.

"Holy crap," she muttered.

If he hadn't been standing close he wouldn't have even heard it, but it made him smile.

They washed up and Tucker loaded them all into his pickup. He didn't doubt for a second that giving Delaney some time to herself was a good move. Plus, the boys loved the big truck and there was no chance they could get it dirty—the truck was made for dirt.

Delaney got into her Jeep with the rented moving trailer behind it, ready to follow him to the farm with all their stuff.

Tucker shifted the truck into drive and pointed it east, feeling a strange contentment as he started toward his farm with Rafe's boys and Delaney.

They were going home.

CHAPTER TWO

Tucker's farm was exactly as she'd imagined it.

The farmhouse was a big white two story with a ton of windows. It appeared newer than she'd expected—she'd envisioned him living in a house that had been passed down through the generations—but it looked perfectly at place in the ring of trees that *had* been there for generations and the land that rolled out in all directions toward fields and pastures. It had a stereotypically wonderful wraparound porch and a porch swing.

Delaney grinned at that. He had a porch swing. That had to be a sign that she was in the right place.

Delaney loved porch swings. Well, she loved the *idea* of porch swings. She'd never actually sat on one. But a house like this had to have a porch swing.

She pulled up behind Tucker's truck in the gravel lane several yards in front of the house and killed the engine.

The sun was shining brightly and she would bet a good chunk of change that she'd hear birds singing as soon as she opened the Jeep's door. The sky was blue, there was a light breeze and the temperature was a perfect seventy-three degrees.

Delaney looked up at the cloudless sky. "Okay, Rafe, it's gorgeous. You made your point. You don't have to…"

She trailed off as she saw the four boys tumble out of Tucker's truck and go running toward the barn and the grove of trees behind it. Three dogs seemed to appear out of nowhere, chasing the boys, barking and jumping.

David stopped and dropped to the dirt and one of the dogs jumped on his chest, knocking him back onto the ground and covering his face with dog kisses. Delaney gripped the steering wheel and just watched. The boys had never had a dog—or any other kind of pet—but they loved animals, especially David. She didn't know much about dogs either, but she did know the big gray thing sitting on David was a pit bull. Who was clearly very happy to see her nephew.

Another dog, who was much smaller and looked to be a mutt, watched them, hesitating to get involved, but with his tail wagging so hard that his whole body shook. David looked over at the dog and reached out a hand. The smaller dog took the invitation instantly, running forward and licking any spot on David's face the first dog hadn't claimed.

The third dog was clearly a puppy, a basset hound or at least a mix, if she wasn't mistaken. His ears were longer than his front legs and his tongue hung out of what almost looked like a grin. He loped from one end of David to the other, as if he wasn't sure where to start. He finally decided on chewing and tugging on the toe of David's shoe.

Jack and Henry were almost to the barn, but Charlie swung around, saw David and the dogs and ran back, his face bright and happy.

"You don't have to push it," she finished softly.

This place was perfect. The boys' laughter and happy faces would have been enough for her to think so. But add in three cute dogs, the endless blue sky and bold-green grass and bright-red barn and the place looked like a postcard promoting the goodness of country living.

And then there was the hot farmer striding toward her.

Damn. He didn't hurt the scenery one bit either.

She pushed her door open, paused for a moment with her head cocked until she heard the birds chirping, shook her head and got out.

"Welcome." Tucker stood inside her open door, his grin almost as big as the boys' had been.

"Thanks. It's beautiful here." She looked around. "The boys know your dogs."

"Two of them," he said with a nod. "I've had Luna for about six years and Tank for five."

"Tank's the pit bull, I assume?"

Tucker shook his head. "That's Luna. Tank's the mutt."

"The *little* mutt?" she asked, watching David, Charlie and the dogs.

"Yep. And he barely barks, has never growled and doesn't know a single command. But he's the sweetest dog I've ever met."

She raised a hand to block the sun shining into her eyes, but she wasn't watching the boys and dogs now. She looked up into Tucker's face.

"What about the puppy?"

His smile was almost boyish.

Well, damn. That was hard to look away from.

"I got him about two weeks ago."

"What's his name?"

"I'm going to let the boys name him."

Oh, man. He was a nice guy. "You got the boys a puppy?"

Leaving at the end of the summer was going to be hard enough.

He nodded, clearly unapologetic—or maybe unaware of how that could complicate things. "Boys need dogs."

"There were already two."

"And those boys can wear those dogs out," he said with a laugh. "We needed a young'un. Boys and dogs go together. They run and jump and play and..." He trailed off, as if he hadn't meant to say what he'd almost said.

"And?" she pressed.

He sighed and looked a little sheepish. "Cuddle."

She blinked at him. Had he just said the word cuddle?

"What did you say?" she asked. She felt the corner of her mouth twitch and try to curl up, but she fought it.

He sighed again. "I said cuddle."

She pressed her lips together. He'd said cuddle. "And the boys need a dog to cuddle with, huh?"

Tucker seemed to recover from his embarrassment. He

flashed her a grin. "Everyone needs someone to cuddle with."

She almost groaned at the jolt of heat that his words evoked. Dammit. They shouldn't flirt.

And in a second, when his grin faded, she would probably remember why.

Actually, she was a fan of cuddling. She got plenty of it from Jack, and even David when he was sleepy and mellow. She read to them each night, they sat together and watched movies, Jack preferred her lap to sitting on a chair of his own. Yep, she got plenty of cuddling. But cuddling with Tucker…well, it was safe to say that SpongeBob would not be the main entertainment.

So it was still there. That feeling of connection, of some kind of string wrapping around both of them and pulling them together. She'd felt it at the bakery when their gazes had met—corny but true—and then when he'd taken her hand she'd felt that string pull tight.

And they did have a connection. A few in fact. They'd both known and loved Rafe, they'd both lost him and their lives would be forever altered because of that. They also shared a love and a determination to do right for the boys. And, yeah, there was a physical attraction. At least on her end. Of course, she was *alive*, and she was pretty sure that's all it really took for a woman to be attracted to this man. But she'd seen something in his eyes too—something that wasn't sympathy or concern. There had been a flicker of heat, of appreciation for her as a woman.

Considering sympathy and concern had been all she'd gotten from other adults for the past four months, she very much responded to that.

She knew that's what it was, *all* it was—being seen as something besides the grieving, overwhelmed executor of Rafe and Chelsea's estate and the grieving, overwhelmed guardian of four little boys. That made Tucker's male appreciation of her feel even better than it would have otherwise. But she still welcomed it.

Delaney knew she looked like a mess. She knew that in many ways she *was* a mess. That's what *she* saw when she looked at herself. So hell yeah, she was going to like it—a lot—if someone looked at her and saw more than that.

But like all the other nice, quiet moments over the past few months, the minute passed quickly. She heard a shout and looked to find that all of the boys and dogs had disappeared from sight.

"Okay, so..." She moved past Tucker, avoiding brushing up against him—because she thought maybe she'd never stop rubbing up against him if she started—and took a few steps in the direction of the barn.

"Whoa there."

She felt a strong hand circle her wrist and Tucker tugged her to a stop.

She turned, eyebrows up. "What?"

"They're fine."

She glanced toward the barn. "But—"

"There is nothing out there that they can hurt. They've been here enough to know the rules about where they can go and what they can do."

He still held her wrist and she did nothing to try to loosen his hold.

"But there are things that can hurt *them*," she pointed out.

"We have a very good doctor in town."

She felt her eyes widen and she pulled on her wrist. "Wha—"

He chuckled and tightened his grip slightly. "I'm kidding. They're fine. They're going to be dirty and tired later. Nothing more." He gently pulled and she took a step closer to him. "I promise," he said, his voice a little lower. "The boys are going to be fine."

Delaney looked up into his eyes and felt something that reminded her of relief trickle through her chest. It wasn't much, but it was the first she'd felt that in a really long time.

He wasn't only referring to them playing by the barn right now.

Lord, the urge to step in and beg him to wrap his arms around her was strong. She thought he'd do it too. There was an air about him that made her think he was used to taking care of people, that it was a natural instinct.

If that was true, she was going to have to constantly remind herself that a huge part of her attraction here was that she had no clue what she was doing in the most important role of her life—mom.

She took a deep breath and nodded. "Okay."

"Let me show you around the house. Grab what you need right now and the boys and I will unload everything later on."

Great. One thing at a time. That was how the school counselor had suggested she approach everything right now. And that worked for Delaney.

Chelsea had been the planner, the organizer, the one with the huge wall calendar, the book-size planner and the little notebook she carried in her purse. Delaney just...went along. Their family certainly hadn't needed *two* hyper, extra-organized, plan-every-second stress balls. And in all fairness, Chelsea had never seemed stressed. She'd thrived on keeping everyone and everything going.

Simply watching her had stressed Delaney some days.

So she hadn't watched. She'd sat back and waited for Chelsea to tell her what was going on and when. Chelsea had run the house, their business and the family. When their parents had first thrown Chelsea out for dating Rafe and then said "fine" when Delaney threatened to go with her, Delaney had lived with Chelsea and Rafe. She had, of course, been in her own apartment since Charlie had been born. But she'd worked with Chelsea, eaten dinner at their house almost every night and had spent many nights on the pull-out couch since Rafe's diagnosis.

"Which bag?" Tucker asked.

Delaney pulled herself back to the moment she was supposed to be in now. She also needed to work on the dwelling-in-the-past thing, according to another grief counselor she'd talked to.

"The big red one," she said.

He still hadn't let go of her, and she got the sense that he wasn't going to. At least, not until he was sure she wasn't going to bolt. Whether he thought she was going to head to the barn or get in her Jeep and drive away, she wasn't sure. And she wouldn't *actually* do either of those things. She knew nothing about barns, so she wouldn't know if the boys were getting into trouble or not, and she would never leave them. Not for good. For a trip downtown for a drink, maybe. If there was someone to stay with them, of course.

She watched Tucker heave her big duffle over his shoulder and knew, deep in her bones, that he was that guy. He'd be with them, for anything, anytime.

So her getting a drink wasn't completely out of the question.

That was good. Very good. She hadn't had a drink of anything alcoholic in four months. And frankly, if there had ever been a time that she'd needed it, the past four months was it.

Tucker faced her, the bag over his shoulder, her wrist encircled by his big hand. "Okay?"

Delaney took a deep breath and nodded. "I think I'm going to be." That was as honest as she could be at the moment. But it felt good to even say that. There had been some recent days when *okay* had seemed a long way off.

"You *are* going to be."

He said it with a confidence in his eyes and his voice that made her heart trip a little. Maybe he wasn't just determined to make sure the boys were okay. Maybe he was going to make her okay too.

She was game. For whatever it took. Being okay, even feeling kind of okay, would be awesome.

"Thanks, Tucker," she said softly.

Something flickered in his eyes, and for the tiniest one-one-thousandth of a second, she thought he might kiss her.

"Of course," he said instead. "Anything. You're here now. It's all good."

That sounded...perfect.

"Let me show you the house."

He slipped his hand from her wrist to link his fingers with hers. And she let him. There was no harm in that. No reason not to.

He led her up the porch steps and Delaney cast a wistful glance at the swing. Later. She was definitely sitting on that thing sometime between now and tomorrow.

Tucker had to let go of her to open the front door and he didn't reach for her hand again after he swung it open. He must have decided she was going to stay. Too bad. Her hand felt cold without his grasp.

He set the bag on the floor at the base of the staircase that sat off to the left of the small entryway. To the right, two steps led down into the living room with two huge couches, a coffee table laden with magazines and newspapers and the biggest television she'd ever seen. There was also a stuffed wingback chair near a stone fireplace and a rocking chair that sat by the large picture window that overlooked the portion of the porch opposite where the swing hung.

Yep, she was going to sit in that rocking chair too.

A rocking chair by the window.

Perfect.

"Living room," Tucker said with a grin.

"Nice."

"Glad you think so. My mom was dying to come over and clean."

Delaney smiled up at him. "You don't clean?"

"Not to her standards, no. Then again, no one cleans to her standards."

He started across the huge living room toward a swinging door that she assumed led into the kitchen.

"Why didn't you let her come clean?" Delaney had to ask.

He chuckled and held the swinging door open for her. "Because she would have made it last all day so she could be here when you got here."

Delaney stepped into the kitchen and looked around, cataloging several details automatically. It was a habit that came from spending ten to twelve hours a day renovating other people's houses for a living. She was especially critical of kitchens. "She wanted to meet me?"

"Oh, you have no idea," Tucker said. "She loves the boys too, of course, but yeah, my family is pretty curious about you."

She turned to face him. He'd let the door swing shut behind him. He had a hip propped against the countertop beside him and his hands tucked into the back pockets of his blue jeans. The position pulled the cotton T-shirt tight across his chest and stomach and Delaney had to force her eyes back to his face.

Which was absolutely as nice to look at as those pecs.

"Why are they curious?"

He gave her a half grin. "You really don't know?"

She shook her head with a frown. She could admit that she'd been in a bit of a fog lately, so she wasn't surprised to feel like she was missing something. "I really don't."

"Rafe has them convinced you're the one."

Delaney's heart thudded at that. "The one?" Surely he didn't mean…

"For me."

That was exactly what Rafe thought. She grimaced. "Sorry. Rafe thinks that I need someone to take care of me."

That sounded pathetic. But it was true. Rafe had always wanted her to find someone, and in the last few months of his life, especially at the very end, it had become an obsession of his. Particularly after Chelsea's death, when it had become clear that Delaney would be taking care of the boys.

Tucker chuckled.

Her eyes flew to his face. The happy sound was in such contrast with what she'd been thinking and feeling, but it made the embarrassment fade.

"He's been trying to set us up for a really long time. Guess he finally got his way."

She studied Tucker's face, a million things going through her mind. She liked that he didn't treat the subject of Rafe as taboo or something to be careful about.

"I'll bet he's feeling pretty damn proud of himself," she said. "I'm finally here in Sapphire Falls, on your farm. After hearing all about it—and you—for as long as I've known him."

Tucker's grin grew. "I can picture that damn smug smile clearly."

Delaney felt her mouth curl.

"He was talking about you bringing the boys to Sapphire Falls even back when he first got sick. He didn't know if he'd be up to it, and he didn't want them to miss out and…" Tucker shrugged and gave her an almost-embarrassed grin. "He thought we'd hit it off."

She tipped her head. "I've never known if I should trust him on this. He has horrible taste in movies, but excellent taste in pizza."

Something changed in Tucker's expression. He went from amused and flirtatious to something softer, affectionate. "You talk about him in the present tense."

Her smile died and she crossed her arms. "I know. I can't help it."

Tucker pushed away from the counter and came toward her. He didn't take his hands out of his pockets, didn't touch her, but he got close enough that she had to tip her head back. "Don't stop, okay?"

She felt something clench in her chest. That urge to ask for a hug was strong, and she felt the words on the tip of her tongue. She swallowed hard and simply nodded.

"It makes it feel…better." Tucker cleared his throat. "A lot better."

And it hit her—Tucker had lost his friend too. This was the first summer without Rafe for him too. In fact, Tucker had known him longer.

It wasn't as if any of those were exactly new thoughts. She knew all of that, had thought about it. But standing here with Tucker, looking into his eyes and seeing his heartbreak up close, made her realize for the first time that maybe Rafe hadn't sent her here only for herself or for the boys. Maybe Tucker needed them here just as much.

She gave in. It wasn't as though she was emotionally strong right now anyway. She stepped forward and wrapped her arms around Tucker's waist, putting her cheek against his chest.

His arms came around her without hesitation, and he rested his chin on her head.

He was six-two or three, several inches taller than her own five-foot-seven. He was hard where she was soft. They were a perfect fit.

He felt strong and warm and…*alive*.

She'd always been affectionate with the boys, and they'd been raised with hugging and kissing and I love yous, but Delaney knew that she'd been overdoing it with them lately. It was as though she was constantly in need of feeling their breathing and wriggling. She even loved the squeals of "ewww" when she got kissy with them. Because that was *alive*, that was normal, that was healthy.

Of course, Tucker wasn't saying "ewww," and he

wasn't trying to get away. But neither did he do anything but hold her. Neither of them said anything. Their hands didn't stray. Hers remained flat against his back, his clasped at her lower back. For several long moments. Several long moments that were the best she'd had in a really long time.

"I'm thinking that maybe this is more of a pizza situation than a movie situation," Tucker finally said, his voice rumbling under her ear.

She pulled back, her chest tight. She wet her lips and managed a small smile. "He has never ever introduced me to a pizza I didn't like."

Tucker looked like he was going to say something—or do something—and suddenly Delaney pulled back and spun away from him to focus on his cupboards.

Cupboards she could deal with. Intense feelings that came in the midst of the most emotional, confusing, overwhelming time in her life for a guy she'd just met, probably not so much. They had all the ingredients for some very bad decisions.

"This kitchen is great," she said.

"You think so?" he asked, apparently letting go of whatever had been between them a moment ago.

"Definitely. Great space. And light. How old is everything in here?"

"Built the house ten years ago."

"You built it?" she asked, glancing over at him. She would happily admit that a guy who knew his way around a tool belt got points with her.

"With my brothers' help," he confirmed.

She looked over the appliances and cupboards, windows, even the table and chairs. "You picked everything out?"

He shrugged. "Yeah. Though I'll confess I didn't put a lot of thought into things in here. Just the basics."

That's what it looked like. It was all fine. Functional.

But nothing special.

"The kitchen isn't a big deal to you?" she asked.

He shrugged again. "Does it make me an ass to admit that I still eat at my mom's a lot?"

She had to smile at that. "Your mom still cooks for you?"

"She loves it." He was quick with his defense. "And TJ still eats there a lot too. Travis did too until he got married." He paused, then said, "Come to think of it, him and Lauren are at Mom's a lot too."

"None of you cook?"

"Not like Mom."

"So you're over there for dinner all the time?"

"Most nights. And breakfast sometimes." He gave her a grin that said he didn't feel one bit bad about any of it.

That sounded like Heaven to Delaney. She turned back to pretend to study the cupboards rather than his grin.

She didn't cook either and had counted on her sister to keep her fed at least four days a week. She got by on sandwiches, frozen meals, takeout and soup the rest of the time—to keep from being completely pathetic. But cooking for one wasn't so great anyway.

There was something so wonderful about a number of people gathered around a table, passing dishes, laughing and talking. Thank God, Chelsea had been a good cook. Of course, Chelsea had been good at everything.

Delaney was going to miss all of that. She'd have to make a point of getting the boys around the table for dinner each night. Somehow. They'd been existing on sympathy food from friends and neighbors and takeout for the past couple of months. That was the thing about having two family members die close together—lots of casseroles.

She didn't blame Tucker for eating at his mom's at all.

"So, you can have free rein in here."

She turned to look at him. His eyes were bright, his smile huge.

"Yeah?"

"Absolutely."

A thrill went through her. She hadn't done a project since Chelsea had died.

Delaney looked at the cupboards, the sink and appliances, the wall that separated the kitchen from the mudroom that led to the back door. This might be great therapy actually. Something she could get involved in, feel productive at, enjoy.

"That would be fantastic," she said, her voice a little breathless when she smiled up at Tucker.

His smile grew. "Then consider this room all yours."

"We should talk about what you like and want—"

"Whatever *you* want," he cut in. "I'll like anything you do, I'm sure."

"Anything?" she repeated. "Really?"

"Absolutely."

She looked around the room again. She hadn't done a free-for-all project since before she and Chelsea had started their business doing restorations and renovations seven years ago. Obviously, they were hired to makeover things for their *clients*. Delaney and Chelsea brought in ideas, but ultimately it was the clients' choice.

"That's amazing, Tucker. Thank you. This might be exactly what I need."

"I know it's going to be a win-win." He gave her another heart-tripping smile. "Let me show you the rest of the house and your room. You can get that shower and maybe a nap."

A shower and a nap. Delaney actually groaned at the thought. Those two simple things had never sounded better to anyone ever, she was sure.

Tucker cleared his throat and held the kitchen door open again. "Right this way."

ॐ

"It's really too bad that Delaney had to miss her own engagement party." Travis, Tucker's older brother, laughed at his own joke.

And so it begins.

Tucker sighed.

His family had said nothing about Delaney's absence from dinner later that day other than, "That's too bad," and, "We were looking forward to meeting her," when he'd told them she was exhausted and he'd left her sleeping to bring the boys to his mom's for supper.

They'd all used their napkins and utensils and manners like normal people. They'd passed the fried chicken and mashed potatoes and fresh green beans and salad like normal people. They'd talked about work and the dirt-bike track they had just finished like normal people. And Tucker had made sure the boys ate all of their beans, and that David and Charlie both had seconds of potatoes, and that the boys all had a chance to talk about their day and what they were looking forward to for the summer—like *normal* people.

But now the boys were finished and had run outside to play in the tree house out back and it was just Tucker and his parents. And his two brothers and his sister-in-law.

Yeah, it kind of seemed like a party.

"Shut up, Travis," Tucker said simply. It didn't matter how old a man got, no one could make him crazy—and immature—like his brothers.

"Well, geez, Mom even got the tablecloth out," Travis said, managing to tease his younger brother and his mother all at once.

The table didn't simply have a white linen tablecloth on it. There was also a huge vase of wildflowers in the center, wine glasses and cloth napkins at each setting, and the dinner rolls were in a basket with another linen cloth. Usually the rolls were thrown on a plate.

Wine glasses. Along with a bottle of red wine. Tucker hadn't even known his mother had that many wine glasses. They didn't drink wine with dinner around here. Beer maybe, once in a while. But only out of the bottle.

Kathy Bennett made a face at her son. "I was hoping to make a good first impression. She's the boys' guardian. She's part of the family now. No matter what."

Tucker felt a twinge in his chest in spite of the "no matter what" that translated to "even if Tucker doesn't marry her". Which he knew his mother was sort of, kind of hoping for. She would never admit it, but when she'd found out that Delaney had become the guardian for Rafe's kids, she had likely conjured all kinds of fairytale scenarios where she became a mother-in-law again *and* a grandmother to four all at once.

If she could get away with it, Kathy would offer TJ or Ty up to Delaney if Tucker didn't cooperate.

But that was part of the major craziness here. He would be happy to cooperate.

He'd met the woman five hours ago for the first time and he'd already come up with a bunch of wacky shit himself. Stuff like her moving into his house permanently and them raising the boys together.

And going to bed together every night.

He sighed and reached for the bottle of wine. It was the only alcohol available and he had a feeling he was going to need *something*.

He and Delaney had simply hugged. In a sort of sad moment. How could he be thinking about taking her to bed? Okay, out by the car when he was getting her bag, he'd thought about kissing her for a split second. But that had also been a sort of sad moment.

One thing was for sure—they were going to cut way back on the sort of sad moments. It was summertime in Sapphire Falls. His favorite time of year. And he had a beautiful woman and four rambunctious boys living with him.

This was going to be the best summer he could make for all of them, and they'd deal with what came after that later. It really did feel natural to think of having the boys around all the time, and he knew that the Bennetts and Sapphire Falls would be so good for them—on a permanent basis—but they had time to worry about what happened in August later.

As for Delaney, what his mom said was true. His family would embrace Delaney, already had even having never met her, because she was part of the boys' life. That was how the Bennett clan did things. If you mattered to one of the Bennetts, you mattered to all of them. Rafe had mattered to all of them. Delaney had mattered to Rafe. So Delaney mattered to all of them.

He had a feeling that would overwhelm Delaney, even though she really needed it. Her sister and Rafe were gone, she wasn't close to her own parents, Rafe's mom was in Mexico. She might not realize it, but she needed the Bennetts. And they'd be there for her.

"That's funny," TJ said, coming into the room with a huge platter of cake. "I don't remember us ever using a tablecloth when Rafe was around."

It was German chocolate cake, to be specific, and Tucker groaned again. A tablecloth and German chocolate cake? Definitely a party.

Kathy shook her head. "We use a tablecloth every Thanksgiving, Christmas and Easter, and Rafe was here for all of those over the years."

It was true. And actually drove home the point even harder—this was a special occasion in Kathy's mind.

"But this is engagement cake," Travis said, taking a piece for himself before his brothers could get to it. He offered Lauren a piece but she passed.

"This is German chocolate cake," Kathy said. "Not engagement cake."

TJ, Tucker and Travis all exchanged a look and then laughed.

Kathy frowned. "What?"

"It's German chocolate," Travis agreed. "But the only time you make it is when someone gets engaged around here."

"It's your father's favorite," Kathy said.

"And you think of dad whenever you make it," Travis said. "I know."

Kathy's cheeks were pink, and Tucker glanced at his dad. Thomas was smiling at his wife of thirty-three years with affection, but also a hint of something more—maybe even heat. But Tucker didn't really want to think about that.

"The last time you made this cake," Travis said, after swallowing a huge bite, "was when Lauren and I got engaged."

"That doesn't mean it's engagement cake," Kathy protested, but it was less adamant than before.

Travis laughed. "You made it when Adrianne and Mason got engaged. You made it when Joe and Phoebe got engaged. You made it when *TJ* got engaged."

TJ's marriage hadn't lasted, and their mother had never liked Michelle, but they'd had an engagement party anyway.

TJ chuckled. "Being subtle has never been your strong suit, Mom. But don't worry, we all know you'd rather have Delaney over for pie and coffee some afternoon when we're all busy so you can *really* grill her—I mean, get to know her."

Kathy narrowed her eyes and pointed at her oldest son. "You're never too big that I won't take a wooden spoon to your backside."

That was hilarious. One, Kathy Bennett had never taken a wooden spoon to anyone's backside in their lives. She'd threatened it—oh, had she threatened it—but she'd never done it.

Of course, the palm of her hand was a different story.

And two, TJ was six-four and two-hundred-some pounds. No one was taking a wooden spoon, or anything else, to him.

"Well, whatever you think you know about my German chocolate cake, sitting down with a tablecloth and the good silver once in a while doesn't hurt any of you," Kathy told them. "At least we showed the boys that we all know how to use utensils and say grace and mind our manners."

Laughter erupted again. The boys had been as confused by the formality as anyone. They had been around enough to know how dinner at the Bennett table went. You sat down, you said grace and you dug in. You didn't use your mouth for talking until you were full or all the food would be gone before you got around to eating.

"You're so good with them, Tucker," Lauren said from across the table where she sat with Travis's arm draped over the back of her chair.

"Thanks," Tucker said. "I've known them their whole lives. They're great kids."

"It's clear they really love you," Lauren said. "And they look up to you."

Tucker felt a warmth in his chest. He wanted to be someone the boys could look up to. Even if Rafe had still been around, Tucker would have wanted to be a role model. But with their dad gone, they would need that male influence in their lives.

"That's a big deal to me."

"It's really nice." She smiled but sniffed at the same time. Her eyes were shiny and she wiped away what he could have sworn was a tear. But this was *Lauren*. Tough, brilliant, world-traveler, businesswoman, scientist Lauren.

Still, tears wouldn't be the strangest change he'd seen in his sister-in-law. Lauren was seven months pregnant. She'd always had an incredible body and had turned pretty much every male head in town. Now she had a round belly

and had given up her high heels and short, fitted skirts—
temporarily, she insisted—and honestly, she was even more
beautiful in Tucker's opinion.

It wasn't that he didn't appreciate a tight butt and perky
breasts and he loved the scent of a woman's body wash and
shampoo and he definitely noticed a sexy pair of heels. But
he found a woman with Play-Doh in her hair, who smelled
like grape jelly and wore beat-up flip-flops, strangely
attractive.

Strangely maybe being the keyword. His friends and
brothers loved to tease him about having a uterus himself.

"You okay?" he asked Lauren.

She waved her hand and sniffed again. "It's the
hormones, I'm sure. But dang, seeing a guy as a dad is hot
and sweet, but seeing a single guy who is willing to step up
for his best friend's kids…you're going to have girls all
over you.

That was interesting. "You think so?"

"Definitely."

"You have a thing for guys with kids?" Travis asked.
"How did I not know this?"

She shrugged. "I have a thing for good guys who step
up to help other people out." She glanced at Tucker. "And,
yeah, it was pretty cute to watch Tucker watching the boys.
He's clearly smitten."

"Stop watching Tucker," Travis told her. "Seriously."
He glanced at Tucker. "It's a good thing my ego is *huge*."

Tucker snorted at that. Because it was. Huge.

Lauren laughed and leaned it to give Travis a quick
kiss. "I love you."

Travis wrapped an arm around her shoulders and pulled
her close, turning the kiss into more than a peck on the lips.

Tucker smiled at them but he knew the smile probably
looked wistful.

It wasn't Lauren that Tucker wanted. It was the
relationship. She and Travis were building a life together.

Tucker wanted that. He knew that most of his friends thought he was just saying that as a way to keep the girls coming around with cobbler and low-cut tops. He knew even some of the girls were skeptical because he never really got serious with anyone. But it seemed as if he figured out pretty quickly when a girl wasn't the *one*.

That didn't mean he wasn't looking for her.

Travis pulled back from his kiss with Lauren and looked into her eyes. "You just wait until you see me with *our* kids. You won't be able to keep your hands off of me."

As if she could now. Tucker rolled his eyes and even his father snorted.

"I can't wait to see that," Lauren said softly, her eyes so full of love for her husband that Tucker felt as though he was intruding on their intimate moment.

Travis kissed her again and then grinned at everyone around the table. "She's talked me into having at least three more."

The genius scientist and cofounder of the world-renowned Innovative Agricultural Solutions, who had been traveling the world and putting politicians in Washington in their place, and living in Haiti for months at a time helping institute programs to rebuild the post-hurricane economy, was now thinking about becoming the mother to four? Or more?

Tucker's first instinct was to look at his brother and think *lucky bastard.*

His next thought was that if Travis could talk *Lauren* into that, surely Tucker could talk sweet, loving Delaney into—

And then he got ahold of his common sense and shut those thoughts down before they could go further. What the hell was he doing? Thinking about having babies with Delaney? On top of the four kids she already had and that were overwhelming her? Within *hours* of meeting her in person for the first time?

Jesus. He really was crazy.

He worked on not giving anything away in his expression or body language. Fortunately, everyone was watching Lauren.

She looked embarrassed as she lifted a shoulder. "I think it's partly this town." She said it with affection but she also rolled her eyes. It was well known that Lauren had been drawn to Sapphire Falls in spite of herself. She'd tried to resist the charm…and had failed. "There's kid stuff everywhere. There's Santa Claus sitting right in the middle of the town square, and the little growing program Mason has going on at IAS where the kids can come and learn about plants, and the kids' menu at the diner and the kids' activities at all of the festivals… It's *everywhere*."

Tucker caught himself again and consciously *stopped* thinking about making a point to take Delaney and the boys to all of the kids' activities at the festival coming up.

"Well, thank God for face painting and pony rides," Travis said.

Tucker looked at Travis with surprise. "You're really into all of the kid stuff too?"

Travis was going to be a great dad, but Travis as a family man was still sinking in.

"Definitely," he said. "Can't wait. But you know what that's like. You've wanted to be a dad since you were like six."

It was true. A well-known fact actually. Tucker wasn't embarrassed about it. He just got tired of the ribbing. Maybe now Travis would lay off a bit since he could relate.

"Do you remember the Christmas he asked for a doll?" Travis asked TJ.

Or maybe not.

TJ hadn't said much so far, and Tucker looked over to find his oldest brother studying him, a strange look on his face. He looked almost concerned.

"Something on your mind?" Tucker asked.

"I'm just a little worried about what's on *your* mind," TJ said calmly.

Tucker frowned. "What do you think is on my mind?"

"You know exactly," TJ said.

And Tucker did. TJ knew them all very well. Too well. It was scary really.

TJ was the quiet one of the bunch. He'd always been more thoughtful, less emotional and reactive than the rest of them. Travis was charming, Tucker was sweet and their youngest brother, Ty, was smooth. TJ wasn't any of those things.

Interestingly, TJ had as much female attention, if not more, than any of them. While Tucker and Travis were outrageous flirts and apparently easy to figure out, according to local girls, TJ was "complex". Of course, that made Tucker roll his eyes.

Travis looked from Tucker to TJ. "What? What's on his mind?"

Kathy and TJ said it at the same time. "Delaney."

Tucker shifted on his chair. So what? There was nothing wrong with being attracted to the woman who was living in his house for the summer and taking care of Rafe's boys.

Probably.

Lauren's eyes got wider, as if she had figured something out. "So this whole thing about you two getting together...that could be real?" She looked at Kathy. "I thought we were kidding around."

Tucker felt a weird flutter of...something he couldn't name. But he kept his features carefully schooled. He didn't need any more shit from Travis or any more reason for TJ to look all concerned.

Yes, Delaney had gotten to town mere hours ago and he didn't really know her. So, no, they weren't actually a *couple* or anything. But his thoughts immediately went back to the moment in his kitchen when she'd hugged him.

That had been…something he couldn't name. They had a connection, and it wasn't just that they had the boys and Rafe in common.

"They just met," TJ said. He gave Tucker a serious look. "There's no way he's giving up cobbler for her already."

"Ah, yes, the cobbler," Lauren said, leaning in with a grin. "Does Delaney make cobbler?"

Everyone knew the first step to Tucker's heart was through his sweet tooth, and that his biggest weakness was cobbler. In fact, he'd been known to call it a deal breaker. A lot of people thought it was a big joke. The women in Sapphire Falls, thankfully, took it seriously, and he could pretty much have cobbler whenever he wanted it.

"I haven't actually had her cobbler," he said, thinking that could be a good euphemism for other things he'd really like—and hadn't yet had—from Delaney. "But she did get pretty excited when she saw my kitchen."

Lauren frowned. "Your kitchen is nothing special."

Tucker shrugged. She was right. And Lauren didn't even cook. "I'm not kidding, her eyes lit up when we walked in there. Said there was a lot she could do in there. I told her it was all hers." He couldn't help his huge grin. Delaney had a lot in the plus column, that was for sure, and if she could make even a halfway decent cobbler, his mother might have to break out the linens and silver one more time before the summer was over.

But even as he tried to think about it lightheartedly, something tightened in his chest.

He was ready for a family. He wasn't apologetic about it and he wasn't keeping it a secret. Having the boys around the dinner table tonight had felt good and, stupid, crazy or whatever it was, it had felt like someone was missing. And that someone wasn't Rafe.

Tucker would miss his friend forever. He would think of him on a daily basis, he was sure. But he would also be as much of a father figure to Rafe's kids as he could be—as he would be allowed to be.

Maybe that was part of the chest tightness. Delaney was in charge of the boys and who interacted with them. He knew that she would let him continue to be a part of their lives but how much? Unless they lived here, where he could see them all the time, it wouldn't be enough. He already knew that.

What about if she met someone? He knew from Rafe that she wasn't involved with anyone seriously, but that wouldn't last forever. She was a beautiful, intelligent, funny, sweet woman. She would find a guy—or a guy would find her—and he would become a father to the boys.

Tucker hated that idea. It was irrational he realized, but still...

"Well, you've got nothing to worry about if you like her," Lauren said. "Delaney will be all over you."

Tucker's gaze flew to her face as his heart stuttered. "What do you mean?"

"The dad thing," she said with a shrug, picking up her teacup. "Told you women were going to go crazy about you being a dad type with the boys. Delaney will be putty in your hands."

Tucker shifted again, but the discomfort was different this time. Delaney and his hands in the same sentence was enough to send his thought is another direction entirely.

"How so?" he asked.

"You're going to be her big hero. You're directly helping her. And she'll see all those moments with you and the boys that other women won't. Trust me, she'll melt. Hell, I practically did when you were helping Jack cut his meat. If she sees you hugging them and playing with them, she'll be all over you."

Laure sipped her tea, completely oblivious to the havoc she'd created in Tucker.

Kathy was nodding her agreement. "And the poor thing

lost her sister *and* her brother-in-law and took on this huge responsibility with the boys. I'm sure she's feeling completely overwhelmed and alone. She's going to need to lean on you hard, Tucker. You guys will have a very unique bond."

Tucker was having trouble sorting one thought from another. He would never use the boys to get close to Delaney. He would never use the boys. Period. That wasn't what this was all about. But if his natural interactions and relationship with the boys was to her what cobbler was to him, who was he to argue?

And he would be there for her. His mom was right that Delaney had suffered a major loss and her world had been blown upside down. Even if he hadn't promised Rafe to look out for her too, he would have. He was able to offer her some help, some stability, support, and he would do it. Even if he never got the chance to kiss her.

But in that moment, he fully acknowledged that he really, really wanted a chance to kiss her.

CHAPTER THREE

The porch swing was everything she'd hoped it would be.

Delaney pushed herself gently with her toe against the porch, letting the swing rock her and the light summer breeze wash over her. She tipped the cold bottle of beer back and sighed. This was practically perfect.

She heard the truck coming up the lane and smiled. Everyone was back. Tucker's note had said they were going to his mom's for dinner but that he'd wanted to let her sleep and he'd bring her a plate when they came home.

She'd slept for hours and awakened slightly disoriented but rested. She hadn't slept well in months, and she never would have expected it the first day at Tucker's. She wasn't much of a napper and never slept well even in nice hotels. She preferred her own bed and own pillow. But she'd slipped into a deep sleep within minutes of lying down in her room for the summer and hadn't stirred until about thirty minutes ago.

The whole place already felt so comfortable, almost as if she had been the one staying here every summer for the past thirteen years. Jack and David would be sleeping in the matching twin beds in the room next to hers. Rafe had always slept with the younger boys, but they were older now and would be fine in a room nearby rather than right with her. Tucker and his brothers had finished his basement, making a bedroom for Henry and Charlie so that she could have a room to herself.

It was considerate, and she had to admit that she'd found it sweet he'd gone to the trouble of finishing off his basement simply because she was going to be there for the summer.

Her awareness of him had climbed another couple of notches when he showed her the master bedroom at the end of the hall. The very masculine bedroom that smelled really good—like fresh air and clean laundry with a hint of cologne that could be sandalwood—and held the gigantic king-size bed with rumpled sheets.

She would admit her heart rate had kicked up a little when he'd shown her the master bath and said, "If you'd rather stay in here so you have the bathroom to yourself and more privacy, I don't mind sleeping in the guest room."

Something about the charcoal and gray ceramic tiles, the deep Jacuzzi tub and the all-glass shower stall with multiple shower heads had her stumbling back out of the door…and over her words.

She'd somehow declined the offer and assured him she'd rather be closer to the boys and sharing the bathroom down the hall with them.

For some reason, his bed had made her breathe faster, but the offer from him to get naked and wet in his bathroom was the thing that sent her over the crazy-attracted edge.

She'd blamed it on sleep deprivation.

In contrast, the guest room had made her relax and smile. There was no heart thumping against her rib cage or lungs that wouldn't fully expand when she looked at the queen-size bed with the homemade quilt on it. Instead of masculine shades of gray, this room was decorated in lavender, light blue and white that seemed cheery but soothing at the same time. She'd taken a deep breath and felt a strange peace.

She would have never gotten any sleep in Tucker's room.

And she'd almost laughed at that thought. If her heart thumped and her lungs constricted *thinking* about being in his bed, actually being in it would be torture. Being in it *with* him would possibly kill her.

She'd fallen asleep, assured that once she was well rested, it would all seem much less…heart-thumping.

And when she was awake again and in the shower in

the *guest* bathroom, she'd blamed thinking about him with her heart thumping on the fact that she'd just read his note and found his gesture of letting her sleep and put off meeting his entire family at once to another time very sweet.

But surely all of her attraction to him so far was simply a crazy combination of the long road trip, being emotionally and physically drained and incredibly relieved to know she was somewhere comfortable and supportive for the next three months?

Her attraction earlier today had surely been nothing more than a projection of a whole host of other emotions.

Surely.

And it seemed she would soon be able to test that theory. Tucker got out of the truck and was coming up the sidewalk. Alone.

Delaney straightened on the swing and took another quick shot of beer before giving him a big smile. "Hi. Hope you don't mind I borrowed this," she said, holding the bottle up.

He smiled and shook his head. "Of course not. Whatever I've got is all yours."

And *any* straight, red-blooded female would have found *that* sentence enticing.

"And beer goes great with my mom's chicken," he added, holding up a plate covered in aluminum foil.

Chicken. *Homemade* chicken. She smiled. "That sounds awesome."

He set the plate on the porch railing and settled his very fine ass next to the plate. "How do you feel?"

"Much better," she admitted. "Sorry I passed out like that. I didn't expect to."

"You needed it. No big deal."

"But you already lost the boys I see," she said lightly, trying to cover that she was actually quite emotional about the fact that she wasn't worried one bit about the boys. She didn't know where they were or what they were doing, but she knew Tucker did, and that was enough.

Damn. He might never get rid of her.

She drank from her beer again to cover up the reaction to that thought.

She wasn't staying. They weren't staying. This was a pit stop, a vacation. Their new life was waiting in Colorado.

She had to be strong. No matter how nice it felt to lean on someone else for a little while, she had to be in charge and make decisions and keep things together. She could do it. She was related to Chelsea after all. She simply needed to channel her sister.

And that might actually be possible. If anyone was strong enough and organized enough to come back as a spirit to ensure that her children were being well cared for, it was Chelsea. She'd make a deal with whoever she needed to.

Delaney wondered if Sapphire Falls had a resident medium.

But she wasn't sure she was ready to talk to Chelsea. Chelsea might not be completely thrilled with the copious amounts of French fries her boys had been eating or that Henry had failed his last math test or that Delaney was taking the boys to Colorado, where she and Chelsea's parents were going to help them get back on their feet.

Yeah, her sister would definitely be yelling at her across the space-time-heaven-earth continuum—or whatever it was. Delaney decided to put the trip to the medium off for a week. Or twenty.

Of course, there was always the chance that Chelsea might simply decide to haunt Delaney if she got really unhappy.

Just what she needed—to be kept up at night by her sister nagging her as a ghost.

Delaney snorted.

"Night crawlers are funny?"

She focused on Tucker. He was watching her with a bemused expression and a half smile.

Oops. "Night crawlers? No. Sorry." She shook her head, clearing it of thoughts of Chelsea in opaque white. "What did you say?"

"I said the boys are catching night crawlers with my dad," Tucker repeated.

Delaney took a deep breath. Chelsea wouldn't be haunting her tonight. The boys had played on the farm, ridden dirt bikes, had homemade chicken for dinner and were now spending time with people who were as close to grandparents as they had ever had.

She shook her head, swallowing hard against the knot of emotion in her throat. "Don't know what that means. Don't need to know what that means," she finally said.

"They're great big, fat, slimy worms that are great for fishing bait," he said anyway, grinning at the way she wrinkled her nose.

"They come out at night when it's cooler," he went on.

And she now officially knew more about night crawlers than she'd ever wanted to know. "They're going to go fishing tonight?" she asked. She also knew absolutely zero about fishing, but she kind of assumed that doing it in the dark would be difficult.

"Night fishing is great."

It had to be her imagination that thought his voice got a little lower at that.

But maybe night fishing didn't mean night *fishing*. Maybe it was one of those excuses to go out and...

Her mind had just started to wander when Tucker moved off the railing and took a seat next to her on the swing.

Wow. She really needed to keep focused here. It was ridiculous the way her mind kept going off on tangents. She needed to concentrate.

On Tucker.

She looked over at him and realized *that* would be no problem at all.

The swing was certainly big enough for them both. They could have easily fit two of the boys on it with them. But it seemed that there was very little space between them when he sat down. He propped his elbow on the arm of the swing and draped his other arm along the back of the seat, his fingertips at least three inches from her shoulder. She still felt her skin tingling.

Delaney tucked one leg up underneath her. She'd changed into simple cotton shorts and a T-shirt. It was early June and the night was cool and yet humid. She'd felt the moisture on her skin and could feel it curling her hair, so she'd pulled the long strands up into a ponytail. The shorts weren't particularly short and the T-shirt was a basic old T-shirt, not revealing or tight, but every inch of her was aware of every inch of him.

She drank again and realized she'd finished her beer.

So maybe she could blame all of this tingling on being tipsy, since she wasn't as short on sleep anymore.

"The boys will be home a little later," he said. "Figured they needed a good night's sleep. Been a big day already."

Home. He meant here. His home. He knew the boys were comfortable and happy here. So maybe just for the summer they could refer to it as home. They didn't really have another one. They'd left Nashville behind and hadn't made it to Denver yet.

"Did you have fun dirt biking?" she asked, instead of dwelling on the fact that she'd turned her four nephews into nomads.

Tucker's grin was immediate and big. Clearly, this was one of his favorite topics. Something else she knew nothing about.

"Oh, yeah. They had a great time."

"Were they good at dinner?" They were all good kids

and got along fairly well, but they were still kids and didn't always say please and sometimes talked with food in their mouths and loved to make one another giggle by putting peas in their noses and other miscellaneous silly, oftentimes disgusting things.

"They were fine at dinner," Tucker said, watching her.

She licked her lips and wiggled on the swing, wondering what he was seeing. Before she'd been almost too tired to care. She had to look better now than she had in the bakery when he'd first walked in. She didn't feel so droopy and on the verge of tears. But she hadn't done anything with her hair and wore no makeup.

Not that it mattered.

She was a houseguest. A friend of a friend. Here because she was the legal guardian to the boys who wanted to spend the summer with Tucker. It didn't matter how she looked to him.

She still wondered.

"Fine doesn't mean good," she said, focusing on talking instead of thinking. And feeling. "Fine could mean they didn't spill anything or throw any food at one another. Fine could mean they were perfect gentlemen and did everything right. Or fine could mean that they had a farting contest and laughed so hard milk came out of their noses."

Tucker was grinning at her. "You seem to have some experience with all of those things."

She shook her head and couldn't help her smile. "Not the perfect gentlemen thing."

"Good. I would have worried they weren't normal if you saw perfect gentlemen very often."

She appreciated that he was laid-back, she really did. Because she loved the boys intensely. But perfect they were not.

"So there was a farting contest?" she asked.

He laughed. "No. Jack burped and Charlie said, 'Good one'. That was as bad as it got."

She sighed. "You sure?"

"My mom and dad raised four boys. My brothers and I *were* those four boys. Lauren has been around us long enough that stuff doesn't faze her anymore."

Lauren? Tucker didn't have any sisters.

"Lauren?"

Jealousy? Really? That was the stupidest thing to feel ever. But in a flash Delaney realized that she maybe had let her imagination—and all of Rafe's talking over the years— convince her that if she spent the summer here, she'd have Tucker's undivided attention at least for a few months. Well, divided between her and the boys. She was sure the women in Sapphire Falls had entertained some impure thoughts about Tucker Bennett over the years, but she really hadn't considered that he might have a girlfriend.

And if he did, what was with the heated looks and hand-holding and he-might-have-been-thinking-about-kissing-her by the car?

He nodded. "Lauren is my sister-in-law, she's married to Travis."

Ah, okay, kind of like a sister.

"Well, I promise I'll be around and on top of things from here. But thanks for taking them on tonight."

Tucker looked puzzled. "I didn't take them on. I took them to my mom's for dinner. It was no big deal. And it's something I hope we do a lot more of. My mom and dad do too."

She smiled. "Thank you."

He turned slightly on the swing, facing her more fully. "What did you mean by you'll be on top of things from here?"

Delaney studied her beer bottle, working at the edge of the label with her thumbnail. "You know—actually taking care of things, of the boys. I'm going to…step up."

"Step up? More than you already have dealing with everything you've already had to?"

She sighed and still resisted looking at him. Tucker had never been alone in his life. And neither had she, actually. She'd always had Chelsea and Rafe. Until she hadn't.

"I'm going to be what they need. Do what needs to be done. I really do know what I'm taking on here and I don't want you to worry. I know you love the boys. You don't have to worry that I'm not doing what I should."

He didn't say anything for several long moments. He cleared his throat and shifted on the swing, the wood creaking with the movement. "Where's all of this coming from?"

She glanced up at him finally. "Me falling asleep and leaving them with you for hours."

He frowned. "I told you I didn't mind. Neither did they." His tone was a little defensive.

Well, she was feeling defensive too. "They're my responsibility, and while I really appreciate your help today, and this summer, I can't lean on anyone else." The defensiveness was completely about her *wanting* to lean on him. Very much. And the fact that her move to Colorado was all about leaning on someone.

"You sure as hell *can* lean on someone else. Me. My family. That's what family is about."

She felt that stupid lump in her throat again. "I'm not part of your family."

"You are," he said firmly and without hesitation. "You are Rafe's family and you're the boys' family, so you're my family."

She just looked at him. Did people really think that way? Feel that way?

"I don't... I can't relate to that."

He nodded. "I know."

She only thought for two seconds about what she wanted to say. She turned to face him, crisscrossing her legs on the swing seat. "How much do you know about my family? My parents?"

He probably knew everything. Rafe would have told him.

"I know that when Chelsea fell in love with Rafe, your parents tried to break them up," he said. "And when she transferred colleges to be closer to him, they cut off her money."

Delaney noticed the hand that was resting on the arm of the swing was clenched. It didn't surprise her that Tucker was angry about what her parents had done, especially because it was about them not approving of a guy who Tucker considered his best friend, practically his brother.

"And then when they got married, your parents disowned her."

Delaney nodded.

Rafe and Chelsea had met when he and Tucker and some other friends had taken a spontaneous road trip to watch the University of Nebraska play Colorado University, where Chelsea was a freshman. They'd met at a bar and it had been love at first sight.

It had taken Chelsea only a month after meeting Rafe to decide to transfer to Kearney, Nebraska, to a much smaller school, closer to where Rafe was still finishing his senior year in high school.

Her parents had been furious. Then two weeks after his graduation, Rafe and Chelsea had gone to a Justice of the Peace and gotten married.

Delaney remembered every detail about that period. "I'm younger than Chelsea by three years," she said to Tucker. "So I was still at home when all of it was happening. They were so angry." And it hadn't been about Chelsea being too young or their concern over her future or welfare specifically. It had all been about the fact that Rafe was half Hispanic. They were horrible racists. Delaney still cringed thinking about some of the things she'd overheard her father saying when he was ranting and raving about Rafe.

"I know you went to live with Chelsea and Rafe," Tucker said. "You went with them to Nashville right away, didn't you?"

She nodded. "When my dad found out they'd gotten married, he went ballistic. Said horrible things, threw things around, vowed to never speak to her again. I couldn't believe how my family was falling apart and how awful my own parents were being. I loved Chelsea and I knew Rafe was making her happy. I figured that was what was supposed to matter. I told my dad that if he stopped talking to and seeing Chelsea, he'd have to stop talking to and seeing me too. He said fine. Even gave me money for gas. I packed up my car and left. Drove straight to Chelsea and Rafe, they took me in and we all moved to Nashville together."

"You were only sixteen," Tucker said.

Delaney shrugged, her heart feeling heavy as she thought about it. "But they didn't care. I guess if they had sent the cops after us or tried to get me to come home it might have been a battle and we might have had some trouble. But they didn't even try."

Tucker frowned. "I just don't get why you're going to Colorado now after all of that. After all this time."

She sighed. She'd had this same discussion with Rafe probably a dozen times. "They're the only family we have now besides Rafe's mom and her family in Mexico," she said. "And after Chelsea died, my mom wrote me a letter. She said they wanted to help however they could and that they wanted to meet the boys. Chelsea's death brought up a lot of regrets, made them realize that there aren't always second chances to fix things." Delaney took a deep breath. "In those two months after Chelsea was gone, I had to face the fact that Rafe would be too eventually and I'd be on my own. The idea of trying to repair things with our family, give the boys grandparents, and yes, have some financial help, is really appealing."

"You're not all on your own, though," Tucker said softly.

She didn't reply to that. She knew that. Tucker was closer to the boys than anyone else still living besides her. But it wasn't his responsibility to take it all on.

"I hadn't finished high school when I left home, so I got my GED. We skated by on things like health insurance and stuff, just never needing it in the early days. I got a few jobs here and there, waitressing and stuff, and then when Chelsea was done with her degree and started working, I worked with her." She breathed deep again. "I don't have much to fall back on. I probably can't get hired right now with my limited work experience and no degree. And even if I could, I can't live like that with the boys—paycheck to paycheck, without insurance or a savings account."

And all of those truths scared her to the point that even asking her father for help was a lesser evil. She needed a backup plan and the only one she could come up with was in Colorado.

Truthfully, Delaney had been fully dependent on her sister forever. Even as kids, Chelsea had been the leader. She'd taught Delaney to read, to tie her shoes, to add and subtract. She had included Delaney in play groups with her friends, had shared her Barbies and had played Legos with her when Delaney had gotten bored with changing the dolls' clothes and shoes.

She'd been Delaney's world.

Delaney felt the tear slip down her cheek and dashed it away.

"I bet you really miss her," Tucker said.

Delaney sucked in a big breath and nodded. "So much."

"Rafe, um…" Tucker stopped and cleared his throat. "Rafe told me a little about what happened to her, but he was—"

She nodded again. "I know." It had been tough for Rafe to even have a phone conversation without ending up

exhausted, and his pain medications had made him loopy
when he was awake. She hesitated for a split second but
knew she could say this to Tucker. "He always said that of
all the places for him to get cancer, his brain was least fair
because he hadn't started with much there in the first
place."

Tucker laughed softly. "He's such a smart ass."

Delaney's heart thumped a little at Tucker's use of
present tense talking about Rafe too. "So what did he tell
you about what happened to Chelsea?" she asked.

It occurred to her that she hadn't actually told this story
out loud to anyone. Everyone in their circle had known
about it from the local news. It had been a big story for a
while. She had informed their parents by letter.

Tucker held her gaze directly when he said gently, "He
told me she was shot in a convenience store."

Delaney wet her lips and nodded. Then she gave a little
laugh and shook her head. The whole thing was still so
bizarre. "It was six blocks from their house. She—all of
us—had stopped in there a hundred times. She went in to
buy a jug of milk for the morning because they were out. It
was a random robbery. Four people were shot. Chelsea and
one other fatally."

Tucker swallowed hard, but he didn't look away, he
didn't flinch. And he didn't say he was sorry. She had
heard so much of that it had started to not mean anything
and, well, of course he was sorry.

"I've been grateful for two things since then," Delaney
said. "That she was shot in the head so she didn't suffer."

Tucker pulled in a quick breath at that.

"And that the boys weren't with her." Delaney felt
another tear escape, and she brushed it away. "She'd just
brought them home and realized she'd forgotten the milk. If
she had remembered on her way home, they might have
been there." She shrugged. "But then I think if she'd
remembered on her way home, the guy with the gun

wouldn't have been there yet. Or she probably would have stopped somewhere else instead." She took a deep breath. "Anyway, that's what happened. A stupid, random act of violence. Nothing anyone could have done."

Again, Tucker let a few seconds pass without commenting, but then he said softly, "But she was supposed to be around after Rafe passed."

Delaney nodded. "We had planned and talked. All three of us knew what was coming and we had a plan. The boys knew too really. Rafe prepared them as much as he could. But everything was about both Chelsea and I being there. In fact—"

She stopped. She wasn't sure she could tell him the rest. She loved her sister, she missed her terribly and she didn't know Tucker well enough for this.

Did she?

Something about him made her want to share everything.

"In fact what?"

She hadn't told anyone her feelings about how things had gone at home during the last months of Rafe's life. But she wanted to tell Tucker.

"Chelsea decided that the easiest thing for the boys was to establish some new routines without Rafe, so that when he was gone, there would be some things that still felt normal."

Tucker frowned. "How did that work?"

"For instance, every Wednesday night, they went out for pizza, just Chelsea and the boys. And on Saturdays, they started going to a sports complex where the boys each played on different teams. Movie nights. Different things."

"And what about you and Rafe?" Tucker asked.

His voice was low and somehow comforting. She took a deep breath. The summer night, the soothing sounds of the frogs and crickets, the swing, the feeling of peace that just seemed to be in the air here—it all worked to loosen the knot in her chest.

"I hung out with Rafe. He really needed someone there all the time, so that was me. Chelsea...she loved Rafe but she...wasn't handling him getting sicker very well. She was a dynamo—always moving and doing and planning and going. It was hard for her to see him weaker and sicker and more and more out of it. And it was hard for her to just sit there."

"So you did it."

She nodded.

"And I'm guessing when Chelsea was working, you picked the boys up. And I'm guessing if one of them was sick, you stayed with them so she could go do her stuff. And I'm guessing if she needed someone to stay late at work so she could go to a school program or ballgame for one of the boys, you were the one to stay."

She frowned. He was right. But there was something in his tone that made her defensive.

"Chelsea was..." She took a deep breath. "Rafe and I used to joke that we were the flashlights, but Chelsea was the batteries. She kept us going. We weren't much good without her."

Tucker opened his mouth, but then he shut it and shook his head. "I know you have a big adjustment to make."

She actually found herself laughing lightly at that. "That's an understatement."

"I hope that you can really use this summer for that adjustment," he said. "We're here to help."

"That means a lot."

She knew she needed to get on her own two feet. She knew she needed to be the ultimate decision maker. But if she could just *breathe*—know the boys were happy and healthy and safe while she made some of those decisions, while she weighed all the pros and cons, while she swallowed her pride and communicated with her father...while she put off some of those decisions until the last possible moment.

The tears welled up fast and hot and she couldn't hold them back. She tried to take a breath but it came out as a little sob. She pressed her lips together.

"Come here."

Tucker didn't wait for her to come to him. He slid over and pulled her into his lap. He wrapped his big arms around her and pressed her cheek to his chest.

Delaney really was cried out. She'd cried and cried and gone through all of the stages of grief. She'd talked it all out with Rafe when he was lucid. She'd talked to two counselors—one for herself and one with the boys. She'd talked to the boys about it.

She had most definitely talked and cried enough about her loss and grief.

The feelings of being overwhelmed and failing though? Yeah, those were still there and actually getting stronger.

"You're not on your own, Laney," Tucker said against her hair. "It's going to be okay. I'm going to help you with all of it."

He didn't even know what all of it was, but there was something about being in his arms, and that low, confident voice, and...being in his arms, that made her believe.

And with that I'll-worry-about-it-later decision made, his warmth and strength and scent surrounded her and completely distracted her from feeling anything else.

It was so nice.

When she hugged the boys, she was reminded that there were lots of good feelings still to be felt—happiness, love, joy, hope. They were here, right now, full of life. There were tough times ahead but there were awesome times too. First and last days of school, spelling competitions, baseball championships and vacations. They would be discovering new books, new interests, new friends. There was a lot to look forward to.

That's how it felt in Tucker's arms. New and hopeful

and exciting. Times a hundred.

She knew that getting physical with Tucker just because she was lonely or tired or because she was grateful to him wasn't smart. She knew that using pleasure—whether it was alcohol, drugs, sex or anything else—to mask or forget about the harder, more painful things was dangerous. She knew that sex with Tucker wouldn't fix everything.

But it *would* fix one thing. It would break her streak of I-don't-know-what-I'm-doing, fly-by-the-seat-of-my-pants, I-don't-know-what-I-want stuff that she'd been living with.

She did know what she wanted in this case and she did know what to do about it.

Delaney pulled back slightly and looked up at Tucker. His gaze met hers and she saw that he knew exactly what she was thinking.

She sat up, twisting to face him. He didn't say anything. He didn't pull her closer. He didn't push her away. He sat and waited, letting her make the decision—and the first move.

Delaney leaned in and put her lips to his.

He still didn't do anything. He didn't resist the kiss. But he didn't deepen it or prolong it when she leaned back.

She got it. He wasn't going to take advantage of her in her weak emotional state.

Well, fuck that.

She was tired of being weak and emotional.

She took hold of his shirt in one hand, tipped her head and went back in. This time she opened her mouth and licked along his bottom lip.

That was the magic touch.

There was a rumbled groan from Tucker's chest and his hand came up to the back of her neck. It was the palm of his hand against her neck, but it was skin to skin, and her whole body responded. He opened his mouth as well and met her tongue with a long, bold stroke of his. Delaney relished the pleasure rolling through her, hot and fast.

Yes. This was good. Pleasure. Taking charge and having it turn out well. Feeling confident. Knowing exactly what she was doing. This was all very good.

Tucker's other hand moved from the back of the swing to her hip, and for a moment, she thought he was going to turn her to straddle him. But when she wiggled in his lap and felt his fingers curl into her neck and hip, she realized he was holding her in place.

Or trying to.

And why was that? The hard ridge behind his fly was pressed against her thigh and told her that him wanting her was not the problem. Was he trying to be a gentleman? Was he afraid she didn't know what she was doing? That she was reacting this way because she was an emotional basket case?

She needed to start convincing people—lawyers and school administrators and doctors and counselors and her parents and *herself*—that she was very much in her right mind and not emotionally volatile.

No time to start practicing like the present.

She leaned back. "I want this," she told him, gaze on his, trying with everything in her to exude confidence.

He hadn't moved his hands off her and she felt his grip tighten minutely. But he pulled in a deep breath and shook his head. "Too fast."

She gripped his shirt harder and gave him a little shake. "Life is short, Tucker."

That got his attention. She could see how his jaw clenched, felt how his fingers definitely curled into her harder and something flickered in his eyes.

"Life *is* short," he finally said. "And if you want something you should go for it."

She sighed. "Yes. Exactly. And I want this."

"I'm just not sure we're thinking of the same *this*."

She wiggled against him again, delighted at the quick intake of air it caused in him and smiled. "Well, it's been a while, but I think I'm being pretty clear here."

"Laney...the thing is, once you're in my bed, you're not leaving it."

His voice was gruff, his gaze intent, and it seemed like the hard body under hers had just heated twenty degrees.

Dang.

She could honestly say that she had no problem with that. "Tucker, I—"

"Tucker." The deep voice from behind them made her jump.

Tucker just sighed.

There was someone standing on the walk in front of the house. She hadn't even heard anyone drive in. Tucker's lack of surprise indicated he had.

But he hadn't pushed her off his lap or stopped touching her.

Delaney pivoted on his lap to look at the guy with the horrible timing.

Wouldn't it be polite to come upon a scene like the one on the porch swing and quietly leave without interrupting?

Tucker groaned softly as she moved on his thighs and gripped her hips with both hands. "Easy, babe."

She looked back at him. Oh, right. The wiggling.

And it occurred to Delaney, too late to really do anything about it of course, that she should possibly be embarrassed about someone showing up while she was on Tucker's lap begging him for sex.

Okay, so not begging. Yet. But still...

She slid to the side, carefully, moving off of his lap and turning so she was sitting on the swing facing forward.

"Who is that?"

"My brother." He didn't sound happy about it.

A big guy came forward into the light spilling from the windows.

"Mom wanted me to bring dessert over since you left without it. It's her famous German chocolate cake, after all."

"You don't have the boys with you?" Tucker asked, shifting on the swing, obviously uncomfortable.

Delaney looked at him. Was he embarrassed at his brother catching them like that?

But it didn't appear to be that kind of discomfort. He was physically uncomfortable. And a little perturbed.

"I got the brains in the family," the big guy said. "Travis is bringing them about five minutes behind me. Just so they wouldn't see anything they shouldn't."

Okay, *now* she was embarrassed. Not so much that Tucker's brother had caught them kissing, but because he had been expecting to catch them kissing. Or something.

Maybe Tucker had women crawling all over him on a regular basis. Maybe he pulled women into his lap every other day. Maybe she looked easy and desperate.

Awesome. On all counts.

But she wasn't only embarrassed. She was intrigued too.

She looked at Tucker again. His brother had expected to catch him kissing her. Why? How? What had he said to them?

Tucker pushed himself up from the swing and went to the top of the porch steps. "Well, thanks for the cake. See you later."

His brother propped a foot up on the bottom step, hooked a thumb in his front pocket and gave Tucker a very clear yeah-right look. Then he swung his attention to her. "Hi, Delaney. I'm TJ."

He didn't exactly smile at her and his tone wasn't overly friendly, and she got the impression that he'd specifically chosen not to say it was nice to meet her.

What was that all about?

She lifted a hand in a little wave. "Hi."

Tucker's eyes stayed on his brother. "Okay, see you later."

"No offer of coffee to go with the cake?" TJ asked.

"You're not getting any cake."

"Then we can have this conversation out here."

Tucker drew himself up tall and Delaney could feel the tension and irritation coming off him. Something was going on between the brothers, and while she was incredibly curious, she wasn't so sure she wanted to witness this.

She got up from the swing and took a step toward the door. "So, I'll go—"

Another truck pulled up in front of the house and all the doors swung open at once. Henry, Charlie, David and Jack jumped out and ran toward the house while a grinning guy, who was quite obviously related to Tucker and TJ, climbed out from behind the wheel.

"We interrupting anything?" Travis called.

"Almost," TJ said.

Delaney wasn't sure if TJ was referring to what he'd almost interrupted on the swing or the conversation/argument that had almost started between Tucker and TJ.

Didn't matter. She now had four very fine distractions from all of it.

"We were in the mud puddles!" Jack told her.

That much was clear. The boys were dirty from head to toe.

"We got so many night crawlers," David told her enthusiastically. "They are *huge*."

And that was all the details about *that* she needed to know.

"Shoes and jeans off out here, then the rest of you in the house," she instructed.

They kicked their shoes off and shed their jeans without argument. She started to herd them toward the door, their chatter continuing.

"We had to use red flashlights," Charlie informed her. "So the white light didn't scare them back into their holes."

She looked at Henry for confirmation. He nodded. "They can't see red light."

And *now* she knew more about night crawlers than she ever wanted to.

"We have to keep them cool," Charlie said. "And we gave them leaves for food."

Delaney stopped. "Food? Why?"

"To keep them alive," Charlie said.

"But I thought you're going to use them for fishing," she said. She did not want the boys to start keeping pets that were smaller than, say, the new puppy. Or more insect-like than, say, the new puppy.

"They have to be alive for bait," Henry told her.

She looked up at him. "You put them in the water alive for fishing?"

Henry shrugged. "Yeah."

She frowned. "That seems kind of cruel."

"It's how it happens in nature," David told her.

Right. Great. The kid was going to be fine on the farm with that kind of attitude.

"So we have to keep them alive," she said, accepting her fate but hoping like hell that their adoptive grandpa intended to go fishing soon. She started toward the front door again. "But all they need is leaves?"

"And to be cool," Charlie said.

"And to be cool," she repeated. "Okay." She looked at Henry again. "You're going to take their temperatures?" Because *she* was not going to be taking their temperatures.

"The refrigerator is the right temperature," David said happily.

He was holding up a Styrofoam cooler.

She stared at it. A Styrofoam cooler, talk of night crawlers, talk of the refrigerator being the right temperature to keep them alive...

"They're going in the *refrigerator*?" she asked.

"We'll put them in the fridge in the barn." Tucker

plucked the container from David's hand. "They'll be just fine out there."

Thank God.

Charlie nodded and David grinned up at him.

"They can stay alive for a month in the fridge with just leaves and dirt in the container," David told her.

She tried to give him a smile, she really did. But she was feeling a little queasy. "Okay, time to hit the showers," she told them.

Jack, David and Charlie all groaned right on cue.

"We showered before dinner," Jack protested as she nudged him across the threshold of the house.

Delaney looked at Tucker.

He shrugged and looked down at the boys with a huge grin. "I couldn't tell who was who they were so covered in dirt. It was a necessity."

He'd had them bathe before dinner at his mother's?

And she'd slept through the commotion?

Wow. On both counts.

"I'm impressed," she confessed.

He leaned in. "Impressed enough to come back out here after the boys are in bed?"

Being impressed wasn't what was going to bring her back out here after the boys were in bed. Sitting on Tucker's lap, she'd felt empowered, daring, not to mention full of endorphins.

She wanted more of all of that.

"Yeah," she said softly.

"Great." He looked like he wanted to say more than that, but they had quite an audience.

"Minus the earthworms?" she asked.

He grinned. "Definitely." He looked at the boys. "Somebody or two use my shower so you get done faster."

She didn't know if he was just trying to be helpful in getting the boys through their nightly routine or if he was really that eager to get her back outside with him, but she appreciated that suggestion as well. For both reasons.

She managed to get all the boys in the house and up the stairs. She was already used to tuning out the predictable complaints and excuses that came around bedtime, so she got Charlie and David into the bathroom and gave them instructions over their quibbling. Charlie was to help David get the shower going and make sure he washed his hair. They both were to brush their teeth and they were to be sure their dirty clothes got put in the hamper in the corner. They would do it all. They would argue and dawdle and get water all over the floor, but they would do it. Eventually. She was thankful on a near-daily basis that Henry was older and so responsible. He took Jack with him into Tucker's bathroom—which meant she wouldn't have to deal with Jack's nonstop talking about earthworms and she wouldn't have to deal with being overwhelmed by being in Tucker's bathroom again.

With a deep breath, she went into the younger boys' bedroom to get their pajamas out and their beds ready.

The bedroom windows were on the front of the house and were open to let in the cool night breeze.

Delaney paused with Jack's pillow in her arms.

She could hear Tucker and his brothers talking.

It wasn't as if she was eavesdropping, she thought as she moved closer to the window. Their voices were raised. And Tucker had been the one to open the window. Sure, he might not be thinking about that right now, of course, or that she might be in the room and able to hear, but it still remained that it wasn't her fault the window was open.

And she had to put the boys to bed, so she had to be in the room.

"What are you *doing*?"

She thought it was TJ's deep voice that asked that question.

"It must have been a while for you," Tucker said. "Because that's called kissing a pretty girl."

"That is what's called kissing *the* pretty girl," TJ said.

The pretty girl? What did that mean?

And with that, Delaney gave up every pretense of *not* listening to the conversation. She plopped down on David's bed, right by the window, and hoped for the first time that the boys would dawdle in the bathroom.

CHAPTER FOUR

"What are you *doing*?" TJ demanded with a scowl.

He'd finished filling Travis in on what he'd seen when he'd driven in.

The short story—Delaney on Tucker's lap. The long story—and the one TJ had told—included them kissing, Tucker's hand on her ass and what he'd overheard Delaney say about wanting this. He'd also overheard Tucker's response.

To which Tucker had said simply, "It's true."

Then TJ had asked what Tucker was doing.

What he was doing was getting annoyed with his brother's butting in.

"It must have been a while for you," Tucker said. "Because that's called kissing a pretty girl."

"That is what's called kissing *the* pretty girl," TJ said.

Yeah, it was. And Tucker felt it down deep. Delaney was the one.

"You can't be shocked by any of this," Travis said. "This has been coming on for like ten years."

Thirteen, but who was counting?

"He just met her," TJ said. "And more importantly, she just met him."

"They've known about each other for years," Travis said. "He's been waiting to meet her forever. Why do you think he hasn't gotten serious with anyone around here?"

Tucker looked at Travis. "What the hell are you talking about?"

"You've been waiting on Delaney," Travis said with a shrug. "In the back of your mind, you've always wondered if she's the one, and it's kept you from getting serious with anyone else."

Tucker looked at TJ and found their oldest brother looking at Travis with the same "huh?" expression he was sure was on his own face.

"Oh, come on," Travis said. "Seriously? This is news?"

"How could he be waiting on someone he'd never met?" TJ asked.

"Because of Rafe. I mean, they hadn't *actually* met, but they knew all about one another, they'd seen pictures. Rafe told Tucker she's the one forever. So of course he thought that deep down. Or at least wondered."

TJ ran a hand over his face. "Jesus."

Tucker couldn't exactly argue with Travis's assessment. He looked at TJ. "What?"

"You already think you're in love with her."

Tucker could not say yes to that. He couldn't. It was crazy. And stupid. And TJ would tell him both of those things. More colorfully probably.

"In the few hours I've known her, combined with the things I already know about her, I don't have any reason to not want to find out if I could be," he finally said honestly.

TJ just shook his head.

"There you go," Travis said. "This is good. He hasn't really given the girls here an honest chance because Delaney's always been in the background. Now she's here and he can find out once and for all if she measures up to the hype."

"The hype?" Tucker asked, not wanting to address the notion that he'd been holding back from other women because of the fantasy of Delaney. It didn't feel as crazy as it sounded.

"Has Rafe ever told you anything bad or negative about Delaney?" Travis asked.

Tucker sighed. "Rafe was crazy about Delaney. Maybe there wasn't anything bad or negative to tell."

"Oh, sure, she's the one perfect human being in the entire universe," Travis said. "Come on, Tuck. You know there's got to be stuff. But Rafe never said any of that. Because he wanted her with you. Which is nice. And I'm not saying any of the negative stuff is really that negative. I'm just saying that the idea of Delaney has been built up in your brain for a long time and it's good that she's now here for real so you can finally find out what she's all about."

"She's not here for a vacation," TJ said. "And she's not a mail-order bride, for God's sake. This isn't some big elaborate, three-month-long blind date."

Tucker kept his mouth shut. It kind of was. Not the mail-order-bride thing, but this was supposed to be a break, a time of regrouping for Delaney. And Rafe had sent her here not just because the boys loved and needed a summer in Sapphire Falls, but because of Tucker. He'd told Tucker so himself.

But TJ didn't need to know that.

"We all know Tucker is the big romantic looking for a wife," TJ said. "And we all know that Rafe picked this one out for him. But this is not the time. This woman just lost everything. She's vulnerable and emotional and she just fucking got here. Maybe he could keep from feeling her up on the very first night she's in his house."

Whoa. Tucker took a deep breath. "That's between me and Delaney," he said firmly. "But fuck you if you think I'd take advantage of her."

TJ took a deep breath then blew it out. "Okay, I'm sorry. I know you wouldn't. But you get caught up in this stuff anyway and you're vulnerable and emotional about Rafe and everything too. This woman shows up here, the fantasy in the flesh, with four *kids* that you happen to love. It's an instant family. A happily-ever-after dumped right on your doorstep."

Tucker shifted his weight and breathed and worked on formulating a response that wouldn't sound crazy but that his brother would believe.

TJ knew him. Both of his brothers did. He couldn't flat-out deny that all of that sounded pretty fucking perfect. They'd know he was lying. But he couldn't say that it was...pretty fucking perfect. They'd lock him up at TJ's house for the duration of the summer if he wasn't careful.

"Look, we've got chemistry, okay? I didn't know that before today, of course. I'd heard all of this stuff about her but I didn't *know* how I would feel. I knew I'd like her. I knew we'd have the same goals for the boys this summer. I knew that I would respect her for what she's taking on. I knew I'd feel empathetic because of what she's gone through and what we've both lost. But..." He breathed again and met TJ's eyes directly. "But I didn't know how I would *feel*. Until today. And now I do and...yeah, okay, it's tempting." There, he'd confessed that much. "But what you didn't see was her naked up against the porch railing screaming out my name," he said bluntly. "And *that* is because I can fucking control myself and I do realize that would be way too fast. But *not* because she didn't want it. Okay? So I'm not taking advantage of her or running away with some fantasy fairytale Rafe told me. I'm not taking her to bed and I'm not proposing and I'm not meeting with any lawyers to draw up adoption papers. So get off my case."

TJ looked at him for a long moment, his jaw tight. Then he said, "Yet."

Tucker stepped forward into his brother's personal space and met his gaze directly. "Yes, *yet*."

"Okay, enough brotherly bonding," Travis said. He took TJ's upper arm. "Let's go."

"He's going to do something stupid because of this woman," TJ said, still looking at Tucker.

Travis nodded. "It's about time he did something stupid because of a woman."

TJ didn't respond to that. But all three of them knew that Travis, the recently in love and married and almost new dad, wasn't the only one who'd been stupid over a woman. The difference between TJ and Travis was that Travis's stupidity had worked out.

And Tucker realized in that moment that TJ's concern over him and Delaney was based on some experience. TJ had been crazy about Michelle at one time. And when she'd come to him, pregnant, insisting the baby was his, he'd built up that fantasy of love and family and forever big and fast. Michelle had told him when she left to be with the baby's real dad that she'd come running to TJ because she'd been vulnerable and scared.

So there were some parallels. That did *not* mean that what was happening with Tucker and Delaney was the same thing.

"Let's go," Travis said again, pulling on TJ's arm.

Finally, their older brother gave Tucker a nod. "Be careful."

Tucker didn't nod. He did, however, say, "Thanks." He knew his brother's words and him being here tonight really were because he was concerned.

But careful wasn't exactly the right word. He wasn't sure that admitting to Delaney how he felt and what he hoped for this summer was *careful*. But he was going to be honest, and he really did feel like he had his eyes open. He didn't expect her to fall into his arms, weeping with gladness and professing her own deep and eternal love. But he hadn't expected her to climb into his lap and tell him that she wanted him on night one, either.

Delaney knew what she wanted, and if he was a part of that, then he sure wasn't going to be *careful* about it.

He watched his brothers drive off and then headed to the barn with the night crawlers. He grabbed a beer from the fridge while he was there. The fridge was immediately inside the barn door and he could see the house from where he stood. He popped the top and started to drink, but the lights in the upstairs bedroom went off just then.

Delaney was done with the boys.

He grabbed a second beer and started back for the house. He got there as she stepped out onto the porch. She closed the door softly behind her and went to the swing. He climbed the steps and crossed to where she sat. He opened the second beer and handed it to her, then settled back against the porch railing directly in front of her.

She took a long drink of the beer. He did like a girl who drank beer.

"The boys all good?" he asked.

He couldn't deny that seeing her rounding them up, listening to each of them, touching their heads or their shoulders as they moved past her into the house, had tripped something in him. She had this way of watching them and talking to them as if she was persistently amused and overwhelmed and totally in love. It made him want to hug her and laugh and help her and yet sit back and watch and enjoy it all at the same time.

It was clear that she was head over heels for the boys even when they exhausted her and made her crazy.

He loved that.

Yeah, it might not be super macho, but he was in love with the fact that Delaney was clearly in love with her nephews.

"They're exhausted," she reported with a happy smile. "They had a great time today. And tonight."

"I'm glad. That's the idea, right?"

She nodded. "Right."

They sat quietly, each sipping their beer. Delaney started the swing rocking with a push of her toe. He watched her, trying to put his thoughts and feelings into some kind of order. He was so happy she and the boys were here. But he couldn't come on too strong.

Suggesting they get married and raise the boys together was probably coming on too strong. For tonight.

But he wondered if it was too much to suggest that they go back to where they'd been when TJ had shown up.

Her sitting on that swing definitely wasn't helping him concentrate on much else.

She was beautiful. He'd known it. He'd seen lots of pictures over the years. But in person—it was so much more. Hearing her voice, seeing her expressions change and soften around the boys, knowing how she felt in his arms, and how her lips felt against his, and how she sounded when her voice got soft and husky and she said, "I want this". Meaning him.

"I overheard you and your brothers talking."

Well, that was certainly one direction their conversation could go.

She pointed up and he realized the window in Jack and David's room were open.

"I shut it and turned on a fan for them."

He sighed. He hadn't intended to hide all of his feelings from her. He'd already told her that his family was interested in her because Rafe had been trying to set them up for years. And she'd felt their chemistry too. She couldn't be shocked that he was thinking about being more than her friend and confidant. Hell, *she'd* kissed *him*. But he hadn't intended for her to hear it like that.

Still, maybe this was good. Get it all out in the open.

"How much did you hear?"

"That you think you could already be in love with me and that you haven't given the other girls around here a real chance because you've been waiting to meet me and that you're romantic and want a wife."

"Okay, so a lot." At least he didn't have to wonder about how to bring this all up.

"Yeah, a lot. Or" she shrugged, "all of it."

She'd heard all of it. Great. But maybe it was. He couldn't tell how she was feeling about any of it. What should he say? What *could* he say? It was all pretty much true. So he didn't say anything.

She took another drink but kept her eyes on him. "You really want all of that?"

"I do."

"And you really think that I…that you and I…"

"I do."

She shook her head. "Wow, you seem very sure."

"Are you really shocked?" he asked. "You haven't ever had any of those thoughts? Never once wondered if maybe Rafe was right? Never once, after a bad date or a breakup, wondered if the perfect guy was waiting here in Sapphire Falls?"

She blew out a breath. "This is crazy."

"Have you had those thoughts? Ever? Even once?" Suddenly it was important to him to know.

He was taking a chance, gambling, but surely he had occurred to her over the years. At least once. She had to have been curious, right? She had to have wondered.

Delaney wet her lips and Tucker gripped the railing and his beer bottle. No grabbing her and kissing her. Not yet.

"Okay, fine. Yes, I wondered."

Satisfaction spread through his chest. "I have too, and now that I've met you, kissed you, I know that I have to find out where this can go."

She shook her head and sighed. "This is crazy," she said again.

"No. What's crazy is a young, loving guy with a wife and four kids getting a brain tumor at age twenty nine and dying just after turning thirty. What's crazy is a vibrant young woman with a family, randomly getting shot in a convenience store while she was picking up milk. Wanting to explore a relationship with a gorgeous woman I'm incredibly attracted to and have been intrigued by for more than a decade and happen to be living with for the summer? Not crazy at all."

She pulled in another breath. "When you put it that way, it makes perfect sense."

"It does?"

She gave a little laugh. "No. But it doesn't sound quite so crazy."

"I'll take that."

They shared a smile, but then she went on, "And I do feel the chemistry."

"The chemistry that prompted you to kiss me."

She nodded. "Yeah, that chemistry."

"I have to tell you, that was definitely one thing I wondered about." He took a drink of beer and watched her think about that.

"Before the bakery or after?" she asked.

He grinned. "Before. The minute I saw you, I knew."

"And would you have been disappointed if we weren't attracted to one another?"

"You have no idea." Full truth. "But the chances were very, very slim, Delaney."

"Because you'd seen pictures."

"Yes, but—" His attraction included her gorgeous, thick dark hair and her bright green eyes and that mouth that made him think very not-just-friends things. Yes, he knew she was beautiful because of the pictures. But it wasn't only how she looked. "But I was ninety-percent attracted before the bakery."

"Really?"

"Everything I knew about you turned me on."

She sipped her beer again, not really reacting to that. Then she nodded. "I know what you mean."

Surprise and satisfaction again spread through him. "Yeah?"

She laughed softly. "I don't crawl into guys' laps every day."

"Glad to hear it." He sipped. "Want to do it again?"

She grinned. "Yes."

He moved to sit beside her. He sat with his body twisted to face her, an arm on the back of the swing. "I was hoping you'd say that."

She turned to face him too, tucking her foot underneath her. "But I'm not sure it's a good idea now."

"Because you know it's going to be the last lap you ever want to crawl into?"

Her eyes widened. "Because I'm afraid you're going to propose afterward."

"Would you rather I propose first?" He tried to make it sound light and laid-back, but frankly, the conversation was winding something tight inside of him. Something he wasn't quite sure he could even label.

"I will admit that I wondered about you," she said. "I probably even wondered about this summer, me staying here, what it would be like to be with you twenty-four-seven. But I didn't expect...this. All of this. That it would be this serious or intense."

He breathed and worked on being cool. He couldn't beg her, he couldn't get on his knees, he had to *show* her. He had time. He had the summer. "Okay, well, I can't take it all back, so what do you need?"

"What do I need?"

"If getting married was what you knew you needed, then you'd be in my lap already. So there must be something else. What can I do? Rafe told me—" He stopped. Maybe he shouldn't tell her what Rafe had said. But surely it wouldn't surprise her.

"What did Rafe tell you?" she asked with a little frown.

"He asked me to take care of you."

She breathed out. "Oh."

"What were you afraid he'd told me?" Tucker had to ask.

"That I was clueless, in over my head, out of my comfort zone, about to screw everything up." Her words came fast.

"Whoa," he reached out and touched her hand. She looked up at him. "No, he didn't say any of that."

"He knows it though," she said. "We talked about it enough."

Tucker studied her. Yeah, maybe she was in over her

head and out of her comfort zone. "You're not clueless," he finally said.

"You have to say that," she told him. "It would be rude to agree that I have no idea what I'm doing."

"With the boys?" he asked, to clarify.

She nodded.

"You're definitely not clueless there," he said firmly. That much he knew. "You're great with them."

She swallowed and shook her head. "I love them. They're still in one piece. And I brought them here. But I know how to be their favorite aunt. Not their m…mom."

She tripped over that last word and Tucker wanted to hug her.

"You'll learn. Loving them is number one. Wanting to do your best for them is number two. I'm not sure there is a number three."

She smiled up at him. "You're giving advice about being a mom?"

He shrugged, glad to see her smiling. "I had one of the best."

She nodded. "Well, I do want to do what's best for them, so that's what this summer is about for me."

"I'd love to know what you need from this summer," he said. "And what you want."

"My plan is to use this summer to practice."

"Practice?"

"Parenting. To read some books, establish some routines with the boys, to make a financial plan and," she took a deep breath before continuing, "to help us all heal and get stronger emotionally. I need to really bond with them before we get to Colorado."

Tucker hated that she truly seemed unsure of herself in her new role. "You and the boys are clearly close. They love you. You're their rock."

She shrugged. "They're stuck with me."

"Delaney—"

"No, listen, I know they love me and they trust me. I know I make them feel safe. But…my parents are…a lot. They always think they know what's best. My dad has a way of steamrollering everyone. If I'm not sure of myself and totally confident in my plan for the boys, and if they don't feel totally secure and bonded with me, then my dad could break everything apart. He's already offered to take custody."

Tucker felt his immediate scowl. "Rafe wouldn't—"

"Neither Rafe nor Chelsea would want that," Delaney interrupted. "I know that. Rafe and I talked about all of this. He knew exactly what my father would be like, and he tried to help prepare me to face him. That's part of why Sapphire Falls was so important to him. He knew I wasn't ready to be around my parents full-time with the boys yet. He said Sapphire Falls would make us a stronger unit."

Tucker's gut was churning, but he made himself relax and nod. "It will. There's no better place for healing and getting to know yourself."

She gave him a little smile and he felt the knot in his gut loosen slightly. "That's what I need. Time. Peace. Focus."

"Done."

She raised an eyebrow.

He did too. "Whatever you need."

She sat looking at him for a long, drawn-out moment. "You know, if I'd come to visit last summer, or the summer before that. Or if you had come to Nashville…something would have happened."

Damn right it would have. Tucker couldn't help the thought. She was completely right. He could feel it now. The timing at the moment might not be perfect, but all of the other ingredients were there.

"Yeah, it would have," he agreed, his gaze on hers.

"But now it's complicated. There are other things I need more this summer." She wet her lips and Tucker couldn't pull his attention from her mouth.

"Maybe those are things you need this summer *too*," he said, his voice husky.

She swallowed hard. "Well, there is the list Rafe gave me."

Tucker met her eyes again. "The list?"

Her lips curled into a half smile. "He knows I'm going to be completely focused on the boys and getting everything organized. So he made me a list of things I have to do or experience in Sapphire Falls myself this summer. He made me promise."

Tucker smiled. "That sounds like him." He held out his hand. "Let's see it."

Somehow he'd known she had it with her. She dug into the pocket on the side of her shorts and produced a small piece of paper. She handed it over.

Tucker set his beer on the porch beside him and unfolded the paper. In small, curly handwriting was a list of five things.

He read them out loud. "Go on the Ferris wheel at the festival, skinny dip, sleep under the stars, drink Booze, have Mrs. Bennett's German chocolate cake."

Something else knotted his gut now. Anticipation.

Rafe knew very well what he was doing when he made that list for Delaney. He'd known that Tucker would be right there with her for all of it.

He looked up at her. "Pretty good list."

"Yeah? That covers the summer fun in Sapphire Falls?" she asked.

"It's a really good start," he said. "But I'm sure Rafe won't mind if we add a few things as we go."

She gave him a smile that made his heart thump hard. "You're going to help me with that list?"

"Well, there's no way in hell I'm letting anyone else do any of it with you," he said honestly. "And you should never drink Booze by yourself, and going on the Ferris wheel alone is a little pathetic."

"Booze is..."

"Potent," he said with a chuckle.

"And skinny dipping alone isn't safe?" she asked. "I'm a very good swimmer."

"That might be more of a preference on my part than a safety issue," he said.

Her smile deepened and the look in her eyes made every pulse in his body thump hard. "And the cake?"

He shifted on the swing. He'd been very upfront with her so far and she already knew that his family was interested in her. "Everyone in town calls it engagement cake. Mom makes it when anyone gets engaged."

"TJ brought German chocolate cake over from dinner," she said.

He nodded. "Yep."

"Is there a reason that your family had engagement cake for dinner tonight?"

He nodded. "There is."

"Me? And you?"

"Yep."

Her shoulders slumped forward and she looked up at the ceiling. "I'm already engaged to you as far as your family is concerned?"

"My mother is...hopeful. And not subtle."

Delaney looked at him again. "Seriously?"

"She said she was trying to make a good impression and that is definitely her best cake."

"But everyone around the table knows what it means?"

He shrugged. "It's a well-known, often-repeated family story."

"Let's hear it."

"When my mom met my dad, she was a terrible cook, but she knew that he loved cake because she worked at the diner after school and he would come in for cake every other day. So she decided that she needed to learn to bake to win him over. She tried several different cakes, but this was the only one that turned out okay. She took it to his house and found out that it was his favorite. He says that he fell in love with her with the first bite, but the truth is, he was going into the diner all the time to see *her*, not because of the cake."

Delaney's smile had steadily grown and now she was grinning. "Nice story."

He nodded. "They had German chocolate for their wedding cake, and ever since it's been her tradition to make it for romantic occasions."

"That's sweet."

"Wait 'til you taste the frosting," he said. "And there's a story about that too."

She narrowed her eyes and tipped her head. "Okay."

"Mom has never confirmed this and shushes us whenever we bring it up, but there is a rumor in town that she frosts the cake extra thick because some of the couples have had some fun with the frosting—besides eating it with a fork."

Delaney's mouth fell open. "Your *mother* puts extra frosting on her famous cake so the couples she gives it to can get sexy with it?"

She didn't exactly seem scandalized. She seemed entertained.

"Like I said, she won't confirm or deny. She blushes whenever anyone brings it up. But she keeps frosting the cakes thick."

Delaney laughed lightly. "Wow. It's my first night in town."

"My mom is addicted to her boys getting married now that Travis has taken the plunge. I mean, she always wanted us to all settle down and be happy, but now that she's got a daughter-in-law and her first grandbaby on the way, she's completely crazy. And she's been—"

"Hearing about me for thirteen years," Delaney filled

in.

He nodded. "Rafe's like another son to her. Once he said that you and I should be together, she was completely on board."

"Oh boy."

"Yeah." He probably didn't need to say that he'd felt the same way. He'd pushed it deep down, but now it had all come out and he had to admit that his brothers were right— he'd been waiting for Delaney.

"But TJ brought it over to me tonight and he doesn't want me engaged to you."

"TJ needed a reason, however flimsy, to come over tonight to make sure I wasn't doing anything stupid."

"Like kissing me on the porch swing."

"He thinks it's too fast."

"It probably is."

"I've been waiting thirteen years to kiss you, Delaney."

She stopped and sucked in a quick breath. "You know, if you do all of those things on Rafe's list with me, it's going to be really hard to resist doing more of that."

He couldn't help his huge grin. "I know."

"Right. You don't really want to resist."

"Nope."

She took another deep breath. "Full-court press, huh?"

He leaned in. "Life's short, Delaney."

She nodded. "Yeah, I know."

"I know you need this summer to get your head on straight and to get stronger," he said. "I know you need to figure things out. And I'm going to help you with all of that. But I don't intend to hide or deny that I want you."

She pressed her lips together and studied him. "You mean it? That you'll help me?"

"The sooner you feel strong and confident, the sooner you'll realize that I'm part of what you want."

"I'm in trouble," she muttered, almost to herself.

Tucker just grinned. He hoped so.

"I feel like I'll be leading you on, getting your hopes up," she said.

"You mean by going out with me and staying up late talking and kissing me and letting me spread frosting all over your body?"

She coughed, her eyes wide. "Um, yeah. For instance."

"Hey, Laney?" he asked, his voice low.

"Yeah?"

"Lead me on. Please."

There was a heartbeat between her staring at him in wonder and her sliding over and into his lap again. This time she straddled him right away, wrapped her arms around his neck and pressed her breasts to his chest.

The first time they'd kissed, he'd held back, let her make the moves, seeing where she wanted things to go. This time, he was going to show her where she wanted things to go.

The kiss was hot and bold. Their tongues stroked deep and firm, her hands roamed over his shoulders and up into his hair, holding on to him as she pressed against his instantly hard-for-her cock. That's all he needed to know.

Tucker slid his hands under her ass and stood up from the swing. She automatically wrapped her legs around his waist and he carried her to the porch railing. He set her down on the narrow railing and pulled back so he could see her eyes.

"I know you have some things to figure out," he said gruffly. "But there are some things I want you to consider while you're making your plans."

Her breathing was ragged, her eyes wide, her lips so tempting. He lifted his hand to the back of her head, grasped her ponytail and ran his hand down the length to where it rested on her shoulder.

She wet her lips. "Things like what?"

"Things like the fact that there are four very happy little boys in the house right now. In part thanks to me."

"I see the humble part of the day is over."

He grinned. "We're to the everything-you-can-have part of the day."

ౠ

She was so in trouble.

She'd meant everything she said to him about needing time to get her head on straight and bond with the boys. She had to be fully confident, know exactly what she and the boys wanted and needed before she walked into her father's house.

Any weakness, any insecurity, and he'd take over.

And Chelsea would *definitely* haunt her then. Maybe Rafe too. She and Rafe had talked specifically about how she had to be fully prepared before going to Colorado.

But Rafe hadn't told her that Tucker would be ready to propose within twenty-four hours of her hitting Sapphire Falls. Or that his mother would be making engagement cake for her. Or that she would be able to picture her and the boys staying here and being completely happy.

Rafe had surely known all of that though. He would have known that Tucker would step up in every single way she needed him to, would take over with the boys, would have a small army of people to feed and entertain and take care of the boys.

Which meant Rafe had hoped she would take the easy way out and stay in Sapphire Falls.

Which pissed her off.

Rafe had doubted her. She knew that. She knew that he was worried about her taking things over, supporting the boys—financially and otherwise. But she'd believed that he thought Sapphire Falls was a great *temporary* stop.

Now it was clear that he'd planned for her to come, fall in love—with the town, the lifestyle, the sense of family and yes, Tucker—and stay.

Dammit.

Just once she'd love to have someone think that she could handle this.

"Hey, you with me?"

She felt a tug on her ponytail and her focus snapped back to Tucker.

"Yeah, sorry. Just thinking."

"I haven't even given you everything to think about."

That was what she was afraid of. There didn't need to be any further temptation as far as she was concerned.

"Maybe I should go—"

He cupped the back of her head and brought her in as he lowered his head.

Okay, she could stay for a few more minutes.

His lips were hot and pleasure zipped along every one of her nerve endings. He had definitely been holding back before his brother had showed up and outed all of his feelings. Tucker tipped her head just right so that he could deepen the kiss. He slid his tongue along her bottom lip and then onto her tongue when she sighed.

She tried to get closer, but sitting on the railing gave her little room to move. So she slid forward, getting her feet on the floor. He put a hand on her lower back, encouraging her to arch into him. She wrapped her arms around his neck and pressed against him, her breasts into his chest, her belly button against the hard length of his erection.

He groaned and moved his hand from her back to her ass. He squeezed her butt cheek, the pads of his fingers stroking along the hem of her shorts, brushing the bare skin just below the edge of the soft cotton.

She gasped, pulling their lips apart so she could breathe.

"Delaney."

No, don't stop yet. That's not enough.

"Turn around."

She blinked at him. She wasn't done…

"Hands on the railing."

Okay, she was curious. She let go of him and settled onto her heels. She licked her lips. "Hands on the railing?"

He pointed to the porch railing behind her.

Hands on the railing. Hmmm. Letting Tucker take over—and take care of her—was so, so tempting. And already getting to be a habit. She had to nip that in the bud if she had any hope of finding her oomph. Her spark, her confidence, her...whatever it was that was going to make her sure of herself and ready to meet this parenting thing head on.

Unfortunately, Chelsea had gotten all the oomph genes. Her father had been overflowing with confidence and oomph. No doubt the reason the two of them had always butted heads. Delaney was more like her mother, happy behind the scenes, in the supporting role.

Well, now the spotlight was hers and this was the role of a lifetime. And she only had one chance.

"Delaney," Tucker said, low and commanding. "Turn around and put your hands on the railing."

Well, she didn't have the oomph thing figured out yet. One more dabble in the just-tell-me-what-to-do pool wouldn't hurt, would it?

She turned, bracing her palms on the wood.

Tucker moved in behind her and ran his hands over her back from her shoulders to her hips. Then he brought her butt back against his erection.

She started to move her hands and he put his mouth against her ear. "No moving."

"Tucker, what—"

"I don't want the boys to possibly come out and see my hand down your pants."

Heat and need. That was all she could really focus on. She cleared her throat and curled her fingers around the railing tightly. "I'm not going anywhere."

He chuckled lightly and the sound rumbled from his

chest through her. "Good girl."

His hands caressed her hips through her shorts, heating her skin and sensitizing every inch of her body from those two points somehow.

Delaney let her head drop forward, grasped the railing and concentrated on breathing.

Tucker's hand came around to her belly and he stroked back and forth above the waistband of her shorts. The motion lifted the hem of her T-shirt and he dipped under the edge so they were skin on skin.

She shivered with pleasure at the feel of his big, hot, rough palm against her stomach, anticipating, *needing* his touch somewhere else, *everywhere* else.

"Tucker," she said with a small groan.

"Oh, we're just getting started," he told her.

She breathed in with relief and pleasure. Relief and pleasure. She couldn't help but want a lot more of both. "Thank God."

He chuckled against her skin just before his lips met the spot where her neck curved into her shoulder. He flicked his tongue against her skin and then kissed her as he moved his hand up under her shirt and over her ribs to the edge of her bra.

His fingertips trailed over the lace underneath her breast and he kissed his way up her neck to the spot behind her ear that made goose bumps erupt head to toe. He pressed his hips into her butt as he cupped her breast. Her nipple happily welcomed his touch, hardening and pressing into his palm like they were old friends. Or would like to get to that point. He moved his hand over the stiff tip and shifted to take it between his thumb and finger.

She gasped. Exactly the right pressure to shoot hot shocks to her clit.

Speaking of areas that wanted to get to know Tucker *really* well.

"I love that sound," he said gruffly.

"I've got better."

She figured she'd surprised him. She knew he saw her as sweet, even—she cringed slightly—maternal. He probably didn't realize that she would be completely upfront about what she liked and wanted.

Well, she loved sex. She hadn't had near enough of it for far too long. But she remembered really loving it. And she had a feeling with Tucker it could go beyond anything she'd had before.

"Do you now?" he asked, tugging on her nipple and pressing against her from behind.

"Oh, yeah," she managed. "But you're going to have to keep those hands busy."

"Can do, babe," he said, proving it as he slid his hand from her hip across her stomach and inside her shorts. "Can do."

She swallowed hard and gripped the railing as he ran his fingertip back and forth along the elastic waistband. She really wanted to move her hands. Really.

She lifted one off the railing.

"Oh, no." His hand came out of her shirt and trapped hers against the railing. "We're just standing here looking at the stars if any short people come out here needing a drink of water."

She huffed out a breath and grabbed the railing again. "Those short people are going to be here all summer."

"Yep."

He put his hand back on her breast. Thankfully. And squeezed, tugged and stroked her right back to near-begging level.

"Which means we're going to have to be creative about how, when and where we do this," he said.

She could only nod.

But then the hand in her shorts moved lower to cup her through her silky panties.

"Oh." It was more of a gasp than a word.

"I do like that sound too."

"Well, I can't get too much louder if we're worried about short people."

And she should be, of course. They couldn't have a hot, spontaneous fling with four kids in the house.

"I can stop if you're going to have trouble controlling yourself." He started to move his hand out of her panties.

"No!" Okay, that was louder than it needed to be. He did stop moving away though. "I mean, I'm fine. They're clear upstairs."

She felt his soft chuckled against her neck. "Good girl," he said again.

He pulled the cup of her bra down as he slid his hand into her panties. *That* was skin on skin.

Her bare breast in one hand, his erection pressing into her ass and his middle finger slicking up and down over her clit. Delaney felt her need building so fast her head was spinning.

This was crazy. She loved sex and had no doubt Tucker was quite good but she never reacted this quickly.

She worked on breathing and even distracting herself a little. She knew that not all women could orgasm easily. She knew for some it could be a rare occurrence even when everything was perfect in every way. She knew some women who just flat-out didn't care about sex. So she was grateful for her sex drive and her ability to climax nearly every time.

But dang.

She studied the stars overhead, the shape of the barn in the distance, the sounds of the breeze in the trees and still her orgasm coiled tight and hard and fast.

And then he moved his hand lower and slid a finger into her.

She actually cried out and then clamped her lips together.

"Ah, very nice."

His breath was hot on her ear, and even that made her clit throb.

He added another finger and thrust deeper.

Yes. Damn, that was exactly what she needed. If he so much as brushed over her clit she was going to go off. Within minutes. That was…unbelievable.

And amazing. Of course it was amazing. Any woman would want to be where she was standing right now. Any woman was going to be completely addicted to a man who could do that to her.

So why was she trying to hold back?

Maybe because she'd felt as if she was in control—right up until Tucker touched her.

He rubbed his thumb over her clit as he thrust his two fingers deep and she came apart.

In spite of the stars and the barn and the breeze in the trees, in spite of herself, Tucker Bennett gave her the fastest orgasm of her life.

Dammit.

At least she didn't scream.

The ripples continued for several seconds, and when they finally quieted, Tucker slid both of his hands to her stomach, resting them against her belly and pressing her back against his erection.

She was stunned. She really was. The release had been amazing and complete. And she was stunned.

Okay, well, at least she could take some control back by making *him* crazy.

She started to turn in his arms, but he tightened his hold. "That was fucking amazing."

Yeah, it was. Dammit.

"And now—" She tried to turn again, but he didn't let her.

"And now that I'm sure you're going to be thinking about me—and all I have to offer—I will say goodnight."

Shock rocked through her.

He kissed her neck, removed his hands from her clothing and stepped back.

She whirled on him immediately. "What was that?"

He didn't seem contrite. He gave her a grin. "Oh, babe, if you don't even know what that was—"

"Was that an engagement orgasm?"

That stopped him with his mouth open. "What?"

"To go along with the engagement cake?"

"That was—"

"A taste of what I could have if I marry you and settle down here."

For just a moment, a flicker of…something…passed through Tucker's eyes. Temptation? Uncertainty? But then in a flash, it was gone, and in its place was that sexy, I-want-my-hands-in-your-panties grin, and he moved in until he was practically on top of her.

"Yeah, I guess you could say that's a taste of what you will have. But if we're comparing sex to cake, that was barely a crumb."

Oh man, she was in trouble.

"So you're going to tease me with only a crumb? You're all big talk about how you know exactly what you want and life's short, but you pull up short when it's time to go for it?"

She was overreacting, but she had never had a guy get her off without getting something for himself and she didn't like the feeling of being vulnerable and at his mercy. She liked sex, she had it when and with who she wanted to and she got what she wanted from it. But no one *gave* her anything. She got orgasms, but that was because she made them happen—either by telling the guy what to do or doing what she needed to make it happen during sex. Where they were *both* involved. Where she wasn't the only one overwhelmed and letting go. It was one area where she was sure of herself and she was in control.

And now Tucker had taken that away.

Well, she was going to get it back.

Tucker crowded her against the railing. He cupped the back of her head with both hands, his fingers in her hair. His gaze tracked over her face, lingering on her lips and then coming back to meet hers. "How long has it been?"

Since I felt good? Since I felt like I knew what I was doing? Since I felt like I was about to do something I was pretty good at that would turn out well?

But she knew what he really meant. And the answer was actually the same. "A long time."

It wasn't completely dark out here. The light shone out from the living room window right behind them. But his face was in shadow. Still, she could feel how his gaze heated.

"How long?"

"Twenty-two months."

He gave a small grin at her very specific answer.

She tried to look as sincere as possible as she said, "You asked me what I need and want for this summer. Well, I was serious when I said I need to figure a whole bunch of things out." She just hoped three months was enough time. "But I think I also need to have a wild, fun fling this summer. I'm not thinking about engagement rings, but I am thinking that some really hot sex with a guy I like and trust would go a long way toward me feeling good again."

Maybe it was stupid, maybe it was wishful thinking, but maybe if she had *one* area of her life where she was taking charge and knew what to expect, it would help the other things fall into place. Or at least help her feel like less of a loser for not knowing what she was doing in any other area of her life.

Or at least remind her what taking charge and being confident felt like.

Sex seemed like her only hope.

That should totally be a slogan for something.

He opened his mouth but no words came out.

So she went on. "I haven't been sure of much lately, but this I *am* sure of. I'm a full-time mom now. I don't know what I'm doing, but I do know that having boyfriends isn't going to work. I can't bring men in and out of the boys' lives. And I'm okay with that. I really am. Like I said, I am going to step up and be everything they need me to be. I also know that you have a bunch of stuff going on in your head that takes this whole thing to the next level."

"I do."

And that also made her feel out of control. He wanted to *marry* her.

Okay, he wanted to see if maybe he wanted to marry her.

Still, the idea that the word marry was being tossed around already was nuts.

She needed some control over things between them as well. She couldn't let him say things like I want to get married and just nod and say oh. She couldn't let him take the boys to his mom's for dinner and kick back and just say thanks. And she couldn't let him finger her to orgasm on the front porch and say that was great and go to bed.

"But you did say I could lead you on, and I can't help but want to enjoy what I can, while I can."

He stared at her. There were a number of things in his eyes, and Delaney realized he needed to process everything she'd said. Probably he had to process the fact that she had *said* it. She knew he saw her as sweet and maybe a little meek. And she was a little meek.

But that had to end now.

And the longer she stood on the porch, with his big hands in her hair and his hard thighs against hers, the more she knew that this was a really good decision—and she *really* wanted him to agree.

"Tucker, say something."

He cleared his throat. "I'm just trying to keep from

starting now."

"Starting what now?"

"Our wild, fun fling."

She felt her smile growing as relief and anticipation and heat spread through her. "I don't want you to keep from starting now."

"Starting *now*. This minute?"

"Yes."

"Even knowing that I want this to be more than a fling."

"As long as you remember I *don't* want it to be more than a fling."

"So I'm more like a stress-relief program." He ran his hand up and down her arm.

"Therapy," she said with a nod, pressing closer to him.

"Therapy. I like that."

"So that's a—"

"Fuck yes," he filled in as he pulled her in and sealed his lips over hers.

CHAPTER FIVE

It was a bad idea. He was going to have sex with Delaney the first night she was in town. He was going to go into this without any guarantee that it would be anything more than a fun hot-and-dirty romp in the hay. Literally.

He'd had plenty of sex with women he wasn't serious about. He'd had plenty of sex with women who were more serious about him than he was about them.

He didn't think he'd ever had sex with a woman he wanted more from than she was willing to give.

This might be therapeutic for him too.

And if that excuse didn't work, then he'd find another.

Like the fact that he was committed to making Delaney happy and giving her whatever she needed. And she said she needed this.

It wasn't like he'd had to talk long or hard to himself.

Her mouth was hot and hungry under his. Her hands were all over his chest and he felt her slip one underneath his shirt. Her bare palm against his stomach was his undoing.

Tucker ripped his mouth from hers. "My bedroom or the barn?"

"Uh." She had a glazed look in her eyes and she was moving her hands up and down over his abs. "God, I can't wait to see you naked."

He gave a short, surprised laugh. "Bedroom or barn? Bedroom is more comfortable." Though for some reason, he wanted to take her on a hay bale. He'd never done that, but he had a few fantasies about the loft in his barn. "Barn will be more private." He'd also never had a woman over with four boys in the house, two just down the hall.

"Barn," she finally said.

He grinned. The girl who didn't want to talk about night crawlers wanted to have sex with him in the barn.

Well, she wanted to have sex with him and she was willing to do it in the barn.

"Let's go." He took her hand and started off the porch.

"Tucker."

She was still on the top step and he was on the bottom. He turned.

"Can you take your shirt off?"

There were lots of really good things about living in the country. The privacy and lack of close neighbors was one of them. He reached for the bottom of his shirt and stripped it off.

"Your turn," he told her.

She was staring.

"Delaney."

"Yeah."

She was still staring, her gaze roaming over his shoulders, chest and stomach.

"Take your shirt off, Laney."

Her gaze snapped up to his. She didn't say anything, but she licked her bottom lip and then pulled her shirt off.

She wore a simple white bra with the lace trim he'd felt earlier. She wasn't overly endowed either. Another fact that he'd felt for himself. But damn, he wanted those breasts in his hands, against his chest, in his mouth.

He climbed the two steps between them, swept her up in his arms and started for the barn.

She gasped and then laughed and wrapped her arms around his neck.

"I've never done this in a barn before," she told him.

"Me either. But I'm completely positive it will work."

Of course it would work. He had multiple sturdy horizontal surfaces and blankets to pad them out there. And Travis had overshared one night about him and Lauren and *his* barn.

He felt Delaney's arm tighten around his neck. "You haven't?"

He wondered why he'd put the fricking barn so far from the house. He didn't have any animals that used the barn. It was storage and workspace. He didn't have to worry about animal noises or smells, so why was the thing so far away?

"Tucker."

He looked down at the woman in his arms. She felt right there. It felt as if he'd been waiting for her, for all this, for so long. "Yeah?

"You've never had sex in a barn before?"

They got to the barn door and he put her on her feet but kept her close. "No."

There was always a utility light on in the barn, but he hit the switch inside the door, illuminating the whole barn. He didn't want to miss the chance to see every single inch of her.

"Seriously? Country boys don't have sex in barns all the time?" She grinned up at him and he could tell she was pleased by the idea that she'd be the first.

She had no idea all the firsts she was going to be—that she already was.

"I'm not saying we're opposed to it," he teased lightly. "But most of us have beds."

"Right. But not kids."

"Right."

She took a deep breath. "So we both might need to get used to this."

He backed her up against the door, taking her hands and putting them on his stomach again. "I also have an air mattress that turns my truck bed into a bed. And there's a gorgeous spot for a big blanket down by the pond for after skinny dipping. And, of course, there are lots of babysitters here."

She pulled in a deep breath through her nose and ran her hands up his chest and then up to his shoulders. "But we're here right now."

"Yes, we are."

"Does it make me a pervert if I want to see you completely naked on a hay bale?" she asked, leaning in to press her lips against his left pec.

Tucker cupped the back of her head and groaned. "Honey, you can have me completely naked anywhere you want."

She kissed her way to his nipple and flicked it with her tongue.

He was hard and ready like that.

"Okay, country boy, take me to the nearest bale."

He couldn't help but tip her head up for a kiss first. She opened her mouth under his immediately and he stroked his tongue in, already imagining stroking deep into her body with other parts. Fingers, for instance. His tongue too. And the rock-hard cock that was craving her after even the little taste he'd had.

He could just take her up against the barn door.

She pulled her lips from his. "I need you spread out," she said. "There's a lot of you and I need my tongue all over you."

She could have anything from him she wanted.

"Loft," he said, pointing to the ladder that led to the loft area over where they stood.

She slipped around him and started for the ladder.

He definitely appreciated her enthusiasm.

And they'd both had time to think about all of this. Was this the best decision he'd ever made? Sleeping with her right away? Getting in deeper with a woman who already had him wrapped around her finger, who he'd had a thirteen-year crush on? Maybe not. But he wanted her. He wanted a lot more from her than this, but this was what she was willing to give him right now. How could he not take whatever she'd give?

Then she climbed up onto the ladder, her sweet ass, her bare legs, her bare feet…and he was going up after her no matter what.

He was a sucker for a barefoot girl.

He grabbed a heavy wool blanket and tucked it under his arm so he could grip the ladder with both hands. Then he was right behind her, unable to look away from the ass that fit perfectly in his hands—convenient for against-the-wall or in-the-shower sex.

"Wow."

She stopped at the top of the ladder, blocking his way.

"Let's go, honey, move it." He put a hand on her butt and nudged her forward.

She moved but she kept staring. He stood in the loft, trying to see what she was seeing.

It looked like a hayloft to him.

"What are you thinking?"

"It's actually got hay bales in it."

"If the lady wants hay bales, the lady gets hay bales."

She turned to him. Again, her gaze roamed greedily over his chest and stomach. "I think I said I wanted you naked on a hay bale."

There wasn't as much light up here. The lights hung about even with the loft, so there were more shadows in the loft. But the subdued lighting made it feel more intimate.

"Gladly." He tossed the blanket onto the nearest bale, toed off his shoes and his hands went to his fly. He unbuttoned and unzipped.

Her eyes were glued on every movement. He'd never been so turned-on by a woman watching him before.

When he paused, she crossed her arms, tipped her head and lifted an eyebrow.

She looked hotter than hell standing barefoot and topless in his hayloft.

His fricking hayloft.

"Are you sure you don't want to—"

She took three steps that brought her right up against him. Her fingers replaced his at his fly and she spread it open and pushed the jeans down. They fell the floor around his ankles, leaving him in his underwear only.

Not that he thought she had any question how he felt about all of this, but it was impossible to hide his arousal now.

He stepped out of his jeans and kicked them to the side. Then he shed his underwear. Fully naked, fully aroused, he moved to the blanket-covered hay bale. He sat down and braced his hands behind him, leaning back.

He had never had any self-esteem issues about being naked or anything having to do with sex, but he was also typically in charge. He took the lead in seductions and he could be demanding in bed.

But he sensed that Delaney wanted to be a little bossy here. She'd had a lot happening that was out of her control. She had already shared with him that she felt in over her head in a lot of things. So if she wanted to order him around during sex, he could definitely live with that.

"Holy crap," she finally breathed.

His eyebrows shoot up. "You okay?"

Her gaze lifted to his. "I'm so okay right now."

He grinned and held out a hand. "Then come here."

She didn't take his hand right away. Instead, she reached behind her to unhook her bra and let it fall forward and drop to the floor.

Tucker's mouth got dry and it was his turn to stare.

Then she hooked her thumbs in the waistband of her shorts and stripped out of them and her panties at once.

He'd already felt everything he was now seeing—her perky breasts with the hard nipples, her bare mound, the smooth, soft skin of her belly and thighs. He'd seen naked women. He thanked his stars that he'd seen lots of them. All shapes and sizes. He didn't really have a specific type other than naked and willing. But he was more turned-on by Delaney than he ever had been by any other woman. He'd also seen enough pictures of Delaney that he could tell she was thinner than usual. Clearly, the last few months had taken their toll on her appetite.

His mom would fix that quick enough.

"Come here, honey." He held out his hand again.

She walked toward him, looking every bit the siren.

But she stopped out of reach.

"You're gorgeous," she told him.

"So are you."

"Put your hands behind you," she told him.

Bossy. Okay.

He leaned back on his hands again.

She put a hand on each of his knees and leaned in, bracing herself as she kissed him.

He started to reach forward, but she pulled back and shook her head. "Hands on the hay, big guy."

He took a deep breath. If he couldn't touch her, this was going to be torturous. But he complied.

She kissed him again, her lips soft against his but moving, stroking her tongue along his lower lip and then meeting his tongue with hers when he swept into her mouth. She let him lead the kiss as far as he could without using the rest of his body. He wanted to grab her, flip her underneath him on the hay and plunge into her sweet, tight body. But he held back, sensing she wanted to be in charge.

Apparently trusting that he was going to keep his hands where he had them, she ran *her* hands up his thighs. Everything in him tightened in anticipation.

Finally, after what felt like a year, she wrapped one small hand around his cock.

He tore his mouth from hers, giving a heartfelt, gut-deep groan. "Delaney."

She stroked her hand up and down his length. "Don't worry, I'm not going anywhere."

He dug his fingers into the blanket and pieces of hay poked through. He barely felt them.

She went to her knees, still pumping him firmly. She looked up at him as she lowered her head. He should probably stop her. She didn't have to do that. But God, he wanted to feel her mouth on him. For just a minute.

She slid him past her lips and over her tongue slowly, swirling the tip of her tongue over his head and then sucking softly.

Tucker tipped his head back and worked on breathing and not grabbing the back of her head and thrusting.

Holy shit.

He had Delaney's mouth on him. And he was thinking that she just might ruin him for other women.

Even in the midst of his cock moving in and out of her sweet, hot mouth, he knew it was only in part due to her technique. This was Delaney. The woman who had brightened his best friend's life and had cared for him in the last months of his illness. The woman who had helped her sister achieve all of her dreams and goals. The woman who might not feel confident in any of it but who was diving into being a mother to the four little boys who had made Tucker sure he wanted to be a father himself.

She was amazing.

And she was giving him a blowjob.

She was beyond amazing.

Her hands worked him at the base while her mouth worked the top. That, along with the fact that he'd been aroused since he'd sat down on the swing next to her, meant Tucker was wound tight.

"Lane—"

She lifted her head and looked up at him. "I'm on the Pill."

Jesus. He hadn't even thought of a condom. Of course, in what fantasy land would he have imagined having sex with her the very first night she was here? Still, he should have thought of it before carrying her to the barn.

He was going to have to start storing them out here.

"I'm totally clean," he told her. If she called a halt to things now because of the lack of a condom, he might not survive.

"Me too."

She stood up and stepped forward with a foot on either side of his feet. She was just ready to climb on.

"Hang on, honey." He did reach for her now, intent on making sure she was totally ready for him.

But she beat him to it. She cupped one of her breasts and ran her other hand over to her mound and then down to her clit.

"I can't wait, Tucker." She put a knee on the hay next to his hip and moved over him.

"I loved having my fingers in your sweet pussy," he told her, leaning in to take a nipple in his mouth. She moaned, and he didn't know if it was the dirty talk or the suction he applied. But it was perfect. She was perfect. He ran his tongue around the hard tip, loving everything from the taste to the way it made her sound to the way she threaded her fingers through his hair and gripped.

"Say something else."

Ah, it was partly the dirty talk.

"The feel of you coming around my fingers made me want to bend you over the porch rail and fuck you right then and there."

She moaned and gripped his hair tighter.

He was talking dirty to Delaney. He'd just said the word fuck to Delaney. Within less than twelve hours of knowing one another.

Her hot opening was right above him and he desperately wanted to thrust. But he was letting her take the lead.

"Take me, Delaney."

Okay, letting her take the lead with a little encouragement.

She reached for his cock and slid her hand up and down. "I love that you're eager for me."

He ran his hand up the outside of her thigh, squeezed

her hip and then moved to cup her heat. "You have no idea."

She squeezed him. "I have a little bit of an idea."

"That isn't the only part of me that wants you."

She stared into his eyes. "You've got to quit saying stuff like that."

"Not gonna happen."

"I should just leave now then," she said.

He knew that part of her didn't mean just leaving the barn. There was a voice in the back of her head telling her that staying here in Sapphire Falls for the summer was going to complicate things.

"You're not going to leave now." And he didn't mean just the barn either.

Somehow, he knew that she knew that.

"No." She shook her head and pulled her bottom lip between her teeth.

He reached up and freed it with the pad of this thumb. "Delaney, I'm going to be everything you need. Even the stuff you don't know you need or don't think you want to need."

"Tucker," she said, mimicking his tone. "You gotta stop saying stuff like that."

Before he could respond, she lowered herself onto his cock.

Her tight, hot grip almost pulled him over the edge right then.

He grabbed her hips before she could move. "Give me a second, honey."

She was breathing hard too, digging her fingers into his shoulders. "Yeah, okay."

She felt it too. The intense, nearly overwhelming reality of their bodies connecting for the first time. It was beyond physical. It was like they were made to fit together and the emotions of it were almost...

"You're so *big*."

Okay, so maybe a lot of it was physical.

"Honey, you're saying all the right things," he told her through gritted teeth. He was working to hold back, to keep from slamming up into her for the three whole thrusts it would take for him to hurtle into a mind-blowing orgasm.

"Yeah?" She was breathless. "Well how about I'm halfway there already?"

"Yep. All the right things."

She grinned down at him. "You're good, big guy. And that nickname means a lot more now."

He swatted her ass. "Flattery will get you everywhere."

She lifted herself and the slow, sweet drag made him grit his teeth again.

"Will it get me another orgasm?" she asked.

"There's no way you're leaving this barn without an orgasm, Laney."

"Well, I'm taking you with me." She put her lips to his and began moving.

Tucker could only hang on. She rode him, controlling the rhythm, tightening her muscles around him perfectly, rubbing her nipples over his chest, kissing him deeply as if she'd never get enough.

He was at her mercy.

And she seemed to know and love that.

She pulled her lips from his and put her mouth near his ear. "I can feel you everywhere. I love how you fill me up. I love your hands on me, your lips on me, your cock stretching me."

He gripped her hips, trying to slow her down. He was going to go right on without her if she kept talking like that. Not that there weren't other ways to be sure she got hers before they left the building. But he really wanted to feel her clamping down on his cock.

He knew dirty talk got her going, but there was something else, something he wanted to test.

He grabbed her ponytail and tipped her head back,

looking directly into her eyes when he said, "I want to know every inch of this gorgeous body. I want to know your taste, all your sounds, how you look when I'm fucking you from behind, how deep I can go when you're spread out wide on my bed, and I already want to make love to you every night for the rest of my life."

She gripped him hard and cried out. Her orgasm grabbed them both and he felt his cock pulsing and then the incredible release.

She slumped against him a moment later and Tucker held her close.

Her hot breath against his chest felt as right as still being embedded deep in her body with her arms and legs wrapped around him.

He stroked his hand up and down her back and waited for her to be the first to speak.

"Tell me that it was the hay bale that made that so good."

He chuckled. "I'm moving a hay bale into my bedroom if so."

She leaned back, pushing an escaped strand of hair away from her face. "Well, we should probably try the bed once to compare."

"No."

She frowned. "What?"

"There's no *once* to any of this."

She pressed her lips together, searching his eyes.

He let her look. He had nothing to hide. Not even the pure, bone-deep satisfaction that he felt knowing that dirty talking and using the word fuck might get her going, but talking about forever and making love could take her all the way.

"You're definitely going to keep saying things like that," she finally said.

"Yes. And I think you're going to keep liking it."

He was going out on a limb, pushing maybe. But the

sooner she recognized and admitted that there was something here, the sooner he could get on with the rest of getting her settled in his life.

"Tucker, I need you. I'll admit that."

"Right."

"But I'm specifically here this summer to work on *not* needing people. You have to understand—and respect that."

He shook his head. "You're in the wrong place for going it alone, Delaney."

"Yeah, I'm starting to catch on to that." She didn't seem overjoyed.

"And you're not going anywhere."

She sighed and shook her head. "Not yet."

He wanted to say more, to argue with that, but he did have some control, as he'd told his brother. Yeah, so he'd also told TJ and Travis that he wasn't going to sleep with her, propose or adopt anyone tonight.

Two out of three wasn't bad.

"We should get back to the house." She pushed up off him.

They both got dressed and Delaney started for the ladder, but Tucker grabbed her hand. He opened his mouth to say something, but he wasn't sure what, so he kissed her instead.

The fact that she melted against him, opened her mouth and gripped his shoulder trying to get closer told him everything he needed to know.

"I'm glad you're here," he told her when they pulled apart.

She looked like she wanted to respond differently, but she gave him a little grin. "I'll bet you are."

She could make light of it all she wanted, he decided as they headed back for the house, but when he left her outside of the guest bedroom he leaned in and whispered, "You know that being that amazing at what we just did is no way to make me *not* want to marry you."

She sighed and shook her head. "You've *got* to stop saying stuff like that."

He leaned in and kissed her. "No chance."

She shut the door in his face, but he was smiling bigger than he ever had.

ళ్జ

Well, crap. That hadn't worked at all.

Her one attempt to regain some control, to exert some take-charge attitude over something had backfired. Completely.

Sex with Tucker had been…out of control.

She'd been on top. She'd defined the motions and the rhythm. She hadn't let him touch her much. She'd even turned the tables and talked dirty to him. But she still hadn't had any control over the way he'd taken her body and mind and—if she was crazy enough to believe something like that—her heart.

She'd been all into him.

Crap.

Well, one good thing about being sexually overwhelmed by Tucker—the four boys would be a fantastic buffer the morning after.

She could hear them as she made her way downstairs. Belatedly, she wondered if she had hay in her hair. She hadn't been the one actually *on* the hay, so she was probably good. She still came up with a possible story in case one of the boys asked why she had hay in places she shouldn't. Or why she had hay anywhere.

She'd taken time to scrub her face and her feet in the bathroom before bed last night, but she hadn't wanted to risk the noise of a shower when Jack and David were fast asleep in the room next door. And when she'd awakened from a dead sleep full of sexy dreams including Tucker and more hay, mud and German chocolate cake frosting, she'd headed straight into the boys' rooms. They were out of bed and out of the room and she'd immediately gone looking for them.

They were eating powdered-sugar donuts and milk around Tucker's breakfast table.

Well, if Chelsea was going to haunt her for not feeding them healthy every meal, then at least Tucker was going to get it too.

"Morning, everyone."

"Tucker said we can go to the field with him today!" Jack told her

"I'm helping make a doghouse for Tater," David said.

"It's not Tater," Charlie said. "That's not a dog name."

"We're not naming him Nashville," David told him.

"Why not?"

"We said we were going to name him Duke," Henry said.

"Yeah, Duke," Jack said. "I like Duke."

"You like Tater too," David said, giving Jack a look.

"Tater is dumb," Jack muttered.

"It is not!"

"We're not calling him Tater!" Charlie yelled.

Delaney was always amazed at how quickly things could go from peaceful to chaotic.

They all started arguing at once and her plan to *not* look at Tucker—ever again—was blown immediately.

She found him over their heads. "What's going on?"

"I'm going to take the boys with me today," he said over the noise, as if there was nothing out of the ordinary going on in his kitchen at all. "TJ has a transmission he's going to look at and he wants Charlie's help, Mason's got some work for Jack and David first thing, and I'm going to give Henry some driving lessons."

"He won't let me drive yet," Jack told her.

That also amazed her—the boys' ability to carry on a

good, loud argument with one another while still never missing a detail going on around them.

"Well, I think *that's* a good idea," she told him. She looked back to Tucker. "What kind of driving lessons?"

The boys had quieted and were now focused on Delaney and Tucker's conversation. She'd learned from Chelsea that sometimes you intervened when they fought and sometimes you didn't. Delaney was still learning which times were which, but a lot of the time, if she left them alone, the boys worked things out. As long as there was no blood and no name calling, she stayed out of their disagreements about things like who could run faster or who could fit the most marshmallows in their mouth— things that were easily tested and proven one way or another. And things like dog names. They needed to learn to make joint decisions.

"The tractor," Tucker said about the driving lessons.

They were talking in the midst of four boys about farm machinery and yet she saw a heat in his eyes that made her start tingling.

Damn.

"And the truck," Henry added.

She gave Tucker a questioning look.

He shrugged. "Just around the fields."

"Your pickup?" she asked.

"Yes, but kids around here drive on the back roads and in the fields long before they're sixteen. It's fine. I started driving at twelve."

"But—"

"It's fine," he assured her. "I promise."

She sighed. What did she know about driving on back roads and in fields? "Fine."

"Yes!" Henry exclaimed.

Jack sighed. "I won't be twelve for eight years."

Delaney looked at him. "How many years?"

Jack shrugged. "Forever."

She laughed. "That's how long it will feel," she agreed. "But let's prove to Tucker that you can actually add numbers up to twelve."

"Six," David said.

Jack slugged him in the arm. "I was gonna say that!"

Delaney reached to stop David's return strike, but Tucker grabbed her hand before she could. David punched Jack in the arm and Jack yelled, "Ow!"

Delaney pulled away from Tucker. "Hey."

"If you're going to hit somebody," Tucker said, though he was addressing Jack. "You have to be prepared for them to maybe hit you back."

"But that hurt!" Jack said, sticking out his lower lip.

Tucker nodded. "Yep. I only ever hit one of my brothers if I *really* meant it and was willing to hurt for whatever I was mad about."

"Like what?" David asked.

Jack was rubbing his arm but he wasn't crying or pouting.

"Like when TJ nailed a board over the hole in the side of the barn so the mama cat couldn't get in and out anymore."

"You hit him for that?" David asked.

Tucker nodded. "Oh yeah. Gave him a bloody nose."

"Did he hit you back?"

"Gave me a bloody nose too," Tucker said. "Hurt like crazy."

"But you were glad you did it?" Charlie asked.

Tucker shrugged. "I don't know. Later that day, Ty and I went out there and took the board off so the cat could go in and out again. That was easier and less painful."

"What else?" Charlie asked.

"Well, I punched Travis over a girl once," Tucker said, with a grin.

David wrinkled his nose. "Over a girl?"

"Yep. A really pretty one."

"Was *that* worth it?" Henry wanted to know.

Delaney wanted to know too. And was very interested in the fact that Henry seemed interested.

Tucker chuckled. "Well, I hit him because he asked her to the sweetheart dance. He hit me back, hurt like crazy and we didn't talk to each other for about three days. Then at the dance, I danced with the girl and she told me that she said yes to Travis because he asked her first. If I'd asked her first, she would have said yes to me. So it wasn't really Travis's fault anyway."

"But then he might have hit you," Henry pointed out.

Tucker grinned. "Yeah, but then she would have been *my* date and it would have definitely been worth it."

Henry grinned at that and something very big and very important hit Delaney—the boys needed Tucker.

She'd known it on one level. They needed someone to hunt night crawlers with and dirt bike with and do farm chores with—boy stuff, stuff she simply didn't know how to do. But that was little boy stuff. Henry wasn't going to be a little boy much longer. None of them were going to be little boys forever. And they would need more than someone to go fishing with. They would even need more than advice about girls. They would need someone to show them how to be men—good, sweet men, good sons and good....husbands.

She felt emotion thickening in her throat and knew she was about to start crying.

She was never going to really handle anything, never going to know if she *could* handle it, because...she couldn't. The boys needed Tucker.

And wasn't that a fabulous excuse? Talk about the easy way out. She should go upstairs right now, move her suitcase into Tucker's room and inform him that she wanted a plain gold wedding band because she wanted to wear it while she worked and a huge diamond would get in the way.

She'd been a single mom for one month. One month. And she was already looking for the easy way out, for someone else to take care of things.

Pathetic. Seriously.

She supposed that she'd always assumed she would eventually grow up and not need her sister and Rafe so much. She'd always thought that she'd eventually have her own husband and kids and home. But Chelsea's husband and kids and home were always there, always so easy. They had filled the gaps in Delaney's life—her need for family and friends, companionship, kids.

Ugh. *Really* pathetic.

She'd known it even before they died. She was pretty sure she'd known it deep down for a long time but had successfully ignored it. But when her last boyfriend had accused her of breaking up with him because Rafe didn't like him, she'd really started thinking about it.

Well, Rafe *hadn't* liked him. Neither had Chelsea. Rafe hadn't liked most of her boyfriends. Neither had Chelsea. And the boyfriends often got frustrated with taking second place to the five other men in her life—Henry, Charlie, David, Jack and Rafe.

It had just been really hard for any guy to give her anything she didn't already have. Except for sex of course.

She really liked sex.

She looked at Tucker again with that thought.

Yep, that whole take-control-back-with-sex plan had really backfired. Basically, she had *everything*—home, family, the kids and now sex.

Well, everything except her self-worth.

She was so screwed.

"So what am I going to do all day while you're out working?" she asked Jack, ignoring the riot of emotions rocking through her. Maybe a sense of self-worth was overrated anyway.

He shrugged. "Watch TV."

She smiled. She wasn't much of a TV watcher.

"I'll be so bored and lonely without you all," she said.

"I thought you could relax, maybe read a book," Tucker said, picking up the milk glasses from the table in front of the boys and taking them to the sink. "Or you could take a long bath. You can use my Jacuzzi if you want. Take a nice long soak. In case you're sore or anything." He said it casually, not even looking at her.

She still blushed immediately. Down to her toes. She even felt her scalp get hot and tingly.

"I'm fine," she said, resolutely *not* meeting his gaze. "And you don't have to take the boys with you all day. Surely you have real work to do."

"Of course I have real work to do. I've been putting a bunch of it off for when they got here. I'm looking forward to the break I'll have now with all this extra help."

"We're really helpful," Charlie assured her.

"The boys who are too weak to even put their towels back up on the rack after their showers?" she asked.

"It's not because we're too weak," Jack said with a giggle.

"Well, I can't think of any other reason those towels never get picked up," Delaney said.

"We...forget," Charlie said.

"Uh huh."

"You know what my mom would've done?" Tucker asked Charlie. "She would have left them on the floor. Then the next time we needed a towel, we would have picked those up and found them still wet and we would have realized why hanging them up was important."

"My mom hates it when things are messy," David said.

Everyone got really quiet and David looked around the table. He sighed and his head dropped. "I mean she used to hate it."

Delaney moved to put her hand on David's head. "I promise you, she still hates it," she said. "You know that she's cleaning up after all those angels who keep tracking mud across the clouds."

David looked up. "Angels don't get into the mud."

She smiled at him. "How do you know?"

"There's no mud puddles in Heaven," David told her.

She widened her eyes. "Well, that doesn't sound like Heaven to me."

Jack nodded. "There has to be mud puddles to be Heaven. And dirt bikes."

"And video games," Charlie said.

"And baseball," Henry added.

There was a long pause, and then David said, "And dogs."

"Oh, definitely dogs," Delaney said.

"And pizza," Tucker added. "And tonight I'm going to show you all exactly how pizza in Heaven tastes. We'll get takeout for dinner and have a movie night."

All of the boys brightened and turned their attention to Tucker, giving Delaney a chance to blink rapidly and pull in a deep breath. She never knew when these discussions of their parents would come up, but she was never completely ready.

"The pizza in Heaven tastes like the pizza here?" Charlie asked.

"That's what your dad always said," Tucker told him.

Everyone was quiet for a moment, but they seemed thoughtful versus sad.

She'd take thoughtful.

"Okay, guys, gotta get to work if you want riding time this afternoon," Tucker said.

"Riding time?" Delaney asked.

"The sooner we get our work done, the more time on our bikes we have," Charlie told her.

"The dirt bikes," she clarified.

"Yep."

They started to file out of the kitchen, but Tucker hung

back.

"They're really going to work and not be in your way?" she asked.

"Of course. They've been doing chores around here for years," he said with a grin. "It's good for them and they actually really like it. My brothers and I were doing farm chores before we were Jack's age."

"Well, I can't stay in the bathtub all day," she said.

Tucker's gaze heated. "I'll still be imagining it."

She took a big step backward, but he caught her around the waist and pulled her in for a long, hot kiss.

She became acutely aware of the fact that she was still wearing the shorts and tank top she'd slept in with only a simple wrap around her. She never had to worry much about a bra. Perhaps the one advantage to being small on top. But with Tucker around, it seemed she was very in tune with her nipples.

When he let her go, she knew she was breathing faster and blushing again. "You have to—"

"There's no way in hell I'm going to stop doing that, so don't even say it," he told her. "But I'll try to keep it to when we're alone."

"Tucker!" David shouted from the front door.

"We're never going to be totally alone," she reminded him.

"That sounds like a challenge."

Of course it did. She shook her head. "Not a challenge. A fact."

"We'll see."

He started for the front of the house and then glanced back. "You could spend your time in here today."

She looked around the kitchen and felt her heart kick when her vision for the new cupboards and countertop and floor appeared in her mind. She could. "That sounds great actually." Just what she needed. She could work off a lot of pent-up energy and emotion in here. She could crank the music up and get into her work and forget about all of the crazy thoughts and regrets and fears that were crowding her mind.

"Knock yourself out," he said enthusiastically. "It's all yours."

"You're really okay with anything?"

"Yep. Anything. I'm easy."

She couldn't help blushing again.

"Good to see where your mind is at," he said with a wink.

How could her mind really be completely anywhere else? She was incredibly attracted to him. More so than she ever had been to any other man.

She was pathetic, but she wasn't stupid. She knew a lot of her attraction to Tucker was physical—he was a gorgeous man with a body that made her so, so grateful she was a woman—but a lot of what drew her to him were the same things that made him think they would make a perfect couple. They had both been close to Rafe and they both loved the boys.

"So I'll just spend the day here in the kitchen," she said, changing the subject. "I have a lot of ideas."

He gave her a knowing look but he let it go. "I can't wait to see what you come up with," he said.

"Have fun," she said as he headed out to join the boys.

"We'll see you for lunch."

Lunch. Great. That gave her a good three hours or so to get a start on things in here.

This was good. This was definitely, without question, something she knew, something she was good at and something that she could look at and be proud of.

Now all she needed was a sledgehammer.

CHAPTER SIX

Tucker dropped Charlie off with TJ to work on a transmission and he planned to take Henry with him to the fields, but first he was going to get the younger boys set up with Mason.

Mason Riley, resident genius, international expert on all things agricultural, the guy who loved nothing more than to spend his days digging in the dirt.

"Gentlemen," he greeted Jack, David and Tucker as they walked up to his greenhouse. "I have a huge job today. I hope you ate a good breakfast."

"Donuts!" Jack immediately ratted out Tucker and his less-than-healthy breakfast.

Mason nodded. "Donuts are good. But I think we'll have to take a coffee break in a bit too."

"I don't drink coffee," Jack told him.

"I do," David said, standing tall. "Black."

Mason didn't laugh. He shook his head. "Dang, I'm sorry. I only have banana smoothies. Maybe Adrianne can bring some coffee out later."

Tucker appreciated his friends and family every single day of his life, but some days and moments he was even more thankful than others. He knew that Adrianne had come up with the idea of smoothies, and he wasn't even offended to think that she'd been so sure he wouldn't have fed the boys fruit.

"Well, I guess we can do banana smoothie today," David said. "Maybe coffee another day."

Mason nodded solemnly. "Thanks, I appreciate you being laid-back about it."

"No problem," David said, sounding much more mature than his eight years.

"Okay, so, this job is dirty and sweaty," Mason said. He took the boys over to a table that was just their height and got them started planting some seeds that he assured them were extremely important and a big government secret.

Though Tucker suspected he was saying it to further the boys' enthusiasm over the project, the truth was, both of those thing were very possible in Mason's work. And it wouldn't surprise Tucker that the guy was letting little kids mess with his project. He had always been great about involving people in his passions, and since becoming a dad himself, he'd become enthusiastic about getting kids excited about science and agriculture early on.

Once the boys were elbow deep in the dirt, Tucker said, "Hey, Mason, can I talk to you for a second?"

Mason Riley was the smartest man Tucker knew. He was the smartest man everyone in Sapphire Falls knew. And he was a straight shooter. That was a nice way to say he didn't have a lot of tact sometimes and he didn't always pick up on the subtle cues from other people—like expressions and body language, for instance—that let most of the rest of the human race know how their messages were being received. And he didn't really care. He said what he thought and felt and didn't apologize for his less-than-popular-at-times approach to situations, even with the White House and the media that loved to cover his company's activities.

So Tucker knew that if he asked Mason for an opinion or advice, he'd get Mason's honest take on the situation.

He also knew that Mason had fallen in love with his wife Adrianne in three days.

It wasn't that he couldn't talk to his brothers or other friends. He could, of course. But he kind of wanted a less emotional reaction. Mason was a wonderful guy, but less emotional was his forte.

"Sure, what's up?" Mason wiped his hands on his jeans and came over to where Tucker was standing.

"It's about Delaney."

Mason nodded. "Okay."

Tucker also appreciated that he could get right to the point. Mason didn't really do beating-around-the-bush. Sometimes that was exactly what a guy needed.

"I think I'm falling for her already. Is that crazy?"

"It makes complete sense," Mason said matter-of-factly.

Okay, this was going well so far. "It does?"

"I assume there is a physical attraction?"

Tucker flashed back to the night before in the barn. He cleared his throat. "Very much so."

"Have you acted on the attraction?"

Was Mason asking him if he'd already slept with Delaney? And if he said yes, would that be bad? Or good? All he could do was tell the truth.

"We did. Last night."

Mason didn't seem shocked. Which made Tucker wonder about Mason and Adrianne. Tucker—well, everyone—knew that things had happened hot and fast between them, but had Adrianne, the girl all the guys had wanted the minute she stepped her cute curvy butt into town, gotten frisky with Mason the first night they met?

Damn. Mason had more game than Tucker had even realized.

"Then it makes sense that you're feeling intense feelings for her," Mason said.

"Because of the sex?" Tucker asked. That was not how it felt. Well, that was kind of how it felt, but he had been feeling some pretty intense things even before that.

"The sex simply confirmed what your subconscious was already telling you," Mason said. "I'd be surprised if you *weren't* falling in love with her."

"Even though it's so fast?" Tucker asked, making sure.

"Time has nothing to do with it," Mason said. "You know what you need to know about her in order to develop deep feelings for her."

Tucker nodded. "Right." He paused. "Things like

what?"

"That she has the same values you do, that she wants to have a family and is a good mother, that you can be physically intimate with her and that you can protect and take care of her."

That sounded very scientific. And maybe a little…cold.

"Are those like things all men look for subconsciously or something?" he asked.

Mason shook his head. "While the need to protect and care for our partners is innate in most of the species, there are differences in what men want and need. Having a family and being a good mother weren't part of the equation for me with Adrianne."

"But you did want to have a family and she is a good mother," Tucker said, confused.

"Of course. But those weren't the things that made me fall in love with her. For me it was the need to have someone who understood and supported me. Who could help me see the direction I wanted for my life."

Tucker thought about that. "I don't think I'm hard to understand."

Mason laughed. "You're not. You're very easy actually."

There was that to-the-point stuff. "I need a direction in my life too," Tucker said, thinking that sounded like something someone mature and enlightened would think.

"You have a direction to your life," Mason said. "A very specific one. Home, family, farming."

"Hailey calls it an Oedipus complex," Tucker said.

Hailey was Hailey Conner, the mayor of Sapphire Falls and a high school classmate of Mason's. Hailey was a gorgeous, sexy, bossy know-it-all woman who ran the town. She was also, strangely, a friend to Adrianne, Lauren, Phoebe and Kate. Somehow. That meant she was often hanging out with their group at the Come Again or at river parties or other social events. She was opinionated, that was for sure, and had no problem sharing that opinion anytime, any place, with anyone.

She was also friends with many of the women Tucker had dated in Sapphire Falls and every time he broke up with one of them, he got to hear about it and how he was actually looking for a woman like his mother and how no woman would ever measure up in his mind.

Fuck, he hated that. But he got why she said it. Maybe that was why he hated it so much.

Mason shook his head. "You don't have an Oedipus complex."

Tucker perked up. Mason was more intelligent than something like ninety percent of the human population. He was definitely smarter than Tucker. He was smarter than Hailey too. So this was a relief.

"No?"

"No. You like your father."

"I love my father."

"Exactly."

Tucker didn't want to seem too needy here. He wasn't needy. He knew he didn't have any kind of complex. Still, hearing it was nice. "So Freud doesn't apply?"

Mason shrugged. "I feel Freud is extreme in his descriptions of the psychosexual development stages. But regardless of that, in classic Freudian psychoanalytic theory, resolution of the Oedipus complex occurs when a child identifies with the same-sex parent."

Tucker blinked a few times. He'd heard *resolution*; that was good. "So I'm fine."

Mason grinned. "You might want a woman *like* your mom, but you also want to be a man like your dad. You're fine."

"Mom's a wonderful woman, mother, wife. The fact that I'm attracted to women that are in *some* ways *like* my mother is normal?"

"Of course."

Tucker really wished Mason was the type to go on and on. In regular-guy English. "So nothing to worry about or be embarrassed about?"

"No."

"Straight-forward, normal stuff, right?"

"Absolutely."

Tucker frowned. "I'm not very complex I guess."

"That's not what I mean," Mason said. "Where I was looking for something to fill a gap in my life, an emptiness I didn't know was there, you don't have gaps. You already know what you want and you've been waiting for the woman who needs you to fill in gaps for her."

A light bulb seemed to turn on for Tucker. The women in Sapphire Falls had all seemed perfect for him. They all had the same background, the same life, wanted the same things. But that was just it—they already had everything he could offer.

Delaney didn't.

She needed home, family, roots.

He could absolutely give her all of that.

And Mason thought it was fine, rational even, for him to already be falling for her. So it must be okay.

"Hello?"

Delaney swung toward the voice coming from the living room. She pushed her goggles up to the top of her head and crossed the room to turn her music down.

"Hi! I'm in here!" she called out, heading through the swinging door between the kitchen and living room as she pulled her work gloves off.

A pretty blond met her with a big smile. "Hi, I'm Kate."

Delaney swiped her forearm over her forehead. "Hi."

A beautiful brunette came into the house along with Adrianne, the woman who owned the bakery in town.

"And I'm Lauren."

She was clearly pregnant and Delaney instantly knew who she was. "Tucker's sister-in-law, married to Travis."

Lauren grinned and looked Delaney over from head to toe. "Tucker's been talking about us."

"Hi, Delaney," Adrianne said. "Nice to see you again."

"Hi, Adrianne." Delaney didn't know what was going on exactly, but Adrianne had a plate in hand. That could only mean something sweet. Delaney was a fan.

"Wait, see her *again*? You've already met her?" Lauren asked Adrianne.

"Met her at the bakery yesterday," Adrianne said, setting the plate on the table next to the couch.

The women all looked great, and Delaney was very aware of her ragged blue jeans, T-shirt, work boots and the bandana around her hair. She was sweaty and was sure she had dirt all over her face.

"You didn't tell us that," Kate said to Adrianne.

"Didn't I?"

"We were talking all morning about how we wanted to meet her and you didn't say anything," Kate said.

"You were talking all morning about how you wanted to get to know her. I don't really know her," Adrianne said, giving Delaney a smile. "I've met her, I've met the boys, I saw how Tucker looked at her. That's all I know."

"How Tucker looked at her?" Kate asked, clearly curious and excited. "How did he look at her?"

"Like he'd just seen the most delicious cherry cobbler of his life," Adrianne said with a big grin.

Lauren grinned too and nodded. "I can see why."

Delaney had no idea what to say or how to react. She thought maybe she shouldn't react at all. But she wasn't sure that was possible. Especially when all three women turned to look at her at once with wide eyes and smiles.

"I'm sorry I'm late!" A cute redhead breezed into the house. "Start from the beginning."

"Adrianne was saying how Tucker looked at Delaney like she's the best cobbler he's ever seen," Lauren filled her in. "And I was agreeing."

"Easy, girl, don't scare her off on her first day." The redhead dropped her purse by the door and headed straight for Delaney. "Hi, I'm Phoebe."

Delaney *really* didn't know how to respond now. "Hi."

Lauren laughed. "What did Tucker tell you about Red, here?"

Delaney grimaced a little. The name Phoebe didn't sound familiar. "Um...sorry."

"Wait, he told you about them?" Phoebe asked, gesturing to the other women with her thumb.

"Just Lauren," Delaney said.

"I met her at the bakery yesterday," Adrianne said.

Phoebe turned to her with a hand on her hip. "You didn't tell me that."

"You already missed that part," Lauren said. "We were to the cobbler part."

Phoebe turned back to Delaney. "Well, even if the jerk didn't mention me yet, I've known Tucker longer than any of these girls. Anything you want to know, ask me."

"Okay," Delaney said slowly. "What did she mean about the cobbler thing?"

It hadn't sounded *bad*, but she was curious—probably too curious—about what *exactly* it meant.

Phoebe grinned. "Cobbler, especially cherry, is Tucker's all-time favorite thing and biggest weakness."

Oh. Delaney blushed and shook her head. "I don't think—"

"That's awesome," Kate said. She looked positively delighted. "He is such a great guy and you are the perfect woman for him."

Delaney blinked at her. Seriously? "We just met." Not to mention that she'd known Kate for about three minutes. How could she possibly think that?

"But you've known *about* each other for a long time, right?" Lauren asked. "And you have the boys and you're beautiful. If you can make cobbler, you're totally perfect."

Cobbler? What the hell was all this talk about cobbler?

"Well, I—"

"Is that a *tool belt*?"

Delaney looked at Phoebe. "Um, yeah."

"That is completely hot," Lauren said. "Total crush going here."

Delaney blinked at her. *What?*

Phoebe patted Lauren on the back. "Don't mind her, she's got raging hormones."

Um, okay.

"So you're actually using those tools?" Kate asked.

Delaney shrugged. "Yeah."

"Are you fixing something?" Adrianne asked.

"Actually, I just started a renovation on Tucker's kitchen," she said.

They all stood looking at her without a word for several seconds.

Phoebe was the first to speak. "A renovation? Like you're painting the walls or something?"

"Eventually," Delaney said. "But there's a lot of work to do before that point."

"This I have to see." Phoebe pushed past Delaney and headed into the kitchen.

The other women were right behind her.

"Oh my God," was the general reaction.

Delaney could admit that this stage was a little messy. The kitchen wasn't huge so the debris was kind of jumbled in the middle of the room and seemed worse than it was. She'd been working for about two hours and wasn't as far along as she'd like to be. She'd had to dig through her Jeep for her tools and goggles and other necessities and then rifle through Tucker's garage, shed and finally barn—while trying, unsuccessfully, to block the memories from the night before—for other supplies. But she'd definitely made some progress in the kitchen. Just maybe not to the untrained eye.

She'd pulled the cupboards off the walls, she had the countertops laying in the grass out back and she was about to start pulling up the linoleum.

Phoebe turned to look at her. "You did all of this?"

Delaney nodded. "Yeah."

"How?" Phoebe asked.

"Why?" Kate asked.

Delaney shrugged again. "It's what I do. And Tucker told me I could go for it. Thought it would be fun to have a project and it needed a facelift in here."

"It's what you do?" Kate repeated.

Delaney smiled. "For a job. My sister is a realtor and interior designer. She either finds fixer-uppers for people or she works with them to consider renovating their existing house rather than buying new. Then we go in and do the work. I do the carpentry, countertops and flooring. Rafe does the plumbing and electric. We both do drywall and all of us do the painting and stuff. Chelsea does the décor. We're a great team."

It wasn't until she'd finished that Delaney heard what she was saying.

A cold ball formed in her chest. She felt her smile fade. "I mean, we were. We worked together for the past ten years or so."

The women all moved in closer around her and Adrianne pulled Delaney into a hug. "We're so sorry for your loss."

Delaney swallowed hard against the lump in her throat and actually returned the hug. She didn't know Adrianne, but she could tell the woman was sweet and sincere and dang, lately hugs just felt really good. "Thanks," she said softly.

"So you're a *carpenter*?" Kate asked after a moment of

quiet.

Adrianne let Delaney go and Delaney wiped her cheeks and faced Kate. "Yep. I learned from one of the best in Nashville. Was his apprentice for almost two years."

"So you can *make* cupboards and stuff?" Kate asked.

Delaney smiled. She knew she didn't look like a carpenter or a contractor, but surely with all the shows on TV now about renovations and remodeling, people were beginning to see women in those roles more easily. "Yep. I like making furniture better, especially coffee tables, but I can do almost anything."

Kate came forward and took Delaney's hands, as excited as she had been when she'd heard that Tucker had looked at Delaney as if she was a cobbler. "Levi bought an eighty-year-old farmhouse. He did some renovations, but what that means is he updated the heating and air, some of the plumbing, got new carpet and had someone paint. We need...more. Cupboards, new flooring, new woodwork, a new banister on the staircase. You can do that stuff?"

Delaney nodded. "Yes, definitely. But surely there's someone else around here who could do the work." She couldn't come into town for the summer and take work away from a local.

"The contractors around here do big jobs like houses and barns, dirt work, cement work, drywall and roofs, yes, but not cupboards and banisters and stuff," Adrianne said.

"There's no carpenter?" Delaney asked.

"There's an older guy who's mostly retired who will do smaller jobs—furniture repairs and things—and there's a guy over in Danbury who would do jobs like this, but no one does custom cupboards and things," Adrianne said.

"And I should mention that Levi is a millionaire," Kate said. "You can totally gouge him for some custom stuff."

Delaney laughed. "A millionaire in Sapphire Falls, huh?"

Kate grinned. "A short visit turned into forever," she

said with a little shrug. "For both of us."

She was clearly over-the-moon happy and Delaney felt her heart flip a little. A short trip that turned into forever. That sounded nice.

"So you could do cupboards and stuff for me?" Kate asked.

"I'd be happy to come take a look." If the boys were going to be hanging and working with Tucker all summer, she was certainly going to have some free time.

"Awesome." Kate looked thrilled.

"It's going to be hard to cook in here, isn't it?" Lauren asked. "I mean, I'm not much of a chef myself, but that doesn't look right." She pointed to the stove that was sitting in the middle of the room, clearly not connected to anything.

Delaney laughed. "Well, that stove will work fine for *me*, but yeah, I'm hoping Tucker was serious about eating at his mom's a lot."

"That stove will work fine for you?" Lauren asked.

"I'm not much of a cook either."

The girls all looked at one another and then back to Delaney.

"You don't cook?" Kate asked.

"Nope. My sister is—was—the cook," Delaney said. "She was great and I was over there all the time. Kind of like Tucker and his mom. But don't worry," she added. "I'm planning to take some cooking classes once we get to Denver."

She didn't know these women well, but she had the impression, maybe just from Tucker, that they would all be concerned about the boys' well-being.

"Cooking classes?" Lauren asked.

"Denver?" Kate asked at the same time.

Delaney nodded at them both. "Cooking classes. In Denver."

"Why Denver?" Kate asked.

"That's where we're relocating." That sounded better than saying it was her best option and she was making the boys go. "My parents live there," she clarified.

"You're moving to *Denver*?" Kate asked. "When?"

"At the end of the summer. A couple of weeks before school starts so the boys can get settled."

Kate looked at the other women. "But—"

"You really don't know how to cook?" Lauren asked.

"Nope," Delaney said.

"Bake?" Adrianne asked.

"I'm fully dependent on bakeries. I leave that all to you pros."

"So you have no idea how to make cobbler?" Phoebe asked.

"Right."

"Oh boy." This came from Phoebe. "Does Tucker know that?"

"Well, at dinner last night, Tucker said…" Lauren trailed off. "Wait a second. What did he say about the kitchen to you?" she asked Delaney.

"That I could do whatever I wanted in here, that he was sure he'd like anything I came up with." She stopped and felt her eyes get wider. "You think he meant cooking."

Lauren started laughing. "He definitely meant cooking. He said you were really excited about the kitchen last night."

Delaney looked around the disaster area she'd created. Oh… "Fuck." Then she covered her mouth with her hand, realizing that had been out loud. "Sorry."

They all laughed.

"You're going to fit right in," Phoebe assured her.

"Except that Tucker's going to kick me out when he sees this," she said. Dammit. It hadn't even occurred to her that he might be talking about her *using* the kitchen. But of course why wouldn't he think that's what she meant? Most people cooked in kitchens. And he wouldn't know that her skills were limited to soup. From a can. In the microwave.

But he knew what she did for a living. Didn't he?

"Tucker is so not kicking you out," Lauren said. "Don't worry about that."

"You sure?"

"Travis came home and told me about his conversation with TJ and Tucker last night. Tucker's already in deep."

Delaney blushed again. She hadn't blushed as much in her entire life as she had in the past twenty-four hours. "Yeah, well, Tucker's a little…"

"Sweet?" Kate asked. "Hot? Charming?"

"Sexy," Phoebe supplied. "Funny."

"Sexy and sweet," Adrianne agreed.

"Crazy," Delaney said.

"Cocky. Confident," Lauren added. "All the Bennett boys are."

"And crazy," Delaney said again in case they hadn't heard her. "He thinks we should get married."

None of the women seemed surprised.

"You probably should," Phoebe said. "It would be hard to do better than Tucker."

Yep, there was another good excuse to just curl up in Tucker's arms and let him take care of her and the boys and everything else forever.

She would never do better.

It would be so easy to let Tucker take over. So, so easy.

And hell, she couldn't even cook. She wouldn't let the boys starve or develop rickets or anything, but staying here would sure take the need for those lessons off her plate.

She didn't really want to take cooking lessons. She didn't really want to cook.

Yep, her list of reasons to stay in Sapphire Falls and marry Tucker kept getting longer and longer.

There were really only two things in the negative column at this point: feeling bad about herself and her abilities for the rest of her life and the fact that Tucker wasn't actually—couldn't be—in love with her.

She'd always found renovations, particularly the demolition part of it, very therapeutic. Today had been especially full of revelations. Like that she'd really missed work. That she would never break up a countertop without thinking of her sister and brother-in-law. That Tucker could no way be in love with her no matter how sweet and earnest he was about it.

That seemed quite obvious, actually, in the light of day when she was alone. But, wow, last night, with the moon and the stars, Tucker's hot body, his sincere promises about helping her and taking care of things—it had been pretty easy to get sucked into the whole thing.

And she couldn't discount the fatigue, grief and beer. Those had definitely played a part.

The sober-light-of-day truth was Tucker was crazy about the boys and the *idea* of her—the family-wife-home thing—not *her.* How could he be? They'd just met. He knew good things about her. He was attracted to her, she was the guardian to four boys he adored, she needed him and he seemed to get off on that and, oh yeah, she was willing to get naked with him within hours of meeting him. Not even on the first date. He hadn't even had to go that far.

But there was no way he could be in love with her, and when he found out that she was nothing like the woman he wanted—underscored by the whole cobbler thing she'd just discovered—he wouldn't be gung-ho about marrying her at all.

"Are you tearing the sink out too?" Adrianne asked, moving around the piles of rubble to where the sink hung from the wall without a cabinet around it.

Delaney didn't know if Adrianne had changed the subject because she read the emotional chaos on Delaney's face or if she really was interested in the sink, but Delaney was grateful.

"Well, I wanted to move it over there," she said, pointing to a different wall. "But I realized that I don't have my master plumber with me." She'd almost started crying then.

"Plumbing shouldn't be a problem," Phoebe said. "All of the Bennett guys can do that stuff."

Kate sighed. "I do love a man who can really work with his hands."

"Levi doesn't know how to do plumbing, does he?" Lauren asked.

Kate laughed. "Um, no. But he keeps trying things."

"Travis told me Levi helped him with a fence the other day."

Kate nodded. "He was so proud of the thumb he whacked."

"And the attention you gave him because of it," Lauren added.

"That too." Kate winked at them all. "And don't think he's not good with his hands. He is. Just not pipes and wires."

It was clear that the women were all friends, and obviously the men in their lives were too. Their dynamic, the way they shared things and knew one another, was nice. And tempting. And made Delaney miss her sister terribly.

"So Tucker can help her with this part?" Adrianne asked.

"Sure, he could," Lauren said, pulling out her phone. "But if you want the Bennett who is best with this kind of stuff, you need TJ." She started typing into her phone. "He can fix anything, take anything apart and put it back together. He's the one I'd call."

Delaney was already shaking her head. "TJ doesn't like me. This will be fine. I'm sure I can do it. I've watched Rafe enough times. I'll figure it out."

"I already texted TJ," Lauren said with a shrug. "He'll be happy to come over."

"TJ doesn't like me," Delaney said again.

"TJ's bark is worse than his bite," Lauren said with a dismissive wave of her hand.

"He's a big teddy bear underneath?" Delaney asked. She really could use someone with expertise on the plumbing job.

"I didn't say that," Lauren said.

Oh.

"He's incredibly protective of the people he cares about, his family in particular, and he's suspicious of anything that happens too fast or easy."

Delaney nodded. She couldn't find fault in either of those things really.

"But in this case," Lauren went on, "it's almost like he's feeling protective of *you.*"

Delaney looked at her in surprise. "Why? He doesn't know me."

"But he knows Tucker," Phoebe said. "And for all of his sweetness and charm and humor, Tucker is…single-minded about some things."

"And enthusiastic," Kate added. "If he gets excited about something, he becomes determined to make everyone else excited too, and has a really hard time letting things go."

"He can also be overbearing," Lauren said. "He'll keep at you until he convinces you or wears you down."

That already sounded about right.

"Like this track project of his. I swear, he should be in sales," Adrianne added. "No one really knew what to think when he first brought it up, but now the whole town is completely excited."

"So he's effective too?" Delaney asked.

"Oh, definitely," Phoebe said. "Pretty much always gets his way."

Great.

"What track project?" she asked, to keep her mind off

of the things Tucker was going to try to convince her of.

"A dirt-bike track," Adrianne said.

"I thought the track was here on his land?"

"He has one here for fun," Adrianne said. "But he's talked the town into building a big one for races and shows. Down off of the highway. Levi's the major investor."

Kate nodded. "Levi knows zero about dirt bikes, but he knows all about entertaining the masses and he's got money. He and Tucker got together on it only a few months ago and it's going to be ready by the middle of the summer."

"They're attracting riders from all over. It's going to bring a lot of people to town," Adrianne added. "The mayor and town council are thrilled."

"Yep, he did it again," Lauren said. "Talked everyone into something that they now all think is brilliant."

This did not bode well for her resisting his enthusiastic ideas about them being together.

And Delaney wasn't particularly stubborn either.

He'd have no trouble convincing her that his ideas were brilliant.

She'd be engaged by the weekend if she wasn't careful. *Dammit.*

This had gotten out of hand quickly.

"TJ just said he'll stop by tomorrow," Lauren told her, reading from her phone.

Delaney thought about that. That might be a good thing actually. Whether TJ was being protective of her or of Tucker, he didn't think this whole thing was a good idea.

It might turn out that TJ Bennett could be her best ally.

"Well, we should get out of your way," Adrianne said. "You're clearly in the middle of stuff. We just wanted to come say hi since you won't be at the barbecue tonight."

"Yeah, Tucker said something about pizza night here at home." She cringed. "Here. At his house." Not *home. Not* home.

Kate nodded. "He called and told his mom a little bit ago. That's why we're all here now. We couldn't let him keep you all to himself indefinitely."

"Keep me to himself?"

Phoebe grinned. "Tucker's never missed a family barbecue before."

"Are you all related?" Delaney asked instead of thinking about the keeping-her-to-himself thing too hard.

Phoebe and Kate and Adrianne all shook their heads.

"With the Bennetts, once one of them loves you, they all love you," Lauren said. "These girls and their husbands are more like family than friends."

The lump in her throat and the stinging in her eyes came on so suddenly it stunned her. Delaney blinked and swallowed hard. Damn. That was so *nice*.

"We've all got stuff to get to," Adrianne said. "But welcome, and we really do look forward to getting to know you better, Delaney." She gave her another quick hug. "Don't worry about the cobbler."

The cobbler. Good grief.

"Bye, Delaney. I'll be in touch about the renovations at the farmhouse," Kate said. She also gave her a hug as she went past.

"I'm so excited you're here," Phoebe told her.

She pulled Delaney in for a hug too. Wow, they were a touchy bunch. And that also reminded Delaney of her sister.

"Tucker is a great guy," Phoebe said when she let Delaney go.

Yeah, he was. Totally deserving of his fan club. And a woman who actually wanted all the stuff he wanted and needed.

She wasn't upset about being the boys' guardian, of course, but she was hardly a natural mother, nor would she ever be the super mom her sister had been. Which she knew she would have to come to terms with. She should probably

add more counseling sessions to the things she needed to
sign up for in Denver. Right along with those cooking
classes.

She couldn't cook or bake She knew nothing about
living on a farm or even in a small town. She didn't know
about dirt biking.

She was most definitely not the perfect woman for
Tucker.

Lauren was last but not least. She moved to stand in
front of Delaney. "And the Bennett boys don't get over the
cocky thing, by the way." She also hugged Delaney. "But,"
she said, leaning back. "They mean what they say and say
what they mean. You can trust the things Tucker is saying
to you. He'll be there for you."

Delany knew that. She already knew she could trust that
he meant what he said. It was what he was saying that was
the problem. "Okay," she said to Lauren, because she
didn't really know what else to say.

The women filed out with promises to see her soon and
invitations to margarita night. As the door closed behind
them, Delaney took a deep breath. There wasn't really any
easing into anything around here, it seemed.

She turned back to survey the kitchen.

It was a huge, crazy mess.

Tucker was in for a big shock when he got home.

But maybe that was a good thing. If her not knowing
how to do anything in a kitchen that didn't involve a
sledgehammer was a mark against her, then this was good.

She headed for the area where she'd already pulled
back a corner of the linoleum, determined to get more of
the floor done before Tucker and the boys came back.

As she worked, her brain reeled through everything that
had happened in the last not-even-quite twenty-four hours.

Bottom line was she wasn't the girl for Tucker, no
matter how much he wanted her to be.

Tucker deserved a girl who cooked and did scrapbooks

and hosted dinner parties and barbecues for his friends and family. A girl who got excited about dirt-bike racing. A girl who was tough and sure of herself on the farm. A girl who had that maternal instinct and wanted to have four *more* kids with him.

Delaney froze and straightened, thinking about that.

Surely Tucker wanted kids of his own. She knew he loved the boys and would probably adopt them tomorrow if he could, but he'd want more too.

She was *not* the type to be the mother of eight. No way.

She attacked the linoleum with renewed vigor.

Ironically, her sister Chelsea would have been the perfect woman for Tucker. Chelsea loved the domestic stuff and was definitely tough. She would have learned, enthusiastically, what she didn't know about farming and dirt bikes. And she most definitely had wanted more kids. The boys were almost exactly two years apart. Although she and Rafe had thought they were done after Jack, she had started talking about having more as the baby got older.

Delaney stopped and wiped her forehead, staring at the subfloor but not seeing the hardwood she'd been envisioning. Instead, she saw her sister, holding a baby on one hip, stirring a pot with her other hand while on the phone making a business deal.

That had been Chelsea.

And it occurred to her that Tucker might actually be in love with *Chelsea*.

Rafe and Tucker had a lot in common and Rafe had been crazy about Chelsea, about everything that made Chelsea Chelsea. Her energy, her imagination and creativity, her optimism, the way she kept everyone in line and met everyone's needs. It would make sense that Tucker would have imagined having a life like Rafe's. With a woman like Rafe's.

And it made sense that Tucker would assume that Delaney had a lot in common with her older sister.

Delaney frowned and grabbed the knife to cut through another piece of linoleum, stabbing into it and pulling with more force than was needed.

Great. So Tucker was essentially in love with Chelsea.

This was getting better and better.

It was a good thing he was about to come home and realize that Delaney was nothing like what he'd been imagining.

The sooner the better, in fact.

CHAPTER SEVEN

"Uh."

It wasn't even really a word, but it was all Tucker could get to come out of his mouth.

His kitchen looked like a bomb had gone off.

And Delaney stood in the midst of it all, looking grubby and grumpy and gorgeous.

"I don't bake cobbler," she said to him, hands on hips that were supporting a tool belt, her eyes flashing behind plastic safety goggles. "I don't bake anything. Or cook. Other than in a microwave."

"Okay." What else was he going to say? It was pretty clear that his lack of countertops and cupboards was because of Delaney and the crowbar and sledgehammer lying off to one side.

Which stunned him at the same time it completely turned him on. He wasn't sure he'd ever dated a girl who actually knew how to use a crowbar.

He wasn't sure why that was hot, but it was.

"It is *not* okay." She was scowling at him. "It's the opposite of okay. You said to knock myself out in here and I heard 'tear out all of my cupboards and flooring' when you really meant 'cook me some fabulous meal from scratch and don't forget dessert'."

Henry and Charlie came stomping into the house then and headed straight into the kitchen. "What's—"

They both came up short, but they were grinning as they took in the sight before them.

"Can I help with the floor?" Henry asked, wading into the debris.

He had work boots and blue jeans on and Tucker didn't think to stop him. But, interestingly, neither did Delaney.

The woman wasn't sure if the boys should play down in the barn but had no problem with her oldest nephews

151

climbing around on broken-up cupboards and pieces of linoleum.

"I was planning to have you do a lot of it," Delaney told Henry in answer to his question. But her eyes were still on Tucker.

Clearly, Henry and Charlie weren't at all surprised to find their aunt in the middle of a demolition zone.

"Tile?" Henry asked.

"I'm thinking wood," Delaney told him.

Henry nodded. "Good idea. Something dark, with light cupboards and stuff. There's a lot of light in here."

Similarly, Delaney didn't look surprised to hear Henry giving opinions about wood flooring.

Tucker was intrigued.

"I think glass-fronted cupboards for the dishes," Charlie said thoughtfully.

"You always say glass-fronted cupboards," Henry said, turning an old cupboard over.

"Delaney likes glass-fronted cupboards for the dishes," Charlie said.

That got a small smile from their aunt. "I do like glass-fronted cupboards for the dishes," she said. "But those are Tucker's dishes."

She pointed to the kitchen table by the window. The table and chairs were the only things made of wood in the room that hadn't been demolished. Yet.

On the table sat his mishmash of dishes. His small mishmash of dishes. It was just him eating here. He didn't need twelve full place settings.

Charlie wrinkled his nose at the plastic thirty-two ounce cups from the Stop, the convenience store downtown. "Oh. Maybe not glass."

That actually got a laugh out of Delaney.

"Well, if *this* is what happens when you try to bake, maybe staying away from the oven is a good idea," Tucker said, recovered enough from his surprise to make his way farther into the room.

She was right back to frowning at him. "I don't *want* to bake. I don't even try because I have *no* desire."

"Okay." That was...surprising. Yeah, that was a good word. He wouldn't go so far as to say it was a *problem*. It was just...surprising.

But a look at Delaney's face told him that she wouldn't appreciate that word.

"It is *not* okay. Stop saying that."

"How do you know it's not okay?" Then he thought about what she'd said earlier about cobbler. "How do you know about the cobbler?"

"That it's your favorite thing and your biggest weakness?" she asked.

He frowned. "Who stopped by?"

"Kate."

Kate had told her about the cobbler. Dammit.

"And Lauren."

Double dammit. Those two were far too interested in his love life. At least Phoebe hadn't come along.

"And Phoebe."

He sighed. Of course Phoebe had been here. What had he been thinking?

"And Adrianne."

"Adrianne?" That surprised him a little. She was much less of a meddler than the other three.

"They said it was because you cancelled with your mom for the barbecue."

Yeah, he'd figured that news and the accompanying curiosity would spread in about five minutes, but he really hadn't anticipated the girls showing up over here.

Though in hindsight, that was stupid of him.

"Luna is covered in cow poop!" David came barreling into the kitchen, skidding a little on the dirty floor.

He also didn't look a bit surprised by the chaos in Tucker's kitchen. Or that Delaney was in the middle of it.

And it flashed through Tucker's mind that this might be a perfect analogy for Delaney in the middle of his life. Perhaps things like cobbler weren't going to go exactly according to his expectations. And it might all end up messier than anticipated.

That was very enlightened, he thought.

"Can you guys handle that?" Tucker asked Henry and Charlie, nodding toward David.

"Yeah sure." Henry started toward the back door.

"Can we wash Mickey too?" Charlie asked.

"We're not naming the puppy Mickey," Henry said, heading out the door.

"Why not?"

"That's a mouse name."

"Mickey Mantle was a baseball player," Charlie pointed out.

"King. We should name him King," David said, hurrying after his brothers over the debris covering the floor as if it was perfectly natural to have dirt and boards and drywall underfoot.

They were still debating it when the door closed behind them.

Delaney stood watching him, clearly waiting for him to be the one to say whatever came next.

"I like a girl who's not afraid to get a little dirty."

Her eyes widened. "Seriously?" she said.

He nodded sincerely. "You look totally hot right now."

"You're coming on to me? Now? Like this?"

He crossed the distance between them and looked directly into her eyes. "I'm going to be coming on to you all the time, everywhere. Get used to it."

She sighed. "I think you're going to get over it pretty fast."

"Absolutely not."

"Tucker, I can patch your roof, recover your couch, build you a deck—but there will be no cobbler."

He got the impression that this had now become a matter of principle rather than an actual lack of talent.

"Damn, I should have waited to finish the basement until you got here."

"You believe me about the cobbler?"

"Well, clearly it's that you *won't* make it, not that you can't," he said reasonably. And as long as she *could* make it, there was hope.

"I've never made cobbler in my life."

"Okay, but a woman who can do drywall and build a deck, can make cobbler."

"Tucker," Delaney said firmly. "It is very important that you understand that I'm not going to make you cobbler, whether I can or not."

He nodded. "I hear you." He heard her saying that she was not going to make him cobbler. Today. Or maybe even this week.

"You do?" She didn't look like she believed him at all.

"Yes." He grinned at her. "This is your way of telling me that you're not the right woman for me and you're not going to change to please me."

She seemed surprised. "Well, um, yeah."

And that should possibly hurt his feelings. Or at least his ego. But it didn't. She had been very clear about what she wanted and needed this summer, and baking and fawning over him and landing herself a husband were not on the list.

Yet.

But no one had ever accused Tucker Bennett of lacking confidence.

"Okay," he said agreeably.

"Really?"

"Sure. It's completely okay for you to think that."

She narrowed her eyes. "It's important for *you* to think that."

"I do." For now. But he didn't add those last two words

out loud. "We don't have to worry about dessert right
now," he assured her, running his hands up and down her
arms.

She moved in closer to him. She put a hand on his chest
and ran it back and forth over the soft cotton that covered
his left pec. Her gaze dropped to his mouth. "I—"

The dog door in the back kitchen door slapped open and
a wet, muddy pit bull came hurtling into the kitchen. Luna
skidded on the dirty linoleum still in place by the door and
table before turning the corner and heading for the living
room.

Four wet, muddy boys came thundering into the house
after her.

Tucker looked at Delaney. She simply sighed, watching
them run through the door into the living room, shouting
and laughing. They heard things like, "Chase her over
here!" and, "Watch out for the lamp!" and then stomping
and banging and finally the front door opening and
shutting.

"I was thinking maybe I should spend some time with
your mom," Delaney said in the relative quiet that
followed.

"My mom?" He couldn't hide his surprise. "To learn to
bake?"

She looked at him with an eyebrow up and he realized
the answer to that was a definite *no*.

"She's the only woman I know who raised four boys,"
Delaney said quietly.

And everything in Tucker softened at that. She wanted
advice on mothering from his mother. "She would love
that."

"You sure?"

"Absolutely," he said firmly. His mother would be
thrilled.

"So maybe we should go to the barbecue after all?"

He shook his head. "No way. For one, you won't get

any time alone with her. Everyone will want to talk to you all night. Pizza tonight. Here. Just us."

She chewed her bottom lip for a moment. "Eventually we'll have to do the barbecue thing, right?"

He sighed. "Yeah."

"I'm not good with big crowds and I'm not great at being the center of attention."

He knew that somehow. The things she'd told him about her life had already shown him that. Her comment about her being the flashlight and Chelsea being the batteries hadn't been accurate. Maybe she felt like her motivation and energy came from Chelsea, but Delaney hadn't been the one shining. Her contributions had all been behind the scenes.

"We'll ease into it," he promised her, already thinking about who to call to babysit if he got a group together for a bonfire at the river tonight after the boys were in bed.

God knew, he loved this town. He loved his friends and family. But they could definitely be an overwhelming group all together.

He felt a tug on the front of his jeans and realized Delaney had hooked her finger in his waistband and was pulling him forward. He went. Gladly. She rose up on tiptoe, wrapped her arms around his neck and kissed him.

It wasn't a sweet, ease-into-it kiss at all. It was a full-on hot, hard, wet kiss.

He was gripping her ass and thinking about backing her up against the wall—since there were no more countertops—when she pulled back.

"But, yes, I definitely like to get dirty," she said.

"It looks good on you." Even the streak of drywall dust on her cheek made him want her.

"Do you think we could get dirty tonight? After the boys are in bed? Like in the barn?"

Tucker stared at her. She was talking about having sex. She was making a date with him for sex. Tonight. Her second night in town.

She was quite possibly the most perfect woman he'd ever met.

"I can do even better than the barn tonight."

She grinned, clearly eager about that. "The boys need to be really tired tonight. Early."

"I can handle that too." They had more work around the farm to do and then the dirt-bike track was calling their names.

She pulled him down for another kiss. "Sorry about your kitchen," she said against his lips.

He grabbed her ass and hauled her up against him. "What kitchen?"

They kissed again, long and hot, his thoughts replaying everything from last night and making plans for a few hours from now. He'd let her take the lead last night, but tonight he was in charge.

Finally, they separated.

She was breathing fast, her pupils wide, and Tucker really wished his countertops were still intact. They couldn't get naked with the boys right outside, of course, but he wouldn't mind getting her up on the counter and getting his throbbing parts against her soft parts for a minute. Or twenty.

But there were no counters.

He looked around, still a little amazed. "So you really did all of this?"

She settled back on her feet, which was probably for the best with the boys running around. But his body missed hers immediately.

"Yep." She looked around too. "Renovations are one of two things I'm really good at and like to do."

He grinned. "Oh, I don't know. Last night you were *really* good."

She met his gaze and nodded. "That's the other thing."

Surprise shot through him but was quickly tamped out

by the jolt of desire and—as crazy as it sounded—affection.

She was telling him she was good at home renovations and sex. Only renovations and sex.

Part of him wanted to hug her and assure her that she had many other talents. But a bigger part of him, the part that was all male and had been witness to just how good she was at one of the two things on her list, pushed right past the affection and into lust.

"Girl, if you're half as good at renovations as you were in that barn last night, this is going to be the best kitchen ever renovated."

She smiled at that. "I'm probably even better at renovations. After all, this isn't the first time in twenty-two months that I've redone kitchen cabinets."

He didn't know what to say. He'd met women who were confident in their sex appeal and not shy when they were between the sheets, but he wasn't sure he'd ever met a woman as matter-of-fact about sex.

"You said you really like both things too," he commented. *He* really, really liked *that*. He knew women liked sex. He'd never had a hard time finding willing partners and they always had a good time. But it seemed that for most women sex was part of a package deal, part of bigger things, sometimes even a means to an end. He couldn't remember the last time he slept with a woman who didn't hope it would lead to wedding bells.

Until last night.

Delaney clearly liked sex just for sex—because she wanted nothing to do with his package. He cringed at that unfortunate choice of words. Okay, she wasn't interested in the *package deal* of marriage, home and family. She wanted to heat up the hayloft all summer and then pack up and move on in August.

"I do really like both things," she said, meeting his gaze straight on.

"So why were renovations the only things you've been

doing in the past twenty-two months?"

She stepped back and took a deep breath, tucking her hands into her back pockets. The move thrust her breasts against the soft cotton of her T-shirt, and Tucker knew for a fact that any avoidance of sex had all been her doing. There had to have been guys lined up to get close to her.

"Turns out I love fixing up houses. Men, not as much."

He chuckled. "You run into a lot of fixer-uppers of both kinds?"

She rolled her eyes. "You have no idea. Lots of men with issues. Women too, I guess," she added.

Tucker thought about that. Interestingly, the women he was used to really were kind of issue-less. Not that they were perfect or anything, but the women in Sapphire Falls tended to be pretty well-adjusted. In fact, Delaney was the first woman with some decent-sized baggage that he'd ever been involved with.

"The women you've been interested in have had issues?" he teased.

She laughed. "I'm happy to say that only half of the general population are candidates for driving me nuts."

He chuckled again. "And I'm grateful for that."

"You're not wishing I liked women too?" She gave him a little smile. "Not into threesomes, Tucker?"

He wasn't *opposed* to threesomes, in theory, but he'd never had one. Again, that was a little outside the norm for Sapphire Falls. "Are you offering?"

She watched him, seeming to think things over. "I don't want to share you," she finally said.

He'd also never met a woman who could make him hot and ready with so few words.

"You won't have to." Ever. But again he bit his tongue before adding the last word. Too much. It was too much, he knew that. But it was hard to hold back.

He had to remember that August was a long way off. A lot could change between now and then.

She gave him a single nod. "Good. This summer. Just you and me."

"Anything you want."

That got a big smile. "You keep saying that and things are going to be fine."

Oh, he'd keep saying it. And proving it. He was going to be whatever she needed and wanted.

He had two things for sure that she wanted—his kitchen and his body. Both were all hers.

"So when you're not ravishing me," he said, enjoying the faint pink in her cheeks at his words. "You're going to rebuild these cabinets?"

She laughed. "I am going to rebuild these cabinets. And redo the walls and the floor and maybe add a center island, if you're okay with that?"

He moved in, put his hands on her hips and pulled her up against him. "I'm okay with anything that puts that happy look on your face."

Her gaze and smile softened and she tipped her head. "You're almost too sweet, Tucker."

"Yeah, well, don't forget that the other thing that puts that happy look on your face makes me pretty damn happy too."

She ran her hand over his chest again. "Wish we could make each other happy right now."

He started to hold back the words that first came to mind, but this time he let them out. "You *are* making me happy right now."

Her smile died, but her gaze didn't waver from his. "Wow," she said softly. "Are you for real?"

He pressed her against his erection. "Every inch of me."

That lightened things up enough that she laughed and stepped back. "Well, speaking of this renovation…"

He chuckled. "We were *not* speaking of this renovation." He was learning—say something serious and deep, then follow it with a flirtation or joke. That way she heard him and the serious stuff would start sinking in, but she didn't get spooked.

She grinned. "Is there a place where I can do some building and painting and staining?"

"Sure. The back of the barn has some empty space. There might be some junk back there but we can move it all out."

"That would be perfect."

There was a spark in her eyes when she talked about the renovation that made him feel a combination of things, including desire. Yet it was the strangest desire he'd ever felt.

Yes, she looked incredibly cute with her hair up and the goggles on top of her head, the tool belt around her slim hips and the work gloves tucked in her back pocket. But the intensity of his want was more about how happy and confident she seemed. She was clearly in her element here. He was more than willing to help her out with that happiness and confidence in the bedroom—or the hayloft, his truck, the riverbank, pretty much anywhere—but he liked seeing her looking tough and cocky like this, because it was clear she liked *herself* in this setting.

He'd seen it last night too. When she'd stripped for him, when she'd been sucking his cock, when she'd straddled him and ridden him, she'd been fully herself and she'd liked herself.

And he sure as hell liked her. More than he would have ever believed—even after climbing down from the loft.

There was something in her eyes when she looked up at him. Almost as if she could hear his thoughts. Her gaze was warm, happy and…mischievous. He really fucking liked that. That combination. He wanted a lot more of that.

His body responded to the memory from last night and he moved in closer.

She smiled up at him. "Maybe you should show me the area of the barn I can use."

He knew exactly what she was thinking. "There are four boys running around out there with three dogs."

She unhooked her tool belt and dropped it to the floor. "Yep, you'll have to be really quiet." She turned and headed out the back door.

It took Tucker another minute or so to follow. He needed a bit of control here. Since he didn't have time for a cold shower, he settled for pulling in deep breaths and going over the list of things he needed to get the bonfire party going down at the river tonight. Ice, beer, Booze. But he definitely followed. He'd follow her anywhere.

The boys were on the other side of the house. Tucker could hear them shrieking and laughing, the dogs barking and the sound of the water from the hose hitting the side of the house. There would be four very wet boys as well, but blood was about the only thing that would keep Tucker from heading straight to the barn. Of course, he hung back enough to watch Delaney walking in front of him.

Plain and simple, the girl did very nice things to blue jeans.

They stepped out of the bright sunlight into the barn and she kept going down the center aisle. "Back here?"

"Yep. Those last couple of stalls are all yours, and there's space behind the last one too. But if you need more room, we'll find it."

He'd move everything out of the freaking place if that's what she needed.

She stopped by the last stall. He'd never had animals out here, though they'd built the barn with the idea that it could work as a typical, functional barn for horses or whatever else he might want. Lately he'd been thinking that the boys would maybe like a horse. Every kid should know how to ride a horse.

However, all thoughts of kids and animals vanished when Delaney stepped into the back stall and turned to face him, her hands going to his hips and pulling him close.

Tucker cupped the nape of her neck and lowered his head.

The kiss wasn't fast and hard like in the kitchen, but it was every bit as hot. It felt as though she was drinking him in, pulling him deeper with every second. He sunk into her sweetness, stroking his tongue lazily over her bottom lip and then over her tongue as she opened for him.

She gripped the belt loops on his jeans, arching close, rubbing against him with needy little sounds that made him want to amp everything up.

But Delaney beat him to it.

She had his fly unbuttoned and unzipped before he even realized where exactly her hands were. She slipped into the cotton and denim and wrapped her hand around his cock, squeezing and sliding her hand along his length.

Tucker ripped his mouth from hers, sucking in a much-needed breath. "Laney, holy—"

She kept stroking him and pressed her lips to his throat above his shirt. "I love touching you," she murmured. "You're so big and hard and hot."

He was most definitely hard and hot. He curled his fingers into her hair. He could lift her up against the wall and be done in minutes, he knew. Could they risk the boys not coming looking for them?

"I want to make you crazy, Tuck," she said.

He felt his cock swell in her hand. It was the first time she'd used anything other than Tucker. Well, she'd called him big guy and country boy but those felt less intimate. Tuck was personal, something the people closest to him called him, and from Delaney's lips it was so, so sweet.

"You do," he promised her. "You make me…" He couldn't even adequately finish the thought.

And it was day two with her.

He knew that was nuts. He did. His brain recognized that. But nothing about this felt anything but sweet and hot and *right*.

Of course, her hand was wrapped around his cock, so he wasn't exactly in a position to form a completely unbiased opinion.

"You make me...too," she told him with a little grin.

Then she pushed his jeans and underwear to his ankles and went to her knees.

"No." He couldn't let her give him a blowjob. Not here, not right now. Not when he really wanted to be buried deep in her hot, tight body with the barn wall behind her and her legs wrapped around his waist.

But they couldn't do that either, because—

He completely lost his train of thought as she licked up and down the front of his shaft. Her pressure was perfect and he instinctively cupped the back of her head and groaned.

She moved to the head of his cock, sliding it past her lips slowly, sucking as she took him in. Tucker's hand went to her ponytail, but he resisted grabbing on and moving her, instead letting her do her thing. And damn, her thing was good. She kept going, sliding him farther into the wet heat of her mouth, shocking him with how deep she was able to take him. She circled the base of his cock with her thumb and first two fingers, forming a snug ring that she moved up and down as she took as much of him as she could. Her other hand cupped his balls, and Tucker knew he was about three minutes away from losing it.

"Laney," he groaned.

She gave no indication that she'd heard him. Or that she had any thought of stopping.

Delaney was giving him the best part of a really good blowjob and she was clearly into it.

She lifted her head and kept stroking over his hard flesh, slick from her mouth. She looked up at him from below her long lashes. Her mouth was shiny, her cheeks flushed and she still had flecks of drywall in her hair.

She looked absolutely gorgeous.

He wanted desperately to plunge into her, to hear her crying out his name, to feel her clamping down around his aching cock that was minutes away from a massive release. But that wasn't going to happen here and now.

"Laney, I'm close, baby."

She met his gaze and kept stroking. "Good."

"Honey, you don't have to—"

"All I want to hear is you saying my name as you come." She took him back into her mouth and increased her speed and pressure.

He shouldn't have been surprised that Delaney was giving him the best blowjob of his life. He should simply be grateful. And hell, he'd warned her.

This was what she wanted.

He felt his climax tighten low and deep, and he gripped the back of her head. "Laney," he ground out. If she wanted to pull back, she'd better do it now.

But her suction increased and she took him deeper, and a moment later, he came with a hoarse, "*Delaney.*"

He was afraid his knees were going to literally buckle with the aftershocks of his climax, so he pulled her back and sank to his knees in front of her. She was grinning at him as he yanked his pants up, and when he gathered her close in a hug, she came against him willingly. He sat back onto his butt, bringing her with him into his lap.

She cuddled close, resting her cheek on his chest, and he stroked his hand over her hair.

Holy shit.

He'd like to think that he was a better guy than to have a blowjob completely push him over the edge into love, but this was no ordinary blowjob. There was something about her—not the technique, though that was stellar—but the way she'd been so eager to get out to the barn, the way she initiated it all, the way she had been so intent on making him lose it and how satisfied she now seemed, that made her mouth the hottest he'd ever been in.

"The least I can do is buy you a drink tonight," he said, consciously keeping his tone light as he ran his hand over her ponytail. The ponytail that he still wanted to grab onto the next time she sucked him off. Or when he took her from behind.

His body stirred again. Already. In spite of the release from only minutes before.

She laughed. "A beer on the porch later before we come back out here?"

Yep, his cock liked that too. He'd certainly had women who wanted him, who wanted to sleep with him, who wanted to please him, but finding Delaney insatiable was like finding out that the frosting on your favorite cupcake was spiked with liquor.

"I actually have a different plan."

She tipped her head to look up at him, and where there had been a flirtatious spark before, now she looked wary.

He bit back his sigh. He did, however, tighten his arms around her, sensing that she wanted to push up off of his lap.

"I thought we were doing pizza and a movie with the boys?"

"We will. Definitely," he agreed. "But after."

"We can't leave them here alone."

"Of course not. I know several fabulous babysitters."

"We can't ask your family to come over to babysit while we go drinking and fucking."

Okay, his body liked hearing the word fucking from her too, but he worked on concentrating on what she was really saying.

"First, I don't think I would put it quite that way even with someone who isn't my family," he said with a small smile. "Second, I was thinking of asking one of the girls who babysit for Joe and Phoebe and Mason and Adrianne."

She managed to get her hands up between them and pushed against his chest. He loosened his grip on her but dropped his hands to her hips, ready to grab her if she tried to bolt.

He wasn't sure where the instinct came from, but he sensed that she would do every intimate sexual thing there was with him, but the idea of spending time with him one-on-one in anything that seemed like a real relationship made her nervous.

And if she thought he was crazy, what did that make *that* reaction?

She'd rather fuck him in the barn than go on a date with him?

"You're asking me out," she said.

"Yes."

She shook her head. "Wow, *that* blowjob and you still don't want to just have hot sex with me all summer?"

He laughed. "I want to have hot sex with you all summer, *but* I'd really like to date you too."

"The relationship thing," she muttered. "They said you were single-minded."

"They?" he asked. But he knew who she meant. So he was enthusiastic about his ideas. His ideas were usually brilliant. And lots of people said so. He wasn't giving up on this.

"The girls," she confirmed.

"They're right," he said. "I'm single-minded when I have a wonderful ideas." And he always ended up getting his way. He wondered if the ladies—and he used the term loosely—had shared *that* tidbit with her.

"What if I say no?"

He narrowed his eyes, studying her face and trying to figure out how serious she was about saying no. He actually wanted to tell her that their fun times in the barn would be over if that's all she wanted from him. He wanted more than that. And that did *not* make him a bad guy. The opposite, in fact. At least with most women.

"Then I guess we wouldn't go out tonight. But I'll keep

asking."

Her eyes widened. "You would let it go?"

"I said I'd keep asking."

"But nothing else would change? You'd still…"

"Let you give me the best blowjobs I've ever had?"

Her face brightened at that and he had to fight not to laugh. Or put her back on her knees in front of his cock. She was *proud* of the blowjob. She liked hearing she was the best he'd ever had.

"You will let me keep doing that?"

"Well, gee," he said dryly. "I guess. If you really want to."

But he sensed that she did really want to. She maybe even needed to. He was a little slow maybe—probably because a lot of his blood had been hanging out down south of his belt—but there was something about her taking charge and leading him around by his dick, literally and figuratively, that was important.

Important enough for him to let her keep doing it. Sure, it probably didn't seem all that altruistic, considering he was going to keep getting off on all of this—again, literally and figuratively—but he did actually want to do it for her.

She pulled back a little farther. "But you don't actually want this to just be about sex."

He ran his hand up and down her back. "No, I don't."

"But you'll let me do things my way."

"Yes."

"Why?"

"Because I told you that I'll give you whatever you need this summer."

That made her pause for a second, and Tucker thought maybe that had finally sunk in.

"But if I want something other than what you want—everything else stays the same? The boys can still hang out with you and ride dirt bikes and I can remodel your kitchen and we can stay with you and—"

"Delaney."

She stopped talking with his low, firm use of her name. She pulled in a deep breath.

"Everything stays the same. I'm here for you and the boys. None of that is contingent on me getting my way."

She licked her lips, studying his eyes. All she would find there was sincerity.

"A superficial, sex-only, casual fling is an option?" she asked.

Was he an idiot? What straight, single guy would look at this woman and *not* say yes? But in the strangest twist in his thirty years, he was saying yes to a no-strings-attached affair that he didn't really want. Because he wanted so much more.

It didn't even sound right in his head, but he knew that Delaney needed this. She needed to feel in control, she needed to have fun, to let loose, to have the physical and emotional release that really hot, no-holds-barred, completely indulgent sex could provide without the pressure of a relationship. Especially a brand-new relationships. Relationships took time and energy and attention, and those were all things she didn't have right now. Or didn't feel like she could spare, anyway. She needed to have only expectations that she could meet. She knew what she was doing in the kitchen renovation and in the blowjob department. Everything else had her feeling confused and insecure and unsure.

So he was going to have a casual fling for the summer. Great.

"But we're also friends, right?" he asked her.

She opened her mouth, then shut it and paused for a moment before nodding slowly.

He frowned. "What's with the hesitation?"

"I was just—" She shook her head, her gaze on his chin instead of meeting his eyes.

"Laney." Again, that low, firm tone worked to pull her

gaze up to his. "You just had my cock in your mouth. I think you can tell me what you were about to say."

Her eyes widened slightly, but she nodded. "Okay. I was going to say that I feel like you're my best friend right now. But I know that's crazy. This is day two of our stay here."

He curled his fingers into her hips and had to resist the urge to propose.

"That's not crazy at all," he said. "I'm here for you. Your friend, your...whatever you need."

She could have said something dirty there. Something flirtatious or sexy about the things she needed that he could be. Instead, she said, "You'd really like me to go out with you tonight? As friends?"

He nodded. "Fun. Casual. Just a good time. No pressure."

He maybe should quit promising the no-pressure thing. He was making promises that he didn't want to keep. He wanted to pressure her, to spell out all of the reasons why a casual fling between them would never be enough.

But he kept his mouth shut. His brothers would be shocked.

"What are you thinking this going out thing would entail?" she asked.

"A few friends, many of whom you've already met," he added dryly. "A bonfire at the river, some beer and Booze."

"So the girls who came over earlier?"

"And their husbands. Maybe a few other friends. But a small group."

"And Booze? Like the Booze Rafe put on his list for me?"

Tucker nodded. "It's a Sapphire Falls party staple."

"And the babysitter is someone you know well?"

"I know her and her older brothers and her parents and her grandparents—both sets."

Delaney smiled at that.

"And we'll be about five miles away. The party spot is over by Phoebe and Joe's house."

She nodded. "That sounds like fun."

He felt a tightness in his chest unfurl. The idea of Delaney hanging out with his friends, in their party spot at the river, made him happy, plain and simple. He'd had so many good times out there, and he wanted her to be a part of these things, these normal, regular, good parts of his life.

Of course, he didn't have a lot of not-good parts to his life. He was blessed, he knew that. He was happy and content and fulfilled. He was surrounded by people and places that he loved, memories and hopes for the future, honest, hard work, laughter, unconditional love, people who wanted the best for him and would do anything for him.

Delaney didn't have most of that.

She was an honest, hard worker. She'd had family and love and support and laughter.

But now everything was messed up, broken or gone.

A deep, gut-tightening—and yes, single-minded— desire to give her everything he had swept over him.

But he'd just promised a casual summer fling.

Fuck.

CHAPTER EIGHT

"We should get back up to the house," she said, pushing herself off his lap as he was lost in thought.

He still wanted to grab her and bring her back into his lap, but she was right—the boys, the dogs, the rest of his work were all out there.

Tucker got to his feet, re-zipping and buttoning his jeans and brushing the barn floor dirt off of his ass.

"After we check on the boys, can you help me bring some of my stuff down here?" she asked.

"Of course." Typically, he would have suggested they get the boys to help unload her stuff, but he wanted more time to talk to her alone.

They headed up to the house. The boys were still wet, but everyone—dogs and kids alike—were devoid of mud and cow manure.

"Tell you what," he said to the boys. "There's apples and peanut butter and bread in the house, or my mom has turkey sandwiches, salad and cookies."

"Cookies!" Jack and David said at the same time.

"You heard the salad part right?" Tucker asked.

"Oh, David and Charlie are allergic to salad," Delaney said.

"Is that right?" Tucker smiled.

"Oh, yeah, it makes their faces scrunch up really ugly and this horrible sound come out of their mouths." She grabbed Charlie from behind, hugging him while she mimicked an I'm-gonna-be-sick expression and a loud, whiny, drawn-out ewwww sound.

Tucker chuckled even as his chest felt tighter watching them.

"I want turkey sandwiches," Jack said.

"I want her lemonade," Henry said.

"Oh, yeah!" David agreed.

"Okay, you guys head over there. You can take the four-wheelers," Tucker said.

And his getting rid of the boys really was not so he could get Delaney naked. He wasn't going to get her naked. At least not until tonight when he had her in the back of his truck and some Booze in her system. He wanted her to let go, loosen up, have some fun. He was hoping to take the edge off of this seemingly constant need of hers to be in charge.

"Four-wheelers?" Delaney asked.

Tucker glanced at her. "Henry and Charlie are really good on them."

"Are there helmets?" She was frowning.

"There can be," Tucker agreed. He and his brothers hadn't worn helmets four-wheeling as kids but that didn't mean it wasn't a good idea.

"Oh, come on," Charlie complained.

"Well, you don't have to," Tucker told them. "But if you don't want to wear helmets, I'll take you over in the truck."

The path between his place and his mom and dad's was a straight shot across the pasture and would take only a few minutes on the four wheelers. The boys knew the way and there was absolutely nothing perilous between here and there, but he definitely respected Delaney's need to know they were safe.

"Fine," Charlie said. "I'll wear it."

"Okay. Text me when you get there," he told Henry.

"Sure."

"And change into dry clothes," Delaney called as they started running toward the shed where the four-wheelers were housed.

They all groaned, but they did stop and trudge back to the house, grumbling but compliant.

When they were finally all dry and on the four-wheelers, heads covered and instructions given for texting when they got there and when they left to come back, to say please and thank you, and to wash their hands before they ate, they headed off.

Tucker followed Delaney to where her Jeep was parked with the trailer behind it. She opened the back door of the trailer, got inside and started rummaging.

When she shoved a bench saw to the back of the trailer, Tucker fell a little further in love.

"This is yours?"

She grinned, that spark back in her eyes. "Yep."

"Nice." He grabbed the edges and started to pull it from the trailer, but then he eyed the distance to the barn. "Maybe we should drive the trailer down to the barn and unload there."

She laughed and jumped out of the trailer. "Yeah, good idea."

They pulled the whole thing up to the front of the barn and together carried the bench saw to the spot in the back of the barn where she was going to set up.

She also pulled out some additional saw horses, an electric sander, several types of clamps, a drill with an elaborate set of bits, and a few things Tucker had never seen.

He wanted to bend her over one of those saw horses.

But he couldn't. He would give her everything she wanted. If she wanted to try to keep things casual, fine. He would make her feel good in every way he could, every chance she gave him. But to him that meant more than sex. He could make her feel good, safe, comfortable, happy in many ways. He wanted more than sex, so when they were together, she was going to have to initiate sex. He was going to initiate getting to know each other better and showing her how much deeper things could be between them.

Delaney was checking out the space around them since they hadn't done much looking at anything but each other the first time they'd been out here. "I'm going to set my saw up over there," she said, pointing. "I can do the cutting and sanding there and then the staining over here." She pointed at the stall they'd been in. "Is there a lumberyard here?"

"Next town over. I can take you tomorrow or the next day."

"Just tell me how to get there. You don't have to take me."

Tucker nodded, watching her move around the barn with a crazy mix of emotions.

She was studying the window above the opposite stall. "I'll need to wash that window for better light, okay?"

"I'll have one of the boys come do it."

She looked at him. "I can wash a window, Tucker."

"They boys need stuff to do. And they seem to be used to you being in the middle of a pile of rubble with tools in hand."

She smiled. "It was always a big family project as much as it could be. The little ones know how to scrape wallpaper and David's not a bad painter as long as you don't have him do edges. Jack is great at sanding and loves to kick through drywall. Henry is actually really good at tiles and grout. Charlie is our main painter, including edges, and he's always the one wanting to crawl into spaces and check out wiring and look for water damage and stuff. We've taught them what to look for and they've all learned a lot about construction and the engineering behind it. It's fun to take everyone to a house and start ripping into things and talking ideas." She suddenly got quiet and, much like David that morning at breakfast, she looked sad for a moment before she said, "It used to be fun."

Tucker cleared his throat, the strength of his emotions surprising. "You're going to keep doing it though, right? I mean, you all obviously love it."

She shrugged. "Probably not. I mean, I'm a one-woman

show now, and it takes time to build a reputation like we had in Nashville. Down there, word of mouth was our best advertisement. Starting over in a new city would be tough, if not impossible."

"So what's your plan?"

"I'm going to get my realtor license. Chelsea handled that part for us, but I learned a lot from her."

"You like the realty part of it?" He couldn't see her as a saleswoman, frankly. She liked the behind-the-scenes. He couldn't see her meeting with clients and driving them all over the city, trying to sell them on properties and dealing with the negotiations.

"I don't know. I haven't done it before."

"But you know what it's about. Was Chelsea good at it?"

Delaney laughed. "Chelsea was good at everything."

He wanted to roll his eyes but didn't.

"She was great at sales," Delaney went on. "People loved her. She was enthusiastic and was great at figuring out what was important to them and then finding a way to give it to them. That was where we came in a lot of times though. If a home was perfect in every way except for the layout of the kitchen or the size of the bedrooms or the number of bathrooms, Chelsea showed them what we would be able to do to make those things happen."

"And you want to do that?" Tucker pressed. "Sell houses? Deal with clients? Go through selling them on your renovation ideas?"

She frowned at him. "It makes the most sense. I can't run a renovation business by myself. I don't know everything there is to know about home construction and remodeling. It's not like I can go out to Denver and teach second grade or fight fires or deliver babies. I kind of need to stick with what I know."

"Would you rather go back to school for something else?" he asked.

"No. I love what I do."

"But that's not what you're going to do out there."

She sighed. "Why are you giving me a hard time about this?"

"I'm just..." *Making sure you'll be happy.* "I'm just curious," he finally said.

"Well, it will be fine."

"It takes a while to get up and going as a realtor too," he said. He assumed that was true. There was one realtor in Sapphire Falls and he did it very part-time. There simply wasn't a lot of moving in and out going on here.

"I'll get in with a big company," she said. "One of those companies where the homebuyers come to the office because of the company name and get assigned a realtor."

"What about until you have your license?" He had no idea how long something like that took.

"I have to take classes and pass the test," she said. "I figured I would start the classes this summer."

"While you're here?"

She nodded. "Part of my plan to get things organized before I move out there."

"Because of your parents." He hated her father and didn't even know the man. That was a foreign concept to Tucker too. He typically liked most people and he tried not to judge people he didn't know personally.

But the man had judged Tucker's best friend based on his race alone, and he'd ruthlessly disowned one daughter and let the other leave home as a minor without protest.

"Yes," she admitted. "The more I have in place, the less likely it will be that they'll try to talk me out of stuff or guilt or scare me into something else."

"Something else?" Tucker knew he was scowling but he couldn't seem to stop.

"Like a job at my dad's firm or something."

Tucker knew he was an attorney. "That would be bad?" he asked, truly wanting to know. It seemed good in some ways. She wouldn't have to take classes, she wouldn't have any lag time between moving out there and being able to work, she wouldn't have to go into a sales job that she didn't really want.

Delaney lifted her chin. "Yes, that would be bad."

"What would he have you doing?"

"I don't know. And I don't care. I don't need him to give me a job and I don't want him playing watchdog."

But Tucker kind of did want him to play watchdog.

He hoped that it wouldn't get to the point that Delaney would even be going to Colorado, but if she was going to be out there, he didn't want her to be alone. If her dad was the kind of guy to give her a job and watch out for her—even if he was a judgmental prick—he wasn't all bad in Tucker's opinion. Delaney needed people looking out for her.

Preferably Tucker. But if it took him longer than three months to convince her that she needed to be in Sapphire Falls, he would actually feel better knowing that her dad wanted to help her out. Tucker would never fully forgive Delaney's dad for how he'd reacted to Rafe and treated his own daughters, but if Tucker had to choose between his higher morals and keeping Delaney safe and well, he'd pick Delaney every time. And the thing about unbending assholes was if they were on your side, they could be real assets. Lord knew where Tucker would be without TJ.

"You should at least hear your dad out," Tucker said.

Delaney had walked into the space behind the last stall. At his words, she came back into sight and faced him. It was clear she was stunned. And ticked off.

"What are you talking about?"

Yep, she planted her hands on her hips. A clear sign he was treading on thin ice here.

He didn't care. He was giving in on the casual sex thing. He *wasn't* giving in on making sure she was safe and supported.

"I'm saying that if your dad wants to help you out, maybe you should let him."

Her eyes narrowed. "My dad wants to take over and handle everything."

"Would that be so bad?" Tucker asked. "Really? You've got your hands full, Delaney. If you have people willing to help you, why not let them?"

"You have no—"

"If you won't let *me* do it, you need to let *someone* do it." Damn, the idea of her out in Colorado—or anywhere, for that matter—on her own, trying to make it work, feeling lost and unsure, made everything in him protest.

"Maybe I don't need anyone to do it. Maybe I'll be fine. Maybe I'll actually figure it all out and do a great job," she said. "I don't suppose *that* ever occurred to you? Or my dad? Or Rafe? That maybe, just maybe, I have the brains and the guts to make it work."

Tucker stared at her. She was so fucking gorgeous. She was breathing hard, her cheeks flushed, her eyes wide. And she looked tough. She was smart and she clearly had enough love to do anything the boys needed her to do. But she shouldn't have to be alone. The urge to protect her, to take care of her, to be her hero, would not leave him alone.

"It's not about what you *can* do or handle, Laney," he said. "It's that there are people who *want* to help you. Who can make things easier."

"Maybe I don't want it to be easier," she said, lifting her chin. "Maybe it's my turn to do the tough stuff."

"Your turn?"

"Chelsea took night classes while she had four boys and worked full-time. She never missed a kid's program or game. She was a room mom at school. She helped them with homework and made sure they had everything they needed."

"Yes, your sister was amazing," he said with barely contained impatience.

"And Rafe...he worked eighty-hour weeks. He took on every job he could get. He coached baseball and basketball for the boys. Even after he was diagnosed and feeling like shit, he showed up for them whenever he could. He...suffered for a long time."

Her voice caught on a sob, and Tucker couldn't stay apart from her for another second. He took the four strides to where she stood and pulled her into his arms. He tucked her head under his chin and wrapped her in a tight hug.

"It's okay, Laney," he said softly. "He was happy. He wanted more time, for sure, but he was happy with every minute he had."

Delaney's arms went around his waist and Tucker felt her press into him, as if seeking even more contact.

"It's my turn, Tucker. They made my life so much easier, so much better than it would have been otherwise. Now it's my turn to do the hard stuff. To prove I can."

"You can. But you don't have to *suffer* for it."

"Maybe I do."

God, was she going through survivor's remorse? Did she wish it had been her to die instead of them?

Everything in him revolted at that idea and he tightened his arms around her even more. She was here. She was alive, healthy, warm and soft in his arms.

He pulled back to look down at her. "This is what you're supposed to be doing. You are supposed to be here, alive, with the boys, with me."

She stared up into his eyes. Then slowly, she nodded. "I know."

"You do?" He looked closely, needing to see that she really meant it.

She nodded again. "I don't feel guilty about being alive, Tuck."

That use of his nickname again made his heart kick against his ribs. "Good." He ran his hand over her hair. "That's a good thing."

"It is. I'm supposed to be here. Because it is my turn to step up." She shook her head and put her hand over his mouth as he started to protest. "You don't really know. Rafe and Chelsea took care of me. They're the reason I had a home, a family, a job. They gave me everything I love— family and friendship, the boys, a job I love and am good at. They gave me a place to be at Christmas. They fed me, helped run me around when my car broke down and did *everything* for me."

Tucker pulled her hand away from his mouth. "*I* want to do everything for you now."

She nodded. "I know. And a *huge* part of me wants to let you."

"Great. Then it's settled. We can go to the justice of the peace tomorrow." Damn, he wanted that. As he said it out loud, he realized how much. "My mom will never forgive us. We might have to do a church wedding down the road too, but let's do it."

"You *have* to stop saying stuff like that."

That frustrated the hell out of him. "I want to help. Chelsea didn't do it all alone. As amazing as she was, she still had help."

"And then he died!"

Tucker bit back his next words. Words like "I meant you" and "she died first". It didn't matter. He knew what she was saying.

"What if I lean on you, Tucker?" Delaney asked. "What if I let you take care of everything and go on blissfully thinking that everything will be okay now that I'm here? And then something happens to *you*?"

Okay, now they were getting somewhere.

"You're afraid of losing anyone else. Of getting close and then going through all of that again," he said. "I get that. Of course. You know firsthand that bad things can happen suddenly. But I don't plan on going anywhere for a really, really long time," he said. "And even if something would happen, you have *a lot* of people here. Not just me. A whole town of people to lean on. You don't have to be scared of being left alone again."

Now she blew out the frustrated breath. "I'm not scared, Tucker. I'm pathetic."

He frowned. "What?"

"It's not that I'm *afraid* of having to do it on my own or that I feel guilty for being here to do it instead of them. I feel *pathetic* that I don't know *how* to do it on my own. Even without the boys, I'd be feeling pretty lost right now. I've never taken care of myself."

Tucker looked at her for a long moment. And he wondered if he'd ever really taken care of himself. He'd always had his family around. His mother still fed him most of his meals, for God's sake.

But he felt like he had been on his own, taking care of things. Maybe because he took care of his family in return. They took care of each other.

"You did a lot for Chelsea. And for Rafe," he said. "You helped them a lot. You were by his bedside every day. He told me."

She nodded. "I helped. Of course. But that's not really the same thing."

It *was* the same thing. It was *more* than the same thing. She'd comforted Rafe in his last days. For that alone, Tucker would forever be in her debt. "You're amazing, Delaney," he said sincerely. "I wish you could see it."

"You're biased by the blowjob," she replied with a half-smile, clearly trying to lighten the moment.

The blowjob had been phenomenal. And had nothing to do with this moment.

"How can I make you see this?" he asked gruffly. "I so need you to see how amazing and strong you are."

This woman was mixing things up for him, things that had always seemed so clear. He actually felt an urge to step back and leave her alone so she could figure these things out, prove what she needed to prove. But that impulse was directly at war with his instinct to make it all better for her. And, yes, easy. He wanted to make things easy for her.

Exactly what she did not want.

She looked at him for a long moment. Then she said simply, "Kiss me."

That he could do. Without hesitation, he lowered his mouth to hers.

And immediately realized she had a point.

How exactly to make things better for her was complicated. But when they kissed, everything seemed simple. It was just the two of them and how fucking amazing things felt when they touched.

Delaney instantly wrapped her arms around his neck and arched close.

He loved that. She responded to him instantly. She seemed hungry for him. Always.

It felt like he had been kissing her for years. Her mouth under his felt as natural and familiar as sinking into his pillow at night or propping his feet up on his porch and watching the sunrise. He felt at home. Right. Purely himself and surrounded by everything that mattered. The epitome of comfort.

Other than the heat pumping through his body, tightening every cell and ratcheting his desire up to the point that he needed her like he needed his next breath.

He moved his mouth along her jaw and down the side of her neck, and she let her head fall back, giving him full access.

"God, Tucker, you make me feel so good. When you kiss me, everything else goes away."

Yes. That was what he wanted. He ran his hands up and down her back. "I hate every time you needed something—a car repair, a ride, a drink, twenty bucks, a neck massage—that I wasn't there to give it to you," he said against her skin.

He felt the vibration of her soft laugh against his lips. "That means a lot to me," she said. "But when you touch me, you make all of those times not matter one bit. I feel strong and sure and happy when I'm with you like this."

If the girl had spent hours contemplating the perfect words to say to make him putty in her hands, she couldn't have come up with better ones. She was giving *him* exactly what he needed—to know that he could give her what *she* needed most.

"Tell me what to do," he said hoarsely against her ear, his hands lifting her up against him more fully. "Tell me how to take it all away, how to make you good right now."

There was a pause, but she tightened her arms around his neck and said softly, "Put me up against the wall and make me come hard."

Tucker drew in a ragged breath, gripping her firm ass in his hands. There was no way in hell he could do anything but give this woman anything she asked for.

He backed her up to the nearest wall and pressed into her, letting her feel how hard and hot he was for her.

"Let me undress you," she told him, kissing his neck as she slipped her hands under his shirt, her hands on his back, drawing the cotton T-shirt up and pulling it over his head.

He yanked his arms from the sleeves and tossed it aside, stepping back to watch her strip.

She pulled her shirt off and quickly tossed her bra in the same direction. Her hands cupped her breasts and she squeezed her nipples between her fingers.

Tucker watched, his mouth watering with the need to suck on the hard tips and make her groan.

She bent and untied her boots and kicked them off. His cock hardened as he imagined bending her over like that, fully naked, so he could thrust into her from behind.

Soon. Very soon.

But when she straightened and undid her jeans, Tucker lost track of anything else as she pushed the denim and her silk panties to the floor. She stepped out of them and the gorgeous body that he could get lost in for hours was completely bare to him. The sunlight from the window spilled over her and he wanted to put his tongue everywhere the light touched.

And a few places it couldn't quite get to.

He needed to taste her. He needed to feel her sweetness on his lips and tongue.

He had visions of going to his knees, but before he could move, she stepped forward and took his hand.

"Touch me, Tucker," she said softly.

"I want my tongue on you." He cupped her breasts, rubbing the nipples with his thumbs as she arched closer. He tugged on one and then bent to suck it into his mouth and swirl his tongue over and around the tip.

She gripped his head with one hand, her fingers in his hair. Then he felt her other hand on one of his, tugging it from her breast and moving it lower. She kept her hand over the top of his as she slid him between her legs and pressed his middle finger into her heat.

"Yes," she hissed, moving her hips against his hand.

As far as hints went, that was a really good one. He added another finger and she pressed harder against him.

"Right here, Laney. My tongue on you right here," he said, circling her clit with his thumb.

"*Tucker.*"

He stroked in and out, but she was moving against him enough that after a second he stopped moving his hand and let her take over. Watching her face, he kept his fingers deep, but her hand was still over his. She pressed him against her more firmly while she ground down with her hips.

"Let me taste you," he said again.

"Don't stop." Her hand pressed harder against his, keeping him in place.

He let her go for a few more seconds, but as her pussy

clenched around his fingers, he walked her backward to the wall again.

"Please," she said softly.

Maybe she wasn't into oral sex. Receiving anyway. Yet.

She would be.

"Lane—"

"Need you," she said simply. She unfastened his jeans and opened his fly, freeing his achingly hard erection from his underwear and stroking her hand up and down the length. "Now, Tucker," she said, her voice husky. "Please."

Fine. But his mouth and her clit had a date later.

He moved his hands to her ass as she lifted herself and wrapped her legs around his waist. He pressed her into the wall and she reached between them to position him at her entrance. He tried to ease into her, but she looked him straight in the eye and said, "Hard and fast."

Well, if she insisted.

He thrust his hips forward, sinking into her heat. For a moment, he had the same flash of *home* that he had when he'd kissed her a few minutes ago.

Delaney felt like everything he'd always wanted all wrapped up in one sweet, feisty, hot, vulnerable package.

And then she squeezed her inner muscles around him and his brain only thought of taking her.

So he did.

He thrust into her, hard and fast as she'd asked. She held on, her fingers digging into his shoulders, her hot mouth against his neck, her pussy gripping him like a silk glove.

It was only a few strokes in when he felt her already beginning to come. She was saying his name over and over, her body clenching around him, and he couldn't have held back if his life had depended on it. He'd happily enter the afterlife just like this.

Delaney cried out and he pumped into her, fast and

deep, his climax building and building until it took him up and over the edge in one of the hottest, most fulfilling releases he'd ever experienced.

He kept her pinned to the wall for several minutes, both of them just breathing.

Tucker took in every detail about it. The feel of her around him, her weight in his arms, her hot breath against his shoulder, the silkiness of her hair against his chest. He'd been in this barn a million times, but for the first time, he felt as if he was really *here*, in the moment, absorbing everything from the smell of the wood and hay, to the creak of the boards underfoot and the sight of the dust swirling in the shaft of sunlight.

Damn. Delaney was making him poetic.

Eventually, she lifted her head. She didn't say anything but gave him a smile and kissed him quickly on the mouth.

He pulled out of her body—that sensation in and of itself erotic and sweet at the same time—and let her feet swing to the floor.

They got dressed without talking and headed back up to the house together.

Delaney stopped by the back door. He faced her. "I'm going to go get the boys and go over to the dirt-bike track."

She nodded. "I'll finish pulling up the linoleum and clean up in here a little."

"Pizza and movie at six?" That would put them out at the river before nine.

Delaney smiled up at him, a little sparkle in her eye. "How about five?"

The sooner they did the dinner and movie thing, the sooner they could head for the party. She wanted more time with him. That was a very good sign.

He knew he should just leave. Or maybe kiss her and then leave. But he needed to say something.

"Thanks for the two orgasms before lunch" didn't seem quite right. "Marry me and have my babies" was also not going to sit well. Especially considering he had heard what she'd said out there about needing to be strong and wanting to prove herself.

So he went for a combo of the two.

"Thank you," he said, lifting a hand and running the pad of his thumb over her lower lip. "For letting me take it all away and make you happy for a little while. I can't tell you what that means to me."

Her eyes went wide.

Okay, maybe he'd gone a little deep there.

"Tucker," she said softly.

"Yeah?"

"You've *got* to stop saying stuff like that."

Then she turned and went into the kitchen, the back door slapping shut behind her.

But Tucker was smiling as he swung around and started for his truck.

He wasn't going to stop. And she knew it.

৵৶

Movie and pizza night with the boys was great.

Until it wasn't.

There was a point in every week, and she was definitely getting better at predicting it, when things just kind of went to hell. There wasn't always a really clear reason either. It was typically a combination of fatigue and too much togetherness and probably low blood sugar or something about kids covered in the parenting handbook that hadn't been handed down to Delaney, that mashed together and resulted in irrational crabbiness from one or more of the boys at once.

"This isn't how I want my popcorn." Jack crossed his arms, getting the obstinate look on his face that made Delaney brace herself.

Tucker looked down at the two bowls in his hands.

"Thought you said popcorn and M&M's, bud," he said easily.

"Peanut M&M's. Not plain," Jack told him. "That's how my dad always did it."

Oh, crap. Delaney sighed. "Jack, your dad liked plain M&M's too."

"That's not what he put in popcorn." Jack's eyes got watery and Delaney felt her own sting in response.

"Stop being a dumb baby," Charlie told him.

Jack was sitting on the couch between Henry and Luna. "I'm *not* a baby!"

"Then stop acting like one," Charlie said.

"Charlie, no name calling," Delaney said sharply. "Jack, you can eat the popcorn the way it is and pick out the M&M's, or you can try it and see if you like it."

"I want it the way Daddy made it," Jack said stubbornly.

"You're making Tucker feel bad," Henry said crossly, nudging Jack with his elbow. "Knock it off."

"He's not making me feel bad," Tucker said. "I understand that he's bummed out. Sorry I didn't get the right kind." He handed the bowl to Charlie. "You want me to make another bowl without M&M's?" he asked Jack.

"I want M&M's in it!" Jack said.

"Shut up already!" David told him.

"Everyone is going to listen to *me* right now," Delaney said firmly.

Delaney appreciated the apology and Tucker's attempt to diffuse the situation, but while Henry hadn't approached it well, he had a point. Jack was old enough to start understanding how his words and actions affected others and that grownups had feelings too.

"David, we don't say shut up to each other. Henry and Charlie, I'm very glad you're aware of Tucker's feelings, but I will handle Jack's outburst, thank you. You be his brothers and I'll be his…" Oh, God, she couldn't say mom or parent. She just couldn't. She didn't think she ever would be able to. "The grownup," she said. She cleared her throat. "Jack, you need to decide if you're going to watch the movie with us or not. Popcorn and M&M's are optional, good attitudes are not."

Jack frowned at her.

"You don't have to smile," she told him. "But lose the frown."

Jack sighed dramatically, but at least tried to ease the scowl on his face.

Delaney glanced at Tucker. He was eating popcorn and staying out of it. But he was watching her with an expression she could only describe as happy and affectionate.

That was weird. But this was Tucker. In his mind, this was probably foreplay. He was the one who wanted a hundred kids, after all. He clearly had a very strong family unit and she was sure he and his brothers had gone at it. Probably not only verbally all the time. This was normal to him and she appreciated that he wasn't bothered by it. She didn't feel judged. She felt secure that this was normal and fine. But seeing the boys fight and her chew them out probably got Tucker hot.

He seemed to be fighting a small smile, and that made her smile—and roll her eyes.

Charlie stuck the bowl of popcorn in Jack's face. "It's good this way."

"It's not how Daddy did it!" Jack swatted at the bowl, clearly intending to move it away from his nose where Charlie was holding and shaking it.

Of course, his hand hit the container and sent it flying out of Charlie's hold. Popcorn and M&M's flew everywhere.

Complete silence reigned for ten full seconds.

Then Tucker burst into laughter.

Delaney and the boys all turned to look at him at once.

"Now *that* is something your dad would have done," he said with a big grin. "He was the messiest guy I ever met."

Delaney felt her own grin spreading, and by the time the boys looked at her with wide eyes, she was laughing too. "He really was," she said. "We never had a meal where he didn't spill something."

The boys all started smiling as well.

"Do you remember the time he was carrying Charlie's birthday cake into the house and Mom opened the door right as he got there and the cake squashed all over the front of him?" Henry asked.

They all nodded.

"I remember the time when I spilled my milk at the restaurant and Dad knocked everyone else's over too," David said.

Delaney nodded. "I remember that. There was milk and water and soda everywhere! Our waitress was so mad."

"And Mom," Charlie said. "And then Dad tipped her water over *in her lap* and she started laughing."

Delaney looked around at her nephews and their smiling faces. And her heart swelled. That was all she wanted. Four happy, smiling boys who knew they were loved, had wonderful memories of their parents and felt secure and *normal*. That most of all. The normalcy. People who had routine lives—boring, predictable, never-changing lives—didn't fully appreciate the beauty of that. She hadn't. She'd taken it for granted. Complained about it even.

She looked over the boys' heads to Tucker.

Tucker didn't complain. His life was pretty routine, pretty unchanging...stable. Solid. Safe. Sweet. And he knew it. He appreciated it. He wanted to give it to her and the boys.

Their voices faded and she just watched Tucker with the boys. They'd all dropped to their hands and knees, Tucker included, and were picking up the popcorn and

candy scattered everywhere. They were still talking about
Rafe but they were all smiling and laughing.

That was, plain and simple, what she wanted for them.

She pulled in a long breath, the truth suddenly so clear.

Not falling in love with Tucker was going to be the
hardest thing she'd ever done.

And that was saying something.

She wasn't good at resistance. She wasn't especially
into denial. Less so over the past few months. Life was
short. So instead of trying to avoid it, she decided right then
and there to let it happen. Hell, it was happening anyway.

So she wasn't going to fight it.

She would simply fight the urge to *marry* him.

Because it was there too. And it was really, really
strong.

Thankfully, she was pretty sure it was less about him
making things *easier* and more about him simply making
things *better*.

She couldn't marry him.

But she could date him.

She knew that her dating life was going to be
completely different now because of the boys. She wasn't
going to put on a man parade through their lives. But
Tucker was different. He was always going to be there for
them, he'd always be involved, always a part of their life
regardless of what—if anything—happened between him
and her. So she could enjoy Tucker and not worry about the
boys being too attached. They were attached, but they had a
relationship with him that wasn't about her at all. They had
a history with him that extended far before her and Tucker.
In fact, he might be the only man in the world she could
date and *not* worry about the boys. She should enjoy that
while she could.

Eventually, every kernel was picked up and they were
all settled on Tucker's couch again. Now Jack was in
Tucker's lap, snitching pieces of popcorn and plain

M&M's from Tucker's bowl. Delaney sat on the other end of the couch with Henry, Charlie and David between her and Tucker. The movie was one of the Transformer movies—she couldn't keep track of which one—but even with the action and explosions, it couldn't keep her attention the way the hot farmer with the little boy in his lap could.

Dammit.

She knew a lot of women were suckers for men with babies and kids. She knew that doting dads made many women swoon, but she'd never put herself in that group. She'd seen Rafe with the boys from the day they were born, through diaper changes, late-night feedings, illnesses and scraped knees. She'd watched him teach them to ride bikes and throw balls, write their letters, and count to one hundred. She'd always thought he was great. She'd admired him. She'd thought it was sweet. She'd also watched his friends who were dads when they came over for birthday parties or barbecues. A few were even single. But same thing—it was great, sweet, nice. But she had never actually felt her ovaries sit up and say, "I have an idea!"

She was pretty sure that was what had just happened watching Tucker.

Was it because they weren't his kids and he didn't *have* to be so awesome? Was it because these kids really needed him and were soaking up his attention and humor like little flowers getting watered after a long drought?

Maybe.

Or maybe it was just Tucker.

And the fact that she was at least partially on her way to maybe, possibly, someday being in love with him a little.

He laughed at something David had leaned over to say in his ear and her freaking ovaries threw confetti. She would have sworn to it.

God, his smile was lethal.

And then he melted her further with a completely juvenile, sweet, silly move—he stretched his arm along the back of the couch where hers was resting behind the boys and laid his hand on top of hers.

That's it. Just his hand on top of hers. And if he would have proposed right then and there she would have said yes.

She took a deep breath and linked her fingers with his. She glanced at him and was rewarded with a big smile and a wink.

That smile and wink made some other things clench—things a little below her ovaries.

She smiled and rolled her eyes but definitely kept holding his hand as she pretended to focus on the movie.

By the time the credits rolled, Jack was asleep on Tucker—and if that wasn't enough to move her a little further into the crazy-for-guys-with-kids camp, he then picked Jack up and carried him to bed behind her and David.

She tucked David in and glanced over at Tucker. His hand was on Jack's head and she heard him whisper, "Sweet dreams, buddy." Then, wordlessly, they both straightened and slid past one another, trading places. Tucker's hands went to her hips as they made full-body contact between the two beds and she felt her whole body give a little yay. But they moved apart—mostly because David was sleepy but not yet fully asleep. And also because things hadn't ended with a simple hug or kiss between them since TJ had interrupted them on the porch swing.

She leaned down to kiss Jack's forehead while Tucker told David that yes, Luna could sleep on the foot of David's bed. She pulled the blanket up over Jack, turned to ask David if he needed a drink of water and patted Luna on the head. Tucker brushed a bit of popcorn from Jack's hair. Their movements were choreographed around the beds and nightstand as if they'd been doing this together for years, and Delaney felt a yearning that she knew was dangerous.

If she wasn't careful, *she* would be the one proposing to Tucker.

They moved to the doorway together and it felt completely natural to link her fingers with his again when he took her hand.

David was asleep by the time they stepped out into the hallway and pulled the door shut behind them.

"I told them that Brittni would be here later on, in case they wake up and we're not here."

She nodded. "Good. Thanks."

"And I told Henry and Charlie they had to ask you about staying up later tonight."

"I'm okay with it, but thanks," she said.

He moved in closer. "I was thinking I might want to sleep in a little tomorrow anyway."

"Oh, yeah?" They couldn't sleep together in his bed, but damn, in that moment she *really* wanted to.

Well, she didn't want to *sleep*.

"I thought I might be out late tonight," he said.

Of course, as they'd proven, beds weren't the only fun places in Sapphire Falls. "You did say something about a mattress in your truck bed, didn't you?"

He grinned. "I did."

"Is truck-bed sex as good as real-bed sex?"

He pulled her in against him and moved his hands to her ass. "Better."

"Better?"

"My brother says it's because of all the fresh air. Makes us hornier."

She laughed. "And here I was thinking it was *you* making me horny."

He squeezed her ass and leaned in until their lips were almost touching. "Maybe I should keep you out of the fresh air. You're already nearly insatiable."

She laughed. She would have never used that word to

describe her sexual appetite before. She loved sex. She enjoyed it immensely and the guys who wanted just that had been her favorite boyfriends. The ones that were fine with her showing up for a booty call and then going home. Or the ones who loved a nooner as much as she did. But she didn't need to *see* them every day or have a conversation every day to be happy. She loved to sleep in her own bed. She liked having dinner with her sister and her family. She preferred to watch TV with Chelsea and Rafe or to go out to clubs to hear bands with Chelsea and Rafe or to go shopping with...

Pathetic.

Until Tucker. She looked up at him as she realized that watching the movie tonight with him had felt as comfortable as she had with her sister and Rafe. Sharing the pizza with him and the boys, sitting on the porch swing last night, just talking down in the barn today—none of that had felt boyfriend-ish. It had felt...natural. And like they'd been doing it forever.

That's what she liked.

She didn't like the pressure of relationships, worrying about the guy fitting in with her family, learning what he liked and didn't like, making sure it matched up with her likes and dislikes at least enough that neither of them was perpetually frustrated, and telling the guy all her stories.

That's what worked with Tucker. He knew a lot of her stories. When they talked about her sister and Rafe, they were both coming at it from a place of familiarity and prior knowledge. She wasn't worried about him fitting in with the people she loved—he loved them too and vice versa. And she felt a definite sense of acceptance from him. Like if he *didn't* like the same music or the same pizza toppings or the same TV shows, it would be fine. It wouldn't matter as much as the stuff they did have in common.

And tonight had proven that they did actually like the same pizza toppings.

"Worried you can't keep up with me?" she finally asked, wondering if her voice sounded funny.

All of this was a little overwhelming.

At the same time, it occurred to her that this was really how it should probably feel to fall in love.

Besides, she had promised herself only a couple of hours ago that she would let it happen if it was going to.

And it was clearly going to.

"I figure it's like training for any physical activity," he said. "You keep on doing it until you're built up."

"And take lots of hot soaks. And massages." A big old bathtub, flavored massage oil and lots of uninterrupted time sounded absolutely perfect.

"Fresh air, here we come," he said.

Okay, so no big old bathtub this time.

He lowered his head for a long kiss that was heating up—and only a few feet from his bedroom—when they heard the knock at the front door.

Tucker lifted his head and gave her a smile. "Party time. And I apologize in advance for my friends and family."

She laughed. "I've already met a bunch of them."

He nodded. "But not all together and not with Booze in the picture."

She was ready.

She was pretty sure.

CHAPTER NINE

"Okay, Phoebe, you said you know Tucker best,"
Delaney said an hour later. They were standing around a
huge bonfire down by the river on Phoebe and Joe's land.
Delaney had her second Mason jar of Booze in hand. And
she was ready for some girl talk.

Phoebe nodded. "And longest. Not to mention I know
all of the girls who have ever dated him."

"Phoebe was everybody's best friend growing up,"
Adrianne said of the bubbly redhead. "Everyone confided
in her, asked for her advice, confessed to her. She knows
what she's talking about."

"Perfect. You said he was very single-minded at times."

"Definitely."

"So he's always intense with the women he dates?" She
realized that all of her information about Tucker had come
from Rafe. A male perspective. Now she had a prime
opportunity to get a female viewpoint. Multiple female
viewpoints.

Maybe there was nothing all that special about how he
was treating her. Maybe this was simply how Tucker was.
Maybe what made things between them feel so powerful
was simply where *she* was coming from. She'd told Tucker
she wasn't used to being the center of attention, and that
was completely true. She wasn't used to be pursued. She
wasn't used to someone being so in tune with her. Like
tonight. No matter where she was or he was or who they
were talking to at the party, she felt Tucker's eyes on her.
And she loved it. She felt important, cared for, wanted.
Tucker made the center of his attention somewhere she
really liked being. She just needed to get used to it. She
didn't get the impression that the intensity of it would ever
fade.

The women all exchanged looks. "No. Intense is not the

word I would use," Lauren finally said.

That surprised Delaney. She looked at the other woman. "But he wants to do the whole wife-and-kids thing and everyone knows it right?"

They all nodded.

"So does he scare the other women off by talking about all of that on the very first date? Does he know how to take things slow at all?" she asked.

The women all looked at one another again but Phoebe was finally the one who spoke.

"Everyone knows that's what Tucker wants," she agreed. "It's always been that way. I'm not sure he really talks about it. He hasn't made a big public announcement or anything," she said with a smile. "It's just always been a thing. In grade school, if the girls wanted to play house, he was always willing to be the dad. In junior high, one of our art projects was to design a house. He designed the one he lives in now. In high school, he was the only one of the guys to get an A in our adult-living class." Phoebe grinned. "You know, the one where we had to carry a bag of flour around for two weeks like a baby."

"He made kind of a public announcement then," Hailey said. "He chewed a couple of the other guys in class out about how they weren't taking it seriously."

Delaney shook her head. "That's what I mean— intense."

Phoebe shrugged. "Tucker is just a really good guy who wants to be a family man. I guess I don't see anything wrong with that. In fact, most of the women around here, who also want families, find it really attractive."

"So when he starts talking about weddings and babies on the first date, they just all swoon?" she asked. "How is he not married already with six kids?"

Phoebe shook her head. "He doesn't talk about weddings and babies on the first date. In fact, the girls he's dated have commented that they wish he moved faster. He never sleeps with them right away. He doesn't take them to family dinners. If they've got kids, he doesn't want to hang out with them until he's sure it's going to work out."

"So how many have gone to family dinner?" Delaney asked.

"None."

Her eyes widened. "How many of their kids has he taken dirt biking and watched movies with?"

But she thought she already knew the answer.

"None," Phoebe said.

Delaney tried to compute what Phoebe was telling her. "But he's the one who wants to get married so badly."

Phoebe nodded.

"And you said he gets really persuasive when he has an idea that he wants everyone to get on board with."

"He does."

"Wouldn't it make sense that he use family dinners and hanging with the kids and sex early on as a way of convincing these women they want to marry him?"

"Well," Phoebe said slowly.

"What?"

"He's never needed to convince the girls of anything. He's never had a problem getting someone on board with dating him and wanting to marry him."

Delaney bit back a growl of frustration. "I think he's crazy."

Phoebe nodded. "He's an enigma."

Adrianne snorted. "I'm not sure that word means what you think it means."

"He's not an enigma?" Phoebe asked.

"Tucker Bennett might be the easiest man to understand in the history of the world. He wants to get married and have kids and farm in Sapphire Falls," Lauren said simply.

"He's a pain in the ass like all of the Bennett boys," Hailey said.

Lauren, the only one in the group married to one of the

Bennett boys, didn't protest that statement.

"The Bennett guys have this very clear, firm idea in their minds of what they want and what's right and heaven forbid someone want something else or not just go along with *their* ideas," Hailey went on.

Okay, Delaney wasn't sure exactly where all *that* had come from, but… "But Phoebe was saying that all of these girls have always gone along with his ideas."

"Yes, all of the girls who bring him cobbler and take off their clothes expect a diamond. They all go along with his ideas. They all want the marriage-home-kids thing. They all want to move to his farm. They all want to cook and bake for him. But Tucker Bennett has never told a girl in Sapphire Falls that he's in love with her," Hailey said.

Delaney stared at the other woman. Tucker, the guy who wanted nothing more than to be a husband and father, had never been in love? "That makes no sense."

Hailey frowned. "I know. The guy who wants to be married the most is the guy who has had the fewest number of true girlfriends."

"But he's already talking about all of that with me," Delaney blurted out.

Then she realized she might have made a mistake.

"Yay!" Kate exclaimed.

But Hailey moved in closer with a frown. "What do you mean?"

Delaney shook her head. "Nothing. Never mind."

"He's already in love with you?" Hailey asked.

"No, of course not." He couldn't be. Delaney knew that. "We just met."

"But he's thinking about marrying you." It wasn't a question this time.

"He's crazy about the boys," Delaney said. "He isn't able to avoid hanging out with them or having us around for family dinners. That's all it is."

For some reason, that realization depressed her. She did

not want to marry him. Falling in love with him would be a really bad idea and a huge complication. But the whole thing—her life, everything about who she was, every choice she made—was now about the boys. She was the guardian/mother to four boys who needed her for everything. She was changing where she lived, her job, her entire life for them. And now an amazing man was in her life—a man who made her feel hot and sexy and beautiful and capable—but only because of the boys.

Tucker was into her because of the boys.

Of course. That made complete sense.

And her ego was just going to have to get over it.

"I don't know," Hailey said. "The boys aren't here tonight and he hasn't taken his eyes off of you."

"He's told himself that it's more than that, but there's no way," Delaney said. She looked around, but the other women didn't appear convinced. "I know nothing about living on a farm. I don't have big family dinners and holidays. I barely speak to my parents. I've never owned a dog. I can't drive a stick shift. I don't cook or bake. I don't—"

"Wait." Hailey put her hand up, stopping Delaney's recitation of her deficits. "What?"

"I'm not a small-town farm girl," Delaney summarized.

"No, the part about cooking and baking."

"I don't do either thing. No cobbler. Not even a cake from a mix."

"And he knows."

She nodded. "He does."

"He's in so much trouble," Hailey muttered. She started across the grass toward Tucker.

"Oh, boy." Delaney turned back to the girls. "Now what?"

Lauren grinned. "Nothing you can do to stop Hailey."

Well, she hadn't said anything that wasn't true. Maybe Hailey would talk some sense into him, convince him that

Delaney was *not* the girl for him.

And that thought stupidly depressed her too.

"I really kind of love this," Kate said. "You don't want to cook for him, you don't want to marry him *and* he wants to be serious. You better watch out," she teased Delaney. "He's going to be trying to get you into bed right away too."

Delaney was grateful for the dark that hid her sudden blush.

But her moment of silence was enough to alert Lauren. Her grin was fast and huge.

"He's already done that, hasn't he?" Lauren asked.

Delaney knew she couldn't deny it convincingly, but she didn't want to confirm it.

Saying nothing was evidently confirmation enough.

"Oh my God!" Phoebe exclaimed. "You've already slept with him?"

Delaney winced and shushed her.

Phoebe lowered her voice, but her excitement was clear. "Delaney, you have no idea—that's huge."

"It's not like he was abstinent before I got here," she said with a frown.

There was no way he'd been abstinent. Still, she held her breath, waiting for them to tell her he had actually been saving himself for marriage. That was exactly how this conversation had been going so far.

"Well, no," Phoebe said.

Delaney let her breath out. "See."

"But he really doesn't sleep with women casually," Kate said. "He's a huge flirt and sexy as hell, and most of the women in town *want* to sleep with him, but he doesn't jump into bed with lots of women."

Yep, this was exactly how this conversation had been going—namely, *not* her way. Delaney sighed. "Seriously?"

"He never has one-night stands and never sleeps with women on the first date," Phoebe said. "Believe me, the girls complain. Some have even offered no-strings, one-night things, but he turns them down."

Delaney shifted her weight and took a long gulp from the glass jar she was holding. The stuff inside tasted like strawberry fire. But she kept drinking. It definitely made her feel nice and fuzzy in the head. She felt like she'd spent *a lot* of time thinking—or trying to avoid thinking and thinking anyway—lately. Just being fuzzy felt good.

"He's slept with girls he's dated, of course," Kate said. "But he doesn't rush into it, and I really believe that he's hoping for it to turn into something serious when it gets to that point."

"So he does date women for a while sometimes?" Delaney asked.

"Always. He doesn't do casual," Phoebe said.

She took another swig of liquor and thought about the most interesting part of what she'd just learned.

Tucker was willing to do things her way. For her. Because that's what she said she needed. When it was exactly what he *didn't* want. He didn't want casual sex. He wanted the whole nine yards. He wanted at least the *chance* at the whole nine yards.

But he was doing casual for her.

Wow.

She couldn't remember the last time someone paid that much attention to what she wanted.

Chelsea and Rafe and the boys loved her, but everything in their lives—Delaney's too—was about the family unit, and Chelsea had been at the center of that. Always. They all revolved around her like the planets around the sun. She'd been their energy and light, their life force.

But Tucker was making this all about *her*.

Sure, he was giving the boys lots of attention and time and energy. But they were easy. They wanted to ride dirt bikes and do farm work and play with the dogs, just like he did. And he had his family and friends helping with the boys too. Their needs could be met by a lot of different people for the most part.

She was the complicated one. She was the one with needs that only he could meet. She was the one doing things he didn't want. She'd smashed up his kitchen. She wanted lots of sex and nothing else.

But he was still here, supporting her, giving her what she needed.

"It's almost enough to make me want to bake a cobbler," she said to herself.

But she'd said it out loud.

"What? You're going to make cobbler?" Kate demanded.

Delaney quickly shook her head, holding up a hand in surrender. Good Lord, these girls jumped on everything. "I might if I didn't think he'd propose—and you would already have the bridal shower planned—before he finished his first serving."

"Well, we want him to be happy," Kate said.

Delaney nodded. "I get that. He's a great guy."

"Would Tucker proposing really be that bad?" Phoebe asked.

Oh, boy, she was going to have to remember that these women were his biggest fans. It sounded like Tucker had many, and that didn't surprise her at all, but Phoebe and Kate and Adrianne and Lauren, and even Hailey, cared about Tucker beyond him being gorgeous and sexy and romantic. Of course, she'd met all of their husbands and boyfriends and she had no doubt that these women were very happy at home. But even single Hailey seemed to have a different level of affection for Tucker. Almost as though they were all his sisters. They loved him because of him, not because they wanted him or because he was perfect husband material.

She was going to have to watch what she said to them

about Tucker.

"It's just…been too fast," she said carefully. "It's hard to trust a proposal that comes within a few hours of meeting each other for the first time."

Phoebe grinned. "But you're in Sapphire Falls."

Delaney shook her head. "What's that mean?"

"Love happens fast here," Phoebe said. "Really fast."

Delaney looked around the circle of women again. "How fast?" she asked, almost dreading the answer.

"About three days for me and Joe," Phoebe said.

"Same for us," Adrianne said.

"Two days," Kate said.

"Two days," Lauren said.

Delaney stared at them. "What the *hell* do you people put in the water around here?"

They all laughed.

"Drink up, hon," Phoebe said. "Falling hard and fast is the best."

Delaney drank up all right. She finished off her jar of Booze and let Phoebe refill it. There was no *way* she was touching the water.

ക

Tucker saw Hailey coming because she'd been standing right next to Delaney, and he hadn't been able to look away from his houseguest all night.

But he'd really thought he had his mayor repellent firmly in place. His younger brother, Tyler, was sitting next to him on his truck's tailgate, and Hailey avoided Ty like the plague whenever they were in the same place at the same time.

Fortunately for Hailey, Ty lived in Denver and rarely visited his hometown.

Unfortunately for Tucker, TJ and Travis had called Ty to let him know Delaney—*the* Delaney, as they'd put it—

was in town. Tyler had shown up a few hours ago and had been waiting at the bonfire with Travis and Lauren when Tucker and Delaney had pulled in.

Also unfortunately for Tucker, whatever had the mayor coming at him was enough that even Ty couldn't keep her away.

"She doesn't know how to make cobbler," Hailey said without preamble. And without looking at Ty.

Tucker saw his brother grin and tip back his bottle of beer, clearly unfazed by the snub.

Tucker sighed. He should have known what this was about. "Yes, I know."

"Yeah, she said that you knew. You're unbelievable."

"How so?"

"Women in this town have been cooking for you and wanting to marry you for years. And now this woman who doesn't know how to cook and doesn't want to marry you is the one you think you're crazy about." Hailey huffed out a frustrated breath. "These are my *friends* that you keep messing with Tucker and I don't like it."

"She doesn't know how to cook?" Tyler asked.

Hailey didn't so much as glance in Ty's direction. "She's been here for *two days* and you're already thinking she's the one. You've known the women here all your life and you don't even give them a real chance."

Tucker just took another drink of Booze. He wasn't going to defend himself to Hailey. "Honey, I told you on Valentine's Day that if you were mad because I've never given *you* a chance, all you have to do is say the word."

Ty's beer bottle thunked against the tailgate as he set it down hard. "What the hell is going on?"

Hailey finally acknowledged his presence. "Men are so stupid."

"How so?" Ty asked, echoing Tucker's words.

"You sit around here thinking that you're doing all the women a *favor* by being sexy and sweet when you're really being huge jerks."

"We're being jerks when we're being sweet?" Ty asked.

"You're being jerks either way, but you're confusing when you're sweet."

Tucker looked from Hailey to his brother. Hailey was usually incredibly articulate and smooth. She was also typically haughty and cool. But at this moment, she wasn't making any sense. She seemed...riled up.

"Is it confusing?" Ty asked. "Really? Or does that sweetness make everything completely clear? Because maybe the right girl naturally brings out our sweetness."

Hailey scoffed. "You guys wouldn't know the right girl if she came up and slapped you across the face."

"And suddenly I'm remembering you slapping *me* across the face the last time we—"

"The *last time* being the key phrase," she interrupted. She pointed a finger at Tucker. "Quit breaking hearts in this town, Tucker." She turned on her heel and stalked away.

Tucker turned wide eyes on his little brother. "*What* is going on with you and Hailey? Seriously?"

His brother lifted his shoulder. "Driving each other nuts. As usual."

Tucker wanted to pursue that. Ty and Hailey had indeed been driving each other nuts, for years it seemed. His little brother loved to push the good mayor's buttons. And was able to. That was part of what was so puzzling about the whole thing. Tucker had never seen anyone rile Hailey up the way Ty could.

He opened his mouth but before he could say anything, Ty spoke. "No way. We're on you and Delaney right now."

Dammit.

But as he took another swallow of Booze, Tucker admitted that having someone else's perspective might be a good thing.

"Okay, so here it is. I think I'm already in love with

her. I want her to stay here in Sapphire Falls. Oh, and she wants nothing to do with any of that."

"So no sex with the girl you've been pining after all these years."

"I didn't say that." He didn't comment on the pining thing. He probably had been. Though he wasn't sure you could pine for something you'd never had.

Now he would pine for her.

"There has been sex?"

"There has been sex." Boy, had there.

"Why do I get the impression there's been *sex* sex?" Tyler asked.

Tucker looked over at his younger brother. "What do you mean?"

"I've seen how you're looking at her."

"How am I looking at her?"

"Like she's yours."

Tucker felt those words, and the truth of them, ricochet through his body. "You can see that?"

Ty nodded. "And that's *sex*."

There was a strange solemnity in his tone. Like he really knew what he was talking about. "Yeah, it was *sex*." No matter if his definition matched Tyler's exactly or not, Tucker knew that what he was feeling for Delaney was not just sex—he'd had sex.

He'd never had what he had with her.

"It's only been two days," Tucker said.

"And that's the other thing," Ty said.

"The other thing?"

"That makes me sure Delaney is different. You never jump in."

He didn't. He'd never had a one-night stand. That might not seem consistent with his playboy reputation, but the truth was he'd known the women around here—and everyone they were related to—all his life. He had approached every relationship with the idea that it might work out. On some level he'd wanted them to work out. Even in high school, he'd dated his girlfriends for months in most cases before they got naked. He'd known for as long as he could remember that his plan was to grow up, meet a nice girl, marry her, settle on the farm and have a bunch of kids. There hadn't been some magical revelation or a turning point where he'd figured his life out. That had always been his plan. Even as a kid, he'd always known that this was where he'd spend his life and these were the people he'd spend it with. He supposed that was why he'd always assumed the woman he'd end up with was someone who was already here.

But had the idea of Delaney been teasing the edges of his subconscious all of these years?

Yeah, maybe.

"I've never had sex with a woman on our first date," he confessed, though Ty knew that. Everyone knew that. It was part of Tucker's reputation. He had sex, lots of it, but it was never casual. "I always buy the woman something before we sleep together," he went on, thinking out loud. "Dinner, a movie, a flower, something."

"Delaney didn't give you the chance to romance her," Ty said.

There was a hint of amusement in his tone but Tucker didn't take offense. It was a little funny. If he could look at it objectively.

"She doesn't want to be romanced."

Ty nodded. "And that leaves you kind of floating in unfamiliar waters, huh, big brother?"

He didn't answer. He didn't need to.

Women always wanted to be romanced. By him. His reputation wasn't just that he was sexy or sweet, he was romantic, dammit. He loved wooing women. Sure, most of them were pretty easy—that went back to the sweet girls from Sapphire Falls who had basic expectations. He could blow the other guys out of the water with very little effort.

Which maybe didn't make him Romeo, but it did make him the most eligible bachelor.

"So what does she want?" Ty asked.

"Sex."

"And that frustrates you why?" Ty asked.

"Because I'm kind of a dumbass apparently," Tucker said.

He should just take the three-times-a-day hottest-sex-of-his-life and the girl who loved to go down on him and who would strip naked in a *hayloft* for him and be grateful.

He should wallow in it. He should take every advantage. He should make it five-times-a-day sex.

But something didn't sit right with him about that.

"So you're giving her what she wants—sex, help with the boys, time to get on her feet and no pressure."

Tucker nodded. "Yep. I'm a fricking saint."

Ty chuckled. "Yeah, well, being patient when you're madly in love is tough."

Tucker looked at his brother again and opened his mouth, but Ty shook his head.

"Nope. Still here about you this time."

Damn.

And then Tucker lost all track of how weird his brother was acting.

Delaney had started toward Phoebe's truck with the girls.

He jumped off the tailgate and headed across the grass. "Hey, ladies."

Phoebe turned and grinned up at him. She was also effectively blocking him from getting to Delaney unless he picked her up and set her out of the way. Which he could do.

"Hey, Tucker."

"What's going on?"

"We're taking Delaney over to Kate and Levi's place."

His gaze went to where Delaney was getting up into

Phoebe's truck. "Why?"

"She's going to redo their kitchen," Phoebe said. "She got all excited talking about it and insisted on seeing it right now."

"Now?"

Phoebe laughed. "She's a little drunk."

Tucker frowned at that, but he could hear Delaney laughing with Kate from the cab of the truck. He sighed. "Fine. I'll follow you over there." He peered down at Phoebe. "You sober enough to drive?"

She laughed again and turned toward the truck. "It's a mile across a field. We're fine."

Ty insisted on coming along. As did Joe, Phoebe's husband, Travis and Lauren, and of course, Levi.

Kate and Delaney went through the house, and it seemed that Delaney's voice got louder and more excited in every room. She was also still carrying a mason jar of Booze and he suspected someone—namely Phoebe—was keeping it filled.

Tucker, Ty, Joe, Levi and Travis sat in the living room.

The women went from room to room like a gaggle of geese.

"The hardwood is amazing," Delaney said. For the third time. This time she was running her hand over the mantel of the fireplace.

Which put her directly in front of Tucker.

He felt himself smiling as she exclaimed over the stonework around the fireplace and the hearth. She really loved this stuff. And she was really beautiful when she was excited. And when she ran her hands over the wood and the stone, his jeans got a little tighter in front.

"You have to let me redo these floors," she said to Kate.

"The floors?" Kate asked.

"There is one hundred percent chance that there is hardwood under here," Delaney said. "This house is old enough that it *has* to have hardwood floors."

"Seriously?" Kate's eyes got wide as she looked around the living room. She eventually focused on Levi. "What do you think?"

"Tear up the carpet and everything to get to the hardwood floors?" Levi asked.

Delaney nodded.

He shrugged. "Okay."

Delaney looked like he'd told her she could have a puppy for Christmas.

"What about Tucker's house?" Kate asked. "Aren't you busy over there?"

She definitely was. Tucker worked on not reacting, since his brothers were watching him.

"Oh, sure, in the kitchen," she said. "But Tucker's house is only ten years old. It needs some updating, but there are no hidden treasures."

Tucker's eyebrows went up at that.

"Hidden treasures?" Kate asked.

"Like the hardwood floors here," she said. "Or the crown molding." She pointed to the top of the doorway behind Kate.

She said crown molding the way Tucker would expect her to say hot fudge—with clear delight and a little bit of a moan.

Tucker shifted on the couch.

"This farmhouse is a hundred years old," she said. "They don't build like this anymore."

Tucker knew she wasn't specifically talking about something *he* hadn't done well in his house, but it was clear that she was far more excited about working at Levi's place than she was about his house. And he didn't like that. No matter how stupid that sounded.

"They told me the house was eighty years old when I bought it," Levi said.

She shook her head. "One hundred. At least. Of course

they maybe didn't have records of all of that back then."

"So you can really do some stuff here?" Kate asked. "Not just the kitchen?"

Delaney nodded. "I would love to reconstruct the banister on the staircase. It looks like they tried to take it out or something at some point. I could restore it back to how it looked originally. And that kitchen..."

She trailed off on a sigh that Tucker knew didn't sound sexy only to him. She was completely turned-on by all of this renovation talk.

Lauren confirmed it when she said, "Definite girl crush."

It was a well-known fact that Lauren had been bi-sexual before meeting Travis. Or still was? Tucker wasn't sure how that worked, but he supposed Lauren still noticed attractive women, and men for that matter, just like Travis did.

Kate looked at Levi with wide eyes. "You up for this?"

Levi was watching Delaney and he nodded slowly. "Uh, yeah."

Tucker wanted to smack him.

"Tell me what you're going to do in the kitchen," Lauren said. "Travis's house is old too."

"Hey, that house is a family heirloom," Travis protested.

Delaney looked at him. "Exactly. All the more reason to preserve it and make sure everything will last for another hundred years."

Travis nodded. "It's got crown molding and hardwood floors too," he said. "And a fireplace. And there's a dumbwaiter."

Tucker frowned at him. It sounded like Travis was trying to impress her.

"No way." Delaney looked intrigued. "Does it work?"

"It does. But we don't use it."

"Where?" Lauren asked. She'd been living in the house

for two years.

"In the pantry. That little door behind the shelves."

Travis gave his wife a smile. "The pantry is the closet thing where we keep the canned food."

Everyone chuckled. It was also a well-known fact that Lauren didn't cook.

"So it's in the kitchen."

Travis nodded, his smile growing.

Lauren looked at Delaney. "I don't care then."

Delaney snorted. And it was adorable.

She, Lauren and Kate headed into the kitchen. Again. Phoebe came to sit on the arm of the sofa beside Joe.

"She's so cute with all of this," she said to Tucker.

He nodded. Cute. Yeah. That was one word.

"I can't believe you horned in on my date like this," he said.

"She's going home with you," Phoebe said with a laugh.

Yeah, she was. Because she had to.

But he squelched that thought. Where had that come from anyway? Did it matter why? She needed him. She was staying in his house because that was her only option at the moment. But he liked that. He liked being someone she needed. He'd always liked being someone people needed.

So what was his problem? He wanted her in his house because she *wanted* to be there. Well, that was stupid because she didn't have a choice right now and there was nothing either of them could do about it.

Maybe it was the Booze. He was getting thoughtful and grumpy.

"I just wanted her to have fun tonight," he finally said.

Ty laughed. "I'd say she's having a really good time."

Yeah, it was impossible to miss that Delaney was totally in her element right now.

Phoebe looked over at him. "Oh, I see. She's not having fun because of you directly."

He scowled. "That's not it."

Plus, it made him sound like an ass.

"That is so it," Phoebe said. "You want to be her big hero, but now she's having fun and making plans with other people."

Tucker sunk deeper into the couch cushions and wished he hadn't finished off his own jar of Booze.

"Aw, it's okay," Travis said. "She still likes you best."

"Probably," Ty agreed. "At least until she sees Trav's dumbwaiter."

Levi chuckled. "Who knew that *old* stuff would be such a turn on? I figured most girls like new and shiny stuff."

"Most of the girls in Vegas probably do," Joe teased his brother. Levi had been a big playboy in Sin City before he'd found his way to Sapphire Falls.

Tucker kept quiet. His instinct was to tell them all to shut the hell up. He didn't need to be Delaney's only friend or the only person who made her laugh. He knew his reaction to all of this was ridiculous. But he couldn't deny that he felt a little restless. Things between him and Delaney were solid—they had a connection that had actually existed for years before they even knew one another—but he also felt that things were very undecided. Tenuous even.

She was planning to leave at the end of the summer. The more people she bonded with here, the more friendships she had, the more projects, the less anxious she'd be to leave. It would increase the chances she'd come back to visit. Maybe, just maybe, she wouldn't even want to go at all.

But, yeah, okay, he wanted to be the real reason she stayed.

"Oh my gosh, this place is amazing," Delaney gushed, coming back into the room and giving Levi a huge, bright smile. "There's an outdoor covered walkway to the garden."

Levi chuckled. "I know."

"That's *amazing*," Delaney said again.

Tucker glanced around. Delaney's grin was contagious. Everyone in the room was smiling, caught up in her enthusiasm.

"Can I see the garden?"

Levi shrugged. "Nothing to see."

Delaney frowned at him. "You don't have a garden back there? No flowers? Nothing?"

"I don't have much of a green thumb," Levi said. "I was going to hire someone to do some landscaping—"

"I'll do it."

Delaney's words stopped Levi. He grinned. "Now you want to plant me a garden?"

She nodded. "And Kate says you can afford the best."

He laughed and looked at his girlfriend. "I can."

"Okay." Tucker got to his feet. He was no less conflicted now. The more she had to do, the more investments she made, the better. That made sense in his head. But he was still feeling damn selfish. Or jealous. Or something.

She was redoing his crappy kitchen, but it didn't excite her like Levi's covered walkway or Travis's stupid dumbwaiter.

"Maybe we should go before you get your sledgehammer out right here and now," he said to Delaney.

She smiled. "I don't need a sledgehammer for a garden."

Right.

He nodded. "These houses and their gardens aren't going anywhere. I think we need to get home."

She glanced at Lauren. "I was hoping we could go to Lauren and Travis's."

"Tonight?" Tucker asked.

"Yeah."

He shook his head. "I think it's time to go."

"But—"

"You have to finish my kitchen before you take on any others anyway, right?"

She shrugged. "Your kitchen will take like another two weeks."

His eyebrows go up. "You're going to make me new cupboards and install them in two weeks?"

"Well, I was thinking now I could buy some new ones and put them in. It would be faster."

That was *not* okay. "I want custom-made cabinets."

She looked surprised. "The ones we can buy will look nice. I'll be sure of it. You won't know the difference."

But he would. "I want to open those cupboards every day and know you made them for *me*."

She blinked at him. No one said a word.

Tucker stood looking at her. He meant it, dammit. Before she moved on to other projects, he wanted those cupboards in his kitchen.

That was probably symbolic of something else, but he had too much alcohol in his system to ponder that with any success.

She must have read something in his expression because she finally nodded. "Okay."

"Time to go," he said again.

She nodded again. "Okay."

He held out his hand and she stepped forward to take it. She glanced back at the girls, who were watching Tucker with surprised expressions.

Yeah, he wasn't known to be demanding or even firm. He was never jealous. And he never *insisted* a woman come home with him.

He'd never needed to.

And that was probably symbolic or something too.

They walked out to his truck without a word and he helped her up into the cab from the driver's side.

He started the truck and drove a half mile before she

said anything.

"Your friends are great."

He nodded. "They are. The best."

"I had fun tonight."

He couldn't help but smile at that. "I know."

"Thank you."

"Delaney," he said carefully. "I will always do whatever I can to make you happy."

Even if that meant letting her redo his friends' houses and plant gardens for other guys. It was stupid to even be slightly jealous of that. It was a garden. And Levi was happily involved and over the moon in love with Kate.

"I know."

He glanced over. She seemed sincere. And that mattered to him. A lot. That she knew he was here for her.

"But we talked about the two things you could give me that would make me the happiest, right?"

He swallowed. "Yeah."

"Your kitchen and your body."

"Yeah." She did not need to remind him.

"And you're worried that I'm finding other kitchens."

He nodded. Having a conversation like this after Booze was maybe not a great idea, but then again, Booze had a way of morphing into a truth serum when it hit the bloodstream. He hadn't had enough to be drunk or impair his driving, but he'd had enough to lower his inhibitions and make him completely honest. And Delaney had *definitely* had enough for all of the above.

"Tucker," she said, when he didn't reply for several heartbeats. "Pull the truck over."

He shouldn't. He wanted to talk and he already knew that tone in her voice. She wasn't thinking about talking.

And what was he going to say? *Please don't ever redo anyone else's kitchen. Don't be friends with anyone but me. Don't let anyone else give you anything you need.*

He couldn't say any of those things. He didn't even

really mean them. Exactly.

"Tucker."

He glanced at her, knowing it was a bad idea even as he did it.

"Please."

Yeah, he couldn't resist that.

He sighed. "Give me a mile." There was a small grove of trees ahead where they could pull in.

A couple minutes later, they were nestled amidst the trees and Tucker killed the engine.

"I'm sorry," he said before she could speak.

"For what?" She slid across the seat and moved into his lap. She straddled him and put her hands on his face, looking directly into his eyes.

They'd both had too much to drink. It had been only a couple of days. He needed to keep his mouth shut.

Of course, knowing that and doing that were two different things.

"I'm sorry that I feel like I need to be the only one who's important to you."

"Do you feel that way?" she asked.

"I do. Which is crazy because I also love seeing you with my friends. I know some of the best people in the world and I want to share the best of everything with you."

"Tucker," she said solemnly—or at least as solemnly as Booze would allow anyone to be. "I want to do those other kitchens and things, but those projects will end. Your body, on the other hand, is something I don't think I'll ever be done with."

"Stay."

Tucker heard the word come out, knew it was his voice, had wanted to say it almost since he'd met her, but blurting it out at that moment was completely the Booze's fault.

"I'm not going anywhere."

She leaned in to kiss him and he did the unthinkable…he pulled back.

She frowned. "What?"

"I don't mean right now. I don't mean tonight. I mean…stay. Here in Sapphire Falls. With the boys. Don't go to Colorado."

She sat back slightly. "You're drunk. We're both drunk."

"That doesn't matter. You know I want this."

"Tuck—"

"I've always wanted it. Always. But it wasn't right. It wasn't time, until you got here."

"It's about the boys."

"No."

"Yes," she said firmly. "This is about the boys, about the instant family, about missing Rafe. You want things to always be like they've always been. And I get that." She took a deep breath. "You have a wonderful life. You have the home, the town, the job, the family and friends that you want and need. You only need to add a wife and kids to have the whole picture. And here we are. Readymade."

He shook his head. "It's you, Delaney. I could have had all of that several times over if I was looking for just any woman and kids to fill in the blanks."

"But you love being the hero, and none of the other girls have *needed* you like I do."

"That's—" Okay, that was true, but it was *not* the whole story. "I'm in love with you. I haven't been in love before."

Delaney paused, clearly surprised by his proclamation. Then she laughed.

That was definitely not what he'd expected.

"Oh, Tucker, that's crazy."

He frowned. "Really? You don't feel it at all?"

"I feel like it could happen, like maybe it's already started, but I know this is about the boys right now. There's no way you could be in love with me. You don't *know* me. I do believe that you're in love with the boys and with the idea of being their dad. Not just a dad, but *their* dad. I do believe that. I also believe the boys would be so, so lucky to have you and there might not be a better man out there for them."

"So stay." Tucker felt his fingers curl into her hips and had to force himself to relax.

"Because of the boys? Is that really enough for either one of us?" she asked.

"It's more than that," he said confidently. "I know it. You'll see over time."

She shook her head and she looked sad. "I'll always wonder if we're only together because of the boys. And that's not enough. We both deserve more, Tucker."

"And if you run off to Colorado, we'll never know. It's not enough time."

He was losing her and he didn't even really have her.

"I—" She started. Then she stopped and shook her head. "You are really good for the boys. This whole town is. But I can't be *with* you just because of that. I want you involved in their lives though."

"I want you too."

"And I want us to both know that we're really in love. Right now, I need to live at your house. I appreciate your help. I love how you are with the boys and how they are with you. I also love sex with you and I love talking about Rafe and Chelsea with you."

"So what else is there?" he asked. Seriously. "Liking each other, enjoying being together, supporting each other. Isn't that what it's about?"

She took a deep breath and slid off of his lap.

That wasn't good.

"You're not going to like my answer."

Somehow he believed that one hundred percent.

"Tell me anyway."

"I want to be like Chelsea."

"What does that mean?" He felt his gut knotting as he

waited for her answer.

"She didn't *need* Rafe. My sister was strong, sure, completely great on her own. She was with Rafe because she *wanted* to be."

Tucker bit back the first words that rushed to his tongue. He couldn't let her devotion to her sister make him crazy. Chelsea was a part of who Delaney was, even more so than his brothers were a part of him. And Chelsea was gone. He knew that after someone died it was easy to focus on the good stuff, to idolize them even more. He couldn't take that away from Delaney.

"So because you think you're dependent on me for a roof over your head and help with the boys right now, you don't think you can also *want* to be with me."

"I just don't know what's really true and it's not fair to you," she said.

"What if I don't care if it's fair?" He wasn't sure he did. He just wanted her.

"*I* care if it's fair," she said. "And how I feel matters too, Tucker."

He sighed. "Of course it does."

"I told you all of this. No matter how I feel or think I feel or what I want, if I get involved with you now, I will always think I took the easy way out. I know *all* about the easy way. I've done *everything* that way. I never got really involved with a guy because it was easier to lean on the relationships with Chelsea and her family that I already had. It was easier to tell myself I was too busy and too committed and that I already had too many people to think about than to really work on a relationship. I never went to college. I never applied or interviewed for a real job. Never had a boss who was hard on me. I never had to worry about bills. Hell, I never even learned how to cook. Trust me when I say that I know very well if I get involved with you right now, it will never be tough or hard or scary."

That was…nice. A compliment of sorts, actually.

Exactly how he would want her to feel.

And it was what was keeping her from him.

Being helpful and supportive and dependable was *keeping* the woman of his dreams from him.

That was so fucked up.

He didn't have anything else to say to that.

He wanted to talk. He wanted to tell her about the track project and introduce her to his mom and dad and tell her his favorite color and song and book. But he knew that if they stayed here, she would only want a quickie in the front seat of his truck.

Delaney didn't want to get to know him. He hadn't had to worry about that before. All the girls he'd dated already knew him. And had met his mom and dad.

Now the one that he *wanted* to want to get to know him was only here for the sex.

And he didn't want a quickie in the front seat of his truck with the hot girl he was crazy about.

His entire world was completely messed up.

His brothers would get such a kick out of that.

Which meant there was no way in hell he was going to tell them.

CHAPTER TEN

The next morning came early. Delaney hadn't been hung over in a really, really long time, and the Sapphire Falls Booze produced a whopper.

It didn't help that she'd barely slept. She'd tossed and turned and stared at her ceiling in between fitful dreams of Tucker. The thing was, she might have been able to convince herself that it was sexual deprivation keeping her awake, but her dreams weren't of the two of them burning up the sheets. They included white dresses and flowers and a church.

A church that looked a lot like the one just off the square in Sapphire Falls.

A church she had driven past exactly once in her life.

How was it showing up in her dreams?

She showered quickly and pulled her still-wet hair up on top of her head and slipped into jeans and a T-shirt. One thing about hanging out on the farm for the summer was that she already had the right wardrobe for it.

She made her way downstairs and, as was becoming a daily habit, was incredibly grateful to Tucker for something. He and the boys were already gone. She could get her headache under control before lunchtime.

She headed for the kitchen and stopped in the middle of the mess that was still taking up the entire room. Oh, yeah. Crap. She needed coffee and this mess—and the lack of an easily accessible coffeepot—was all her fault.

There was a loud knock at the back kitchen door and a hello a moment later.

She'd taken one step to answer the door when TJ Bennett let himself into the kitchen.

"Um, hi."

The guy was so big. And intimidating. But he had two Styrofoam cups of coffee, so she decided she needed to be really nice to him. He was also the plumber who was going to help her put a new sink in Tucker's kitchen. Not a small job.

"'Morning," he said. And he smiled.

Delaney actually sucked in a quick breath. Damn. Intimidating wasn't the first word to come to mind now. The Bennett smiles should come with a warning.

"I didn't expect you so early," she said. Stupidly. Until she'd seen him, she'd forgotten about him coming over to help completely.

"It's nine-thirty."

Right, and this was the farm. The day started as soon as the roosters were up. She didn't know what time that was, exactly, but she was guessing it was before nine-thirty.

"Long night," she said.

He handed her one of the coffee cups—bless him.

"Booze is tough the first time."

She nodded and sipped. Then she thought about that. "How'd you know about the Booze?"

"I know everyone who was at the party."

"And you've talked to them all already?" And what had they said about her?

"Two of them." He shrugged. "And it's nine-thirty."

Right. Half the day was apparently done according to him. Great.

She took another big drink of coffee.

"Is your head going to be able to handle my music?" TJ set a boom box that looked like it had been new in the early nineties on the table.

"Music?"

"Country."

"I love country."

He looked at her. "Good country."

"I lived in Nashville for thirteen years. I know good country," she said.

"You lived in Nashville in the last thirteen years. I'm

227

talking *good* country."

"Such as?"

"Such as Johnny Cash and Waylon Jennings and Willie Nelson."

She wrinkled her nose. "No one from the last two decades?"

"There's a plumber in Langley who likes Garth Brooks."

"I love Garth Brooks."

"And Dierks Bentley."

"Great."

"And Kip Moore."

"Awesome."

"And Justin Timberlake."

"That's…oh." She frowned. Justin Timberlake was hot, no question, but his music was definitely not her style. She could not listen to that all day while working. "How is that even possible?" Kip Moore and Justin Timberlake weren't even close.

TJ shrugged. "I could call him for you."

"Uh, no." It wasn't that she didn't like Willie and Johnny. It was older country, from before she'd realized that she was a country-music girl at heart, but it was guitars and husky voices and songs about drinking and partying and falling in love. She could do that. Besides, it should only take TJ a day or so to move the pipes she needed. "Let's just keep the volume at like medium level until the coffee kicks in, okay?"

"You got it." TJ held out his hand.

She looked and saw two orange capsules in his palm. Ibuprofen, she would bet.

She took them gratefully and swallowed them with a shot of not-wonderful-but-hot-and-caffeinated coffee.

"Okay, so." She surveyed the room. "I'm thinking about putting the new cabinets all along this wall," she said, pointing. "So I'm thinking we could move the sink over to this wall." She pointed at the perpendicular wall.

TJ shrugged. "Can do. But you'll lose the window."

"Well…"

He cocked an eyebrow. "You're going to cut a new window?"

"I was thinking about it."

He chuckled. "This is great."

"Yeah?" Maybe he'd even help her cut the window and install the glass. If she let him listen to more Johnny. "Have you ever installed a window before?"

He nodded. "Yep. But I was referring to the fact that you're completely not what Tucker expected."

She bit her bottom lip. Yeah, she obviously wasn't. "I'm driving him crazy already?" she asked. Tucker had evidently confided in his brother.

"Oh, yeah," TJ said. "You're driving him crazy all right. And it's all about a kitchen that won't be producing cobbler for a very long time."

"Or ever," she said. "If it's up to me."

TJ laughed. "Even better."

Her head hurt too much to pursue that. They had at least a couple of days together. TJ Bennett didn't strike her as the talkative type. That was a really good thing. People around here talked *a lot*.

∽∾

They all fell into a predictable pattern over the next week. Delaney, Tucker and the boys had breakfast together in the mornings—mostly cereal and fruit since those were no-cook items. Then the guys headed out for work and play. TJ showed up around nine-thirty or ten and stayed until about two. The plumbing was done in two days as expected, but he continued to show up and help her with bigger projects, like the new window. Before and after TJ was there, Delaney worked on other smaller projects she could do on her own, like the flooring and painting.

Tucker and the boys came back for lunch each day, and at the end of the day, Delaney tried to be finished and cleaned up by the time they got home from dinner at Tucker's mom's house. He always brought her a plate and it was always delicious, but she heard zero about joining them over there for dinner and she wasn't about to bring it up.

It was fine. Tucker didn't take girls to family dinners. He also didn't do casual sex. And he was mad at her.

She'd said no to staying in Sapphire Falls with him, so her dinner invitations and her quickies in the barn had apparently been revoked. In spite of him repeatedly saying he'd give her whatever she needed, they hadn't even kissed since the night they'd gone to the bonfire. The only time they spent together was with the boys. She went to the barn every night after the boys were in bed to work on the cabinets, but Tucker never followed her out there.

And it was fine. Easier really. Lord knew, saying no to him had gotten progressively harder.

By Friday, the floor and painting were all finished.

"Looks good," TJ said, coming in through the back door, as always. With two cups of coffee, as always.

Delaney really liked him. She'd gotten used to the not-wonderful coffee, she'd developed a new liking for Willie Nelson and TJ was a great work partner—who didn't ask a lot of personal questions or talk a lot. They chatted, of course. Casually. About a variety of things. He made it comfortable to talk about Rafe and Chelsea. He asked about her work in Tennessee. They talked country music. He was smart and funny, like Tucker. But unlike Tucker, he didn't talk about her staying in Sapphire Falls and he hadn't proposed even once.

"Thanks. I'm happy with it," she said. "Countertops, sink and cupboard doors and we're done."

"Well, let's go," he said. "Got a call from the place in

Grand Island. We can pick the countertop and sink up today."

That improved her mood vastly. "You don't have to go with me," she said. "I can go get them."

"How are you going to unload that countertop when you get back?" he asked.

The guys at the marble place would load it for her, but, yeah, there was no way she was getting it into the house by herself. "I can call you when I get back."

"You can't get any of that into your little Jeep," TJ said. "Come on. Let's go."

She admitted he was right about that too. "Okay, fine. Let me grab my purse."

They were back in Sapphire Falls a few hours later and Delaney was excited to get the new stuff into Tucker's kitchen. It was only about one in the afternoon. She could maybe get it all in before they were home tonight.

She looked at the clock again. Damn. It was one in the afternoon. She hadn't been home for lunch. She grabbed her phone and, sure enough, there were two calls from Tucker and two texts.

Crap. She should have left a note.

"Hey, want to see something?" TJ asked as they passed the *Welcome to Sapphire Falls* sign at the edge of town.

"Sure. What?"

"Just hang on." He turned into town.

Delaney decided she'd rather text Tucker than call so she typed in a quick message. "Sorry, forgot to leave a note. Had to pick some stuff up. I'm fine. See you tonight."

She hit send just as TJ pulled the truck to a stop and shifted into park.

"What do you think?"

She looked at him and then around at where they were parked. They were at a curb on a residential street lined with huge trees. The houses were a combination of old and new, two-story and ranch. It was clear the town didn't have any ordinances about what kind of structures could be built in various areas like some did. Obviously anything went.

It was a typical all-American, small-town street. And something in her ached strangely at the sight.

"What am I looking for?" she asked.

"This one."

He pointed to the house across the street from where they were parked. It was an old house—probably close to a hundred years. It was two-story, mostly brick, with six steps leading to a porch that occupied two sides of the house. There was a two-car garage with a long driveway and six large trees around the perimeter of the huge yard. The paint and roof were in good shape but the lawn was overgrown and the flowerbeds were empty.

"It's beautiful," she said. Or it had been anyway. It looked neglected but had clearly been a nice home in its day.

"The Griffin place. It's the second-oldest house in town," TJ said. "And it's for sale. Has been for a while."

She looked at him. "What are you thinking here?"

"It's a historic house. It's been here forever," he said. "But the woman who lived in it passed away and has no family. No one wants it. But no one wants to see it crumble and no one wants to tear it down either. I think it could be a really nice home again, but it needs some work."

"Okay." She studied the house again. She agreed with him. It looked like it needed some updating, and depending on how well the house had been cared for inside, could be restored to a gorgeous home.

"Was thinking I might buy it," TJ said.

"You have a house. On a farm," she said. "You're not looking to move into town."

"No. But I could buy it, hire someone to fix it up and then resell it. Flip it, right?"

She knew all about flipping. Her heart thumped. She knew what TJ was thinking now. A whole house project she could do her way? She had done several whole houses with Rafe and Chelsea, but she had always been outvoted when she and Chelsea had differing opinions. It wasn't fair that Rafe was always the tiebreaker and he was sleeping with one of them. Delaney never won. If she was on her own, she could do whatever she wanted.

"You could definitely flip this place."

"And I know someone who's kind of expert at this kind of thing."

She smiled at him. "You don't owe me any favors, TJ."

He shook his head. "Not a favor. The bank now owns the house. They want to get rid of it, so they'll give me a really good deal. I've been thinking about it for a while because it bugs me that it's just sitting here. But I didn't want to take all the work on myself."

She turned on the seat and looked at the house. "You really want to do this? You're serious?"

"I do. Why not? We need to preserve these old houses."

She pressed her lips together. The only drawback was that she would still be working for someone else. TJ didn't strike her as the type to argue color palates, but she didn't really know him that well.

"Can we see the inside?"

"Yep."

TJ must have been serious about considering buying and fixing the place up because he had a key. He let them in through the front door.

Forty minutes later, Delaney was in love.

The house was gorgeous. It had been magnificent in the day. It hadn't had anything done to it in decades, but there was potential everywhere she turned. There were window seats in two of the bedrooms, a sunroom at the back of the house, gorgeous woodwork, hardwood floors in the dining room that she was positive would extend under the carpet in the living room and it even had a dumbwaiter.

She grinned. It was a silly thing to be excited about, but

those special little quirks were what made old houses so much fun to restore.

"I love this place," she finally said with a huge sigh when they were back out on the porch.

TJ chuckled. "No kidding. You were…pretty worked up going through it."

She blushed and put her hands to her cheeks. Rafe had always teased her about getting turned-on by renovations. She would flush and breathe fast and the adrenaline would pump like it did with any good physical arousal.

"Sorry, I get carried away."

TJ shook his head. "It's great. That's exactly why people will want you working on their houses. Your obvious passion."

She didn't know what to say to that. She didn't intend to work on people's houses anymore. But that was such a depressing thought, especially after coming out of the Griffin place, that she decided to ignore it at the moment.

"So you want to do it?" he asked, pocketing the key.

She did. She really, really did. The house would be a big project. But now that she knew it was here, now that she had seen all the nooks and features, she couldn't stand the idea that it would sit and slowly decay or that someone might come in a bulldoze it. Or even that someone might come and live it in without really letting the house shine. What if they carpeted over the rest of the hardwood floors? What if they painted the woodwork? What if they took the wood-burning fireplace out and put in a gas one instead? No, she couldn't let someone else mess with this house.

"Yeah, I do." She knew she sounded breathless and was again a little embarrassed by the physical effects her desire for projects like this brought out. But she couldn't control it and the endorphin release felt good.

Especially since she hadn't had a good dose of endorphins from Tucker in several days.

"How did you know I would like this house?" she

asked, pushing Tucker to the back of her mind. Or trying to anyway. That was one negative about working every day with TJ—he reminded her a lot of his younger brother.

"Someone told me about your reactions when you were looking over Levi's house the other night."

She didn't remember every detail about that night but she could only imagine what her reactions had been like if she figured in the liquor she'd had in her system on top of her usual signs of arousal. "Tucker?" she asked.

"Uh, no." TJ chuckled. "I think Tucker might be annoyed by this actually."

"Annoyed? Really? Why?"

"Because he wants to be everything that makes you happy. And flushed," TJ added with a little wink.

Delaney shook her head. Damn, some girl was going to have to really watch out if TJ Bennett ever turned his attention on her full force.

"Well, I love this house," she told him.

"Great. Let's go talk to the bank."

"Right now?"

"Yes. Right now. I'm ready. How about you?"

"I've got some other projects I've committed to with Kate and Lauren." Her heart was racing. This was big. This would be all hers. Kate's and Lauren's projects would be fun but they would also be for *them*, not for her. They were smaller, simpler, less-expensive projects than this house. That meant they were safer. It was hard to tell what kind of issues an old house like this might have once they tore into the walls and floor. And what if she did something that no one else liked? They'd never sell the house. Or if she went over budget fixing things and TJ got in deeper than he wanted to be financially?

"You can do those after this," TJ said. "Kate and Lauren will understand we needed to move on this and get it flipped so it can attract a permanent owner."

"Are you sure, TJ? This could be…big. More

complicated—"

"I trust you, Delaney," he said. "Sure it's a risk, but that will make it even better when it's done and amazing."

She thought about that. Everything she was in the midst of was a risk in some way—raising the boys, figuring out what she wanted to do with her life, moving to Colorado. There had been a whole host of things that had come at her over the past several weeks that she had not been ready for—some good, some bad. But they had all led her to where she was at this moment. And yeah, it really would feel amazing when everything was worked out.

She took a deep breath. Could she handle this big project all by herself, making every decision, dealing with every problem, being completely in charge?

She looked up at TJ. "Okay, I'm ready."

Tucker took the boys to the diner for burgers for lunch on Monday. Not only were the burgers pretty good, but he liked showing the boys off around town and giving the kids a taste of small-town life where everyone knew who they were and cared.

And he wasn't sure he could stand yet another lunch with Delaney—being around her, seeing her smile and hearing her laugh and watching her hug on the boys and not being able to touch her or hug her himself. Of course, the ban on touching was self-inflicted. But it was still driving him crazy.

"Hey, guys," he greeted the older men who clustered in the middle of the diner with the Formica-topped tables pulled together and chairs arranged haphazardly.

They were wrapping up their morning business as it was almost eleven and settling their bills. Though what these guys, who had all lived together in the same town all their lives, could talk about for almost four hours every weekday morning was beyond Tucker. Then he laughed. He and Travis and Levi and Joe and the rest of the guys would likely be right here taking over these chairs one day, and he didn't expect any of them would run out of things to say to one another.

He chose the big curved booth in the corner where all five of them could fit comfortably. Dottie brought water for everyone, and Tucker agreed on milkshakes *after* their meals were finished. They placed their orders, then Henry went to check out the jukebox, Charlie had his iPad to keep him busy, and Jack and David set to work coloring on the back of the placemats.

"Heard TJ cosigned that loan for the Griffin place," Frank, the ex-postmaster, called out from where he was third in line at the cash register.

Tucker had no idea what he was talking about, but there was only one TJ in town. Why would his brother care about the old Griffin place? Tucker swiveled in the booth to look at Frank more directly. "Oh, yeah? Cosigned for who?"

TJ was as conservative with his money as he was with his humor. He'd share it with family and those close to him, but it was still in small increments.

"That pretty Callan girl," Frank said. "You know her."

Yeah, he sure did know that pretty Callan girl. What the *fuck* was Frank talking about? Delaney? The Griffin place? With TJ?

"You sure you got that right, Frank?" Tucker asked. But that was a dumb question. These guys had an uncanny accuracy in their gossip.

Frank chuckled. "Heard it from Willis myself. He was in for fried eggs and ham earlier."

Willis was Denny Willis, the only realtor in town. What his breakfast choice had to do with the conversation, Tucker couldn't say though.

"He had bacon," Conrad, one of Frank's cronies, said.

"And the eggs were scrambled," Albert, another of the

regular breakfast crowd, added.

Tucker really didn't care about Willis's egg preference. Except, of course, that it might mean what Frank was reporting about Delany wasn't one-hundred percent accurate either. "What did you hear from Willis exactly?" Tucker asked.

"That TJ and that Callan girl—"

"Delaney," Tucker said, in harmony with Conrad, Albert and Ben. Clearly, Frank was the only one who didn't know her first name.

"That TJ and *Delaney*," Frank started again, "took a look at the place on Friday and went to talk to the bank that same day."

"So glad TJ can help her out," Conrad said. "So sad that she's all on her own now that Rafe and her sister died."

"That was such a tragedy," Albert added at that point.

"I was so sorry to hear about it," Ben added.

Tucker nodded. They had all offered their condolences when it had first become known that Rafe had passed too. "But she's not alone," Tucker felt compelled to point out.

"Well, clearly," Frank said. "TJ is helping her with everything."

TJ.

As far as the town knew, Delaney wasn't alone because of *TJ*? Just what the hell had been going on?

Tucker opened his mouth to respond to that but noticed Henry next to the jukebox listening intently. Tucker thought about his words before replying. "Delaney and the boys have been staying at my place," he said. He'd honestly thought that was common knowledge. It was difficult to sneeze in this town without someone asking if you were feeling better a week later.

"Ogden told us they'd been in for supplies together because they're working on your kitchen," Ben said.

George Ogden ran the hardware store. So the only thing about Tucker's place that mattered was that his kitchen was being remodeled? "Did he?" Tucker knew TJ had been helping Delaney with some of the plumbing, but honestly, how long did that take, and how involved did that have to be?

"Yep, said they'd been in a few times. And they headed over to Grand Island together the other day."

Grand Island. That was over an hour from Sapphire Falls. Making a run for supplies for the kitchen didn't exactly equate to a date but it sat wrong with Tucker. What was that all about? And why didn't Tucker know about it? Or about the Griffin place?

Tucker supposed that TJ and Delaney might need some supplies from a hardware store for the restoration project. It simply hadn't occurred to Tucker that there would be multiple errands, *together*, or that those errands would extend outside of Sapphire Falls or get so much notice. Or that the town would assume that meant TJ was the one who was there for Delaney, helping her with everything.

And it certainly hadn't occurred to Tucker how pissed off he would feel hearing that was the case.

Of course, now it seemed obvious that those assumptions would be there and that he'd be pissed off about them.

Maybe what hadn't occurred to him was that his own *brother* could be moving in on Delaney.

Dottie emerged from the kitchen with the food and the boys all immediately put electronics and crayons away and dug in. The fresh air and hard work had been good for their sleeping habits and for their appetites. But suddenly, Tucker didn't care about his burger or the best fries in six counties.

Sapphire Falls was speculating over Delaney and *TJ*. Speculating was a favorite pastime in Sapphire Falls. There was speculation over everything from what Adrianne's cupcake flavor of the month would be to what Cari and Brandon Sutter were going to name their fourth baby.

"They make a cute couple," Conrad said. "That TJ will make some girl a great husband. Michelle did a number on him. I've always thought that was such a shame."

Michelle had indeed done a number on TJ. But his brother's broken heart wasn't going to be healed by Delaney.

No way.

"That girl needs some help with those four boys," Conrad agreed. "What's she gonna do without a husband?"

And *that* sat wrong with Tucker too.

Delaney didn't need TJ. Delaney didn't *need* anyone. That fact was what was making *his* life so difficult.

He kind of wished she did need him. Kind of. It was a little part of him. Tiny. And not one he was really proud of. But it was there.

Maybe it was old-fashioned. Caveman-like. Chauvinistic even. But dammit, yes, he wished she would lean on him. That she needed him to fix everything for her. That she'd even *ask* him for help and then be grateful and thank him every day with a home-cooked meal and hot sex.

Okay, so none of that was something he would *ever* say out loud to anyone. He would *never* admit it to her—or his mother or his sister-in-law or any of the other strong, independent, amazing women he knew. Or really ninety percent of the women he knew. But it was a natural instinct to look at her and want to take care of her and be her everything. And yeah, okay, have her *realize* it.

He could certainly live with the woman in his life being completely fine without him, but *wanting him anyway*.

So far, he wasn't convinced that Delaney wanted him for anything more than sex.

ॐ

Delaney heard the guys come home. It was hard to miss even over the radio playing an old Loretta Lynn song. The four boys made noise wherever they went. She grinned as she turned the music down. She had finished the tile backsplash behind the sink and along the length of the countertop. She stepped back and wiped her hands on the cloth she had tucked in her back pocket. It looked great and she was excited. The colors and patterns were really coming together. The sand-and-coffee-colored tiles interspersed with the predominantly cream tiles really brought out the rich brown and tan marbling in the granite countertop. The soft browns worked beautifully with the wood that was already present in the house. She had the base of the counters built, the counter in place and now just needed to put on the cupboard doors. Similarly, the upper cupboards were built but needed shelves and doors.

All she needed to do to complete them was figure out what she wanted to do on the doors. She kept getting stuck. She had them cut, sanded and stained, but now she wanted to carve something or do some kind of decorative marking on the front to make them special. Every time she went out there to do it, she found herself just staring. And thinking.

What was holding her back was the idea that this was permanent. This was going to be a part of Tucker's house—his life even, though that sounded pretty dramatic for cupboard doors—for years to come. He would think of her every time he looked at them.

She wanted it to be significant.

Which was way overthinking her woodworking. It was more thought and emotion than she'd put into her work in a very long time. She did custom cupboards and things all the time for clients, but they were...clients. They were not...Tucker. Whatever he was.

Her friend. Her lover. Her landlord.

None of those were adequate. None of those encompassed the idea that she wanted there to be a permanent mark from her in his life.

Maybe people should always want to permanently mark

241

the lives of the people they shared their bodies with, but she wasn't naïve enough to think it really happened that way all the time. And she was self-aware enough to know that she hadn't wanted to permanently mark any of her past boyfriends' lives. Or vice versa. They had been passing through her life and somehow she had always known that.

But Tucker had put the kibosh on the lover thing over a week ago after the bonfire anyway.

Was that why the cupboards had suddenly become more important? It was the thing she was going to leave behind when she left?

Delaney rubbed her forehead. This was ridiculous. She was making way too big a deal out of this.

Which probably meant that the temporary part of the living situation was a good thing and made her think the house in town was an even better idea. If she could get the kitchen and bathrooms working and the bedrooms repainted and re-carpeted, they could move in there sooner rather than later if things got more complicated with Tucker and her.

She heard the boys' feet on the steps pounding upstairs, likely to change out of their dirty things and wash up. She had a casserole from Adrianne in the fridge, which was now back in place, and soup for the crockpot from Phoebe. Not that she'd realized what time it was or even thought about putting either in ahead of time to get done.

Dammit.

One of these days soon, she was going to have to figure out a way to feed the boys and get her work done at the same time.

The crockpot seemed like a promising idea. Phoebe had included a print-off of about six other recipes that seemed simple enough. Get the ingredients, throw them into the pot and turn it on, eight hours later, dinner was ready. She could handle that. Or teach Henry to handle that maybe.

"You *bought a house*?"

Delaney turned to face Tucker, who stood in the kitchen doorway looking big and delicious and pissed off.

And he'd already heard about the house. "You heard about that?"

"Yes, at the diner. First thing when I walked in practically."

She and TJ had talked to the bank on Friday, but it took until today, Monday, to get everything ready for signatures.

Sunday her father had called.

He'd set up an appointment at a private school in Denver for her and the boys. For Wednesday.

Her stomach in knots, she'd told him they couldn't make it on such short notice, and he'd insisted she make it work because the spots would surely go to someone else if she put off the meeting.

Suddenly, it had all become clear. The boys couldn't go to a private school in Denver, with a grandfather they'd never met and who had never wanted to know them making all the decisions. They needed Sapphire Falls.

They needed friends they would meet in grade school and stay close to their entire lives. They needed an annual summer festival where they could get sick on the Tilt-A-Whirl and have their first kiss on the Ferris wheel. They needed to skinny-dip and sleep out under the stars and, as much as she hated to think about it, get drunk on Booze around a campfire at the river. And someday, they needed to celebrate falling in love with Mrs. Bennett's German chocolate cake.

All of the things on Rafe's list were meant for his boys as well.

She needed to keep them here and give them the same childhood that had made some of the best men she knew into who they were—Rafe, Tucker, TJ, and Travis.

If she wanted to do her best for the boys, she needed to raise them in Sapphire Falls.

She'd told her father as much and had hung up on his

blustering and shouting.

Then, at eight a.m. Monday morning, she'd been the one carrying the two Styrofoam cups full of coffee when she'd met TJ at his house. She'd greeted him with, "*I* want to buy the house for the boys."

They'd gone to the bank, gone through the entire loan process again—including TJ cosigning for her—and redone all the paperwork. But TJ had done it with a smile, and Delaney had done it with happy butterflies in her stomach.

"It *just* happened."

"Like four hours ago," Tucker said. "In this town, that's like two weeks."

She smiled at that. "Oh, well, yeah. The Griffin place." She shrugged. "Seems everyone in town knows it that way."

"Everyone in town does know it that way. Betty Griffin lived in that house for fifty years. It's been empty for about five years now."

She nodded. "And Betty didn't update anything in the house since nineteen sixty-something. But it's got a lot of potential. TJ thinks we'll need to update plumbing but agreed the foundation and roof look good."

Tucker was clearly gritting his teeth. She frowned. "What?"

"Oh, don't mind me. I mean, you haven't in over a week."

She put her hands on her hips. "What's that mean?"

"It means that you work in here all day while I'm out, and then when the boys and I get home, you get them busy doing stuff in here. And after the boys head to bed, you go out to the barn and work."

"On *your* cabinets."

"I've barely seen you."

"You could come out to the barn anytime," she shot back.

She missed him too, terribly. But it was better this way.

He'd asked her to stay. And she wasn't sure she'd ever wanted anything more in her life. It was already so comfortable here, so happy, felt so much like home...it would be so, so easy to stay.

And there was that word again—easy.

"You know what would happen if I came down to the barn," he said. He sounded pissed but turned-on at the same time. Turned-on enough to get that little growl in his voice that made her tingle.

"I do know. I'm not the one who has a problem with that." And she didn't. Having sex with Tucker was one of the best things that had happened to her in months, and she would happily keep doing it all summer.

"You used Rafe's life insurance money for the house?" he asked, clearly changing the subject.

She nodded. "For the down payment and everything. But they still wanted a cosigner on the loan for the rest since I'm not from here and they don't know me."

He didn't say anything right away but she saw his jaw tense. Finally, he said, "I didn't even know you were interested in any other houses besides doing the work you and Kate and Lauren talked about."

"I wasn't. It probably wouldn't have even occurred to me if TJ hadn't wanted to show me the Griffin place. And I just intended to help him flip it. But then..." She took a breath. "I just decided to buy it myself last night, Tuck. I didn't know if TJ or the bank would go for that. Once it was a done deal, I planned to tell you as soon as I saw you."

Tucker was quiet for a moment. When he spoke again, his voice was low and tight. "It was TJ's idea?"

She nodded. "Yes. He said that he knew I'd love it. And he was right. It's a gorgeous old house that just needs some TLC."

"And why is TJ suddenly so interested in what you love and where you live?" Tucker asked.

She lifted her chin, somehow knowing what she was about to say was going to upset him. "Because I told him the reason I love doing renovations. And he understood that it's about more than the projects for me."

Tucker crossed his arms, his biceps bulging, looking pissed off and badass. And damn if her stomach, and other parts, didn't flip at the sight. "Tell *me* the reason you love doing renovations. I'd love to hear all about it."

And even though he was clearly quite angry, she believed him. She'd never doubted that he was interested in her. She might question some of the *reasons* he was interested, but the interest was real enough.

"I love fixing things. I love giving something that's broken or worn out or used up a new chance to shine."

He stood staring at her. He still looked angry, but he also looked surprised, if that was possible.

Delaney felt emotions building inside of her, bubbling up, rushing through her, things that she wasn't going to be able to hold back, things that had been tickling at the back of her mind over the past several days but that she hadn't really examined. Until right now.

"And you understand that, don't you, Tucker?" she asked. "You love fixing things too. But instead of furniture or houses, you fix things in this town and for the people here. You might think you're fixing a truck but you're really making things better for that person. You might think you're bringing a dirt-bike track here because you want it, but the truth is, it's something that will make this town better in a lot of ways—visitors and revenue and attention."

He didn't say anything, but some of the anger in his expression eased.

"And that's our problem," she said, the realization hitting her as she spoke. "You want to fix someone who wants to fix herself. There's no way for us to both be happy. Either I fix myself and I'm happy but you're not, or you fix things for me and you're happy but I'm not."

Tucker's jaw tensed again and he swallowed hard. "You want a second chance to shine."

His quiet words hit her directly in the heart. He got it even better than TJ had. TJ got that she liked the idea that things didn't become worthless just because they were broken or worn. But Tucker got how it applied to her.

"My family got broken up. But we—me and Chelsea and Rafe—put it back together, in a new way, and it was still good. Maybe even better. And now we're broken again, but there's a chance that we can fix it and make it good again. I have to believe that."

"And you'll do it."

His voice was gruff with emotion, though which emotion was hard to name.

"And you really want to help me do it," she said.

He nodded.

But she really wanted to do it by herself.

Chelsea and Rafe had been there the first time, doing it for her. Now she needed to know she could do it herself. She wanted to know that, even though she was incredibly grateful to her sister and Rafe for all they had done for her, she had learned from them and had grown up since they'd saved her from life as a sixteen-year-old runaway.

She remembered when she first realized that she'd left her parents' home with no plan B. If Rafe and Chelsea hadn't been willing or able to take her in, she would have been screwed. She had essentially crashed their lives—as newlyweds, as new parents, as a couple. She might not have had a typical, traditional experience, but neither had they. It had never been just the two of them. She'd always been there, the third wheel, the extra, the additional burden on the young couple's life.

Now she didn't want to be an extra or a burden or an obligation or responsibility.

She wanted to take care of herself. And the four boys that Rafe and Chelsea now needed her to take care of for them.

"If I wasn't a project, something to be fixed, do you think you'd be as attracted?" she asked Tucker.

He opened his mouth to reply, but she rushed ahead before he could. "None of the other girls here, the girls who should be perfect for you on paper, need fixing. And you haven't wanted any of them long-term. But with me, not knowing much besides the fact that I *do* need fixing, you were ready to get married on day one. That seems telling to me."

He didn't say anything at first. When he did, he completely surprised her.

"You and TJ have been spending a lot of time together."

Delaney felt her eyebrows rise. TJ? What did he have to do with anything? "He's been helping me with the kitchen."

"Yes. He's a saint."

There was a weird tone in his voice. "What are you not really saying?" she asked. "Clearly, there's something on your mind."

"You went to Grand Island with my brother."

"Yes, to get the countertop." She stepped out of the way and swept her hand over the smooth granite. "And the sink. For *your* kitchen," she added. He'd already seen it, of course, but he was acting as if they'd been on some big secret mission.

"My brother, who is a lot like me in some ways but who does *not* want to fix anyone. Who's completely over fixing women and who would be attracted to your strength and your desire to not lean on anyone."

She frowned. "What are you implying?"

"Did you eat while you were together?" he asked.

"What's that got to do with anything?"

"Did you?"

"Yes."

"Where?"

"Some steak place."

"Timothy's?"

"Yes, that was it."

"So you went on a date with my brother."

She laughed. She wasn't exactly amused. It was more that she was amazed by where this was going. She couldn't help it. He was acting ridiculous, and the idea that she and TJ had been on a date that day was crazy.

"In Sapphire Falls, as soon as you eat with someone you're on a date?" she asked. "You guys should print brochures up with all of these rules for newcomers so we don't accidentally have a cookie with a married guy or something."

Tucker didn't find that funny. His frown deepened.

She sighed. "We were there and hungry and he asked if I wanted to eat and I said yes. It wasn't a date. We were in jeans and T-shirts, we had just picked up a granite countertop and were coming back here to install it. Not exactly romantic."

Tucker scowled. "But it wasn't *not* a date because you didn't want it to be a date, only because of what you were wearing?"

She sighed. "No, of course not. I meant that no one thought it was a date. For any reason."

"You're not getting involved with my brother, Delaney."

She scowled back at him. "Of course not," she said again.

TJ was a good-looking guy, and they'd actually turned out to be a good pair with the renovation stuff. But she had no desire to date him. Or anything else.

The only person she had desire for was the one frowning at her right now and making her whole life and everything she thought she wanted muddled and confusing.

"Why didn't you tell me about it?"

"About Grand Island?"

"Yes."

"Where did you think this sink and countertop came from?"

He looked at the countertop and then back to her. "Yes, I assumed you had to pick it up or had it delivered. I didn't realize TJ was part of the whole thing."

"I didn't realize you didn't know and didn't realize you *needed* to know."

"Well, I do. Just like you should have told me about the Griffin place."

She moved in closer and looked up at him. "About buying the house or that TJ was involved?"

"Both. Especially the second."

"Why?"

He looked at her for a long few seconds, took a deep breath and said, "Because all you want is to fuck me, while you're letting my brother get to know you."

CHAPTER ELEVEN

Delaney reared back as if he'd slapped her. Or kicked her in the heart. "I…don't…I don't want… We get along and we've been working well together. That's all it is."

"I know it makes me sound like an asshole," Tucker said. "I know it sounds incredibly over-the-top, but I want to be the one you tell your stories to. I want to be the one who helps you when you need to pick something up in Grand Island. I want to be the one you go exploring old houses with."

She felt herself nodding. "I know."

"You're letting TJ closer than you're letting me."

In some ways, that was true. They'd talked music and tools. She'd told him about some of her favorite projects in Nashville. He told her that he'd injured his shoulder and was afraid he was going to eventually have to give in and have a repair done on it. "Yes," she said quietly.

"Why?" Tucker demanded, his tone and expression full of frustration. And hurt.

Because TJ didn't propose to her every other day. Because they could spend a nice afternoon together without it meaning anything more. Without her wanting it to mean anything more.

She sighed. She was so tired of fighting it—the urge to just give in to everything Tucker was promising, everything he wanted to give her. And the urge to sit on his front porch swing every night and hold his hand and tell him everything she was thinking and worrying about and dreaming of. For the rest of her life.

She met his gaze directly. "Because if I started doing those things with you, I'd never want to stop."

It seemed to take a little bit for that to fully sink in. But then his eyes widened and he moved in closer.

"That's—"

"Delaney, you said I could stain tonight!" David came charging into the room, Charlie and Jack not far behind.

She felt bad about being relieved that she and Tucker had been interrupted. Not only did he need to stop saying things that made her want more, but she had to be careful about the things *she* said too.

"Me too!" Jack reminded her.

She remembered. Stain was hard to get off skin, but this summer it didn't matter. The streaks of stain on their little legs would blend right in with the dirt that was always there.

"I sure did. I definitely need your help." They were going to do the wood trim on the baseboards and the doorways. It was easily fixed if they over or underdid something, and she had plenty of wood if there was a huge problem. But for the most part, the boys all did a pretty nice job. They'd all been helping out since they were old enough to hold a paintbrush. "And I have a surprise," she told them. "Where's Henry?"

"Right here."

Delaney looked to the doorway. It seemed Henry had grown four inches in the past few months. He looked so much taller. And older. The death of his parents had matured him quickly. But Sapphire Falls had been good for him. He was visibly less tense, he laughed more and he talked more. So far, so good. The Griffin house would be great for Henry too. He was ready to learn a lot of the things Delaney and his parents had done and this could be the perfect time.

"Guess what?" she asked them.

"We're having ice cream for dinner?" Jack guessed.

She grinned. "No. And nice try."

"What are we having for dinner?" David asked.

"I don't..." She looked around. "I don't know. But this isn't about dinner."

"We could have pizza," David suggested. "I love the

pizza here."

The pizza here *was* awesome. "This isn't about pizza."

"They have dessert pizza," Charlie said. "I saw the menu."

"What kind of dessert pizza?" David wanted to know.

Delaney kind of did too. The talk of pizza was making her stomach growl.

"A chocolate chip cookie with a brownie on top of it *and* chocolate frosting," Charlie said.

His brothers all stared at him as if he'd just told them Santa was coming in July.

Delaney knew how they felt. A chocolate chip cookie with a brownie on top *and* chocolate frosting? Seriously?

"We have to get that!" Jack said.

"I want one all by myself," David declared. "I'm *starving*."

"Can we just go to town to get the pizza?" Charlie asked her. "It's faster that way."

They all turned to look at her and she wondered for three seconds how this had gone from her house surprise to them being sure they were having pizza for dinner.

"Um, I bought a house today," she said.

They all blinked at her.

"A house. Here. In Sapphire Falls. We're going to makeover the whole thing. All together. Like we used to," she said.

The boys all continued to just stare at her.

Maybe it was low blood sugar.

"A house," she repeated slowly. "A big old house on Plum Street in Sapphire Falls."

Finally, Jack started jumping up and down. "Yay! We're going to live in Sapphire Falls!"

"Yes!" Charlie shouted. "That's awesome!"

"Really?" The quiet question, asked with big, hopeful eyes and a wide smile that she hadn't seen enough of for far too long, came from Henry.

Hope. She loved seeing that. That was the final piece, the final thing that made her *know* she had made the right decision.

The house was hers. She could fix it up and flip it. That had been the plan right up until she'd signed her name to the paperwork. But then it had hit her—they could stay. They had their own place. She *owned* it. She could provide for the boys. She could stay in Sapphire Falls, *they* could stay in Sapphire Falls, for all the reasons that was a great idea, but she'd be independent. She wouldn't be leaning on her father or Tucker.

"Did you hear that?" David asked Tucker. "We're gonna live here!"

Delaney hesitated to look at Tucker. He hadn't been happy to not know about the house in the first place, and she wasn't sure how he'd feel about this. Actually, she wasn't really sure how he felt about anything at this point.

She lifted her eyes to his and saw a strange combination of things—sadness was one of them though.

"You're going to live here? You're going to stay?"

They all turned back to her.

She licked her lips and nodded, forcing a smile. "Yes. I talked to my father last night and told him. We're going to stay."

She couldn't read Tucker's face in that moment and was hugely relieved when Henry broke into the long stretch of silence.

"How big is it?" he asked.

"Huge," she said with a smile.

"How huge?" Charlie asked.

"Five bedrooms, three bathrooms," she said. "About three thousand square feet. Two stories." With a big backyard and a huge oak tree that *needed* a tire swing and a driveway that would be perfect with a basketball hoop at the end and a quiet street that would be great for riding their bikes.

Charlie's eyes got big. "We could each have our own room!"

Yeah, she'd thought of that too.

And the master bathroom was big enough to put in a Jacuzzi tub. She'd always wanted a Jacuzzi tub. Like the one in Tucker's bathroom.

"Would you guys help me fix it up?" she asked. "We can do each of your bedrooms however you want. I could use you. Henry, I was thinking I could teach you to use the saw."

All the boys loved the bench saw. Well, they loved all of the power tools.

"Sure!" It was more enthusiasm than Henry had shown in a long time. They all started chattering about what color they wanted their rooms and asking a million questions.

She answered them all with a big smile, but it felt more and more forced the longer Tucker's brooding presence stayed, watching them silently.

"Okay, hey, guys, go check on the dogs. Make sure they've got food and stuff and then we'll figure out some food for all of us, okay?" Tucker asked after several minutes.

"I'm feeding Scout!" David shouted, running for the door.

"We didn't decide that was his name." Charlie was right on his heels. "I still like Einstein."

They still hadn't decided on a name for the little puppy. But he came when any of the boys called out anything at all, so it hadn't been a problem so far.

The door slammed behind them and Delaney braced herself for being alone with Tucker again.

He turned back to her. "You're staying."

"Yes."

"In a one-hundred-year-old house that needs a ton of work rather than with me."

"Tucker—" She took a deep breath. "I'm hoping the

boys can stay here while we fix things up. At least until it's more livable."

"And you?"

"I'll stay here until we can get a bedroom and bathroom remodeled. Then I'll go back and forth. I want to see them every day, of course."

"But you don't want to live with me."

"It's making things complicated."

"I was trying to make things easier."

"Okay, it's making things tempting."

"Good."

He was impossible. And it was entirely on purpose.

"Maybe we could just—" She wet her lips. "Eat cookies together for a while."

He didn't smile at her attempted joke. But living in Sapphire Falls and *dating* Tucker seemed like the best of all worlds.

"I just want you happy," he said, his voice lower.

"I know," she said honestly. "So let me do this."

They stood looking at each other, the air around them heating, a thousand unspoken things swirling in the hot currents, clearly wanting to touch…and to more than touch. In fact, Tucker started to reach for her as the front door banged open.

"Hey, Tucker!" Henry called from the porch.

He didn't look away from her. "Yeah?" he called back.

"There's a bunch of people here."

Tucker frowned. "Who?"

She shrugged. "I have no idea."

"Me either."

They started for the front together.

As they stepped out onto the porch, they saw that the drive was filled with pickups and the front lawn was now covered with tables, chairs and people.

"Of course," Tucker muttered.

"What is going on?" Delaney knew her eyes were wide

as she looked around.

"I'm guessing my mother got tired being the only person in town who hadn't met you and decided that if we weren't going to go to her house for a barbecue, she was going to bring the barbecue to us."

"Oh." Delaney didn't know what else to say to that.

And as more people pulled into the driveway and the tables were covered with plastic cloths and then loaded down with pots and pans and plates of food and someone cranked up some country music and three guys she didn't know set to work stringing twinkle lights from the branches of Tucker's trees, across posts they stuck in the ground then to more of his trees, that there simply wasn't anything else *to* say.

"Brace yourself," Tucker said.

"Wha—" But a second later, it was clear what he meant.

"Delaney, darling." A woman with a bright smile and twinkling blue eyes came up the porch steps. Blue eyes that were very familiar.

This had to be—

"My mother." Tucker sounded annoyed and affectionate at the same time.

Oh, wow. Tucker's mom. Delaney put a hand to her hair, or rather to the bandana she was wearing over her hair. She was a mess. She'd done nothing to her hair or her makeup. She was wearing jeans with a T-shirt, both of which were dirty.

It occurred to her that she'd never been in a situation where people might just randomly drop by before Sapphire Falls. It seemed to be a regular thing around here.

Kathy Bennett came straight to Delaney and pulled her into a hug. Kathy was a lot like her son—she did things big. It wasn't just her arms that wrapped around Delaney, but also a sense of kindness and warmth and the smell of cinnamon and sugar. Delaney took a big breath of it and thought she could maybe stay in that hug for the next few weeks. In mere seconds, she felt cared for and protected. The woman was a stranger to her, but Delaney actually felt the prickling of tears behind her eyes as Kathy put a hand on the back of her head and said softly, "It's so nice to finally meet you, sweetheart."

Dang, what *was it* about these Bennetts?

Delaney couldn't reply past the lump in her throat, but she did return Kathy's hug. She hadn't been hugged much by motherly types, but she could get used to it.

"Mom."

Tucker's voice separated them and he pulled Kathy into a hug of his own while Delaney quickly swiped her thumbs under her eyes. She looked up and caught him watching her over his mother's head with a small smile that seemed happy and sad at the same time.

"What are you doing here?" Tucker asked his mother as he set her back from him.

"Bringing dinner," Kathy said, as if that should have been obvious.

"And a party," Tucker commented.

"Well, I can't help if everyone wants to hang out with me all the time," Kathy said with a laugh.

Tucker grinned down at her and Delaney caught her breath. She'd seen Tucker's grins—at her, at the boys, even at the dogs, but there was something special in the way he looked at his mom.

It was pure, unconditional love that lit his face now.

Dang. Seeing that pointed at her for the next eighty years or so wouldn't be all bad.

Delaney shook her head. Whoa. Maybe she was going into a Bennett overdose and was getting loopy with it.

"Tuck!"

She turned at the booming voice from the porch steps to find a large man with a huge grin that was so obviously all Bennett that Delaney felt her eyes widen. So this was the father.

"Hey, Dad." Tucker took his dad's hand, but they leaned into a hug as well, and the older Mr. Bennett slapped his son on the back.

Then all of his attention zeroed in on Delaney.

"And you're Delaney."

She hadn't even nodded by the time he wrapped his arms around her in a bear hug that lifted her a few inches off the floor.

"My dad, Thomas," Tucker explained, though there was no need.

"Hi," she said breathlessly when Thomas set her back down.

He was built like TJ, had Travis's twinkle in his eyes and Tucker's smile.

Holy crap.

"So glad you're here, sweetheart," he said.

The words were obviously sincere, and Delaney felt her heart soften even further toward all people with the last name Bennett. The endearment, the same one his wife had used, made Delaney have to swallow hard before she nodded and said a quiet, "Thanks."

"Take it easy, Dad," Tucker said. "Don't want her scared off."

"I'm the charming one," his dad said. "Never scared a girl off yet."

"That's for sure," Kathy said with a laugh. She put an arm around her husband's waist and he hugged her against his side.

Delaney watched it all with fascination and a bit of yearning, if she was honest. Chelsea and Rafe had acted like that. They were sweet and affectionate and publicly demonstrative with one another—sometimes too much so. But even when she'd been uncomfortable with it, she'd also been envious of it. She knew that affection like that between two people was very reassuring to those around them. It meant the two were a solid unit and would be for a long time.

No wonder Tucker was all about marriage and home and family.

Seeing his parents together and with him, it all made perfect sense.

Tucker would be exactly like them. Not only because his parents had obviously modeled the behavior, but because he had a hard time keeping what he was thinking and feeling inside. If he wanted to hug someone or kiss someone or more, he would. Without worrying too much about who else was around.

"Oh, and watch out for the sweet tea," Thomas said, indicating the huge jug he'd set down on the porch before hugging Tucker.

"Is it spiked?" Delaney asked.

His booming laugh said she hadn't covered her hopefulness well.

"No, but Kath made it and that means it's addictive," he said. "You may never be able to get enough. And trust me, I know all about getting addicted and this woman."

He winked at his wife and she blushed a pretty pink, and Delaney's only thought was that Kathy hadn't stood a chance when Thomas Bennett decided he'd wanted her.

Definite Bennett overload. She obviously needed to watch out tonight.

"I'm going to go clean up," she said, inching toward the door to the house.

Please let me escape for a bit, she silently pleaded with Tucker. She knew that he wanted to pull her into all of this, surround her with these people and all these good vibes— and it was working—but she needed to wash the grime off so she could feel good about her appearance too. And she just needed a chance to breathe.

Was she feeling a little claustrophobic? Maybe. Or maybe she was feeling like she was about to propose to

Tucker for a change.

She definitely needed a minute alone.

"Oh, you look just fine, honey," Kathy said. "Adorable. I'm so fascinated with the work you do."

They'd been talking about her. She wasn't exactly sure who *they* were, and it could have been a number of people, but it didn't matter. She smiled. "I just—"

"Go on," Tucker said, stepping between her and his mother as if playing defense. "We'll all still be here when you come back out." He sounded resigned with that mixture of irritation and fondness she'd heard before.

"Well, don't go sneaking out the bathroom window or anything," Kathy said with a wink.

"The showers are on the second floor," Tucker said.

"Like that ever slowed you or your brothers down," Kathy scoffed.

He flashed his mom a grin and then turned it on Delaney. "That's true. But I've got Delaney's Jeep keys hidden and you all have her Jeep pretty well trapped."

She knew he hadn't really hidden her keys. At least, she was pretty sure he hadn't hidden her keys. But it was true that her vehicle was surrounded by trucks. And more trucks.

As if she could have gotten in it and driven away without being noticed.

The four-wheelers were another story though.

"The shed's not locked is it?" she asked. Why was she teasing with him? Why wasn't she escaping inside?

He gave her an amused look. "You know how to drive a four-wheeler?"

"I'll get Jack to help me. He can be bought with candy you know."

Tucker laughed. "I know. But Jack's on my side."

"Your side?"

"The big fun party. And having you here with us."

It wasn't only the words, but the way he said them and

the way he was looking at her and *something* that made her melt a little at that.

"You'd use my nephew against me?" she teased, trying to lighten the moment and not throw herself into his arms.

Moving out was the right thing. Fixing up the house was the right thing. Proving she could do it was the right thing. She needed that. But she wanted him too. It wasn't that she didn't. She just didn't want to change her last name yet.

"Delaney, one of these days you're going to fully understand and accept the fact that I'm going to do whatever it takes to make you smile and relax and have fun and realize that there are a whole bunch of people who care about you very much," Tucker said.

Whoa.

And in front of his mom and dad too.

She didn't need any other Bennetts to put her into overload—Tucker was more than enough to make her head and heart spin.

She took a deep breath. And didn't dare look at his parents. She already knew from her very first night in town that they were hoping this was going to be more than a friendly houseguest situation this summer. They were probably going to be disappointed about her move to town as well.

"Speaking of taking it easy," Kathy said dryly. "Relax, Tucker. Let the poor girl breathe."

Surprised, Delaney glanced at the other woman after all. Kathy gave her a sympathetic smile. "Tucker can get a little single-minded."

Delaney actually snorted at that. "I've…heard," she said. She didn't need to admit she'd experienced that firsthand, repeatedly. There had hardly been ten minutes between them that he hadn't reminded her of all he wanted from her.

"Fine," Tucker said, his intense gaze still on her.

"Breathe. Shower. Then get your butt back down here and have a good time."

She rolled her eyes but smiled. She kind of liked the fact that he hadn't argued with the statement that he was being intense about her. He acknowledged it. That didn't mean he was reining it in at all, but at least he was aware of it.

Tucker's gaze shifted and landed on someone else out in the yard. "In fact, I have something I need to do at the moment."

Delaney followed his gaze.

TJ had just arrived.

Oh, crap.

Being a little bit chicken and a whole lot not sure how to handle *that*, and even more sure that Kathy and Thomas had a lot of experience handling squabbling between the brothers, Delaney pivoted on her heel and headed inside.

ৎচৎ

TJ saw him coming and must have read his expression, because he visibly tensed as Tucker approached. He didn't look concerned exactly, but he did look as if he'd been expecting a confrontation.

He was going to get one.

"You know, the first night you showed up here, I thought you were overstepping, but I believed that you were worried about her. Maybe even me," Tucker said, coming to stop right in front of his big brother. "But now? You're way out of line."

Travis had appeared beside Tucker and Levi and Joe moved in a bit behind TJ.

"What's going on?" Travis asked.

TJ didn't answer. Tucker did.

"TJ's getting in my way."

"Your way of what?" Travis asked.

"Me and Delaney."

Travis laughed before he realized Tucker was serious. "What are you talking about?"

"TJ is helping Delaney buy a house in town."

Travis's eyebrows shot up and he looked at TJ. "Is that right?"

TJ nodded. "Cosigned the loan this morning."

"Why?" Travis asked.

Tucker crossed his arms and waited for TJ's answer.

TJ frowned. "I thought you'd be happy."

Tucker barked out a laugh. "Why the fuck would I be happy that you're helping her *not* need me, that you're essentially helping her move out of my house and away from me?"

TJ had a long fuse. But no one could eat it up faster than one of his brothers. His frown deepened and he leaned in. "I'm helping her *stay*, you idiot."

"In Sapphire Falls," Tucker admitted. "But not with me."

"It's better than Colorado, isn't it?"

It was. But why did TJ care? "Why do you care anyway?"

"Because *you* care," TJ said as if it should have been obvious.

Tucker took a deep breath.

"What's going on exactly?" Travis asked.

"Delaney isn't ready to pick out wedding cakes yet, but our boy here can't seem to slow down long enough to see that he's pushing her toward Colorado instead of making her want to stay."

"She wants to stay," Tucker said. He was sure of that. Okay, he was about sixty-two percent sure of that. "I'm not pushing her away." He was about forty-four percent sure of that.

TJ ignored him and told Travis, "She hasn't done a project since her sister died. She's been in this kind of daze and she's aware of it. She couldn't trust herself in that state. But doing Tucker's kitchen got her going again and snapped her out of it. Now, the idea of doing a house has her excited and happy and *staying*."

"You tricked her into staying?" Travis asked. "For Tucker? I'm kind of impressed. You talked her into buying a house that would take so long to redo that she has to stay and Tucker will have more time with her."

TJ shook his head. It was clear in his expression that he thought he was surrounded by idiots. "She wanted to stay. But she needed to trust that she was doing it for a good reason and not just because of Tucker or because it was the easy thing to do. She needed a way to be independent. To stay because she *wanted* to, not because she *had* to."

Tucker felt the jolt of realization through his whole body, deep in his bones. Delaney had been basically telling him all of this, but hearing TJ say it made it completely real and, dammit, believable.

It also made him kind of an asshole. Why hadn't he listened when Delaney said it? Why did TJ have to be the one to get it to sink in?

"Why are you doing all of this?" Tucker asked. "Why are you so involved?"

"Because I'm a hell of a nice guy," TJ said. "And she's a nice girl. And because she's important to *you*."

Tucker wasn't sure what to say to that. That was pretty sentimental for TJ.

"Are you going to help her redo the house?" Travis asked TJ.

"Yeah, we talked about the plumbing and some wiring stuff."

Travis glanced at Tucker. "I'd be happy to help out too. That okay, Tucker? If we help her get away from you?" He gave Tucker a huge grin.

Tucker slowly started nodding. "Yeah, it's okay. In fact, I think I'll help too."

"You're going to help make Delaney a place she can happily and comfortably live without you?" Travis asked.

"Yep." It could be the best decision he'd made in— ever. Helping her get some distance from him might actually be the best and only way to bring her close.

Wanting him. Not needing him.

Yeah, he could definitely work on that.

Delaney finally remerged from the house. She looked gorgeous, and Tucker felt the familiar craving stir. He wanted to run his fingers through her hair, put his nose against her neck and breathe in her scent, put his lips...all over her. But he was also aware that while his blood thumped hot and hard with desire, it wasn't pounding and racing with the wild need he was used to feeling. The frustration and desperation were gone. In their place were confidence and love.

She might not trust the love yet, but she would. And he'd wait. He'd prove it. For however long it took.

In any way he needed to.

The next two hours were torturous. He wanted to get her alone, but they had to put the time in at the barbecue. Delaney talked with his parents, laughed with the girls and even danced with a couple of Tucker's buddies.

Tucker drank and listened to his brothers and friends talk about stupid crap.

Or maybe it was brilliant. He had no idea. His attention had been on nothing and no one but Delaney. He'd barely even tasted his mother's locally famous potato salad.

Finally, everything had gone on long enough.

Tucker found Kate.

"You want me to be happy and in love, right, Katie?" he asked, using the nickname that drove Levi crazy. Since Levi was sitting right there.

She smiled up at him. "I really, really do."

"Then you and Levi are babysitting for a while."

She looked around. "Where are the boys now?"

"That's the first thing on your to-do list," he told her.

She rolled her eyes but nodded. "Okay. Fine. Go."

He started across the grass to where Delaney was chatting with TJ and his dad. He turned back though. "Hey, Levi, there are *four* boys. I'm going to need all four of them happy, healthy and clean when I get back."

"Hey, three out of four is seventy-five percent. That's a passing grade," Levi told him.

"Yeah, not in this school."

Levi grinned at him and Tucker counted his blessings—most of whom were human—as he went to retrieve Delaney.

He walked up behind her, wrapped his arms around her and said in her ear, "Let's go for a ride."

He could tell he'd surprised her by the public display of affection. She was going to have to get used to those.

"We can't. We're kind of the hosts here, aren't we?" she asked, putting her hands over his on her belly.

"Hell no, this was all my mom's idea. You were the entertainment," he said. "But now everyone's gotten a good look at you and been introduced. They'll move on to something else by tomorrow."

"Why are my feelings stupidly hurt by that?" she asked with a laugh.

"Oh, they're not," he said, starting to pull her away from his dad and TJ. "You do *not* want to be the center of attention around here."

TJ and his dad pretended not to notice him sneaking her away from their conversation and Tucker made a mental note to up his expenditure on their Christmas gifts come December.

They headed around the side of the house to the back where he had moved his truck earlier.

"People are going to hear it start up aren't they?" she asked, getting in and sliding across the front seat.

"Don't care." He followed her in and turned the key,

put it in drive and started for the road that would get them to the highway and to the edge of Sapphire Falls.

"Where are we going?"

"You'll see."

"Okay," she said. "*Why* are we going?"

He glanced over at her. "Because you're going to get to know me."

"In the Biblical sense?" she teased.

Oh, yeah, there was going to be some of that too. "In a lot of senses. You've gotten to know my family and friends. You've seen every inch of my...house," he said with a purposeful pause and a grin.

She laughed. Clearly, she was in a good mood after the party, and that was definitely a good sign. He couldn't be with a woman who didn't like a good front-yard barbecue with everyone he knew.

Snoopy bastards.

"But there are things about me you don't know."

He looked over again to see that her smile had faded. She shifted on the seat. "You seem like a pretty open book. What you see is what you get right?"

That was right. For the most part. "But you've been trying to avoid getting closer to me. Finding out if there is more than what you see."

"What makes you say that?" But she wasn't looking at him.

"The fact that you're uncomfortable right now. For one thing," he said.

She didn't reply.

"You're trying to keep from knowing me too well because you're trying to keep from getting attached to me. But you're already attached even without knowing my favorite color—green, by the way, like your eyes—or my favorite football team—the Chiefs. Now I think there are some things about me you need to know."

She was quiet for almost a mile. Then she said, "Why?"

"Because I want you to want me."

He felt her surprise.

"I do want you, Tucker. You know that."

"I want you to want *me*. Not to sleep with me. Not to help out with the boys. Me. Because whether you like it or not, you want more than my body and my kitchen."

She was quiet again for a long time. Finally, she said, "I don't need a list of your likes and dislikes to want more than your body and kitchen."

He bit back his smile, but he heard and rejoiced at each of her words.

They drove the rest of the way with Toby Keith, Carrie Underwood and Dierks Bentley filling the silence. Finally, a half mile from the main street in Sapphire Falls, Tucker turned onto the brand-new pavement of a parking lot.

They rolled to a stop and he put the truck into park with his headlights shining on the newly installed sign. The spotlights weren't up yet so he kept the headlights on.

He looked over at Delaney.

"The Raphael Williams Castillo Memorial Raceway," she read softly. She turned to face him. "You named it after Rafe?"

He nodded. "Some of my best memories are of me and Rafe riding our dirt bikes. We're going to have multiple races each year. But annually, on the weekend closest to his birthday, we're going to have a charity ride to raise money for cancer research."

He could see Delaney's eyes sparkling with tears. "Wow."

"Yeah, well, tell Levi wow too. He's funding most of this thing. And he loves when women say wow about things he does."

She laughed. "I can do that."

"Want to see the whole thing?" He really wanted to show her the whole thing.

Levi was footing the bill, but the design of the track and

the spectator areas, even the painting of the interior walls, were all his idea. Like her and his kitchen. Or Kate's kitchen. Or Delaney's new house. He understood how fun it was to be creative and see a vision from your imagination come to life.

"I definitely want to see the whole thing."

"Okay, but there's only one really good way to see a dirt-bike track."

"Okay."

"Do you trust me?"

The air between them seemed to fill with unspoken words and emotions. She wet her lips and took her time answering, but when she said, "More than anyone," Tucker knew she meant it.

He got out of the truck and came around to open her door. He didn't give her much room to slide to the ground, wanting to be close to her, to smell her hair.

He took a deep breath and contemplated pushing her up against the side of his truck. But they would have time for that. Or something better. An idea had been forming ever since he'd realized that she had to want him instead of need him. He could make her want.

So he took her hand and pulled her around to the truck bed. He had the bike covered with a blue tarp and he heard her chuckle as he flipped the tarp back.

"Of course you have to see a dirt-bike track on a dirt bike," she said.

He grinned and let the tailgate down. "Exactly."

"I don't know how to ride."

He grabbed one of the helmets and turned to set it on her head. He took his time fastening the strap, looking into her eyes as his fingers brushed her throat. "I've got you," he said. "Nothing to worry about."

She swallowed hard but didn't say anything.

Tucker kept his big grin to himself this time. He'd never thought about the seductive qualities of a dirt bike, but he knew that women around here were turned-on by the whole thing. The power, the speed, the dirt—he wasn't sure what it was exactly, but Delaney was going to be one of the girls who found dirt bikes, and their riders, hot.

He got the bike to the ground and then rolled it toward the big industrial door around the side from the front entrance. He looked over his shoulder at her. "You comin'?"

She nodded and followed.

He unlocked the panel on the keypad and punched in the numbers. The big door lifted, giving them access to a short corridor that led into the arena. Steps to the left would lead up into the stands, straight ahead was the entrance to the track. He rolled the bike down the hall and stopped at the room where the electrical board was housed. He flipped on a few lights and then re-joined Delaney. "You ready?"

She simply nodded again.

Fifty yards later, they stood at the edge of the Raphael Williams Castillo Memorial Raceway. Tucker turned to see Delaney's reaction. She was staring, her eyes wide. But she was smiling.

"I've never even seen a dirt-bike track," she said. "This isn't what I was expecting."

"Well, this isn't something you would see in little towns like ours very often."

The track was inside a three-hundred-thousand-square-foot building with bleachers for spectators, a concession area, restrooms as well as full locker rooms with showers for the riders and a high-tech PA system from which they could make announcements and pump music.

"A lot of tracks are outside. They stretch out more that way and you have to figure the elements into races, which can be fun, don't get me wrong," he said with a grin. "But this indoor track means we can race no matter the weather or the time of year.

"It's hard to tell from here," he went on, "but from

above, you can see the track swirls around through the building with lots of turns and twists."

She nodded. "And those hills?"

He grinned. "Those are the fun part. The rises and dips vary in size. There are other obstacles too. We can change the track up, depending on if the riders are beginners or advanced." This was the part he was really excited about. "We can vary the path by changing the barriers along the sides and we can play with the height and incline of the hills." That was the really cool part. Being friends with a millionaire could definitely be fun. "We have mechanisms under the bigger, steeper hills that can raise and lower them so we can change the track up depending on the race."

He glanced at her and found her watching him instead of looking at the track.

"And this was all your idea," she said. She wasn't asking.

He nodded. "Most of it. We had a contracting company that specializes in motocross tracks brought in, but it looks pretty much like I sketched it."

She shook her head. "That must be an amazing feeling. To have it built and almost operational."

"It is." He moved in closer to her and put a hand on her hip to draw her up against him. "But you know that feeling. The feeling you have when a room or a house comes together like you envisioned."

She put her hands on his chest, not to push him away but to run her hands over his shirt, rubbing the soft cotton over his chest. He felt his body heating.

"I do know that feeling. But it's different when you're doing something for someone else," she said. She glanced at the track. "It's…bigger when it's all you. When it's truly yours."

"Like the house."

She looked back into his eyes. "Yes. Like the house." She wet her lips. "And the boys."

He shook his head. "What do you mean like the boys?"

"Parents have plans for their kids, dreams about what their lives will be like, how things will turn out."

Tucker nodded.

"I have that for the boys. And it's so sweet and rewarding when things turn out the way you planned."

"Like you want Henry to be a professional baseball player and Charlie an astronaut?" Tucker asked with a smile.

She laughed and shook her head. "No. I know some parents do that—plan that their kid will go to medical school or law school. But my visions for the boys are a lot simpler."

"What are they?" he asked softly. "I'd love to know."

Hell, he'd love to know what her favorite book as a kid was and if she liked Brussels sprouts or not. Dreams and plans for the boys? Yeah, definitely.

She took a deep breath and moved her hands, linking her fingers together behind his neck. "I want them to go to sleep every night feeling safe and happy. I want them to smile and laugh every day. I want them to know that someone loves them. And I want them to do something with their lives that they can make money at but that they can also put on their list of blessings when they count them. Which I hope they do. Often."

He looked into the green eyes that he hoped to watch slowly crinkle at the corners with laugh lines as she aged.

And God, he wanted to be a part of making those things come true for the boys.

"The house is part of that too," she went on. "And this town and your parents and the dogs...and you."

He tightened his hand on her hip. But he stayed quiet. Somehow, he sensed she had more to say.

"I realized it before now, of course. But watching your family and friends together tonight...I realized that I want that for the boys. If I can give them the love and security that is all around them here, then I've really done something amazing for them."

"Is there a but coming?" he asked. His chest felt tight—hell, his whole body felt tight—with anticipation.

She shook her head. "No but." She took a deep breath. "I do want to marry you."

CHAPTER TWELVE

Tucker froze. That was definitely not what he'd been expecting. "You'll marry me?"

Delaney nodded. "It's the best choice. For sure. By far."

She was going to marry him. She'd said yes.

Basically.

But it didn't feel like he'd thought this would feel. "For the boys. It's the best choice for the boys."

She nodded. "Absolutely."

She started to arch closer, but Tucker pushed her hip back, holding her away from him. He was still holding the bike up with his other hand so he couldn't completely control her movements. As she pressed against him, part of him wanted to give in, to say to hell with it, they'd work it all out.

But would they?

He actually pushed her away then.

She took a step back, blinking at him in surprise.

"Fuck," he muttered, turning to prop the bike up with its kickstand so he had two hands free for whatever was about to come.

"Tucker?" She was clearly confused.

And why wouldn't she be? He'd been talking about getting married since she'd first set foot in Sapphire Falls, and now that she was saying they should do it, he was hesitating.

Was he an idiot?

Probably.

"What changed your mind?" he asked.

He'd just realized that he needed to give her more time and space. That having her stay in Sapphire Falls was a perfect first step and that he needed to be satisfied with that and patient. That she had to want him, not need him. And somewhere in that time, he'd realized that's what he wanted too.

Being her hero was great. Being the love of her life was better.

She took a deep breath. "I don't know if it was your mom's hug or how happy your parents clearly are or the best potato salad I've ever had or what. But it became clear tonight with everyone there at the house, the boys running around, everyone happy and together, the way this town seems small from the outside, but once you're here you realize the huge things going on—the work and businesses, the relationships, the way everyone works together..." She trailed off and shrugged. "I want all of this for the boys."

Tucker took a deep breath too. And counted to ten. "So you want to marry me because of my mother."

She frowned. "What? No. I mean, I wouldn't put it that way."

"Her hug, her relationship with my dad, her potato salad."

Delaney considered that. "That was her salad, huh?"

"Yeah."

She sighed. "Those are things that illustrate my feelings here. I'm happy here, comfortable, secure."

"And I'm your best bet for staying close to all of those things."

She studied his face for several long seconds. "I need you, Tucker. Is that what you want to hear? We both know it's true. It's been true since day one. It's been true since Chelsea died, really."

He thought about that. He pulled in a lungful of air. He blew it out. Then he said, "That's not enough."

Her eyes widened. "Excuse me?"

"It's not enough. Because the things you need, you could get from any guy in town. You could get from TJ. And you don't really *need* anything. You're tough and smart and full of love and you could, and will, do whatever you have to do to make those boys safe and healthy and happy. You don't need anyone."

She propped her hands on her hips. "Well, there is one thing that you've been very helpful with that I don't want from anyone else."

He knew exactly what she was talking about. And she didn't need him for that either.

But she was going to want him. And only him.

He turned to the dirt bike, straddled it and kicked the kickstand up. He started the bike and looked over at her. "Get on."

She was going to say no, he could tell. He revved the engine over her response. She glared at him, but she also sighed. She came forward and threw her leg over the bike, settling in behind him.

Dirt bikes weren't really made for two passengers, and there was no way he could take her over the obstacles fast and hard like he liked to ride, but they drove the track at a reasonable speed, her arms around his waist, her knees pressing into him as she hung on.

Finally, he drove to the middle of the track and parked. He killed the engine, put the kickstand down and took off his helmet. He got off the bike and stood, towering over her.

Delaney took her helmet off as well and shook her hair out.

"Now what?"

"Now I show you a little bit about needing and wanting," he said gruffly.

Tucker turned her on the bike seat and she brought her leg over so she was facing him. He pulled her to her feet and held her still for his kiss with his hands on her face.

In the past, Delaney had taken the lead and he'd let her. It had been sweet and hot and just what she needed.

But things had changed.

Now it was about wanting. And she might think she

wanted to be in charge—but he was going to change her mind.

The kiss was full and hot, like always. But he held her head, tipped her when he wanted her tipped, licked when he wanted to lick, nipped at her bottom lip when he wanted her to moan.

She was clutching his forearms when he finally lifted his head. She was breathing hard, her cheeks flushed. Perfect.

"Take your shirt off," he said huskily.

"What? Here?"

"Yes, here. Now. I want to think about your pretty pink nipples every time I ride around this track."

Her pupils dilated and she pulled in a quick breath.

"Delaney. Do it."

She reacted to his command, perhaps without even knowing it. She pressed her lips together and her fingers flexed against his arms.

Her gaze locked on his, she finally let go and stepped back. She whipped her shirt off and then her bra, without being asked.

He liked that. But he was also going to like her following *his* commands.

Her fingers went to the button on her shorts.

"No."

His short firm word stopped her.

"No?"

"Come here."

She stepped forward. And reached for *his* pants.

"No," he said, more firmly this time. "You do what I say."

Her eyes narrowed slightly. "I don't like being bossed around."

"But you will, honey. You will," he promised her.

He lifted his hands to her breasts, brushing his thumbs over the stiff tips that belied her claim that she didn't like the bossiness.

"Tuck—" Her protest ended on a soft moan.

He dipped his head and took one of her nipples into his mouth. He licked and then sucked. Her hands went to the back of his head, holding him close.

"Hands by your sides," he told her.

"But—"

He lifted his head. "Hands by your sides." He tugged on her wet nipple. "Or we're done here."

Her hands dropped. She didn't look happy, but she was complying. He hid his smile and went back to sucking on the sweetest nipples he'd ever tasted.

Her hands were gripped into tight fists by the time he lifted his head.

"Now you can take your pants off," he told her.

She stared at him. "Oh, really? Well, thank you very much."

He shrugged. "If you don't want to, you don't have to."

"Maybe you should take your shirt off. Even things up here."

He shook his head. "This isn't about evening things up. I already want you. This is about you wanting me."

Her eyes widened. "Tucker, I *want* you."

"You can't. You don't even know what I've got to offer."

"You do remember the barn, all three times, right?" she asked.

"I remember every second," he told her huskily. "But I also remember you being all about me. Not the other way around."

"And you're upset about that?" she asked.

He dropped his voice and crowded close to her. "I'm not upset about one damned thing that's happened between us. But that was about you needing to get lost from your life chaos for a little bit, needing to feel powerful and in control. And that's all great. You got what you needed. Just like you've got what you need for the boys. You've got friends and family, potential income and a home. Now it's about wanting. Things are going to start being about *you* and what you *want* now that the needs are taken care of."

"Tuck—"

"And furthermore," he went on. He wasn't sure if it was the determination in his tone or his use of furthermore, but she pressed her lips together and waited. "I acknowledge that you took care of most of your own needs and that other people were also a part of meeting those needs. "But," he brushed his thumb over her bottom lip, "*I'm* going to be all about what you *want*."

"I don't—" She had to clear her throat. "I don't follow."

"Take your pants off."

She looked around. They weren't exactly in public. There were only three other people in town who had keys to the place at the moment and they were all at his house drinking, dancing and having fun. They were alone. But it was a big wide open place.

"Here?"

"Right here. Right now. This place was my dream. You are my new dream. And having you naked and squirming on my dirt bike in the middle of this arena would be a really nice way to combine the two."

She glanced back at his bike. "Really?"

"Oh, yeah." He'd never be able to ride again without getting hard, which could possibly be a problem, but he'd deal with that when it came up. He grinned. "Pants off. I'm not going to ask again."

"I had no idea you could be so demanding."

"There might be several things you don't know about me."

She nodded, the playfulness muted. "I think you might be right."

"Pants. Off. Now."

She undid the front button and zipper and slid the denim shorts and silk panties to her ankles. She kicked her sandals off and stepped out of her clothes.

Gloriously naked. The arena lights were perfect for showcasing her smooth, creamy skin and the curves that had filled out a bit since she'd been in town. He ran his hands from her hips to the dip in her waist and then up to her breasts to cup them, to rub the tips. He brought her in for another hot kiss. As he stroked his tongue lazily against hers, he backed her up until her thighs hit the bike.

"Sit back," he said against her lips. "I want your sweet pussy on the seat of my bike."

She pulled in a shaky breath but sat down on the leather seat.

He stepped back to take in the sight. Oh, yeah, that was the picture he wanted in his head every time he got his bike out. Her dark hair spilled over her shoulders. Her eyes were bright, cheeks pink. She wasn't tall enough to keep her feet flat on the ground, but her toes touched, her calf muscles flexed to keep her balanced and she put her hands on the seat on either side of her, holding herself up.

"Fucking beautiful," he muttered.

"Now your clothes, please," she urged him.

He shook his head. "Nope. Spread your legs."

ᔦᵒ᪽

Delaney knew where this was going. And everything in her turned to a hot, wet mess.

She loved being in control. She *needed* to be in control.

But she *wanted* Tucker to be in control.

He'd been talking about needs versus wants. Okay, so he was right. When she'd first come to Sapphire Falls, to his house and his life, she'd had a list of needs seemingly a mile long. But so many, maybe even all of them, had been taken care of.

So now there was time and room for wants. If she was brave enough to go there.

She hadn't thought about wants much for a long time. She'd had a happy life. She'd loved her job with Chelsea. She'd loved being part of their family. She'd loved helping out with the boys and even with Rafe at the end, but wants? Yeah, she didn't remember the last thing she'd just flat out wanted and gone after.

"Delaney, I can't do the things I want to do if you don't spread your legs for me, honey."

His voice was rough and the look in his eyes made her melt even further.

This hot, sweet, sexy boy wanted to go down on her while she was perched naked on his hot, sleek, sexy dirt bike? What the hell was she hesitating for?

She hadn't even known she was turned-on by dirt biking.

But she was hesitating for two really good reasons. One, this was going to change…something. She couldn't explain it beyond that. She just felt it. Wasn't even sure what *it* was exactly. But Tucker was going to take a part of her that wasn't simply physical.

Two, she hadn't done this for a really, really long time. She didn't let guys do this. It was too intimate, too much.

And it would be beyond too much with Tucker.

She might never recover.

"Oh God," she said quietly.

And she spread her legs.

She had never felt more vulnerable in her life, but when Tucker dropped to his knees in the dirt, the look in his eyes one of lust but also of almost…reverence…she'd never felt more beautiful. And strangely powerful at the same time.

He ran his big palms up and down her inner thighs, the roughness of his hand delicious against her sensitive skin. She felt her body getting even wetter from that simple touch.

He looked at her as his hands moved. They came close to her center but didn't touch her. She wiggled on the seat, the smoothness and warmth from the leather another amazing sensation.

"Tucker," she said softly. "Please."

"I'm trying to decide where to start," he said, lifting his eyes to hers. "I want to lick you. I want to plunge my fingers into you. I want to fuck you so bad my cock has never been harder."

She squirmed again and moaned. "All of it. Any of it."

"I have to taste you," he said, almost to himself.

"Yes. Yes, please." Vulnerable or not, too much or not, she had to get his tongue on her, *now*.

He leaned in and kissed her inner thigh, then licked lightly. He moved higher and did the same thing. Until finally, *finally*, he came to her center. He licked her clit first. Delaney jerked with the flood of sensations that coursed through her with that first touch.

He moved his hands, using his thumbs to part her folds, further exposing her to his eyes. And his tongue.

He licked again, with firmer pressure this time, then he sucked softly.

Delaney cried out. She was going to come in about ten more seconds.

But he seemed determined to draw it out and spend lots of time.

He eased a finger into her and she wished for something firmer under her so she could thrust against him. But she was afraid she was going to tumble off the other side of the bike or knock the whole thing over. That meant she had to hold herself fairly still and let Tucker do what he wanted.

She was sure that had been his plan all along.

He moved his finger as he continued to lick and suck on her clit, and Delaney felt her orgasm building.

"Tucker, Tucker." She was more or less gasping his name at this point and wasn't beyond begging.

Or crying.

Which is what she almost did when he pulled his finger and his mouth away. He grabbed her hand and put it where his mouth had been. "Finish it," he told her gruffly.

She stared at him. "*What?*"

"Finish it, Delaney. Do it."

She was so close, she was so desperate. She pressed two fingers deep and then pulled out and circled her clit with the pressure and speed she knew so well. It wasn't as if *this* was new.

Her orgasm came hard and fast and she cried out as she went over the edge.

But before the ripples had even completely faded, she shoved him back.

He nearly fell onto his ass but caught himself at the last moment and stretched to his feet.

"What the hell was that?" she demanded.

He came forward, practically on top of her, caught her chin between his thumb and finger and looked her directly in the eye. "*That* was the difference between want and need. You don't *need* me to do that for you, but you *want* me to. Remember that."

She stared at him. She knew her mouth would have dropped open if he hadn't been holding her chin.

The…*asshole.*

"You've *got* to be kidding me," she said.

"Not at all."

She pulled away from his hold, grabbed her clothes from the dirt and got dressed quickly. Then she faced him, hands on her hips. "You know what, Tucker? Thank you. Thank you for the reminder that I can take care of myself…in all ways."

"Uh huh."

"And," she added, putting as much haughtiness into her tone as she could muster. "I take back my yes."

She actually didn't have much practice with haughty.

"Your yes?"

"The yes to marrying you. I take it back. I don't want to marry you."

He gave her slow smile. She frowned. He wasn't supposed to smile.

"You don't *need* to marry me," he corrected. "But you do want to."

"No. Actually, I don't."

He looked at her for several beats before finally saying, "Okay, well, when you do, let me know."

He put his helmet back on, fastened the strap and then threw his leg over the bike seat. The bike seat where he'd just made her come—correction, where he'd *almost* made her come—a few minutes ago.

She did *not* want to get back on that bike. Maybe ever. And she didn't really want to ride back to the farm in the close confines of the truck.

But it was a long walk back to the farm. And she was pretty sure she'd end up lost in a cornfield somewhere even if she did try to hike it.

Dammit.

She put her helmet on too and climbed on behind him.

But that was going to be the last climbing on him, or around him, she was going to be doing.

At least for a while.

Because there was one thing she couldn't deny...she did want him.

❧

It was amazing how much work could get done in a month's time even when the workers were part-time, mostly volunteer and drank beer while they worked.

Still, the house was in really good shape by the one-month mark.

In fact, Delaney and the boys had been living in it for

about two weeks. The boys still spent a lot of time on the farm with Tucker and everyone else. They even spent the night there two or three times a week. But they were officially moved into the house on Plum Street. Delaney knew it was official because she'd gotten her first bills at the address.

She stood in the middle of the kitchen, turning in a full circle for the fourth time. It was gorgeous. It had been essentially functioning for two weeks, but now all the details were in place. The backsplash and floor and painting were all finished and looked amazing.

TJ, Travis and Joe had all been hugely helpful. Mason and Levi and all of the girls had come in to help with painting and other things as well. But most of the help had come from Tucker. He'd been there every day, for hours, and had done everything from installing flooring to sanding and staining the new banister she'd put on the stairs to pulling out and reinstalling the ceiling in two bathrooms so they could redo the light fixtures.

She couldn't believe how much progress they'd made. And how helpful the man who had been asking her to marry him since they'd met had been in getting her settled in a house that wasn't his.

He was frustrating as hell.

And she was sexually frustrated as hell.

Because, damn him, ever since the dirt-bike incident, she'd cut *him* off. And had been trying to make do on her own.

And it absolutely was not the same. It might give her a *needed* orgasm, but it wasn't the orgasm she wanted.

She studied the cabinets that she had finally finished installing that morning. It had seemed a bigger priority to get the bedrooms and bathrooms finished and the appliances hooked up in the kitchen so they could be used than it had to get the cupboard doors on.

And in the midst of it all, she hadn't forgotten that the

cupboard doors at Tucker's place still needed to be finished and put on. She also didn't miss the fact that cupboard doors seemed to have become strangely symbolic in her life. She was hesitating with his because she wanted them to be perfect and significant. As long as she didn't actually commit to anything and actually put them up, they couldn't be wrong. She had hesitated in here, not because the cupboard doors were truly less of a priority, but because once they were up, the kitchen would be done and would no longer be a fixer-upper. It would be hers.

She also didn't miss the significance of the fact that she didn't really like these cupboard doors. She hadn't made them. She hadn't even needed to stain them. They'd arrived in a box and she'd hung them.

But now that they were up, she had to wonder why she hadn't picked more carefully.

She heard pounding overhead. Not the hammer-and-nail type of pounding, but the running-feet kind of pounding. It was early afternoon and only she and the boys were in the house, so there were no hammers and nails being used upstairs anyway. They were just roughhousing. Nothing out of the ordinary, especially when they had been cooped up in the house all day due to rain.

Nothing out of the ordinary until she heard the loud bang followed by an even louder crash.

She held her breath listening, but there was no sound for several seconds.

She was already halfway across the living room by the time there were more pounding feet and then a shouted, "Delaney!"

That wasn't good. Especially when it was Henry who was calling her. He wasn't tattling. He was worried.

She ran the rest of the way across the room and up the steps. She skidded to a stop in front of David's bedroom.

The place looked like a murder scene.

There was blood everywhere—on the floor, down the

front of Jack's shirt and shorts, David's shirt, the wall, the bedspread.

"Oh my God! What happened? Who's hurt?"

David and Jack both had blood on them. Henry looked worried. Charlie looked scared. All of them were crying. She hated those expressions and she hated crying but she *really* hated blood.

"Me," Jack said in a small voice. He pulled his hand away from his stomach. He had a huge gash down the middle of his hand. "It hurts." His face was pale and he was breathing hard.

"Okay, baby, okay." She pulled him close, wrapping one arm around him and pressing the bottom of her T-shirt to his hand. "Henry, I need you to call 9-1-1. Charlie, I need you to get towels. David, I need you to go get some ice."

She'd figure out what happened later. She could put him in the car, but she had no idea where the doctor's office was or even how bad the wound truly was. She just knew she needed to try to stop or slow the bleeding and deal with his emotions and the fact that he was possibly on the verge of going into shock.

She yanked the bedspread off of David's bed and wrapped it around both her and Jack. She wasn't letting him go until a medical professional was there to take over.

She applied the towels and ice to Jack's hand as the boys brought them in and sat rocking him in the middle of the floor.

"They're coming," Henry said a minute later.

She smiled up at him. "Great. Now I need you to call Tucker."

He had her cell phone and dialed immediately. Through the fog of worry, she noted that he knew Tucker's number by heart. She liked that.

"Voice mail," he said with a frown.

That was weird. Tucker always had his phone.

"Okay, keep trying. Who else's number do you know? I have TJ's in there." She knew she was babbling a little and she made herself stop and take a deep breath. She didn't need Jack any more wound up than he already was and knew her emotions would directly impact his.

Henry found TJ's number and dialed. "What do I tell him?"

"That Jack's hurt," she said. "That's enough."

Evidently, TJ answered, because Henry delivered the message exactly as she'd told him. And she was right. It was enough. Henry hung up and said, "He said okay."

"He'll let everyone know and meet us...wherever?"

She heard sirens in the distance and her heart thumped but she kept rocking Jack. "Keep trying Tucker," she told Henry. "Leave him a message and then text him too. Maybe he has the sound turned down."

"Does he need to take us?" Jack asked, looking up at her from her lap.

He wasn't even crying anymore. She couldn't believe how brave he was.

"No, sweetie. The ambulance will take us if we need to go somewhere. But Tucker will want to be here." And that truth struck her hard. Tucker would want to be here. Would *need* to be here even. She was handling it. She didn't need him to come save the day, but she wanted him here because *he* would want to be here. God knew, if she was somewhere else, away from the boys, and found out one was hurt, she would need to get there, be there, see that they were okay.

The EMTs knocked on the door and Henry and Charlie ran to open it and show them upstairs.

The next few minutes were a whirlwind. They checked Jack over and then decided he definitely needed stitches and would need to go to the hospital about twenty minutes away. One of them picked Jack up and started for the stairs.

"Henry, you're in charge until someone gets here," she

said, kissing each of the other boys on the head as she followed the EMTs.

"Who's coming?" he asked.

She smiled. "I'm not sure. But someone is." She knew that for a fact. Their friends and *family* would make sure the boys were okay. As she stepped out onto the porch, a car pulled up. Kathy Bennett and Travis got out.

Delaney felt tears sting but she gave them huge smiles.

"I was at mom's having lunch. How can I help?" Travis asked, coming up the steps.

"We're okay. Going to get some stitches. The other boys needs some reassurance."

"And cleaning up, I'm guessing," Kathy said, taking in their appearances through the doorway.

"We've got it." Travis put a hand on Delaney's shoulder.

She smiled up at him. "Thanks." She dropped her voice to a whisper. "Maybe find out how exactly this happened."

"They were playing sword fight with two of the saws," Charlie said, pointing at David.

Delaney looked at David. "No."

He looked miserable and didn't deny it.

"Are you hurt?" Travis asked him.

David shook his head.

"Okay, then let's have a talk about IQ points and hand tools," Travis said.

Kathy smiled at Delaney. "I'll make sure he scares them just enough."

Delaney sighed. "Thanks for coming."

"We wanted to."

Kathy kissed her cheek and Delaney headed for the ambulance.

There it was again. That want-to thing. People around here really did *want* to help and be there and do what they could. They didn't have to. Travis and Kathy didn't both have to come.

But they'd wanted to.

Delaney climbed up into the back of the ambulance, hoping that Tucker might already be at the hospital when they got there. Just as they were about to slam the door, Travis came jogging out of the house.

"Hang on, Brandon!" he called to the paramedic next to her. "Here," he handed her back her phone.

"I wanted Henry to have it in case he needed to call anyone."

"We're here now. I've got things covered. You might need it."

"I might?"

He pointed to the screen. She had four missed calls from Tucker. She felt better just seeing his name. Maybe she didn't *need* him right now—Travis and Kathy and the EMTs were covering pretty much everything—but she most definitely wanted him.

"Thanks."

"Hey, Jack," Travis said.

Her nephew looked over at him from the gurney the guys had him lying on. "Yeah?"

"Don't worry. Girls dig scars."

Jack wrinkled his nose. "So what?"

Travis laughed and slammed the back door to the ambulance and they pulled out.

Delaney texted Tucker. *"I really WANT you to come be at the hospital with me."*

There was nothing he could do, no way he could fix this, no real reason for him to be there. She wanted him there anyway.

His answer came back quickly. *"Good. Because I really NEED to be there.*

And it became official. She was fully in love with Tucker Bennett.

ॐॐ

There was a big good-looking Bennett waiting for them at the hospital all right, but it wasn't Tucker.

TJ met the gurney as they came through the door.

"Hey, Delaney. Hey, Jack." He ruffled Jack's hair and then met Delaney's eyes as they rolled past. "He was about twenty minutes away from Sapphire Falls. He's on his way."

"Thanks."

The next thirty minutes were a blur of people and explanations and procedures. One of the explanations included words like "lucky" and "no tendon damage" and "easy to fix". Delaney did a lot of nodding and signing during that part. One of the procedures included a big needle that was going to numb Jack's hand for the stitches. Another included another big needle that was going to stitch the skin of his hand back together. Delaney did a lot of smiling and looking anywhere but at Jack's hand during that part.

Finally, Jack was back together, a little groggy from some medicine they'd given him to calm him down for the stitches, and they were lying on the emergency-room bed together.

"I'm glad you're here," he told her, snuggling close and putting his unbandaged hand on hers on top of her stomach.

She turned her hand up and linked their fingers. "I'll always be here when you need me, Jack."

He was quiet for a minute, and she wondered if he'd drifted off. But then he said softly, "Mommy and Daddy can't be here when I need them."

The pain in his voice knifed through her and she had to blink back the tears and clear her throat before she could reply. "I know. You're right. But I'll always do whatever I can to be here when you need me." There was no sense in sugarcoating it. The kid knew firsthand that people couldn't always keep their promises.

"But Tucker and TJ and all of those guys will be there if you can't."

She blinked hard again. "Yep. Exactly."

And again, the point Tucker had been trying to make came home sharp and clear—she *wanted* to be there for Jack. He had lots of people to meet his needs. But she wanted it to be her.

That was how Tucker felt about her.

It seemed so clear.

Jack took a big, deep breath beside her. "You make me feel better," Jack said.

She ran her hand over his hair. "I'm so glad." He would have felt better with TJ or Tucker or Kathy or even one of his brothers here too, but dang, it felt good to be the one that was here.

She felt a huge weight lift off of her chest. She got it now. This love thing was complicated, but she got it. Or was at least in the process of getting it.

Jack drifted to sleep and Delaney felt herself dozing as well.

Five minutes later, the curtain pulled back and Tucker came into their little cubicle. He came straight to the bed, leaned over and touched Jack's head with one hand, closing his eyes for just a second, and then wrapped his arms around Delaney and scooped her out of the bed.

He sat down in the chair next to Jack's bed with her in his lap. He hugged her close and put his face against her neck.

God, he felt good.

She absorbed the strong, warm, solid feel of him, and the fact that he was here.

"Thank you for wanting me here," he said, his voice soft and gruff against her ear.

"Thank you for needing to be here," she whispered back.

They sat together, just holding one another, until the

doctor came in and said everything was fine. They awakened Jack and, after strict instructions about how to change the bandages and keep the wound clean and when to come back to remove the stitches, they were dismissed.

Tucker carried Jack and held Delaney's hand as they headed for the ER exit. They came to the waiting area and stopped. TJ was still sitting in the waiting room, but now his dad was with him, as were Lauren and Adrianne.

They all fussed over Jack and he grinned shyly at the attention and climbed into Thomas's lap, accepted a cookie from Adrianne and happily launched into a graphic description of the amount of blood and gore involved in the event.

He was definitely perking up.

"They didn't all have to come," Delaney said, a little stunned to see them all here and yet not surprised in the least.

"They wanted to." Tucker pulled her in and kissed the top of her head. "I need to talk to Adrianne for a second, okay?"

She nodded and he and Adrianne stepped outside of the waiting room.

Delaney sank down onto the sofa next to TJ.

"You okay?" he asked softly, letting Jack continue to attempt to gross Lauren out with the tale of his injury that was already getting taller.

Lauren was tough though, and had seen a lot between living and working in Haiti with her and Mason's company and living on the farm with Travis. Delaney had heard that Lauren had once helped pull a calf and had shot a mountain lion. On the same day.

"I'm good," Delaney said, giving him an honest smile. She watched Jack, realizing he seemed one-hundred percent recovered already. "It might be the easy way to go, but I can't imagine doing this without all of you," she admitted.

TJ looked over at her. "The easy way to go?"

"Yeah. You know, leaning on friends and family instead of doing it on my own."

He laughed. "Who said letting family in is the easy way out?"

"How is it not? Always having people around to help?"

He shrugged. "Sure, they'll babysit, but they'll also give you advice. I guarantee my mother has rearranged your kitchen cupboards already. They'll come over to help you drywall, but then they'll waste an hour of your life arguing over who knows the best way to do it. They'll overstay their welcome and drink all your beer. They'll disappoint you and piss you off and you have to forgive them. They'll meddle in everything. They'll try to set you up on dates that you don't want—" He stopped and shrugged. "Okay, maybe that last one doesn't apply to you. But trust me, the *easy* way is alone, doing it your way, however you want."

"I've never done things alone," Delaney said. "My sister and Rafe were always there. They were my best friends, my roommates for a long time, my bosses forever. They gave me everything. I never really had to work for anything."

TJ laughed again. "I don't know about that. I mean, so they gave you a job. But then you could never get away from the job. You were living with and having dinner every night with your bosses. If something wasn't going well, you'd hear about it at work and home. And you can't bitch about what an ass your boss is because the ass is sitting across the table."

She thought about that and she had to chuckle. "Okay, you're not wrong."

"I'm not wrong," TJ said firmly. "And I can tell you from personal experience that *this* group is not the easy way out." He paused and looked at his dad and Lauren and Jack, then glanced over as Tucker and Adrianne came back into the room. "But they're worth it," he added. "Every last nosey one of them."

Delaney grinned. Yeah. She could see that.

Tucker cross the room. "Can I talk to you for a second?" he asked her, holding out his hand.

"Of course." She took it and let him pull her up. She noticed he was holding a white box in his hand. A white bakery box.

Her heart started pounding, almost as if it had been a velvet ring box.

Tucker was going to give her cobbler.

She covered her mouth with her hand, torn between laughing and crying.

This was even more romantic than a ring in many ways.

He stopped once they were in the hallway where he and Adrianne had been talking. He turned to her and focused on her face. "I—" He frowned. "Are you *crying?*"

She nodded. "A little."

"Why?"

"Because of that." She pointed to the box.

"This? Why?"

"It's so perfect, Tuck," she said, sniffing and giving him a huge smile at the same time. "You've realized that you already have everything that the cobbler represents— home, family, friends, comfort and security—and that it's all yours to give to someone rather than looking for someone to give it all to you."

He looked from her to the box and back. "Huh."

"What?"

"That really would have been perfect."

She laughed. "That's not cobbler?"

He shook his head. "No. But maybe I'll take this home and I'll get a cobbler and—"

She grabbed for the box, but he held it up out of her reach. "No way. You can't steal that idea now. Besides, you've had more than enough cobbler," she said. "I think it's time for something new." And she didn't mean cobbler in the literal sense. And she knew he knew it.

He raised an eyebrow. "Well, then maybe you should let me go on with what I had planned."

Okay, he had planned something. That involved a white bakery box. That had to mean good things. "Fine. Go ahead."

"This is a box of *cookies*," he said. "Because I intended to tell you that I accept your proposal to eat cookies with you, to date for a while and not rush into things. I have visions of coming to pick you up and ringing that doorbell and watching you come down that staircase and kissing you on that porch when I drop you off."

Oh, that was sweet and symbolic too. "That's also really good," she told him, feeling teary again.

"Yeah?"

"Yeah. And I accept the proposal to date you."

"I thought I was accepting *your* proposal to date you," he said with a grin.

"Okay, it was my proposal," she agreed. "Because I figured out why none of the other girls worked out for you."

"Because they weren't you."

She smiled at that. That was the truth. But she'd worked out this speech while she'd been cuddling Jack, so she wanted to say it. "You love to dirt bike and get muddy and play with dogs and go hunting and you're always involved in something, busy doing something. You're used to having a bunch of people in your house and in your life all the time. A woman with no kids would be way too quiet and organized for you. Even a woman with a couple of sweet, quiet little girls who wanted to have tea parties wouldn't provide enough craziness and mud and blood. So of course the only woman for you would be the one with *four* rough, loud, dirty boys who will be arguing and wrestling and making a mess from sunup to sundown."

He brought her in close and kissed her softly. "It's true. My life has been without enough mud and blood for a long time."

She grinned and put a hand over his heart. "So I'll eat your cookies for now. But I do intend to marry you one day, Tucker Bennett."

He gave her one of his best slow, sexy grins and opened the top of the bakery box. She looked inside.

There were at least two dozen chocolate cookies in the box, each with a dollop of coconut pecan frosting on top.

Her gaze bounced back up to his. "German chocolate *cookies*?" she asked.

He nodded.

"Adrianne made these for you?"

"Oh, no." He shook his head. "These are my mother's. Adrianne just picked them up for me."

"Your mom made German chocolate cookies for us?" Wow.

"Upon my request," he said.

"Just today? When Jack got hurt?" That made no sense. There hadn't been time.

"Last night. I had this all planned out before Jack figured out that saw blades and hands don't mix."

"Aw, you did?" She knew she looked like a dope. An in-love-head-over-heels-for-this-man dope. And she didn't care.

"I did. I was going to try to talk you into another dirt-bike ride."

She frowned even as her body heated. "That last one didn't end the way I wanted it to."

He put his lips against hers. "Me either. We need a do-over."

"With German chocolate cookies."

He gave her a wicked grin. "At least with the frosting."

"You know what your mom's thinking now," Delaney said.

"The same thing I hope *you're* thinking."

"That there's going to be an engagement soon," she said happily.

He nodded. "I'm giving you to the end of the summer before I propose again."

She grabbed a cookie, took a bite and then pulled him in for a chocolate-and-coconut-flavored kiss. "Unless I propose to you before that," she said against his lips.

He settled his hand on her butt and squeezed. "And I'll say yes…as soon as I have cupboard doors again."

 formatting_ornament

"I want you at home tonight," Tucker said twenty minutes later as he drove her and Jack back to Sapphire Falls.

They hadn't said much since getting into the truck. The emotions of the day were still spinning through them all and they were both lost in thought.

She looked over at Tucker. She knew what he meant—he wanted them at his house tonight. She had no arguments. "I want to be there tonight," she said.

He gave her a single nod in answer, but she saw the flash of heat and possessiveness in his eyes before turning back to the road.

They didn't say anything else after that either. They didn't need to. She doubted very much if she'd be spending any more nights in the house on Plum Street.

Jack was asleep before they were halfway home and Delaney had to admit she wasn't far behind him. The adrenaline—both the stressful kind and the elated kind—had taken its toll and the idea of relaxing at Tucker's house was already comforting her.

Of course, it would be another few hours until things were really relaxed or quiet.

Kathy and Travis brought the other boys out, along with

tons of food. The rest of their friends and family showed up as well, and everyone did a great job of ooh-ing and aah-ing over Jack's bandages. Almost too much, in fact. Delaney hoped Jack didn't think bodily injury was a good way to get the spotlight in the future. Jack's brothers, however, were the most attentive of all. The boys clustered around Jack the minute he was out of the truck, clearly concerned and needing reassurance.

It was David, though, who ended up needing the most care. David gathered with his brothers, but hung back slightly. Delaney's heart clenched at the sight of the little hell raiser, who typically looked mischievous and happy, looking sad and guilty. Delaney didn't pull him aside then, not wanting to call the other boys' attention to his emotions, but she did sit next to him at dinner and told him all about the hospital visit from her point of view—how Jack had thought the big needles were cool and how the doctor had to tell him three times that he didn't need a blood transfusion and how he flirted with the nurses and that it had gotten him nothing but chocolate pudding cups. Five of them. David laughed with Delaney at that. They all knew Jack didn't like chocolate pudding.

Eventually, David was smiling, convinced that Jack had not been traumatized by the experience. She also made a point of asking David to cuddle with her on the couch during the movie they put in at the end of the evening to help wind everyone down after the guests left. She made it sound as if he was doing her a favor, but she suspected he could use some extra loving tonight as well.

Jack got to choose the movie, so they settled in for *How to Train Your Dragon*. Delaney sighed with contentment as the movie started. She could absolutely do this every night for the rest of her life—right here, with these guys.

The next thing she knew, Tucker's arms were under her and he was lifting her off the couch.

She rubbed her eyes. "What's going on?"

"You crashed," he said with a smile as he cradled her against his chest. "So did everyone else. The boys are all in bed asleep."

She wrapped her arms around his neck and smiled up at him. "Can we go to the barn for a little bit?" She'd missed him. More than his body, more than the orgasms, she'd missed feeling connected to him, giving him pleasure and having moments where it was only them.

He laughed and started toward the steps. "We're going upstairs."

"I'm not that tired. I want—"

"And we're going to make love in my *bed*."

Her eyes widened and her whole body perked up at that. "Really?"

He strode down the hall to his bedroom door and nudged it open with his foot. "Really."

Her body began tingling and she wiggled a little in anticipation. A bed. A whole big, wide, soft bed and Tucker. The perfect combination.

The bedside lamp was the only light in the room. His sheets were rumpled like the first day she'd been in here and she cast a glance at the bathroom door. They were going to have to try that shower out together as well. The one that had made her stumble over her words and her feet. She had a feeling her reaction would be different this time. In fact, some words were already coming to mind. Words like "more" and "harder" and "yes" and "I love you." Especially those last three.

He stopped next to the bed and set her on her feet. "No quickies, no hay or wooden walls, no reason to hurry. You, me, a bed and all night long."

Delaney suddenly felt the urge to cry. That was so stupid. But she hadn't had sex with Tucker since realizing, once and for all, that she was in love with him and would be for the rest of her life. This wasn't going to be sex. They were going to make love.

301

"One night won't be enough," she said softly, putting her hand against his jaw.

"Good thing we have forever then."

He dipped his head and kissed her. The kiss was hot and sweet, not a preamble to anything but tasting one another. He cupped the back of her head with his hand, and she ran her palm over the evening scruff on his face.

He lifted his head several amazing minutes later. "If you're worried about the boys in the night, I'll let you go back to your room, but I would love to sleep with you tonight. Every night. For the next hundred years or so."

She looked up into his eyes, amazed by him and her new life. "If the boys need me in the night and can't find me in the guest room, they'll come in here to you," she said. "And then they'll see us sleeping together like Chelsea and Rafe always did. I think that will just make them feel even more secure and happy."

Tucker's eyes blazed with new heat at that. "I'm in charge tonight."

She pressed her lips together.

"I know you needed to be before," he said. "I know that was important. But now it's my turn. Let me love you."

Delaney pulled in a quick breath. Dirty talk had always gotten her going and made her hot, but she'd had no idea that hearing words about love and forever would be an even stronger turn-on.

She nodded. "Please."

"Take your clothes off."

Bossy too though. That would totally work for her.

She pulled her T-shirt off, shed her jeans and kicked them to one side. Tucker did the same. Her eyes were glued to his chest and abs while she unhooked her bra and slid her panties off.

"On the bed, babe." He stepped out of his underwear, his cock hard and ready.

Delaney sat on the bed and scooted up until she could

put her head on a pillow. She turned her head and took a deep breath of his scent on the pillowcase.

"Arms up." Tucker climbed up on the bed with her, his gaze hungry as it roamed over her.

She stretched, sliding her hands under the pillow. She hadn't been a passive player in sex for a long time. Probably ever. She was usually the one giving directions and setting the pace. But it felt so good to be at Tucker's command. She would do anything for him, let him do anything he wanted to. She trusted him completely.

Besides, every single attempt she'd made to keep from being completely overwhelmed by him had failed spectacularly. No one had ever amazed her like he did. No one had ever understood her like he did. And no one had ever loved her like he did.

"Anything you want, Tuck," she said breathlessly.

He gave a low growl at that, then knelt over her to press a hot, lazy kiss to her lips. He traced her bottom lip with his tongue, then stroked along hers as she opened for him. He dragged his mouth to her jaw and down her neck, leaving a tingling trail behind that had her shifting restlessly against his sheets.

Things had been hot in the barn, no question, but this was *really* nice.

"What I want is every single inch of you against my mouth and burning up for me," he said as he closed his lips around one nipple.

She arched closer. It was strange—she would have expected to want to move her hands, to get them on him, tangled in his hair, grabbing his fine ass, but she was very content to leave her hands up and let him have full reign over her body.

"I'm always burning up for you," she told him honestly.

He lifted his head and gave her a heart-stopping grin. "Wow, I really am good. Because you haven't given me a chance to really show you what I've got."

She laughed and her heart swelled with love. "I'm all yours."

He looked at her for a moment, then he shook his head. "I wasn't going to do this tonight. I just wanted this to be slow and romantic. But damn, girl—I fell in love with you at the bakery when you had chocolate smeared on your arm and sugar on your face. This seems completely appropriate after all."

Her heart tripped in her chest and her eyes stung. "That's completely romantic. What do you—"

He shifted and reached for the side of the bed. He pulled the white bakery box he'd had at the hospital onto the mattress beside her.

She arched a brow. "German chocolate frosting."

He grinned. "German chocolate frosting."

Delaney laughed and then gasped as he scooped the frosting from a cookie with two fingers and painted it onto her nipple. He sucked it clean, swirling his tongue to catch every bit. He did the same on the other side and she felt the shocks of pleasure and need heading straight to her clit.

His mouth still on one of her nipples, he reached for another cookie. But this time he turned it upside down and dragged the frosting over her ribs to her belly button. His mouth followed the sticky trail and he licked up every bit of that as well.

"Tucker." She lifted her hips. "More."

Slow and romantic sounded so nice, but in reality, there were only a few minutes between his mouth touching her *anywhere* and her wanting him thrusting deep and hard inside of her.

He continued to take his time though. He spread frosting over her mound and down onto her clit and his tongue followed in long, hot licks that she felt in every cell in her body.

He slipped a finger into her, pumping in and out in steady, *slow* thrusts as his tongue continued to torment her.

Delaney propped herself up on her elbows. The sight of Tucker's head between her legs was enough to make her inner muscles clench hard. She pulled one of her knees up, planted her heel on the mattress, and lifted up against his mouth. She was rewarded with another low, hot growl and another finger. Her head fell back and she let the sensations wash over her. She felt her climax gathering and when Tucker sucked on her clit a moment later, the orgasm rushed through her body in an intense wave of pleasure and heat.

Tucker continued to lick lightly and pump his fingers in and out as she came down from the crest. When she sank back into the mattress, he climbed up her body. His eyes were locked on hers as he put his fingers to his mouth and licked them clean.

Her pussy clenched again at the sight and she thought she just might be on the verge of another climax that easily. She watched as he palmed his cock with a firm, easy stroke and *knew* she was on the verge again.

Without a word, he put his hands under her, lifted her hips and slid into her inch by glorious inch.

Delaney gripped the sheets in her fists and gasped at the feel of him filling her completely, as deep as he could go, as close as two people could be.

"It's deeper this way," she said softly, watching his face.

His eyes were full of heat and love.

His mouth lifted in a knowing smile. "It feels like you never want to let me go."

Her eyes filled with tears and she gave him a wobbly smile. "Exactly."

He leaned in and kissed her, and Delaney wrapped her arms and legs around him, pulling him into her, hanging on with all she had.

"I love you, Tucker," she told him, a tear rolling down her cheek.

He lifted his head. "I love you too, Laney."

Then he started moving. His strokes were deep and touched a place in her that she'd never felt before. Together, their eyes locked on one another, they made the slow, sweet climb to the best, most soul-deep orgasm she'd ever had, in the bed where she would make love to this man for the rest of her life.

Afterward, Tucker pulled her against his side. She curled into him and listened to his heart go from racing to thumping. She thought about everything he had given her. His love for her and the boys, a home, a chance to be proud of herself even when it took her away from him, the encouragement to be a mom her way, a huge, loving family, and true friends. He'd given her things she hadn't even known she wanted or was missing.

And German chocolate cookies.

She giggled.

He ran his hand over her hair. "What are you thinking about?"

She propped her chin on his chest and looked up at him. "I'm trying to figure out how to compliment my future mother-in-law on her German chocolate cookies without blushing."

He laughed and hugged her close. "Oh, please blush when you say it. And if you love me, you'll say it in front of my brothers."

She grinned. "Oh, really?"

"Travis has been rubbing the German-chocolate-cake thing in for a couple of years now. And trust me, he doesn't care if Lauren blushes about it one bit."

"And what about TJ?"

"Ah, he'll just be jealous. Which is awesome."

She shook her head. "Poor TJ. He needs a good woman."

"Yes, he does," Tucker said with a nod. Then he grinned down at her. "But please promise me you'll mention the cookies in front of him anyway."

❦

A week later, Delaney hung the last of Tucker's new cupboard doors.

She stepped back and felt a thrill dance through her looking at all the new doors with the custom-engraved design on them.

She definitely liked these better than the ones in the house in town.

The intricate swirling design was beautiful and unique even without knowing that there were six letters hidden in the loops. There was a T for Tucker, a D for her, and an H, C, D and J for each of the boys.

Her cell phone rang and she pulled it out of her back pocket without looking away from the cupboard in front of her. "Hello?"

"Is this Delaney Callan?" a deep voice asked.

"It is."

"I understand that you might have a house for sale in a few months."

She frowned. No one but their friends and family knew that she was planning to finish the details on the house on Plum Street and then look at listing it.

Of course, their friends and family knew everyone in the county.

"Yes, that's right. Not for a couple of months as we're still finishing some renovations."

"Wonderful," the man said. "Can I make requests if things aren't completely finished? Like a Jacuzzi tub for the master bath?"

She laughed. "Sure, why not? But I'll have to figure it into the price."

"Of course."

"Do you have bank financing or will you be talking

with a realtor?" she asked.

"I'll be paying cash. I'd be happy to put half down now and then pay the other half at closing."

Cash? Seriously? He hadn't even asked the price.

"What's your name and email?" she asked. "I could send over the details and some ideas."

"Tyler Bennett."

Delaney froze. She shook her head. "Wait, *Bennett*? Tyler? As in Ty, Tucker's brother?"

"One of them," he confirmed.

She'd seen him at the bonfire a several weeks ago and had briefly said hello but hadn't had a chance to really talk to him.

"The one that doesn't live here. That lives in Colorado?"

"That's me."

"But you're buying a house here?"

"I'm moving back."

She blinked. She had heard *nothing* about Ty moving back, and she was absolutely certain Kathy would have been talking about it. Nonstop. "Seriously?"

He laughed. "Seriously. Though it's a bit of a secret at the moment."

"Okay." She was going to eventually be this guy's sister-in-law. Did that make keeping secrets all right?

Sister-in-law. She liked that term. She'd be TJ and Travis's sister-in-law too. Kind of a sister-in-law to Lauren as well, though further removed.

"What are you asking for it?"

She was jerked back to the conversation with Ty. "Oh, um." She named the price and then held her breath. It was a steep price in Sapphire Falls. But she was putting a lot into the place.

"How about I pay you ten thousand on top of that if you promise not to tell my neighbor to the east before move-in day?"

Delaney knew instantly who he was talking about. The mayor lived on Plum Street, right next to Delaney's new house. "You don't want Hailey to know that you're moving in next door?"

"Right. Let's just let it be a surprise for her."

Oh, she was very intrigued now. "I think I'd rather have ten thousand less and the chance to see Hailey's reaction."

Ty chuckled. "Oh, you'll be aware of her reaction either way, I'm sure. Talk to you soon."

Delaney couldn't help but smile. This guy was going to be her brother-in-law. It seemed that there were fun times ahead.

Three dogs, four kids and one hot country boy came barreling into the house as she and Ty disconnected. The noise and the dirt was out of control. And so was the depth of the happiness and love that welled up in her.

"Someone grab Teddy!" Charlie yelled as the puppy, who they'd finally named, sprinted under the coffee table."

"Luna's going after him!" David called in delight as the much bigger dog tried to follow the puppy under the table.

The table tipped and the magazines all slid to the floor. Henry grabbed the table before it fell over. Tank slipped on the slick magazines as he tried to keep up with the other two, barking happily. As the boys and the dogs ran and shouted and laughed, it was clear to Delaney that the fun times were already upon her.

Tucker stepped through the chaos and swept her up in his arms for a big, hot kiss.

She knew the chaos was always going to be a part of her life. But the big, hot kisses and the happiness and love would be too.

Tucker kept his arm around her as they watched the boys chase the dogs back outside, leaving muddy footprints, grass and hay in their wake.

She took a deep breath. Contentment. That was what this feeling was. She really hadn't expected to feel it for a long time from now, and she was still getting used to it.

"Hey, I've got kitchen cupboards again," Tucker said, turning to survey her work.

Looking up at him, she realized that love and lust she was quickly getting used to.

He took it all in. Then his arm dropped from her shoulders and he took a step closer to the cabinets, studying the elaborate design she'd etched into the wood.

She bit her bottom lip as he traced over the swoops and swirls with a finger.

"This is gorgeous," he finally said, turning to look at her.

"You think so?"

"Really, really gorgeous. Amazing. Thank you for doing this."

She smiled, her heart full. "It was my pleasure."

"Will you be able to add letters for our other kids?"

She stared at him. He'd found the letters. And…their other kids?

"Oth—" She cleared her throat. "Other kids?"

"Just three or four."

He gave her a grin that kind of made her want to start on those other kids right then and there. She felt herself grinning in response as her heart thumped again. But it wasn't with fear or panic as she might have expected, thinking about becoming a mother of seven. Or—wow—*eight.*

"Okay," she said. "If we add one at a time this time around."

She could definitely add more letters to the cupboards.

As if *that* would be her greatest concern.

But heck, she had all kinds of help and support now.

Tucker looked down at her with so much love in his eyes, her heart beat in a way she'd never imagined it could.

He cupped her face. "It's official."

"What is?"

"I've got it all."

She wrapped her arms around him and blinked against the happy tears that threatened. "Everything but cobbler," she agreed.

He laughed and gave her butt a little swat. "Well, you might be surprised to hear this, but I think I'm over the cobbler thing."

And with those words, Delaney decided that she was going to make Tucker Bennett the best damn cherry cobbler he'd ever had.

Once. Just to prove that she could.

ABOUT THE AUTHOR

Erin Nicholas is the author of sexy contemporary romances. Her stories have been described as toe-curling, enchanting, steamy and fun. She loves to write about reluctant heroes, imperfect heroines and happily ever afters. She lives in the Midwest with her husband, who only wants to read the sex scenes in her books; her kids, who will never read the sex scenes in her books; and family and friends, who say they're shocked by the sex scenes in her books (yeah, right!).

You can find Erin on the Web at www.ErinNicholas.com, on Twitter (http://twitter.com/ErinNicholas) and on Facebook (https://www.facebook.com/ErinNicholasBooks)

Look for these titles by Erin Nicholas

Now Available at all book retailers!

Sapphire Falls
Getting Out of Hand (book 1)
Getting Worked Up (book 2)
Getting Dirty (book 3)
Getting In the Spirit, Christmas novella
Getting In the Mood, Valentine's Day novella
Getting It All (book 4)

The Bradfords
Just Right (book 1)
Just Like That (book 2)
Just My Type (book 3)
Just the Way I Like It (short story, 3.5)
Just for Fun (book 4)
Just a Kiss (book 5)
Just What I Need: The Epilogue (novella, book 6)

Anything & Everything
Anything You Want
Everything You've Got

Counting On Love
Just Count on Me (prequel)
She's the One
It Takes Two
Best of Three
Going for Four
Up by Five

The Billionaire Bargains
No Matter What
What Matters Most
All That Matters

Single titles
Hotblooded

Promise Harbor Wedding
Hitched
(book 4 in the series)

Boys of Fall
Out of Bounds, Erin Nicholas
Going Long, Cari Quinn
Free Agent, Mari Carr

Enjoy this Excerpt from

Getting In the Spirit
A Sapphire Falls novella

by Erin Nicholas

It's Christmas time in Sapphire Falls!

At least one good thing has come from Levi Spencer's car accident—it seems to have knocked some sense into him. He's ready to leave his wild Vegas playboy ways behind and become a new man. And he knows just the place to do it...his brother Joe's new hometown. He's never spent time in a place described as quaint or idyllic, and now he intends to revel in every charming, sweet thing he can find. Like the homegrown country girl his brother sets him up with for the Christmas formal.

Kate Leggot wants just one great Christmas. After a childhood without Christmas at all and three failed attempts to find the seasonal magic on her own, she agrees to spend the holiday with her friend Phoebe in Sapphire Falls. The Christmas-crazy town is a far cry from San Francisco and Kate quickly finds herself drawn into everything from the snow to the hot cocoa. And, of course, the sweet country boy Phoebe has set her up with for the formal. Looks like she's going to get everything she wanted—and more—under the tree this year.

A not-so-little mix-up, a hot kiss under the mistletoe and a candy cane or two later and December in Sapphire Falls has never been so hot.

This is a novella, about half the length of the novels in this series. Read only if you like fun, small town contemporary romances where they talk dirty and act even dirtier.

Excerpt

"Thank you for agreeing to do this," she said, softly.

She was looking into his eyes like she had been at the bar and he was hit by the punch of desire he'd felt then too.

What was he agreeing to do again? There wasn't anything he wouldn't agree to for this woman, but he couldn't recall the details at the moment. "The formal?" he asked finally.

She nodded. "I know it seems silly, but I'm starving for a nice, normal, traditional Christmas."

The word *starving* made him think of things *he* was feeling hungry for come to think of it.

"I completely understand," he managed while he was really wondering what would happen if he grabbed her chin and kissed her again. This time minus the mistletoe and with tongue. And with less than sweet, gentlemanly intentions.

"And, um…" Her gaze flickered away from him for a moment and she seemed hesitant.

"Anything." He meant it. His tone might have been rougher than it needed to be, but he suddenly wanted to be the one making everything just right for her.

She met his gaze again. "Would you want to spend some time together tomorrow? We could—"

"Yes."

Again, firmer than needed, but he did like the way her eyes went round and her mouth curled.

"You don't know what I was going to suggest."

"Doesn't matter. I'm in."

Her expression shifted quickly from surprised to amused to sly. "What if I want to tie you up in tinsel and keep you at my mercy until New Year's?"

There was a thud somewhere in the vicinity of Levi's heart. A thud that rocked through his whole body. Just as quickly as he went from warm to burning up, it was clear that she'd realized what she'd said out loud to a near stranger.

She started to pull back, but he put his hand between her shoulder blades and brought her in. "Fucking love tinsel," he said against her lips and then took her into a kiss that definitely heated things up.

She didn't hesitate, which further fired his blood. In fact, when he parted his lips and stroked his tongue into her mouth, she moaned.

Tinsel and anything else she wanted. That was the only thing he could really think as she pivoted to lean closer. But they were sitting on a bench, and that meant she had to fold a leg up between them. Neither of them really wanted anything between them at all, so when she made a frustrated little sound, Levi took hold of her hips and picked her up to put her in his lap. Their cups of hot chocolate tipped over into the snow, but they barely noticed.

Thanks to the tight skirt on her dress, she had to sit sideways—pulling the dress up any farther would have put her at risk for frost bite in some very unpleasant places— but they were definitely closer now. And warmer.

She gripped the front of his coat in her hands like she had before. Levi kept his hands on her hips, loving the sweet weight of her against the suddenly noticeable fly of his jeans.

She tipped her head one way, he tipped the other,

deepening the kiss, the tongue stroking getting bolder and faster.

She moved her fingers to the buttons on the front of his coat and as the first released, Levi caught her hands. "It's too cold here for this." Not to mention public. In a nice small town where everyone knew his brother. He really didn't have any problems with public displays of many kinds—including some with far more skin showing than he and Hailey were—but his behavior reflected on Joe and Phoebe.

And he was a little afraid of his petite, red-headed sister-in-law.

He planned to stay in Sapphire Falls for several months, hopefully the whole year, to really soak it in and let it change him. He couldn't afford to be on her bad side.

Hailey sat staring at him, pressing her lips together, looked bewildered and turned on.

He could work with both of those things.

"Let's go somewhere warmer."

He started to shift to get up, but she didn't move. Since she was on top of him, that meant he didn't get far. She was light. He could have easily picked her up and carried her off to his—Joe's—truck. But he sensed her hesitation.

Considering they'd just met, that made some sense.

Joe and Phoebe had set them up. They had no reason to fear that the other was a serial killer or anything, but that didn't mean they should hop into bed together.

Did it?

Levi pondered that for a moment. Why not? Joe wouldn't set him up with someone crazy. And Lord knew, they had the chemistry for it. He was turning over a new leaf, but he wasn't becoming a priest. Having sex with a nice girl who might expect him to show up at her grandmother's for Sunday dinner and take her to the movies on Friday night would definitely be different.

Different was what he needed.

"I have one question," she said. "Before we go to your place."

Yes.

"Whatever you want," he told her sincerely. "And if it involves tinsel, all the better." At her little grin, he leaned in and said softly, "But turnabout is fair play. Remember that."

"What if you never want to see another piece of tinsel again in your life?" she asked.

He gave her what Phoebe had labeled his bad-boy grin. "There's always candy canes if I can't take the tinsel."

She seemed to be considering that. Carefully. And thoroughly. Much to his delight.

"I may never be able to look at a candy cane the same way again. And that's just based on my imagination."

He stared. Completely surprised and as turned on as he'd ever been talking about candy. "I'm buying every candy cane in this town."

Enjoy this Excerpt from

She's the One
Counting On Love, book one

by Erin Nicholas

Sometimes you see love clearly. And sometimes it has to smack you in the face.

When a stranger walks up and punches him, Ryan Kaye assumes there's a good reason. But he's stunned to learn it's over a one-night stand that never happened—with his friend's sister, straight-laced Amanda Dixon. When Ryan confronts her about the lie, Amanda apologizes, but Ryan realizes he doesn't want her to be sorry…he wants the night they supposedly spent together.

Amanda's not looking to add anyone to her long list of commitments, so she was only trying to let a nice guy down easy by telling him a fling with Ryan broke her heart. So what if the fling only happened in her dreams? But when Ryan Kaye tempts her with the chance to go crazy and fulfill a few fantasies, she can't resist. Thank goodness one night isn't enough time to fall in love…

Warning: Contains a hot paramedic who knows how to get a girl to let her hair down, a girl who thinks she prefers her hair up, some naughty laser tag, some naughty role-playing and a lot of falling in love.

Excerpt

Ryan signaled Carrie, the waitress. "Two of whatever each of the ladies want," he said, pointing to Emma, Isabelle and Olivia. He looked at the girls. "Stay here and mind your own business. Or at least mind someone's business other than mine and Amanda's."

Emma grinned. "You and Amanda have business in common?"

He looked down at the woman beside him. He still held on to her elbow, and he became aware that she smelled really, really good. Yes, it appeared that he and Amanda had business in common. How interesting. "Just stay here," he finally said to Emma.

He tugged Amanda through the crowd to the corner near the back door. It wasn't exactly private, but it would work for a few minutes. That was all he would have, he was sure, before Conner realized one of his friends had one of his sisters off in a dark corner alone.

"I talked to Tim Winters," Ryan said when they were as alone as they were going to get. "Right after he clocked me and knocked me on my ass."

Amanda gasped. "He hit you?"

"Yeah, because I slept with you."

"I... Oh... Um..."

Ryan fought a smile. "But it's weird. That really seems like something I'd remember."

She rolled her eyes. "We all probably blend together after a while."

She said it quietly, more of a mutter really, but he heard it.

"What's that mean?" he demanded. He put a finger under her chin and tipped her head so she had to look at him. "Amanda, what does that mean?"

She shrugged and pulled her chin away from his touch.

"It means that it's got to be difficult keeping track of everyone in and out of your bed without making them all wear name tags."

He grinned. He couldn't help it. She was sassy too. He liked that. And liked even more that it didn't show all the time. He liked knowing that there might be layers to Amanda Dixon to discover.

"Where would they pin the name tags?" he couldn't resist asking.

For a moment, Amanda seemed surprised. Then she smiled. "You'll have to get the adhesive ones, I guess."

"Might cover up something I need to see."

"You could try only dating women named Jennifer or something."

He smiled. "But then Tim Winters wouldn't believe whatever you told him about you and me."

Amanda pressed her lips together. Then said, "I'm really sorry he hit you."

"I'll live. What I want to know is why he did it."

"I thought he…told you."

She actually blushed and Ryan wondered if he could remember the last time he'd seen a woman blush. Not off the top of his head.

"I want to hear it from you."

She looked at the collar of his shirt instead of his eyes. "I told him I had a one-night stand with someone and had feelings for him."

"Me."

"Yes." Amanda wet her bottom lip and looked up at him and said softly, "Sorry."

He didn't want an apology. He didn't want her to be sorry for having the idea of the two of them burning up the sheets one night. He wanted her to keep that idea firmly in mind, in fact.

"Did you tell him it was a one-night stand?" He liked the idea that she would think he was so amazing that one night would cause her to be head over heels. Even if it was only in her imagination.

Amanda took a deep breath. "Yes, just one night."

Ryan moved in closer, wanting her full attention on him. "Okay. Make it up to me."

"How?"

"Give me that night."

Made in the USA
Middletown, DE
04 August 2015